EDWARD'S

EDWARD'S OUTLAW is the ... ... potter's daughter, Mathilda of Twyford and the Folville brothers; criminals from the fourteenth century nobility.

Book One - The Outlaw's Ransom
Book Two - The Winter Outlaw

The Outlaw's Ransom can also be found within the timeslip contemporary fiction novel, Romancing Robin Hood, written under Jennifer's romantic fiction pen name Jenny Kane.

JENNIFER ASH

EDWARD'S OUTLAW

Littwitz
PRESS

COPYRIGHT

Littwitz Press
Dahl House, Brookside Crescent
Exeter EX4 8NE

Copyright © Jennifer Ash 2018
Jennifer Ash has asserted her rights to be identified
as the author of this work in accordance with the
Copyright, Designs and Patents Act 1988.

First published in Great Britain by Littwitz Press in 2018

www.littwitzpress.com

A CIP catalogue record for this book is available
from the British Library.

ISBN: 978-1-9993501-0-9

All rights reserved. No part of this book may be copied,
or transmitted in any form or by any means, electronic, electrostatic,
magnetic tape, mechanical, photocopying,
recording or otherwise, without the written permission of
the author: Jennifer Ash and Littwitz Press.

Acknowledgements

Edward's Outlaw is dedicated to Chris Averiss.

Fellow *Robin of Sherwood* fan and all round good guy, Chris was the winner of the Littwitz Press 'Name a Character' competition. He chose the name 'Bettrys' for one of the females within this tale. Read on to discover more about her.

Chris, I hope you enjoy Mathilda and Bettrys' adventure.

Love,
Jennifer x

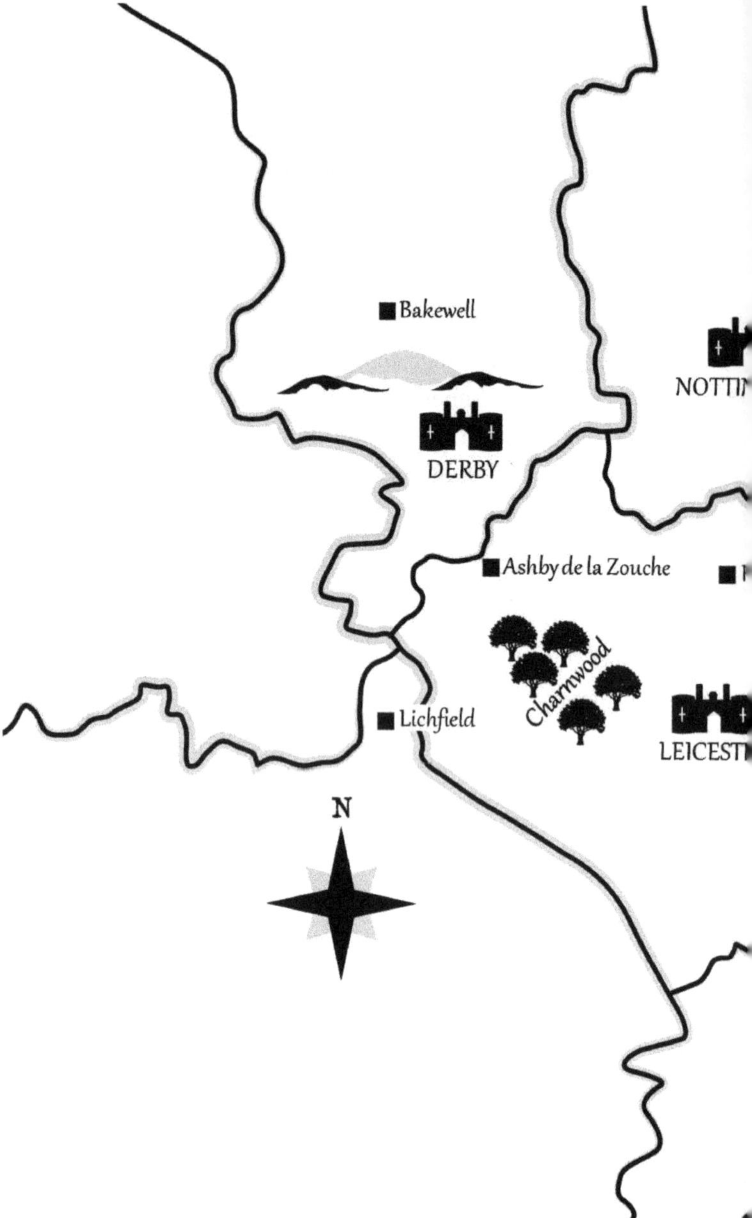

Bakewell
NOTTIN
DERBY
Ashby de la Zouche
Charnwood
Lichfield
LEICEST
N

■ Sempringham

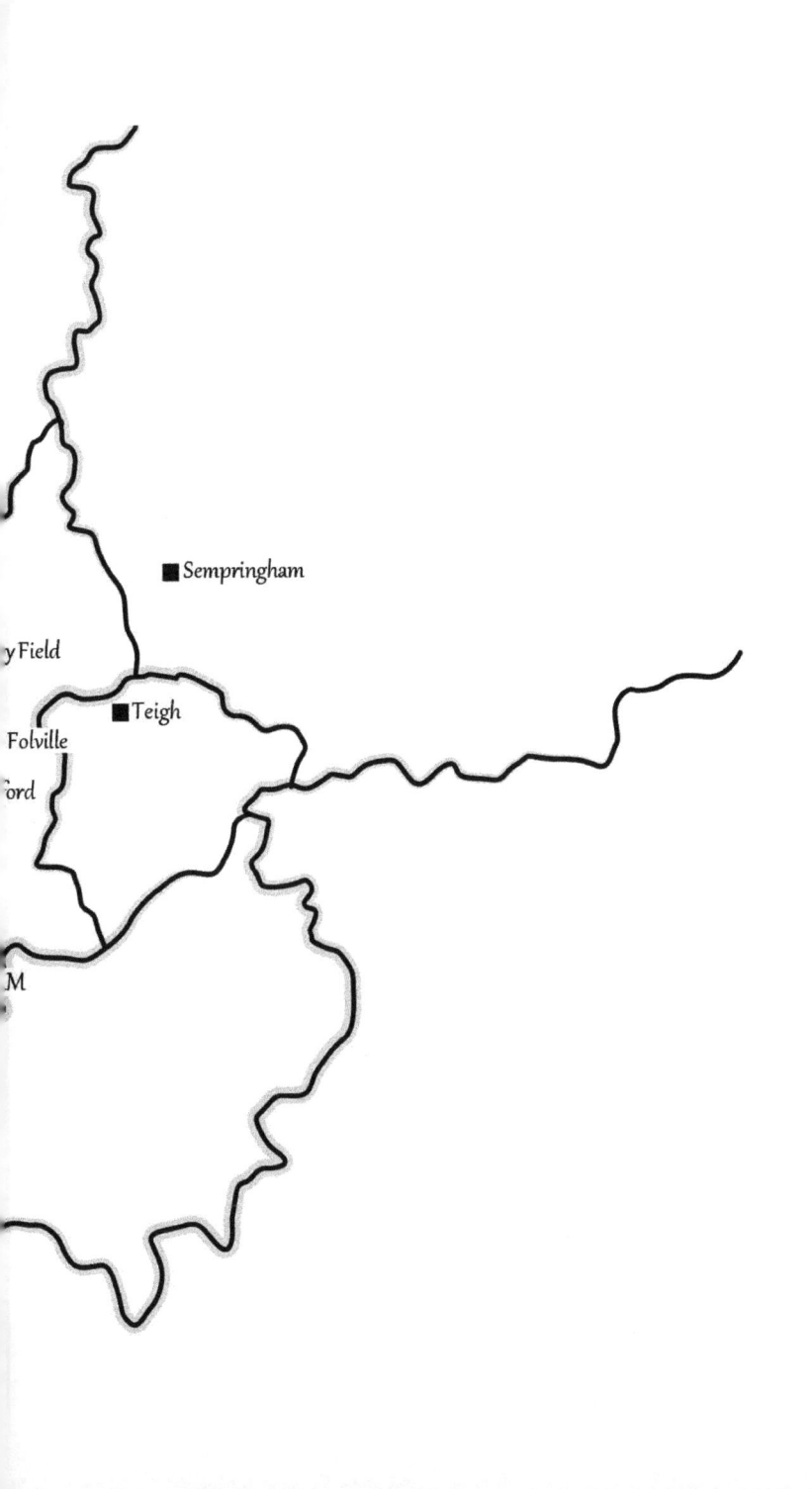

y Field

■ Teigh

Folville

ord

M

~ *Prologue* ~

30th December 1329

Roger Wennesley took a draught of honeyed mead. As he drank, his eyes remained fixed upon the man hovering before him.

Taking pleasure in making Garrick, the king's messenger, wait for his response, Wennesley tapped an annoyingly arrhythmic beat against the side of his cup with a single fingernail.

King Edward had, after years of being in the shadow of his mother, Queen Isabella, taken control of his throne. Now, in a bid to show the reach of his power, the King was attempting to curb the widespread breakdown of law and order which threatened to bring England to its knees.

Garrick tried again, his words beginning to show his impatience. 'I have to take word of your compliance back to the King, Wennesley. Your reply?'

Gesturing to a servant to pour the messenger some ale, Wennesley broke off his unblinking examination of Garrick's pale countenance. 'Be seated. I would be interested to hear how you found me?'

'Found you?'

'I am not at home.'

Garrick shuffled uneasily. 'Sheriff Ingram told me where to find you.'

An amused smile crossed Wennesley's face, but the humour failed to reach his eyes. 'Did he now?'

'He did. My orders were to inform Ingram that he is to help you on this mission. As he resides further north of London than you do, it was sensible for me to call on him first, and then weave back south to you.'

'Which *would* make perfect sense, except that you thought I'd be in Bakewell...' Wennesley let his words hang in the air before adding, 'interesting that Ingram knew I was here. He was only reinstated as sheriff a few days ago.'

Unwilling to acknowledge the implied questions, Garrick looked at the worn furniture and the mess of linen on the bed, 'You mean to spend the New Year celebration here?'

'I meant to go back to Wennesley today.' Roger's eyes dropped back to the document in his hand, unease rising in his gut. 'I must admit, Master Garrick; you are not the manner of visitor I had hoped for on this penultimate day of 1329.'

'And yet I travelled from London, through the worst of the winter frosts, to be here on the orders of King Edward himself.'

'Which is a curious thing, don't you think? I am no one, Garrick. The youngest son of a down-at-heel knight. This makes me insignificant in royal circles, yet you are sent to hunt me down - even to here, a tavern in Leicestershire, when I live many miles away in Derbyshire. A few more hours, and I'd be heading home. Why does King Edward send you out of your way to ensure I undertake this undesirable task?'

Garrick stabbed a finger towards the parchment in Wennesley's hand. 'You know why.'

'I still find it curious that the King would send you out in the midst of winter to find me. Kinder to you and easier for me, if this must be done, to attempt such a hazardous mission in the spring or summer. The urgency for the monarch to prove himself must be keenly felt.'

The messenger thought better of commenting as he listened to Wennesley read the list of men he'd been detailed to apprehend on behalf of the Crown.

'Nicholas and John Coterel... Eustace, Walter, Laurence, Robert and the Reverend Richard de Folville... are things so bad that Edward needs to send a murderer to catch murderers?'

Garrick took an involuntary step backwards, making Wennesley laugh. 'I was not the only man in the room when I despatched Laurence Coterel; and I only did so because I was backed into a corner. I had no choice. This decoration I wear,' Wennesley rubbed at the short scar which ran across his right cheek, 'is proof of that! To my mind it was self-defence, not murder - but the law didn't see it like that, did it? Too ready an opportunity to fine me. To take almost every penny I had to maintain my liberty. And now the King threatens me anew with the loss of my freedom if I do not comply with his wishes!

'Survival makes men do things they later regret.' Wennesley met the messenger's unhappy gaze as he went on. 'Even the surviving Coterel brothers act as though Laurence did not exist rather than admitting to the weakness of having had their kin snuffed out in a brawl.'

Privately wishing he was carrying a weapon, Garrick said, 'The King believes you have special knowledge of the Coterel family. Your home is but a few miles from Bakewell and...'

'And the Folvilles? What does King Edward believe I know of them, beyond the fact that they control Leicestershire with a fierce loyalty?'

'A fierce, violent loyalty,' Garrick confirmed, 'which is why action is required.'

'The Coterels and Folvilles are dangerous, ruthless and uncompromising. What is more, the local people are on their side, because, however violent they may be, they are not as cruel as the law. I am but one man; how does the King suggest I go about dealing with such experienced felons?'

Garrick drew himself up straight, his spine a determined ramrod. 'That, my Lord, is your concern. King Edward expects to have word from you by the last day of January. If you have not arrested the men listed on that document by then, I would advise you to consider your own future.'

'Brave words from an unarmed man, many miles from home.'

'Do not think to threaten me, Wennesley.' Garrick brushed his tunic nervously, pulling his cloak tighter around his shoulders in a gesture designed to announce his departure. 'This task is your punishment. If you would rather I issued a warrant in your name for the murder of Laurence Coterel instead, then all you have to do is ask. After all, I'm the one the King trusts to control his pen and ink.'

Wennesley frowned. 'And is it legal to punish a man for the same crime twice?'

'Do you really want to be the one who asks the King that?'

Roger struggled to bite back his frustration. 'Has Ingram read this?' He waved the offending parchment under Garrick's nose.

'He has not. My orders were to show it to you and you alone.'

'Yet he knows of the contents?'

'The relevant information has been shared with His Lordship.'

Wennesley smiled despite himself. 'You'll go far, Garrick.

~ *Chapter One* ~

The sound of a fist hammering at the door to the bedchamber broke through Mathilda's contented slumber. Slower to react than her husband of just three days, she blinked the sleep from her eyes as Robert de Folville leapt from their bed. Wrapping a cloak around his naked frame, he responded to the urgency of the rapping by flinging the door wide open.

'Adam, whatever's wrong?'

Clutching the bedclothes to her chest, Mathilda tried to hear what was so pressing that their steward had had to wake them so unceremoniously. The draught, which shot with cruel enthusiasm through the open doorway of the manor house's second-best bedchamber, made the new Lady Folville shiver, but not as much as her suspicion that something was wrong.

One look at Robert's expression as he turned from the door confirmed Mathilda's fears. 'Something's happened.'

Instead of elaborating, he threw open the clothes chest in the corner of the room and began piling garments onto the bed. 'There is a linen roll under the bed; could you fetch it?'

Recognising the determined set of her husband's face, Matilda hooked a layer of bed linen around her shoulders and dragged a bundle of bound material from beneath the bed. 'You're packing?'

'We're packing.' Robert stopped moving as fast as he'd started and beckoned her to his side. 'I'm so sorry, Mathilda. This isn't the start to married life I'd imagined for us.'

Engulfed in his arms, relishing the closeness of his flesh, Mathilda concentrated on remaining calm. 'What do you mean?'

'We have to go away for a while.'

He stroked a hand through her wavy hair, teasing out the stubborn red tangles that had formed overnight. Even through the tenderness of the gesture, Mathilda could feel the tension rising in him. 'Away?'

'I'll explain while we pack.' Robert produced another roll from beneath the bed. 'Separately.'

Determined not to neither shout nor give in to the tears that unhelpfully threatened to escape from the corner of her eyes, Mathilda spoke firmly. 'Husband, the road to our marriage was not a smooth one. Are you telling me that, only three days after our wedding, we have to part?'

Robert's eyes flashed with both regret and devilment. 'Wife, you married into a family of felons. You didn't expect we were going to live here happily ever after, did you?'

Ignoring the twinkle in his eye that could so easily have diverted them from the task at hand, Mathilda crossed her arms. 'I knew exactly what I was marrying into. I learnt the hard way if you remember.' She rubbed at the bruises that littered her skin after her run in with the murderer Rowan Leigh. 'And the lesson I grasped fastest of all is that Folville men act first and think second. Therefore, I am not shifting one limb from our chamber until you tell me what's going on.'

Mathilda's hands went to her hips. The result, rather than making her appear more determined, caused the sheet to fall from her body, giving her husband an appreciated, but ill-timed, view of her naked form.

Before Robert allowed desire to take over, he grabbed Mathilda's shoulders and spun her around so she faced away from him. 'If you stand there like that, woman we'll get nothing done. Get dressed; time is short!'

'Why? Why is it short?' Grabbing her chemise from the back of a wooden chair, Mathilda pulled it over her head, followed by her workday tunic, before replacing her hands on her hips. 'I am not dressing properly or moving again until you tell me what Adam said.'

Robert returned to pulling cloaks and tunics from the wooden trunk, passing them to Mathilda to fold. 'For now, just be aware we have to leave Ashby Folville.'

'But…'

'For Robyn Hode's sake, Mathilda! Amongst other things, my unholy brother, the Rector of Teigh, is back in England. Does that sound urgent enough for you?'

At the mention of the only Folville brother she was afraid of, a man who had tried to have her killed, Mathilda froze.

Her mind raced. Richard de Folville, that most unlikely cleric, had, almost a year ago, nearly destroyed her, her family in Twyford and Robert. As a consequence, he had been exiled to France to fight for the King; a bargain his brothers had struck with the sheriff to save his skin. Mathilda had never dreamt he'd survive his time on the battlefield, nor be allowed to come back to England.

Seeing his wife's ashen complexion, Robert reached one hand out to her, while continuing to pack with the other. 'I can't say I'm thrilled he's in England, but I'm not surprised. Richard can Bible-talk his way out of any situation.'

Folding her most practical gowns, Mathilda asked, 'Why do we have to leave here, though? Richard will hardly invade us with force of arms. He's a cleric!'

'He is a man on the run. My brother, Lord John, will never admit him into the household at Huntingdon, nor would Eustace allow him at the house in Leicester. Where else would he come but here?'

'On the run?' Mathilda frowned. 'But surely, if he is back in England, he must have been pardoned for what he did to us?'

'This is for another crime.'

She rolled her eyes. 'Hardly surprising. I can't imagine your reverend brother managing a week without causing someone harm just for the sheer fun of it!'

Robert paused before he added, 'And he is not the only one. On the run, I mean.'

Mathilda stopped suddenly, in the act of folding a gown in half. 'You?'

Robert sighed. 'And Eustace, Laurence, and Walter.'

'But...'

'Adam has just received word from Nicholas Coterel in Bakewell. Coterel and his brother John have got wind of a warrant out for their arrest - and ours too. As soon as they heard, Nicholas sent a messenger to us overnight. It is clear that it would be wise for none of us to remain at home awaiting that particular knock on the door.'

'But why? You haven't...' Mathilda was about to say he hadn't done anything, but the words caught in her throat. Of course he'd done something, he was a Folville: one of the brothers who ruled the area with a strong, albeit criminal, hand. Instead she said, 'But no warrant against my Lords John or Thomas?'

'For some reason my eldest brother has escaped this time; probably his status as Lord of the Manor has afforded him protection. As for Thomas, I'm not sure why he slipped through the net. At the moment I am unaware where the exact spark for this particular warrant ignited, and I'm not going to stay here to find out.' Robert stooped to kiss the top of Mathilda's head. 'Don't worry. We've weathered worse than this. We'll be home in a few weeks, but it's best to be prepared.'

Mathilda folded a thick fur wrap into the second roll. 'Where are we going?'

'It's best I don't tell you where I am ultimately bound. That way you can't tell anyone if pressed. But before I go, I'm taking you to Rockingham Castle. The constable, Robert de Vere, will keep you safe.'

Not wanting to sound as frightened as she felt, Mathilda said, 'Can't I come with you? We work better together.'

'We do, but this time it wouldn't be wise; not until I've heard the details of the charges laid against us. I don't know what I'm to face and I wish to keep my wife safe.'

Seeing Robert was in no mood to argue, Mathilda asked instead about their household staff. 'What about Sarah, Adam, Ulric, and Daniel?'

'Daniel will come with us. I'm leaving him with you as company and as an emergency messenger. The others will stay here. They are not under suspicion, and I wish this place to remain occupied in our absence.'

'I could stay with them. I'm not under suspicion, surely?'

'You are not, but you are known to be dear to me. If King Edward's appointed man takes it upon himself to torture anyone for information about our whereabouts, I'd sooner that person wasn't you.'

'But you're comfortable with risking Sarah to be tortured?' Mathilda snapped. 'And what about Adam and Ulric?'

'Eustace is leaving men to guard them and the manor.'

'But if men do come and torture…'

'I spoke hastily to try and get you to hurry; that will not happen.'

'But…'

'Please, Mathilda, pack faster.'

Selecting a handful of head linens, trying not to think about anything beyond the task in hand, Mathilda realised how little she knew of her husband's life before she'd been so unceremoniously dropped into it.

When she'd been offered up as a ransom against a debt of her father's, the last thing Mathilda had expected was to fall in love with one of her captors. A potter's daughter should not marry into the gentry - not even to a younger son. And she certainly should not have married into the most notorious noble family in the county.

Mathilda's eye fell upon the leather girdle belt that hung over the back of her chair. Pausing in her labours, she ran soft fingers over the exquisite butterfly decoration. Robert had presented the belt to her not long after they'd met. It had been made for him by a friend to give to the girl he'd marry one day; a friend who'd been murdered soon after Mathilda had met him.

'Let me.' Seeing Mathilda stroke her favourite possession, Robert looped it around her waist. 'I confess that I prefer unclasping this to clasping it, but I have to say Master Hugo couldn't have designed it better.'

'I will keep it with me always.'

Robert saw the bravery in her smile. 'We won't be parted long, I -'

Mathilda placed a finger over his lips before he'd finished. 'I know what you were going to promise me, but please don't. We can't afford promises we may not be able to keep, however much we mean to.

~ *Chapter Two* ~

Sarah, her floury sleeves pushed up past her elbows, leant against the oak table and poured steaming broth into a row of five ceramic beakers.

Every surface in the kitchen was covered with signs of activity. The housekeeper had been working since the Coterels' messenger had arrived just before dawn. She was determined to send her masters into the ice-covered world with full bellies and panniers bulging with food. If they had to face an uncertain future, at least they wouldn't face it hungry.

Having raised six of the seven Folville brothers since they were pups, Sarah was as much a mother to them as their servant. The dark cast of concern that shadowed the housekeeper's usually serene face spoke volumes to Mathilda as she came into the kitchen.

She wondered if Sarah was thinking about the only brother she hadn't raised. Richard de Folville had been sent to the Church for his education from an early age. Naturally cruel, his separation from his family had caused him to harbour a grudge against his brothers and, more specifically, against Sarah. This irrational bitterness had already had devastating consequences. At least two murders had occurred as a result of the Rector of Teigh blaming Sarah for sending him away as a child, though she'd had no say in the decision whatsoever.

Raising her eyes from her work, Sarah gave Mathilda a brave smile. 'Good morning, Lady Folville.'

The formality of her friend's welcome alerted Mathilda to the fact that they could be overheard. 'Good morning, Sarah, are my Lords Eustace and Walter ready to leave?'

'They're in the main hall with the sheriff.'

Mathilda grabbed hold of the table. Her last encounter with Edward de Cressy, Sheriff of Leicestershire and Nottinghamshire, had not ended well. 'De Cressy is here?'

'No, it's Robert Ingram.'

Mathilda was confused. 'The former sheriff?'

'Reinstated.' Sarah looked satisfied by this development. 'I don't know the details, but apparently De Cressy saw the wisdom of leaving the area for a while. Sensible, don't you think?'

Mathilda's reply was barely more than a whisper. 'At least Ingram will deal fairly with us.' Her mind pushed down the images of Edmund de Cressy's treacherously gloating face, not to mention the horror of his expression when he'd paid the price for crossing the Folville brothers.

Following Sarah's gaze as she peered along the corridor which linked the kitchen to the manor's main hall, Mathilda forced her thoughts back to the matter in hand. 'Are Daniel and Adam preparing the horses?'

'Yes, my Lady.' Sarah glanced around. 'Do you know what's happening? You aren't really leaving, are you?'

'I fear so.' Mathilda allowed a glimmer of the unease she felt to show on her face. 'Robert hasn't said much. I know a warrant has been issued for five of the brothers' arrest -'

Before she could say more, her husband arrived, placing their pack rolls on the bench. 'Ingram is here?'

Mathilda passed him a beaker of ale. 'He waits by the hall fire with Lords Eustace and Walter. Did you know he had become sheriff again?'

'As of ten minutes ago.' Robert held his arm out to his wife, 'Let's go and learn the extent of the problem.' He took a few paces forward, before turning back to the housekeeper. 'I think you should hear this too, Sarah. Fetch Adam, Daniel, and Ulric, and bring them to the hall along with the refreshments. You are all entitled to know what's going to happen. There is no point having Ingram tell the tale twice.'

Robert Ingram, newly reinstated Sheriff of Leicestershire and Derbyshire and Mayor of Nottingham, sat by the roaring fire. His booted feet were stretched out before him, resting on a stool. His slim calloused hands cupped a tankard of Sarah's ale. His face was calm and unruffled. The activities of the Folvilles neither surprised nor disturbed him as he waited for his audience to fully assemble.

'Lord and Lady Folville, it is a pleasure to see you so soon after your most entertaining nuptials.'

Mathilda curtseyed; thinking that 'entertaining' was an interesting choice of word for a wedding which had ended in a terrifying hostage situation. Had that really only been three days ago?

'My Lord, you have news?' Robert sat opposite the sheriff, with Eustace and Walter to his right and Mathilda to his left. The household staff stood mutely behind him.

Eustace de Folville, second in line to the family title after the absent Lord John, addressed the sheriff in turn. 'This news has been confirmed, Ingram? We are not the subject of ill-founded rumour or malicious hearsay?'

'You are not.' The sheriff steepled his hands together as he spoke. 'A messenger came to me early yesterday. There is no doubting the seriousness of the situation.'

Eustace gave a humourless smile. 'I think we're all grateful that you're the one holding the reins of the county again. Can you imagine the delight in which De Cressy would have received this news!'

'I hope that feeling remains through what follows, my Lord.' Ingram held Eustace's gaze, something few men were brave enough to do. 'We have little time. As you know, King Edward has shaken off the influence of his mother and taken full control of the throne. This can only be good for England, however...' He paused, as if unsure how to proceed. 'However, in order to stamp his mark upon the Crown, Edward is making a great show of clearing up the lawlessness that swept the country under the rule of his mother and her rebel lover, Mortimer.'

Robert grunted with annoyance. 'Let me guess. King Edward is making sure he's seen to be taking a stand against all felons, without any regard for the fact that many of us did what was necessary to rule justly while England was in chaos.'

Eustace gave his brother a sharp stare. 'Trust you to make this sound like a line from a Robyn Hode story.'

The sheriff raised a hand to stop the escalating argument. 'Whatever the rights and wrongs, the situation is clear. King Edward has ordered the arrest of Nicholas and John Coterel on the charges of the murders of John Matkynson and Sir William Knyveton, at Bradley in Derbyshire.'

Swallowing against her suddenly dry throat, Mathilda found herself picturing Nicholas Coterel. Jet black hair framing his weathered face, his piercing eyes finding everything he saw both amusing and challenging. He was a ruthless man; but a ruthless man with principles she respected. Nicholas had cared for her brother, Oswin, and had saved her life. Yet he wasn't the sort of man who worried about being praised for his acts of kindness, however oddly they displayed themselves. He simply did what he believed to be right and to hell with the consequences; good or bad.

Grateful that Oswin no longer lived in Bakewell with the Coterels, but was at home in the village of Twyford with her father and other brother, Matthew, making ceramics for sale in the local markets, Mathilda braced herself to hear the rest of Ingram's news.

'We received an early warning from Bakewell, did you send word to them too?' Robert slipped a hand into his wife's.

'No, but I am not surprised they know. Nicholas has as many informants as I do.'

Robert nodded. 'And the implications of this warrant for my family, Lord Sheriff?'

'As the church bells strike noon today I will be meeting with King Edward's chosen man to discuss the capture and arrest of Nicholas and John Coterel, along with you, my Lords Eustace, Robert, and Walter, as well as your brother Laurence Folville and the newly returned Richard, rector of Teigh.'

The crash of a pottery pitcher as it hit the stone-flagged floor was followed by a torrent of ale leaking across the hall. Adam caught Sarah's arm as her body sagged. Grasping her friend close, Mathilda addressed the men. 'My Lords, if you'll excuse us. I will look after Sarah. Please continue.'

Ushering the housekeeper and Adam out of the room, nodding to Daniel and Ulric to clear up the mess, Mathilda cursed herself for not having warned Sarah about Richard. Seating her friend by the kitchen fireplace, Mathilda wrapped a blanket around her shoulders. 'Are you alright?'

The housekeeper rubbed her right arm where she'd been

stabbed in an attack some months ago. 'Richard is truly back in England?'

'I think he must be.' Mathilda scowled, 'I don't know any more than you.'

Adam pointed along the corridor to the hall, 'Go back, my Lady, please. I'll take care of Sarah. We need to know if that cursed cleric is on his way here.'

With a quick reassuring glance at Sarah, Mathilda hooked up the hem of her gown, and dashed back to the meeting.

Acknowledging the Lady Folville's return, Ingram broke off from what he'd been saying. 'Is your housekeeper well? Forgive me; with recent events moving so quickly I had forgotten how badly the rector treated her.'

'Adam is caring for Sarah. It was the shock of knowing Father Richard is in England again, my Lord.'

Swiftly, Robert bought Mathilda up to date. 'We have approximately six hours until the five of us, and Nicholas and John Coterel, are fugitives. King Edward has ordered not just our arrest, but our imprisonment in Nottingham Castle until trial.'

Eustace barked a harsh humourless laugh. 'You have to hand it to Edward; he's an optimistic one.'

'And yet he is in deadly earnest.' Ingram drained the last trace of ale from his cup. 'I bring you this news as I have worked with your family for some time, an arrangement that has served us all well. However, from midday I'll have no choice but to sever that agreement for as long as needs be. I will, of course, only act against you when I have no choice, but I fear that must happen. For I am not the man our King has entrusted with your imprisonment. I am but the appointed helper.'

Eustace pulled a face. 'Not you?' He drew a dagger from his belt and played it through his hands thoughtfully. 'That puts a different shine on things.'

Ignoring the weapon, Ingram said, 'Giving another this most difficult assignment is a clever move by our monarch, who is probably aware of my connection to you.'

'Enough of the suspense, Ingram.' Eustace continued to fiddle with his blade, a sure sign of his growing impatience. 'Who is this other man?'

'From noon I will be under the guidance of Roger Wennesley, of Derbyshire.'

Eustace was on his feet, slamming his palms on the table as his dagger point stabbed into the worn oak. 'That man is a cold-blooded murderer! He killed Laurence Coterel over something less substantial than a puff of air.'

The brief silence that followed was only punctuated by the guttering of the fire and Mathilda's sharp intake of breath. 'The Coterels had another brother?'

'They did, until Wennesley stabbed him in the heat of an argument.' Robert got to his feet. 'It seems there is little time. The King has been clever. A killer to catch killers. I assume that if Wennesley is unsuccessful in his task, Edward will see him either outlawed or executed as punishment for Laurence's murder?'

'Exactly.' Ingram too stood. 'Wennesley's future depends on his success.'

Eustace growled, before saying, 'We are on this list, but I am more intrigued by who isn't on it.'

Robert agreed, 'My Lords John and Thomas -'

'I was thinking more of James Coterel.'

'Another brother? But...' Seeing Robert's expression Mathilda stopped talking and listened.

Ingram gave a weak smile. 'You predict my next warning, Eustace. Yes, James Coterel is also missing from the warrant. He is, I suspect, too useful to the Crown to be included in this operation. There are rumours that Queen Philippa herself has a liking for the man.'

'A soft spot for the most violent and controlling man I've ever met,' Eustace scoffed. 'How sweet!'

Confusion threatened to engulf Mathilda. She and her husband was about to leave the manor, her new family was under the threat of arrest, and now she'd discovered that the Coterel family was not exactly as they had seemed to her, not if Eustace, a man with a fearsome reputation of his own, was calling James Coterel most violent man he'd ever known.

Her desperate desire to ask a great many questions was curtailed as the sheriff got to his feet. 'I must leave. It is important that you remember I was never here.'

'Before you go, my Lord,' Mathilda spoke fast, not wanting to delay their progress from the manor. 'The Rector; do you know where he is? And my brother-in-law, Laurence de Folville? Has he been informed there is a warrant out for his arrest? And for that matter, what are the charges against my kin?'

'What is lodged against this family, as yet I don't know. You must find and warn Laurence yourselves. As to the rector… my sources tell me Richard arrived from France last week. I imagine only the length of the journey from Dover to Leicestershire, and the slow going of the winter weather, prevented him from joining your wedding celebration.'

Thanking God that Richard hadn't been there, Mathilda muttered, 'So he could arrive any day now.'

'Indeed he could.'

~ *Chapter Three* ~

Roger Wennesley ate his breakfast. His fingers massaged the scarred flesh of his right cheek as he chewed. He wasn't foolish enough to think he could simply ride into the Coterel and Folville manors, asking politely that the inhabitants allow him to arrest them then accompany him to Nottingham Castle.

However, King Edward's instructions had been clear. He was to capture, arrest, and imprison the felons listed. The consequences of him not doing so had been implied, if not stated. His own arrest, imprisonment, and death.

Sipping at the warmed ale the inn's maid had delivered to his table, Wennesley snorted. He would wager the King had no idea how many miles lay between Bakewell and Nottingham; not to mention the distance between Nottingham and Ashby Folville in Leicestershire. Catching these men would be challenging enough. Transporting them without being ambushed by their supporters would be another issue entirely. At least not every Coterel and Folville needed rounding up, he thought grimly.

'Brydon!' he called across the room to where the innkeeper's son was helping his mother.

'Master Wennesley?'

Roger pulled some coins from his money pouch. 'You

will ride to the dwelling of Thomas Sproxton for me. Inform him that the time to repay the debt he owes me has come. I require his assistance immediately.'

Pocketing the money without delay, the boy paused only for directions and ran from the smoky room.

Running his eyes over the document the King's clerk had left, Wennesley frowned. Sproxton, his friend and occasional business associate, would be reluctant to join him in this enterprise. He'd be even more reluctant if he read the full contents of the commission from the King. Yet Sproxton owed him, and Wennesley wanted help in this enterprise from someone he could rely on - and that didn't include Ingram, who was in the pay of the Folvilles and possibly the Coterels as well.

The Coterels... There was one less of them now. Laurence had been the most brutal of the brothers, but not the fastest-thinking. The livid scar on Wennesley's cheek, which still itched, was testament to that. He wasn't foolish enough to think taking in Nicholas and John would be any easier; after all, they already hated him for killing their brother.

He had to hand it to the King. One way or another Edward was going to take visible charge in the midland counties but whether that was by the deaths of Coterels, Folvilles, or through his own demise, Roger Wennesley didn't want to hazard a guess.

Jamming the last of his breakfast bread between his teeth, he chewed purposefully. He had no doubt that Sheriff Ingram would already know what the King was up to. The man had spies everywhere, and it would be unwise to underestimate him. In fact, if Wennesley had judged the situation correctly, Ingram would, by now, have alerted both families involved of the farce to come.

'Farce.' He played the word around his lips, pulling his

winter cloak around his shoulders as he headed to the stables. 'I wonder…'

Richard de Folville was in no hurry to rise from his bed. He lay where he was, appreciating the clean blankets and the sensation of comfort after months of camping out and being frozen to the bone, night after night, on the edges of various French fields.

He'd crossed the border into Leicestershire yesterday, finding a room at the Black Horse Inn in Market Harborough. Although he'd been tempted to rush straight to Ashby Folville, his time abroad had taught him an overdue lesson in the benefit of stopping to think before he acted.

It grated that Mathilda of Twyford had outwitted him; causing him to be exposed. He'd been arrested and sent to France to fight for the King in lieu of arrest, even though he hadn't been the killer; not this time anyway. Richard had whiled away his absence from England by stewing over the manner of his eventual revenge.

There was no way he was going to allow a potter's daughter to believe she'd got the better of him. Richard didn't care that his brother Robert had developed an affection for the girl. Nor would the virtues of charity and forgiveness encouraged by his clerical status interfere with his well-honed characteristics of distrust, hatred, and grudge-bearing.

The Twyford girl was of a lowly status. By now, she'd have been used for whatever purposes his brothers saw fit and passed over in favour of a more suitable woman. That is, if Robert hadn't gone back to his unholy preferences for the male of the species.

Richard sniggered into his linen, until he remembered that it was only his belief that Robert had harboured vile feelings for a local craftsman - a belief which had led to his scheming and later his exile. Yet, despite everything, Richard remained convinced there was something to it, that Robert was incapable of loving women.

A voice at the back of the rector's head asked if he was wrong. If perhaps he was the one incapable of love. He quashed it. Personal doubt wasn't worth wasting time on. Anyway, if that was true, it was not his fault. It was that cursed housekeeper Sarah's fault, for not loving him as much as the others.

The growling of his belly told Richard it was time to leave his blanketed haven and go in search of food. Then he'd head to Ashby and, from there, onto Mathilda's family home in Twyford. The plan he'd formed as he parried and thrust his sword against the French nudged at the inside of his skull. He'd waited long enough for retribution. It was time to send the women who'd sent him to France to witness hell on earth, to Hell itself.

'Thomas.' Wennesley raised a hand in welcome.

'Roger.' Sproxton didn't bother dismounting as he watched his companion climb into his saddle. 'You're still here?'

'Apparently.' Wennesley grimaced. 'That's why I called you.'

Thomas Sproxton's expression began to display a little of the anxiety he'd felt when Brydon had come to find him. 'Where are we bound?'

'Leicester. To start with.'

Sproxton levelled his eyes on the tall man on the grey stallion. 'You called in my debt sooner than I'd expected.'

'If I hadn't needed to, I'd have let it go. A situation has been thrust upon me that requires delicate handling. I would be grateful of both your strength of arm and your counsel.'

'I see.' In fact, Thomas saw nothing, but he hadn't survived twenty years of life without knowing when to ask questions and when to hold his tongue. 'The lad told me to be prepared for some nights away.' He indicated the pack behind his saddle. 'You don't expect this situation to be swiftly concluded?'

'It's unlikely.' Roger fixed his friend with a hard stare, suspicion at what lay behind the question pricking at the back of his mind. 'You have a matter to attend to?'

'Not at all. I wanted to be sure I have enough supplies.' Thomas circled his impatient horse. 'Time is short, I take it?'

'It is. I'll explain as we ride.'

They were a mile outside the town before Roger considered it safe to speak of the challenge ahead. Ducking under the cover of the forest edge, he beckoned for Thomas to draw his horse closer. 'You recall our run in with Laurence Coterel?'

'I could hardly forget it.' Thomas gestured to the slash on his companion's cheek. 'I was only inches from having a matching ornament on my face. If I hadn't struck him on the head when I did, then…'

Roger raised a hand, as if to brush away the obvious end to Sproxton's sentence. 'Well the King has decided I need to be punished for Laurence's death after all.'

'But you paid a fine, and -'

Roger cut across his friend. 'I know, I know, but young Edward is clever. He has seen how to use our run-in with a Coterel as an opportunity to clear the region of noble felons.'

'And?' Thomas's expression darkened.

'And if I don't orchestrate the capture of Nicholas and John Coterel by the end of January, then I am to be declared outlaw and hunted until I'm dead.'

Thomas was incredulous. 'How on earth…?'

'You haven't heard the best bit yet.'

'Go on.'

'I have to arrest Eustace, Richard, Laurence, Walter, and Robert de Folville as well.'

Thomas pulled his horse to an abrupt halt. 'That's suicide.'

'Yes, it is.' Roger nodded solemnly. 'Why else do you think I've asked for your help?'

~ *Chapter Four* ~

'Are you insane?'

Mathilda was stunned at her friend's outspokenness. Sarah had the respect of the household, but that did not mean she had liberty to speak her mind in her masters' presence. Especially not in anger.

'I beg your pardon?' Robert growled. 'Explain yourself, woman!'

Undeterred by her master's ire, Sarah spoke on. 'Are you really taking your new wife into that den of thieves? Do you honestly believe De Vere will see her kept safe?'

Mathilda's pulse quickened as she looked from Robert to Sarah and back again. She couldn't imagine Robert deliberately putting her in harm's way, but equally Sarah would never speak out in such a manner unless she was frightened.

Everything was happening so fast. After the sheriff's departure the brothers, acting as though Mathilda wasn't there, had discussed her disposal. Eustace had agreed with Robert that she would be safer with their associate, Robert de Vere, the constable of Rockingham Castle, than with them. The words 'in case we never return' hung in the air unspoken. She also noted how Eustace had used the word 'associate' rather than 'friend'.

Amused rather than annoyed by the outburst from the

housekeeper, Eustace ripped a lump of bread off a fresh loaf to put in his scrip. 'You give the women in this house too much rope, brother.'

Ignoring the familiar jibe, Robert reined in his temper. 'Sarah, if you haven't worked out that I'd never do anything to endanger Mathilda then you don't know me at all.'

Far from content with his reply, Sarah's hands fixed themselves to her hips. 'You say that, yet jeopardy follows your family like a stray dog. There are hazards everywhere; surely they are better faced when we all stick together?'

Robert held Sarah's gaze, glad that Adam was in the stables; otherwise he'd be backing her up. He could feel Mathilda's eyes on him. For once she wasn't asking questions. That told him how worried she was.

Bored of the moment's theatre, Eustace grunted, 'Walter and I are going now. I'll leave five of my men to watch the manor and keep Sarah, Adam, and Ulric safe. They can also be used as messengers. We'll see you in the agreed location, Robert. Do not tarry in Rockingham too long.'

The silence left by Eustace and Walter's hasty departure felt heavy as Mathilda sat next to her husband. Refusing to be hurried despite the atmosphere of urgency, she said, 'I am not happy about leaving Sarah, despite the presence of Eustace's mercenaries. If Richard is truly on his way... well, it isn't too hard to guess what he'll have in mind for her. Husband, I am not setting one foot towards my palfrey until you tell me everything I need to know about Robert de Vere. And before you shout and say time is short, I am acutely aware of that. Talk quickly, my Lord.'

In truth, Robert wasn't happy about the arrangements being thrust upon them either. 'If I thought it was safe, I'd leave you here, Mathilda. I trust few people with your welfare as much as I do Adam and Sarah, but you are too obvious a hostage. Wennesley is not a stupid man. He would know the quickest way to capture me would be to take you. With you as his prisoner, all he'd have to do is wait for me to try and rescue you, before catching me too. Then my brothers would come to save both of us and... well, you can imagine the rest. It would be a perfect trap, neatly baited with you.'

Mathilda hated that he was right. 'And Robert de Vere?'

'We've made use of de Vere's services on a number of occasions. I will not lie and tell you he is a good man. He is not. But nor is he evil. He will keep you safe, because I will pay him to do so. Nothing speaks louder to the constable of Rockingham Castle than money.'

Sarah shook her head, but she kept her counsel as Mathilda listened to Robert. 'De Vere knows that crossing a Folville would not be a good idea.'

'And if you don't come back for me?' Mathilda spoke the words boldly, hoping she was successful in hiding how afraid she was of that prospect.

'I will be back.'

'But...'

'I *will* come back for you.'

A hush fell across the kitchen before Mathilda steered the conversation back to the returning cleric. 'What of Sarah's safety from the jealous rage of your reverend brother?'

'I will send one of Eustace's men out to try and intercept Richard before he sets foot across the threshold, plus another two to his church at Teigh. I have no intention of letting that man near any of the people I care for.'

Mathilda didn't let herself look back at the manor as her palfrey trotted through the courtyard gateway by Robert's side, with Daniel following behind on his pony. She couldn't shake the sensation that they were leaving Ashby Folville for good.

She didn't see Adam slip his arm around Sarah's shoulders as they'd bid them farewell at the kitchen door. It was hard to remember that four days ago she and Sarah had been talking excitedly about wedding food, gowns, and their hopes for a bright future. Now Mathilda, fresh from that wedding, was leaving her friends behind. Soon she'd be alone but for young Daniel, in the trust of a man who only cared as long as he was paid to care.

Robert's final words as they'd left the kitchen rang in Mathilda's ears. 'I'm sorry; but this is what it means to marry a Folville.'

No one spoke as they travelled the road that led away from Ashby Folville, towards the castle at Rockingham. Occasionally Mathilda glanced at her husband. He looked as far as it was possible to be from the contented man he'd been the night before, when they'd taken a private supper in their room and discussed their mutual hopes and dreams for their life together.

As they steered the horses off the main road and under the cover of the forest trees, Robert finally spoke. 'De Vere has been a help to my family on many occasions. He mixes with rough company and it is true he usually takes payment for his protective services, but let us be plain: he is nothing compared to Eustace or the Coterels. And De Vere has connections everywhere.'

Remembering how frightened she'd been of Nicholas Coterel before she'd met him and how she'd found him to be a man with a dry sense of humour and a sense of honour that many officials could do well to copy, Mathilda sighed in resignation. 'I'm sorry I questioned you like I did. I was frightened. It's so soon after our marriage and…'

Robert held up a hand. 'I know, my love. I feel the same, but difficult decisions needed to be made in haste. I can only hope I have made the right ones.' He peered into the trees on either side as he spoke.

'You are expecting to be arrested already?' Mathilda's breath caught in her throat.

'It is possible, but I gauge I'm safe for a few hours yet. Ingram and Wennesley set the time for our pursuit from noon. They won't deviate from that.'

'You are so sure?'

'Ingram I am very sure of. Of Wennesley, I am less certain. Yet he is not a stupid man, nor is he free from felony himself. I am intrigued as to how he is going to play this game.'

'Game?'

'To him it will be a game. Trust me.'

Ever since they'd watched Robert, Mathilda, and Daniel disappear from sight, Sarah had attacked her household chores like a woman possessed. Adam knew she was afraid to stop, that if she kept moving, kept cleaning, prepared more food and worked harder, the time would pass quicker and they'd all be riding home again.

It had taken both his and Ulric's strength of will to make Sarah stop. Only by wrenching the kindling basket out of the exhausted housekeeper's hands had Adam got her to sit at the kitchen's scrubbed oak table.

Laying his large palm over hers, the steward waited for Sarah's racing pulse to ease under his reassuring touch before he said, 'I am not going to promise that they'll be alright because that would be foolish. I can promise though that they will do everything they can to remain unmolested.'

Sarah patted Adam's arm. 'You know that's why, don't

you?'

'Why what?'

Not given to displays of emotion, Sarah squeezed his hand. 'Why I agreed to marry you. You don't pretend everything will be alright when you can't possibly know. You don't make promises you can't keep.'

Adam brushed a stray hair from Sarah's face. 'I wish we'd had time to tell them.'

Sarah, some of her usual resolve returning, said, 'Well, it will be a nice surprise when they get back.'

Adam kissed the tip of her nose. 'The end of the month. We'll marry as soon as we can after that.'

~ *Chapter Five* ~

Lady Isabella de Vere pulled her favourite cloak around her shoulders. There were times when she was grateful for her father's dubiously funded lifestyle. It meant they could afford luxuries that their status would otherwise not allow. One of those luxuries now swaddled her against the chill of late December.

The pale green cloak's ermine collar hugging her neck would have been the envy of women of far nobler birth than she. Isabella tucked her hands beneath the folds of the heavy fabric, glad that she'd escaped the castle before her maid, Agnes, had trussed her hair up beneath its linen. This minor rebellion against protocol allowed Isabella's neck and shoulders the extra insulation that her long raven black hair afforded.

Her stomach gave an unladylike growl. Cold and hungry, Isabella waited, anxious but unafraid. The hour for his arrival was overdue. A restless impatience gnawed at her mind as much as her hunger gnawed at her belly. Thomas had promised he'd come and so he would; but there was no escaping the fact that he'd claimed he'd be there just before midnight and yet dawn had already broken.

Isabella wondered if she should go home, but if her father had noticed her absence there was a chance he'd never risk letting her out of sight again. Anyway, it was so dark. The hours of winter light seemed to get shorter every day, despite Cook's wittering about how the days were already lengthening towards spring. Either way, Rockingham Forest was not a place to cross alone at night.

Anyone could be out there. Unseen, waiting for a chance to strike against an unwary passerby. Thanks to her father, Rockingham Castle and its outskirts had become a focal point for criminals, making the woodland which surrounded the dwelling in which Isabella hid one of the most dangerous places in England.

Perching on the rough cot that ran along the edge of the hut's one room, wishing she'd had the common sense to bring Agnes with her to light the fire, Isabella dismissed the motion. A maid's absence would have given rise to people noticing her own departure from the castle. Isabella realised with some shame that now her survival was in her own hands she didn't even know how to get a fire going.

No one noticed Isabella around the castle unless she was needed to greet some odious earl or passing nobleman. On the other hand, if Agnes didn't clean the grates or prepare the chambers, her absence would be spotted within hours. It was a chilling reminder that her status as the daughter of an unwanted wife made her invisible. At least, that had been the case until Isabella's father had decided to marry her off.

Her mind drifted to William Trussell. He wasn't a bad man; he just wasn't the man she wanted. After a lifetime of playing second best to her half-sister, Lady Helena, she was determined to have her own way concerning the man she married.

Leaping to her feet, Isabella wrenched her shoulders back. Her chin jutted out as she remembered her father's reaction when she'd found the courage to tell him that betrothal to Trussell was something she intended to resist with every fibre of her being. Robert de Vere's flinty eyes had narrowed as he'd harangued Isabella. Telling her that, as she was only a woman, she should accept his decision and be grateful for it.

Marriage to William Trussell would take her to the manor of Hothrope in Leicestershire. William's parents, Edmund Trussell and his harridan of a wife, Margery d'Oserville, would ensure both protection for Isabella, and the noble status her father desired for her - and for himself by association. It would also bring her wealth and security.

It would not, however, provide happiness, nor allow her any of the limited freedoms she currently had. Freedoms that went hand in glove with being an unwanted female child from a loveless marriage.

Isabella couldn't understand why her father was so willing to condemn her to the same fate he had suffered until he'd been, in his words to her, 'saved by your mother's convenient death,' which had allowed him to wed a woman he loved - Juliana, a woman Isabella suspected he'd been in love with all along. Fate however had not agreed with the marriage, and Juliana de Vere had died a few years later - leaving her only daughter bitter and her husband heartbroken.

Lighting a candle, hoping that the crack she opened in the hut's shutters would not alert anyone outside to its glow, Isabella decided to be practical. She had two choices. Go back to the castle, or make the best of her situation and wait for Thomas. He'd probably been delayed by unwanted guests and would come for her as soon as it was safe to do so. It was the last day of the year after all.

Moving around the forester's hut, hunting for blankets and anything edible, Isabella wondered if she'd feel the same about her proposed betrothal if she hadn't met Thomas. But she had, and for her, there was no going back.

It was her father's fault anyway. If he didn't allow felons to use their home as a hideaway, then she'd never have laid eyes on Thomas Sproxton in the first place. She hadn't asked him what he'd done wrong. Everyone who sought temporary accommodation in the castle had done something. It was safer never to know what that something was.

Isabella had seen Thomas watching her. This was not unusual; most of the men that passed through her home watched the women. Usually it was with the hunger of an animal who knew what it wanted, but wasn't stupid enough to risk the wrath of the hand that fed it. The price of being of evicted from Robert de Vere's protection could mean arrest or even death.

Thomas was different. He'd only glanced in her direction when he thought she wasn't looking. His expression was inquisitive and gentle. When after seven days under her father's roof he'd eventually had cause to speak to her, Isabella had struggled to respond. All week she'd tried to ensure she remained around so Thomas could address her, but by the time he finally did she'd become so tongue-tied she came across as a babbling villager rather than the eldest daughter of the constable.

Many of the men who came to the castle arrived in groups, but Thomas has been alone, keeping himself withdrawn. There was a sadness about him that Isabella found herself wanting to alleviate. It was a sadness she recognised. He was every much as alone as she was.

Once they had spoken that first time, no discussion had been required for them to know that they'd be talking again. Within two days Isabella had confided her dissatisfaction at being forced to marry a man she found indifferent and he'd told her he intended to leave the area behind. Only a week later he'd asked if she would like to go away with him when the time was right.

So here she was, at last, waiting for Thomas. He'd said he'd be here before her, but so far there was no sign of him. Surely he'd arrive soon? He'd left Rockingham two days ago, his fee for accommodation paid and her father satisfied that the agreed protection period was at an end. He'd planned to collect some possessions and come straight back to the hut.

She shivered and gripped the sides of her cloak. *Even if he'd been held up, he should be here by now.*

Refusing to consider that Thomas could have been arrested for whatever he was fleeing from, Isabella concentrated on her father. Robert de Vere of all people should understand her defiance, given his own disregard for the proprieties of his station. The castle constable of Rockingham was supposed to ensure the area and the castle itself were safe on behalf of the King, and to keep the lands maintained and the livestock un-poached. He was not supposed to use the castle to harbour outlaws and protect felons, nor to charge vast amounts of money for that service.

In the poor light, Isabella found a loaf of bread and a small flask of ale under a rough blanket beneath the bed. With a grateful sigh to Thomas, who must have hidden the supplies for her on his way home in case he was delayed, Isabella laid the blanket around her shoulders and took a swig of the drink. Holding the candle in one hand, she took the bread back to the window.

Seconds later Isabella blew out the candle and ducked back as three horses rode past the cottage.

Not one of them carried Thomas Sproxton.

Mathilda stared at the twin drum towers that dominated the entrance to Rockingham Castle's gatehouse. The pale limestone appeared ghost-like in the dull morning light, a dullness enhanced by the dark ironstone of the curtain wall which ran off to either side. A shiver of disquiet trickled through her veins as they crossed the moat. She didn't look into the water. It smelt bad enough for her not to want to see what might be floating in it beyond ice.

Reining his horse in beneath the archway that connected the stone towers, Robert gestured to the nearest of the two guards on duty. 'Tell De Vere that Lord Robert de Folville, Lady Mathilda, and their servant, desire admittance.'

'My Lord,' the guard gave a scant bow of acknowledgement. 'Come within; His Lordship would not wish me to keep you waiting.'

With a nod to Mathilda and Daniel, Robert followed the guard into the outer bailey, where a stable lad took their horses by the bridle.

Dropping the authoritative tone he'd used on the guard, Robert addressed the lad. 'I'm not staying, but please see that my horse is fed and watered. Lady Folville's palfrey and Daniel's pony will require bedding down for the night. Daniel will help you before he follows us inside.'

With a mumbled 'my Lord', the stable lad led two of the three horses towards a drinking trough, so he could go and inform the groom of the household's newest four-legged guests.

Holding out his arm for his wife, Robert spoke under his breath so he wasn't overheard. 'You will be treated well here because you are a Folville. Never forget which family you have supporting you and you'll be safe.'

Mathilda swallowed as she gripped her husband's arm. 'Are you telling me I have to play the haughty lady of the manor?'

'If you have to.' Robert gave her a smile that almost melted Mathilda on the spot. 'But the best thing you can do is to be yourself, as hard and as much as you can.'

'Are you sure?' She green eyes flashed at him in surprise. 'Wouldn't you prefer me to keep out of trouble?'

'Do your best not to get mixed up in any mysteries while I'm gone. Life is complicated enough without you attempting to right a wrong.'

More earnest now, Mathilda asked, 'And what about the wrong that is being done to you right now? And your brothers? What about Richard's return? If I hear anything about those wrongs, would you have me sit at my tapestry and pretend they are matters for others to handle?'

Slowing his step, so they didn't reach De Vere before he'd finished speaking, Robert whispered, 'Why do you think I really brought you here?'

Mathilda's eyes widened. 'You intend me to find out what's going on from here?'

'I can think of no place better.' Robert leant closer. 'But be under no illusion, Mathilda, the people who pay to stay here have the ability - and the will - to make my clerical brother seem saintly. I'm taking you into the lion's den. Which is why Daniel is staying as well.'

'A fitting name for my saviour, then.' Realising she'd misjudged her husband, Mathilda felt her resolve harden. She'd already decided to discover as much as she could about the arrest warrant that had been issued and the man, Roger Wennesley, who was due to pursue it. Now that Robert had told her he expected her to do just that, Mathilda was relieved they wouldn't have to part with the knowledge that any promises she made to play the demure wife would be quickly broken.

'Can I ask you about James Coterel? What did Eustace mean about him being the most violent man he'd ever met?'

Robert was about to reply when the steward to the constable of Rockingham Castle appeared. 'My Lord de Vere will see you now.'

~ *Chapter Six* ~

Robert De Vere stood in the middle of Rockingham's Great Hall. His authoritative presence filled the room.

Mathilda fought the instinct to look at her husband. With their first step into the room, the chatter at each of the hall's crowded tables dimmed. Every pair of eyes swivelled to stare at the newcomers with blatant and occasionally hostile curiosity. One glance was enough to know that the majority of those partaking of breakfast were not the type of guests normally to be found in a royal residence.

'A Folville!' De Vere pronounced the name with an unmistakeable awe, mingled with distrust. Mathilda could almost hear him wondering how much trouble this unarranged visit was going to bring, 'and his lady no less. To what do I owe the pleasure, my Lord?'

'De Vere.' Striding to the middle of the room with Mathilda at his side, Robert got straight to the point. 'I have no doubt you are aware of the current challenge my family has been presented with. While my brothers and I rectify that situation, I would entrust you with the care of my wife.'

'Is that so?' De Vere's eyes narrowed. 'I haven't heard of any business concerning your family. I do know that King Edward has been calling in favours. This is a related issue, I assume?'

'You assume correctly.'

De Vere's gaze landed on Mathilda. 'And what will you pay me to keep this treasure of yours safe from the hounds which snap your heels?'

Unflinching at the manner in which his wife was being addressed, Robert said, 'We will discuss that in private, de Vere, or the only price being paid will be by you.'

'Bold words from a hunted man.'

'A hunted man related to Eustace de Folville.'

De Vere's swallow would have gone unnoticed if Mathilda hasn't been watching for it. Nor had she missed that de Vere had given away that he knew they were being hunted after all.

Breaking the stillness that hung around the room, the constable snapped at a servant girl heating a flagon of mead by the fire. 'Agnes, come here.'

The threat to his tone was enough to spark everyone in the room into resuming their own conversations, while the maid scuttled forward. As Mathilda watched the girl move, she saw that scuttle was precisely the right word. Her walk was awkward, as if one leg was a fraction longer than the other.

'Me Lord?'

'You will escort Lady Folville to the Fire Room. A room fit for the Queen of Leicestershire.'

With a dipped curtsey, the girl tilted her head at Mathilda as if to indicate she should follow her.

Mathilda turned to Robert; his eyes spoke unuttered words. This was it. They wouldn't be seeing each other again until this matter was closed. Her task had already begun. She was to find out as much as she could about the arrest warrant issued against his family.

Trying not to show she minded that her new husband

was departing without the chance for a private goodbye, knowing it would do Robert no good if she weakened his hand by showing to be anything less than an obedient wife, Mathilda said, 'Stay safe, my Lord,' before following Agnes from the overcrowded hall.

As she moved, every single pair of eyes in the place observed her retreating back.

The girl didn't speak as they walked up a steep narrow set of stairs at the back of the Great Hall, which led to the second, and top, floor of the inner bailey.

The lightness of the limestone used to construct the drum towers would have been better employed within the castle, for the ironstone corridor which ran along the curved side of the upper floor of the bailey was dark, despite plenty of lit candles.

Tapestries coated much of the exterior wall in an attempt to trap any warmth. Along the interior wall Mathilda counted three closed doors, presumably leading into separate rooms, before they reached the end of the corridor and one final entrance.

Producing a ring of keys from beneath her apron, Agnes unlocked the door. Expecting to be given the key, Mathilda was perturbed to see it replaced beneath the many folds of the maid's skirt. Not relishing the prospect of being locked in like a prisoner, Mathilda was about to ask why this place was known as the Fire Room, when the question was answered for her.

The combination of red, yellow, gold and orange that hit Mathilda's eyes as she walked through the stone mullioned doorway was startling. Gone was the corridor's feeling of cold darkness. Swathed in a comforting array of tapestries and fabric, the draughts of the outside world were blocked from the bedroom. A modest fire was already glowing in the hearth, and Agnes immediately set to encouraging it from a suggestion of heat to a satisfying blaze.

Mathilda realised her mouth was opened in surprise; she closed it quickly, taking in her comfortable surroundings. The bed was small but well made, with an adequate mattress and drapes to trap the heat. A carved wooden chest stood to the side of the bed, affording a place for her clothes and a surface upon which to place a candle at night. The brightness of the tapestries was astonishing. As she peered more closely, Mathilda saw showed images of dancing fire birds illuminated by the roaring flames. The way the light reflected off the golden threads woven into the wall hangings was magical.

'It's beautiful. Thank you for bringing me here.'

The girl's face broke into an expression of surprise, which highlighted all her freckles and caused a strand of red hair to escape from her loosely wrapped coif.

'Are you alright? Agnes, isn't it?'

'I, umm. Yes, thank you, me lady.' She switched her attention back to the fire and gave it an unnecessary poke; in a move Mathilda was convinced was to hide her face.

'Are you sure you're alright? You appear worried. Can I help?'

''Elp me?' The question wasn't a plea. It was shock that anyone of a higher status than herself should enquire of her well-being.

'That can't be so strange, can it? Surely you have people who help you sometimes?'

'Thank you, but I don't need no 'elp. I... I don't get thanked very often. Only Miss Bella...' Agnes stopped talking, and bobbed a curtsey. 'I'll be leaving you to settle in. Yer belongings will be up soon as I 'as them from yer lad.'

'Only Miss Bella, what?'

The girl was spared being forced to give an answer she clearly didn't want to share by a knock on the door. Daniel had arrived with Mathilda's pack roll.

Agnes took her chance to flee. 'I'll be in the kitchen if you need me, me Lady. I'll come back to attend to yer clothes later.' She'd gone before Mathilda had the chance to respond.

'Come in, Daniel.' Mathilda moved to the fire, toasting her palms. 'Any word from my husband? Has he gone yet?'

'He has, my Lady.' Daniel placed the roll on the bed, before facing the welcome embrace of the fire.

'Warm your hands and tell me all you've overheard so far.'

'There is little enough to share, my Lady.' Daniel wiped a hand across his forehead, pushing his scruffy fringe from his eyes. 'Lord Robert bid me remind you to be careful, and - to stop short of getting yourself into trouble.'

Mathilda couldn't help but laugh, 'Believe it or not, Daniel, I don't court trouble, but sometimes I fear it courts me. Did his Lordship leave word about James Coterel?'

'Nothing, my Lady. Oh, I am to take word to Adam if you discover news of any account.'

Mathilda's head snapped up from the fire and turned to Daniel. 'So Adam does know where my husband is bound after all?'

'I suppose he must, or at least he knows a way to find out. I truly don't know.'

'It would make sense for Robert to confide in Adam. I imagine he has withheld that information from Sarah however.'

'Sometimes it is safer not to know things.' Daniel spoke into the flames and Mathilda wondered if he was thinking of the recent death of his friends, Allward and Owen, Ashby Folville's former kitchen hand and steward. Murdered not long before the wedding, they had made the ultimate sacrifice to protect the women of Ashby Folville. Their demise had hit the youngest member of the household hard.

'Daniel, I want you to be wary while we're here. The people in the hall - I don't know who they are, but I can guess what manner of people they are. I know trouble when I see it.'

'Not the sort you would expect to find in one of the King's castles, my lady.'

'Indeed.' Mathilda frowned. 'Where will you sleep?'

'I have a cot above the stables. It's rather crowded, but with staff rather than guests.'

'Good.' Mathilda was uneasy. 'Don't trust anyone.'

Daniel bowed and reluctantly went to leave. 'I've been tasked to act as a stable lad while we're here. I'd better get on.'

'Keep your eyes and ears open.'

Only after Daniel had gone did Mathilda allow herself to think. When she'd gone to her bed last night she had assumed that today would involve little more than a trip with Robert to see her father and brothers, at their pottery in Twyford. Now, only twelve hours later, the future was a very different place.

Moving the room's only chair nearer to the fire, Mathilda mumbled into the dance of the orange flames. 'King Edward has ordered the arrest of two Coterels and five Folvilles. Why? And who is Roger Wennesley? If he murdered Laurence Coterel, then why did he do that, and how come he didn't hang for it? And why have Thomas and John de Folville been spared the king's retribution?'

Speaking into the fire, Mathilda's mind leapt back to the

spectre of Richard, Rector of Teigh. Her assumption that he'd never return, simply because she couldn't imagine him surviving a battlefield, entered the forefront of her mind.

'Did I wish him dead?' The idea made her shudder, but not as much of the thought of him being alive and heading her way did.

Tugging off her hair linen and shaking out her wavy red hair, Mathilda teased out its knots. Pushing her thoughts back to her husband's potential arrest, she asked the flames, 'Where is Laurence? How can a word of warning be got to him about the hunt at his heels? Perhaps he already knows.'

Mathilda sighed. 'How does Robert expect me to discover anything here? The prospect of wandering amongst the den of thieves below does not appeal.' She laughed at herself. 'And yet I live day to day in such surrounds!'

Her musing switched to her host, de Vere. If she was to learn anything from the constable, she'd have to persuade him to trust her; something she didn't think would be easy. Then there was Agnes. There was definitely something bothering the girl.

Mathilda was considering how to get the maid to trust her, when a hesitant knock at the door was followed by it swinging wide open.

Agnes, holding a large wooden tray upon which was balanced a jug of weak ale, some soup and bread, and a plate of cut pork, tottered in. 'Cook thought thee might be 'ungry, what with travelling so early, me Lady.'

'Please thank Cook for me. That's very kind.'

Putting the tray down on the side, the maid headed to the bed. The worry in her eyes was sharper than it had been before.

'Are you sure you're alright, Agnes? Can I help? I'd like to.'

Without glancing up from the clothing roll she was undoing prior to sorting out Mathilda's garments, Agnes muttered, '*I* needs no 'elp.'

'But you know someone who does?'

'Forgive me, me Lady, but thee asks a lot of questions. That ain't always safe 'ere.' Then, blushing scarlet, Agnes busied herself with her temporary mistress's gowns.

'My husband says I am too curious.' Mathilda let her words hang in the air, hoping Agnes would be brave enough to respond, but the girl kept her silence and carried on smoothing out the clothes.

Agnes worked fast, her fingers nimble. A tress of red hair poked untidily from the bottom of her head linen, showing that it had been tied in a hurry. Mathilda sat quietly until the girl was ready to leave. 'If you decide you require my help, just ask. You have been so kind to me.' Mathilda gestured towards the tray of food and the fire.

The maid said nothing, but Mathilda thought she saw a brief flash of desperate hope in her eyes before she left.

It was only after she'd gone that Mathilda realised she hadn't asked for the room key that still hung at Agnes's waist.

~ *Chapter Seven* ~

Noon tolled from the distant church, echoing through the trees as Robert urged his horse out of the safety of the woods. As he headed towards the crossroads which led away from Melton Mowbray and towards Lincoln, each peal of the bell tripped apprehension down his spine.

Kicking his mount into a canter, he made for the welcome shadows of a short stretch of woodland that he knew lined the road only a mile ahead. Confident that the sheriff would have kept his men as far away as possible while he escorted Mathilda to safety, now Robert had her stowed he was less certain. The appointed hour of Ingram's meeting with Wennesley had arrived. It was only a matter of time before his ally had no choice but to dispatch men to round up his brothers. And him.

Robert cursed under his breath. He had stayed in Rockingham far longer than planned; but not with Mathilda. He'd hoped to have a chance to speak to her again before leaving, but the opportunity had not arisen.

Taking a bite from the chunk of pork Rockingham's cook had wrapped up for him, Robert slowed his horse to a walk as he attended to his empty belly. He hoped his wife wouldn't get into trouble. Letting out a cough of laughter, Robert smiled. Of course she would. If she didn't, then

Mathilda of Twyford wasn't the woman he married.

Wiping crumbs from his lips, Robert steered his mount so that he was facing the open road towards Lincolnshire, and paused. A long ride awaited him. He could see no one, and hear nothing more than the distant sound of men and women working the land. Nonetheless, not wanting to risk drawing attention to himself by galloping, he set his horse to a steady trot and kept his eyes firmly fixed upon the horizon and his mind on his final goal, Sempringham Priory.

As he rode, Robert's thoughts strayed to the Coterel brothers. He was sure Nicholas and John would head for Lichfield to shelter in the cathedral's chapter. For a house of holy men, the place was rife with corruption. The Coterel family had run a protection service from there for years. If his brother Richard survived the next month, perhaps he'd consider joining that ungodly household, where he would be out of everyone's hair and amongst his own kind.

Ducking under a low-hanging branch which jutted into the road, Robert pictured his wife. He'd been away from Rockingham for two hours. Knowing Mathilda, she'd be asking questions already.

Surveying the thinning woodland on either side of him, which was beginning to give way to a small village, he recalled lines from one of their favourite Robyn Hode ballads.
"A gode maner than had Robyn;
In londe where that he were,
Euery day or he wold dyne
Thre messis wolde he here.

The one in the worship of the Fader,
And another of the Holy Gost,
The thirde of Our der Lady,
That he loued allther moste.

Robyn loued Oure der Lady;
For dout of dydly synne,
Wolde he neuer do compani harme
That any woman was in..."

'If you are out there Our Lady, then please, for all that's good in our land, look after my wife!'

The strike of the noon bell woke Mathilda with a start. She hadn't intended to sleep, but the early start to the day and the post-dawn ride, combined with the lull of the fire and a full stomach, had sent her into deep slumber.

Noon. Ingram would be hunting them by now.

Mathilda's eyes blinked against the brightness of her tapestried surroundings. While the vigorous golden glow of the dancing phoenix gave the room a cosy feel, it also assaulted her tired eyes.

Where was Robert?

She had no doubt that, wherever it was they were heading, Eustace and Walter were already there. Robert however had travelled an extra four hours, presumably in the opposite direction, to get her to safety. Sacrificing his own security in the process.

'Why didn't he ask Adam to bring me here?' Addressing the exquisite detail of the nearest phoenix, Mathilda brushed away crumbs from the bread she'd been eating before falling asleep. 'There must have been something here Robert thought he could discover. Or something he wants me to discover.'

She moved closer to the tapestry. Running a fingertip over the neat stitches, Mathilda studied the scene more closely. The fire bird, its beak open, flames pouring forth as if ascending from its nest of rebirth, was not alone. There were other, smaller, phoenixes dancing alongside.

Surely you only got one fire bird at a time? That was what Mathilda's mother had told her. Such magical creatures had formed part of a story she'd shared with her only daughter before famine and illness had taken her to an early grave. Yet there were six different firebirds dancing in the stitching.

Looking again, Mathilda realised she was wrong. There was only one bird, but the seamstress had captured it at six stages of its lifecycle; from its birth in the flames, to its disappearance in a puff of ash, and back to the egg from whence it came, so the process of its short life could begin all over again.

'It's alright for you. You get another go if it all goes wrong.' Mathilda spoke with no resentment as she caressed the work. She'd had so many brushes with the final dust of her existence; suddenly she was determined to make every day count. And she was going to start right now and ask for an audience with Robert de Vere. At the very least, she wanted to find out who Miss Bella was, and what Agnes was so worried about.

Battling down her anxiety as to what, or whom, she might encounter as she searched for her host, Mathilda decided the fact her bedroom door hadn't been locked was a good omen. Giving her leather girdle a stroke for luck, she stood up, shoulders back, and did her best to give the impression that she was a haughty lady of consequence - if not consequences.

Even from the foot of the stairs, as Mathilda stared across to where the constable was standing, she could tell he was uneasy. The confident swagger that had been presented to her and Robert on their arrival was gone - as were the menfolk who had been eating their breakfast.

Stepping into the hall, Mathilda saw de Vere sit himself at the bench nearest the fire, his brows drawn in concern.

'My Lord, forgive me disturbing you.'

The constable looked up in surprise, as if he'd forgotten he was harbouring the wife of a known felon and, from the stroke of noon, a hunted outlaw. 'Lady Folville, I trust your quarters are satisfactory?'

He spoke as if he was amazed she'd left them.

'More than satisfactory, my Lord, thank you.' Mathilda gave a curtsey. 'Your maid has taken good care of me. I am grateful.'

'Then how can I help you?' His eyes scanned the hall before he spoke again, 'I'm sure Lord Robert informed you that this is not always the safest place for a woman to roam alone. Although if I ever caught a guest mistreating a female under my roof...' De Vere raised his voice as if he was making a point to anyone who happened to be listening, 'then they can assume their protection within my walls immediately forfeit.'

Not giving into the temptation to survey the hall herself, to see if anyone in particular was the focus of de Vere's warning, Mathilda followed the wave of her host's hands, and took a seat.

'I don't know how long I'm going to be here, my Lord, so I thought I'd ask if I could be of service to you in some way during my stay. I am not one to be idle, and as I am sure you'll appreciate, keeping busy would limit the amount of time I spend worrying about my husband.'

De Vere's gaze remained fixed on the cup he cradled in his hand. 'There is no reason for you to have to work off the debt of your stay here, my Lady. The Folville family have assisted me many times. I consider this a fair price for the protection that association has always afforded me.'

'May I ask what manner that protection took, my Lord? I am not long married and although I am not blind to the nature of my new family's activities, I still do not know everything I should.'

The smile that crossed de Vere's face was genuine, instantly lightening his ferret-like features. 'Robert told me you were a curious one.'

'Indeed.'

'And of course, I have heard about your role in the removal of the Rector of Teigh from the country.'

Mathilda felt her breath snag in her throat. 'And had you heard he was back in England, my Lord?'

The constable's smile dissolved, leaving a shadow of grey in its place. 'I'd hoped, for all our sakes, that the Devil would claim his own. But it seems Hell hasn't room for the Rector of Teigh yet.' De Vere paused before changing the subject. 'I thank you for your kind offer, Lady Mathilda, but the Folville brothers would not thank me for putting you to work. Far safer for you to keep to your room until Robert's return. Agnes can accompany you for an occasional walk in the grounds when the weather improves.'

'My Lord,' Mathilda, who'd been expecting this response, spoke in a manner she'd copied from Sarah when she'd been trying to persuade one of the brothers to do something they didn't want to do. 'It may be many weeks before my husband comes for me. To keep me within one place, you would have to instruct Agnes to use the key to the chamber that she keeps beneath her skirts.'

The blush that crossed de Vere's face came and went with speed, but Mathilda hadn't missed it. 'Ah, so you did intend for her to secure me. I wondered if she forgot to lock the door, or if you forgot to issue the order for my captivity in the first place?'

'It would be for your own safety. All manner of felons seek refuge here.'

'And they pay handsomely to do so; with, if I heard your warning just now correctly, clear rules and consequences if any abuse comes to a female within your walls.' Agnes's worried face came to mind, 'Has that always been a rule, my Lord, or has something happened to cause you to implement it?'

Ignoring the question, de Vere got to his feet. 'I'm glad I've met you properly, Lady Folville, but if you'll excuse me, I have to attend to my work. As you can imagine, being the constable of a royal castle such as this requires many reports to the Crown.'

Watching her host stride away, Mathilda became aware of how fast her heart had been beating during their exchange. She'd learnt very little, but on the other hand, she hadn't been escorted back to her room and the door slammed behind her. Deciding it would be perfectly legitimate for her to check on her servant, she headed towards the stables to find Daniel.

Gripping her cloak closer around her shoulders, Mathilda stepped into the crisp air of the year's final day. She watched the stable hands as they moved from stall to stall, grooming and feeding the horses that were housed in the busy stable block. There were far fewer than when they'd arrived. It took a few minutes before she spotted Daniel. He was on his hands and knees in the far corner of the courtyard, scrubbing at the stone floor.

'Are you well, Daniel? You look exhausted. Have you been given food yet?'

'No, my Lady. I spilt some whitewash. I'm not allowed to eat until I've cleaned up the mess.'

Mathilda's eyes narrowed. 'The head groom is a bully?'

'I was used to Owen's ways. He was firm but gentle. That is not the case here.'

Knowing that interfering could make her young friend's life harder, Mathilda bit her tongue as Daniel spoke again.

'There is a rumour that a girl has gone missing.'

'A girl?'

'A nineteen-year-old called Isabella. The eldest daughter of the house.'

'Is that so?' Without another word, Mathilda gathered up her skirts and headed to the kitchens to find Agnes. The missing girl had to be Miss Bella.

~ *Chapter Eight* ~

Agnes was nowhere to be seen as Mathilda stepped beneath the archway which ran from the hall to the kitchen. Heat from the room billowed towards her as half a dozen servants dashed around, performing their duties with red-faced efficiency.

This wasn't like the friendly space of the kitchen at Ashby Folville manor, where Sarah would welcome her in, sleeves rolled high, flour dotting her arms and face as she kneaded dough and prepared pie after pie. This was cooking on a grand scale for a never-ending supply of people who could come and go at any minute. After all, this was a royal castle; you never knew when the King would arrive on the doorstep.

Mathilda rested her back against the wall as she watched, keeping to the shadows, not sure if she wanted to be seen. The atmosphere, while not openly hostile, did not feel friendly; she was conscious of not wanting to get in the way.

She needn't have worried.

'My Lady Folville, welcome to my domain.'

Cook, bedecked in tunic and hose more normally associated with a man than a woman, stood by an oak table which made the one Sarah was so proud of look dwarfed by comparison. She brandished a knife in one hand and an apple in the other.

'I didn't wish to disturb you.' Mathilda smiled at the broad-featured woman as a voice at the back of her head reminded her of Robert's warning. She should trust no one. 'It's like a beehive in here. You're all so busily at your labours.'

Cook threw back her hand in a raucous laugh. 'A fair comparison, my Lady. Although, I've never seen myself as Queen Bee before.'

Mathilda returned the infectiously feminine grin that was at odds with the masculine attire and hefty muscles that had probably grown through years of throwing bread dough into shape. 'You know me?'

'Agnes took some food up to you.'

'Thank you, of course. I'm most grateful. I hadn't realised how hungry I was until I was faced with your delicious cooking.'

'You flatter me, my Lady.'

'I speak the truth. My housekeeper, Sarah, would, I'm sure, gladly swap a recipe or two with you should fate ever bring you together.'

The cook was as surprised as Agnes had been when Mathilda had offered her help. 'You are on first-name terms with your housekeeper my lady?'

'Of course. She works hard and the manor is often busy. I help whenever I can.'

The cook stopped peeling the apple she'd been skinning, 'I had heard you were an unusual mistress. A potter's daughter.'

'Yes.' Mathilda was uncertain. 'How did you know?'

'Rumour runs rife here, my Lady.' She began to peel the apple again, dispatching the skin with a skill that proved she was born to her job.

'I'm sure.' Seeing an opportunity to discover some information of her own, Mathilda added, 'I bet very little misses you.'

Cook's face creased a little as she listened, but she said nothing as her eyes flickered around her hive of workers.

'I wondered if you could send Agnes up to me when she has time.'

Relaxing a fraction, the cook said, 'Of course, my Lady. Is there anything I can assist with in the meantime? I can send more food along to your room if you are hungry.'

'Thank you, but I'm fine.' Mathilda rubbed her stomach to emphasise her point. 'I wondered if Agnes was alright. With the Lady Isabella missing, she must be worried. Not just about her mistress, but for her own position. If her mistress has gone, then…'

Her host laid down the knife with a clatter that caused the whole room to pause. For a split second the atmosphere in the kitchen froze. Cook had dropped something. The buzz of disbelief was tangible.

'Carry on.' The words were spoken with authority, but the woman was clearly shaken. Speaking under her breath, she picked up the knife and sliced through the pile of apples as if they were made of thin air. 'My Lady, please be careful. I'm only a cook, so if I speak out of turn then I ask your forgiveness, but the fact you are a potter's daughter is not the only information that has come our way about you.'

Mathilda went pale, 'Tell me.'

'You are known to have had a hand in the capture of two murderers, maybe more. That means, to most of the people who pass through this castle, you're a troublemaker. Your very presence here puts you in peril. If you start to ask questions, then…'

There was no need for Cook to continue. Mathilda understood all too well what she was saying. 'Hence, Agnes being instructed to lock me in my room.'

'To keep you safe from those who stay here who may fear you peering rather closer at their lives than they would like you to.'

'I was to be locked in so that I didn't hear things that others would rather I didn't?'

'You aren't a prisoner, my Lady, but my Lord de Vere has a worthy fear that your life could be in danger within these walls, simply because of what you have accomplished in the past.'

A sense of disquiet added itself to the unease Mathilda had felt since she awoke that morning. Despite Cook keeping her voice down and the noise level of the activity around them being just short of a din, she could see her companion feared being overheard.

'Has Lord de Vere asked you to provide me with all the comforts I need, beyond my freedom?'

'For your own safety.'

'And his.' Mathilda spoke bluntly as comprehension dawned. 'If the wife of a Folville was killed on his premises the consequences would not be worth contemplating.'

Inclining her head in mute agreement, Cook diced the last apple into tiny cubes with barely a glance in the fruits' direction.

'Yet,' Mathilda gestured around her, 'here I am. Agnes did not lock me in. I have just spoken to Lord de Vere. He did not usher me back to the Fire Room, nor have you called a guard to escort me away from your kitchen.'

'I would never dream of doing such a thing, my Lady.'

'Agnes didn't follow her orders...' Talking to herself now, Mathilda muttered, 'And now I hear that Isabella de Vere has gone missing...'

'And so has Agnes.'

'What?'

The cook surveyed her troops as if in hope of seeing Agnes's untidy presence amongst them, but the maid wasn't there. 'She didn't come back from delivering your breakfast. I assumed she'd started to clean the grates, but she can't be found.'

'Has someone searched the castle for her?'

'Naturally.'

'Is Agnes close to her mistress?' Mathilda felt a sense of foreboding steal over her.

'I always thought so.'

'You think Agnes has gone searching for Lady Isabella.'

'Possibly, although I credited the chit with more sense.'

'Perhaps she has got more sense.' Mathilda made ready to leave. 'Maybe Agnes hasn't gone searching, because she knew where her mistress was all along.'

Gathering her skirts in her hands, Mathilda swept back to the hall. She strode to where she'd last seen de Vere, in the hope that someone would tell her where to find the constable now.

'The guests are afraid of me taking too much interest in why they are here. De Vere is afraid of what will happen to him if something happens to me and now two women are missing,' Mathilda murmured to herself as she walked. 'And there I was thinking all I'd have to do was listen at tables for any stray information about Roger Wennesley; about whom I've heard not so much as a whisper.'

Roger Wennesley sat opposite Robert Ingram and next to Thomas Sproxton. 'I believe you have met my colleague before, Sheriff.'

'I have.' Ingram acknowledged Thomas' presence before

the inn's fire with a curt nod. 'A professional acquaintance from the wrong side of the court bench. He is here because?'

'Because, I asked for his help.' Wennesley leant forward; his face was only inches from Ingram's. 'King Edward himself commanded me to lead this pursuit. Me. And I have decided that Thomas will be useful to us. I trust you are in agreement with that, my Lord?'

Unruffled, Ingram said, 'I am. I imagine that the more criminals we have aiding us, the easier it will be to track our quarry. A felon to catch a felon is always an efficient way of achieving success. A fact our new king clearly understands.'

Wennesley's eyes narrowed, but he said nothing. Ingram was no fool; it would not do to treat him like one if they wanted to get out of this alive. 'The noon bell has gone. The Folvilles will know we are pursuing them.'

'As will Nicholas and John Coterel.'

'You think word will have reached Bakewell already, Sheriff?'

'Don't you?'

Wennesley conceded the unspoken confession. 'There are spies everywhere, and of course both families have retained informants across the midland counties. You could say, that between them, they rule the area.'

'You could. And to an extent you'd be correct.' Ingram steepled his fingers before his face. 'The task you've been given will not be easy. I am instructed to help you, Wennesley, and I will. However, I am not convinced that the region would be any better off once these men have been so judiciously culled.'

Roger raised his cup of wine in a mock toast. 'I'm inclined to agree, but it makes no difference. King Edward has issued his orders. Orders he sent to me. We have to obey.'

'Yes we do. So, where do you suggest we hunt first?' The

sheriff switched his attention to Thomas. 'You're good at hiding, Master Sproxton. Any ideas?'

~ *Chapter Nine* ~

Richard, Rector of Teigh, had cursed his horse to Hell for a full ten minutes when it had gone lame only four miles from his goal. Having abandoned it and continued on foot through the village of Beeby, he was now glad he'd been forced to slow his pace.

The rumour that a posse of the King's men was in the area reached him half a mile ahead of the news of who that posse was hunting for. A royal warrant had been issued against members of his family - including himself.

Slipping into the village church, hiding at the back of the building within the silhouette of the worn pews, Richard felt his anger rise. Hadn't he been through enough? Sent to France on the word of an unworthy woman and his worthless brother, so he could help a greedy king make sure the flow of claret from Gascony to his royal table was not disrupted by the constantly squabbling Gascons, Richard had seen horror aplenty, although not always on the battlefields he was sure Mathilda had imagined him facing. It felt good to have cheated her expectations after only a few weeks of combat, even if more by luck than by any cunning on his part. He'd been saved by his ability to convince people that administering to the souls of dead soldiers, was better than becoming a dead soldier himself. Now, having secured his passage back to England via threats and bribery, he wasn't going to find the peace he craved at home either.

He needed to think. Wondering whom the King had seen fit to lead the hunt against his family, the rector considered all the places where his brothers might take refuge until the guards got bored and gave up their quest.

A smile overtook the dark shadow which had cast itself across Richard's complexion. He rubbed at the heavy beard which a lack of shaving opportunities had stopped him trimming. His brothers might have fled the manor at Ashby Folville, but it was unlikely they'd left the house completely empty. The housekeeper and steward would be there.

Richard's grin grew wider. That useless steward, Owen, was no match for him; especially now he'd had his fighting skills refined across the vineyards of Aquitaine. As to Sarah: well, she'd been due a visit from the point of his knife for a very long time. With none of his brothers in the way, it would be so much easier! Perhaps this arrest warrant wasn't such a curse after all…

Sarah dipped her rag into the bucket of warmed water for a third time and wrung it out. The hall table bore the marks of spilt ale from Sheriff Ingram's dawn visit. As she worked on eradicating every stain, Sarah concentrated on her desire to have the manor spotless and operating as well as ever when the family came home.

As the final ring mark, denoting where Eustace had banged his beaker against the oak surface, disappeared, Sarah felt a lump rise in her throat. They would be back. They'd been through worse than this and survived, so they'd come home again. All of them.

Irritation ached in her chest as she scrubbed harder, the heat of the fire egging her on. It was all very well for King

Edward to make a show of rounding up the felons, but if the man stopped to think, surely he'd see that families like the Folvilles and Coterels had been allowed to thrive under his father's reign with good reason. Without them, far more corrupt officials, like that scoundrel Roger Belers - who the Folvilles had dealt with three years ago, much to the relief of the local people - would still be bleeding the people dry.

Sarah's ire evaporated into fear as she thought of Mathilda. The girl, so new to their lives, had become her friend, confident and mistress in the space of only a few months. Mathilda had been through so much and yet she kept that resilient spirit which made her the perfect wife for a Folville. Sarah just hoped she'd get to be a Folville wife for a long time. The way things were going, there was a chance Mathilda would be a widow before a month of marriage was out.

Caught up in her thoughts, Sarah didn't hear Adam as he entered the hall. She jumped as he called out across the unnaturally quiet house.

'I've finished in the stables.' Adam brushed his hands down his tunic, 'Not having fresh orders is going to take some getting used to.'

Sarah dropped her cloth into the bucket and dried her hands on her apron. 'We'll have to carry on as though they're here. I was thinking that maybe Lord John or Lord Thomas would come and stay until Lord Robert returns.'

Adam picked up a broom. 'We should prepare in case they do.'

The question that Sarah had been doing her best to suppress suddenly couldn't be held in any more. 'Do you think Richard will come here?'

Watching as the housekeeper's hand automatically went to the scar on her arm which the Rector of Teigh, although in France when it was administered, was responsible for, Adam shook his head. 'He'd be a fool to do that.'

'But if he doesn't know of the arrest warrant... He may not even have heard about the wedding. He's a bold one, Adam; you don't know him. Richard de Folville has more guile than the Devil.'

Unable to promise Sarah a protection he couldn't guarantee, Adam said, 'How about I go and check on Lord Eustace's men? They'll be glad of some of your soup by now, don't you think?'

Grateful for her future husband's practical outlook, Sarah gave him a smile. 'I've finished here. I'll help.'

Slipping a hand into hers, Adam gave Sarah a proud look. 'You're an amazing woman. Come on, let's show the Hundred that it can try its best, but it can't beat us. Then, once we have reassured ourselves the manor is secure, we'll bank down the fires and go to bed. It has been a long day and if I know those Folville brothers, we won't be left in peace for long. We should make the most of it.'

Richard tugged off his right boot and glared at the sole. A sharp stone had pierced the worn leather and sealed his footwear's fate. Having to walk was bad enough, but now one foot was wet and cold from tramping along the border of the road to Ashby Folville semi-unprotected. He was beginning to feel as lame as his abandoned horse.

Pushing the boot back on, he took a thick leather belt from his pack and wrapped it around the sole to keep the worst of the stones and gravel out. It made for uncomfortable walking, but at least he wouldn't have to pause every few hundred yards to dig grit from his toes. Taking comfort from the fact he was but a mile from his goal, and should get there before the grey evening plunged into night, Richard stumbled on through the shadows.

He was surprised he hadn't seen any guards out hunting for his kin, but then again, this was Ingram's territory and Ingram was firmly in his family's pocket. Perhaps he didn't have to worry about being arrested so close to home after all.

Eustace's men were loyal. They were paid enough to ensure that; but they were also sullen and uncommunicative. Hired for their bulk and the purposes of intimidation rather than good company, they took Adam and Sarah's offered broth and bread with barely grunted thanks. Eating eagerly, they nonetheless didn't cease in their endless task of surveying the surroundings for any sight of trouble.

'They may be miserable devils, but at least they should keep Richard away.' As they reached the kitchen, Adam added, 'Lord Eustace told me we need not worry about their sleeping arrangements. They are to take it in turns to use the stable boy's quarters.'

The steward sat at the table, rubbing his hands together to revive them from exposure to the winter evening. 'At least they had no news for us. That means nothing has happened. I'd rather they had nothing to tell us than to hear bad news.'

Sarah passed Adam a bowl of broth before starting on her own. 'You're right.'

'But?'

'I can't stop thinking about Mathilda. De Vere's castle has an ill reputation for good reason.'

'I have heard of the constable's service to the criminal community. Even when I was living in Nottinghamshire, they whispered word of Rockingham being a safe place for those wishing to stay out of sight.'

'That's what concerns me.' Sarah pushed her meal away, her appetite gone. 'The sheriff knows that. Wennesley knows that. It won't be long before Rockingham Castle is searched from top to bottom in the quest to find the King's quarry.'

Adam's eyes narrowed. 'You think they will take Mathilda if they find her there?'

'The chances of that are good, and yet...' Sarah paused, 'why would Master Robert take Mathilda there? He is no fool. He knows the place will be searched. It is the obvious place for any such investigation to begin.'

Adam sipped his soup. 'Perhaps that's why he took her there.'

'What do you mean?'

'Well, he told Ingram that he was taking Mathilda to Rockingham, didn't he? He said that was what he was going to do.'

'Which means what?' Sarah tore a piece of her bread, but merely crumbled it into pieces between her fingers.

'If word has got round that the king was sending a posse of men to hunt down two of the most well-known families in the region - and you were a criminal in hiding - what would you do if you heard that a member of one of those families was coming to use the very safe house you were sheltering in?'

'I'd get out fast. I'd run, just in case they decided to capture extra criminals along the way.'

'Precisely.' Adam pushed the soup bowl back towards Sarah. 'I bet that Robert took Mathilda there as a favour to de Vere.'

'Favour?' Sarah felt out of her depth. Her mind was normally as sharp as a needle, but since the messenger had arrived that morning, she didn't seem to be able to keep a grip on events.

'One look at Robert Folville and his lady; one whisper that the brothers were being pursued, and I suspect every felon in the place melted away. That means that -'

Sarah jumped in, 'When Ingram arrives there will be no one in residence that he'll feel duty bound to arrest.'

'And as Mathilda is hardly one to sit idle, she's probably out of harm's way working in the kitchen or something.'

Sarah felt comforted for the first time that day. 'You're right. There is no way she'll be sitting on her hands doing nothing. Mathilda isn't afraid of honest hard work.'

Adam nodded approvingly as Sarah picked her spoon back up. 'You'll see; Mathilda will be fine. I bet that right now she is teaching the cook at the castle how to make your apple pie.'

~ *Chapter Ten* ~

The chill to the stone corridors, as Mathilda made her way through the castle towards where she'd been informed she might find de Vere, told her the long day was almost over.

Despite her afternoon nap, tiredness clawed at Mathilda's bones, but she knew there was no hope of sleeping until she'd spoken to her host. There was too much going on in her mind. Not only did Mathilda want to discuss the disappearing women, but she required an assurance that, if she went to bed in the Fire Room, she wouldn't wake up to find the door locked and her exit barred.

It had been difficult to find anyone to tell her where she'd locate the constable. The Great Hall, which had positively hummed with life in the early morning, now held no one. Somehow the quiet of the place was even more foreboding than when her every move was being followed by dozens of devious eyes.

Where had they all gone? Was there somewhere else they went at night? The pallets that doubled as beds were lined up at sides of the hall, unused. It seemed too much to believe that all of the guests had left at the same time... or did it?

A Folville arrives. A Folville's wife remains. A wife with a reputation for getting to the bottom of things...

Mathilda swallowed. Had de Vere been right? Were the felons afraid of her? Were they afraid enough to just give her a wide berth? Cook's words rebounded around her skull. Or was she in danger?

'They've gone. Stop seeing problems when there are none to see.' Talking to herself, Mathilda focused on Agnes. She couldn't stop picturing the worried expression she'd seen on the young maid's face.

Finally, Mathilda found the steward. He was directing a young maid to see to the constable's bedroom fire. With pursed lips and the air of a man who wondered if he'd pay for the information he was giving Mathilda later on, the steward reluctantly pointed her in the direction of his master.

Moments later Mathilda knocked on the door she'd been told led to De Vere's private room. She listened hard for a response, but as the door was fashioned from solid oak, she hadn't expected to hear one. Mathilda was about to give up on the door ever opening, when it swung open.

His face flushed in annoyance, de Vere's mouth was already open as if to shout, but he clamped if shut when he saw who his visitor was. 'Lady Folville, I was not expecting you.'

'But you were clearly expecting someone, my Lord.'

'Well, yes... but that doesn't matter now.' Rather than inviting her inside, he maintained his ground by the door, his body blocking the view beyond the threshold to his private domain. 'How can I help you, my Lady?'

Holding her hands together, remembering the importance of appearing to be in control, Mathilda said, 'You are aware that two women have gone missing from this castle? I wish to know if that is the real reason why you'd see me locked up.'

De Vere went pale. 'Two women?'

Mathilda tilted her head to one side enquiringly. 'You believed there was only one missing?'

Shaking his head, as if he was trying to dismiss what he'd just been told, de Vere groaned. 'Lady Folville, I must ask you to leave this situation alone.'

'What situation would that be, my Lord?'

The constable couldn't prevent the grin that crossed his face, but it struck Mathilda that it was more a hysterical expression than a friendly gesture. 'Lady Mathilda, your reputation for meddling is well known. That was all well and good when you had your family around to protect you, but they aren't here.'

Not rising to the implication that she meddled on purpose, Mathilda pressed her point home. 'Your daughter and her maid are missing. Your daughter, my Lord. Don't you want her found?'

'Your impertinence is not wise. You may have married into a powerful family, but as I mentioned, they are not here. I'd hate an accident to befall you.'

'Threats don't work on me, my Lord. I am, as a guest, offering you help in locating your daughter. I am stuck here with you and you with me, whether we like it or not. And for some reason your castle, usually teeming with life, is all but empty. I may as well use my meddling constructively.'

De Vere held Mathilda's defiant stare, before he swung back the door and ushered her inside. 'Take a seat by the fire, Lady Folville. I will tell you what I know and I will tell you why I will not be asking you to help me. But only on the understanding that you confine yourself to investigating what I'm sure you have been told to, which is to discover as much as you can about Roger Wennesley's immediate plans.'

'You know of them?'

'Your husband told me; before then, I knew nothing beyond King Edward's plans to restore order to England.'

Richard's eyes narrowed as he leant against the trunk of a particularly broad ash tree. He could see the gateway into the courtyard of Ashby Folville manor house, along with two men he recognised as belonging to Eustace. Feeling perversely pleased, sure that the guards' presence meant that the house was empty but for the servants, Richard silently moved on.

Making his way around the manor, keeping to the dark tracks that concealed the entrance to the rear of the house, Richard took the belt off the sole of his boot. He'd rather have a wet foot than risk the leather strap catching on a root or making a noise. Eustace paid his mercenaries as much as he did not just to ensure their loyalty, but because they were highly trained and very good at their job.

Adam couldn't settle. He could hear Sarah's snuffling snore coming from the pallet she'd fallen asleep on near the kitchen fire.

Too tired to use her private quarters and anxious not to be away from her domain should any of her charges return to need her help, Adam had sat with Sarah, stroking her long grey hair until she'd slept.

Restless, knowing his body would not forgive him in the morning if he didn't let it rest as well, Adam headed into the courtyard for a final check of the premises before allowing himself sleep.

There was only one man guarding the main entrance.

There should have been two.

Every hair on the back of Adam's neck stood up. He

whispered, knowing the guard, Borin, would be aware of his presence even though he hadn't moved. 'Something has happened?'

'A man in the trees. We are checking.'

Adam held his tongue. There was no point asking Borin if he was sure it was a man and not a deer. Eustace had recruited men who had raided the Scottish borders and tortured the French - and they were still alive. If they said there was a man in the woods, then there was a man in the woods. They could probably tell you how tall he was, when he'd last eaten, and where he was from, without even seeing him.

Adam felt unease run down his spine as he retreated into the manor. He'd been in this position before. The manor had been attacked only a few weeks ago; Mathilda had been kidnapped and the steward Owen killed... Sarah?

He was by her side in seconds. Mercifully she slept on. There was no one else there.

Mathilda pulled the covers over her head. She missed the heat of the Fire Room's tapestries, even if the warmth they supplied was largely an illusion. Until she'd gained de Vere's trust, however, she wasn't going to risk sleeping anywhere that could so easily become her prison; albeit a comfortable one.

With the exodus of all the felons in hiding she'd had no trouble in finding a vacant room, but the lack of a lit fire was making sleep difficult. Lying with her knees tucked beneath her chin, Mathilda considered what de Vere had told her.

Lady Isabella had only been noticed missing an hour before Mathilda's arrival at the castle. How long his daughter had actually been absent was debatable. If Agnes hadn't visited into her mistress's room to collect a gown she'd been asked to mend and found Isabella gone, complete with three dresses, her travel cloak and roll, then it may have been many more hours before the lack of Isabella's presence was noted.

From beneath the pile of blankets she'd thrown over herself, it bothered Mathilda that the girl might not have been missed for so long. She knew if she had a daughter, she'd have noticed if she hadn't appeared for meals.

A daughter. Mathilda smiled briefly. Would she and Robert have a daughter? She knew he'd like a son. He hadn't said as much, but all men wanted sons - but she hoped a daughter would come along too. Closing her eyes, she squeezed the vision of happy family life away. If she'd wanted that, she should have married elsewhere.

Mathilda recalled her conversation with de Vere in his study. He had talked into his cup of ale rather than to her as they'd sat next to the fire. Lady Isabella's mother, Katherine, he'd told her, had died when Isabella had been six years old. He'd never loved her, nor she him. The marriage had been political and he'd found it difficult to mourn for a woman who'd been prickly and difficult to like.

Katherine's death had left the way clear for him to marry the woman he'd wanted to wed in the first place. A spirited woman called Juliana, who'd given him another daughter, Lady Helena, before succumbing to a fever two years ago, leaving de Vere with Isabella, who couldn't understand why her sibling was happy to sit at her needlepoint until he could secure suitable husbands for them.

Remembering her own inability to settle at her embroidery when adventures waited in the world beyond her home, Mathilda made no comment. She couldn't help wonder however, who would willingly take Isabella as a suitable wife. The protection racket her father ran from the castle was something of an open secret.

Suddenly, Mathilda sat up, her cloak tight at her shoulders. No wonder de Vere was so worried. Not only had his eldest child run away - it was unlikely a kidnapper would have waited for her to pack some clothes - but he had another daughter to find a husband for, and now the King of England was putting his foot down. If King Edward was prepared to go up against the Folvilles and Coterels, what would he do to the likes of de Vere, who ran his criminal undertaking within one of the Crown's own castles?

Shivering, Mathilda pulled the blankets back up around her shoulders. She was sure Agnes had known where her mistress was and now she'd vanished too.

Tomorrow she would visit the maid's quarters. Agnes probably didn't own much, but if she had a spare tunic she might have taken it with her. Mathilda decided she'd also retrieve her own belongings from the Fire Room. 'Then at least I'll have enough clothing to prevent freezing to death if I have to hide in fireless chambers on a regular basis.'

Once she had proof of Agnes's defection, she would go back to de Vere and persuade him to let her help him find his daughter.

~ *Chapter Eleven* ~

Sarah couldn't believe she wasn't shaking. Nor was she shouting, screaming, or punching the unconscious man that was sprawled on a straw cot before her.

Lying there, unaware of where he was, the rector of Teigh was no longer a spectre; a figure of fear that had given her nightmares since he'd declared his tendency to cruelty, rage, and even murder was her fault. Here and now he looked pathetic: a man old before his time, in tatty clothing and worn-out boots. If Sarah hadn't known who he was, she'd have taken him for a beggar.

It had been one of Eustace's men who'd knocked Richard de Folville's senses from his body. A single blow with a fallen branch to small of his back had sent the cleric to the ground, his head hitting the earth with enough pace to knock him from the world, but not enough to kill him. Sarah wasn't sure if she was glad about that or not.

The mercenary stayed next to his prisoner, his unblinking eyes assessing every heave of the rector's chest, every twitch of the closed eyelids.

If he hadn't been there, Sarah would not have stayed. She'd told Adam she was fine and was no longer afraid of this miserable excuse for a man. The lie had sounded unconvincing as she'd uttered it; but if there was even the smallest chance that Richard was aware of her presence, then Sarah was damned if she'd give him the satisfaction of overhearing her admit her terror.

After speaking to the guard on the front gate, Adam joined Sarah, acknowledging the jug of water and plate of bread next to the cot. 'As the rector has food and drink for when he wakes I suggest we lock the door and go to our beds. A closed bolt will keep him secure until morning.'

With one final stare at the man who had caused so much trouble, the housekeeper turned sharply and walked from the room. Only after the door and been locked and Adam had positioned another cot outside the door so the guard could sleep there, an extra barrier between Richard and the world, did Sarah let go of a ragged sigh.

Her words wouldn't come out at first. They caught on Sarah's tongue and twisted in her throat in their hurry to rid them from her mouth. 'A toad. A snake. That's what he's like! And I...' Sarah gulped. 'Why does he live when Owen and Allward are gone? He as good as killed them and he doesn't even know. He doesn't know they are gone and it's his fault. Poison flows through him, thick and evil and...' The housekeeper's fists balled in her hands, hating the oblivious man in the room behind them, hating the person he made her become when he was around.

Taking Sarah's hands, Adam unfurled her fingers. Crescent moons patterned her flesh where her stubby nails had dug into her palms. 'He doesn't know, but he will. His actions will cause his death, if not now, then one day. You'll see.'

'He thinks being a cleric will protect him.' Sarah clasped Adam's hands, using them to keep her from pummelling her fists against the makeshift cell door.

'So did Thomas Becket back when old King Henry was

alive. I believe he was also proved wrong.' Adam was solemn as he guided Sarah to her chamber. 'You need a proper bed. I will sleep in the kitchen. If anyone comes I can fetch you straight away.'

'I wish if all this had to happen, that it had waited until after we were wed. The comfort of your shoulder would be…' She broke off, her cheeks crimson. After so long as a spinster, Sarah hadn't yet become accustomed to the sensation of wanting to be with one particular person all the time. It was strange not having to rely on her searing independence.

Adam brushed the hair from Sarah's eyes. 'I know. And if you want me to lie next to you, I will, but I can't promise I would stop at offering you a shoulder. I love you, and so…'

He stopped talking. Neither of them had any need for the issue of temptation to be spelled out.

Dawn was on the cusp of rising through the fog as Robert dropped a silver penny into the stable boy's palm and took his horse's reins. He hadn't intended to stop on his way to join his brothers, but fatigue and the vision of a group of Ingram's men on the road, several miles adrift of their usual terrain, had forced Robert to veer off the main route to Sempringham.

The village of Morton-by-Bourne had offered him a secluded inn with, mercifully, a single bed available for the night from a taciturn innkeeper and his disinterested wife. Grateful for their lack of questions and for the bowl of stew he was handed along with the ale he'd asked for, Robert had slept fitfully, his mind active while his tired muscles rested.

Now, hopefully up before Ingram or Wennesley roused their men, taking advantage of the early morning fog, Robert pressed his mount on towards the priory. If he rode fast he'd be there in less than two hours; if he rode carefully, he'd be there in three.

Sarah moved around the kitchen on silent feet, trying not to wake Adam. The fact he was sound asleep despite recent events testified to how exhausted he must have been.

Watching the steward's slumbering body, Sarah resisted an urge to stroke his greying hair. 'You're getting sentimental in your old age, woman,' she muttered as she assembled a mental list of the day's tasks.

Deciding they should assume that either Lord John or Thomas would arrive to take up the reins in Robert's absence, Sarah was determined to have the manor in perfect condition. The fact that they had the Rector of Teigh in custody only reinforced her belief that the brothers who'd evaded the king's ire on this occasion would come to their aid.

'Now that's a nice sight first thing in the morning.' Adam rested on his elbows and looked across to where Sarah worked. 'I could get used to that.'

'Which is probably as well in the circumstances.' Sarah fetched Adam some ale. 'I was contemplating the food for the day. Lord John may well come if we send word that the rector is here. Or do you think we should let Sheriff Ingram know? It goes against the grain to hand one of the family to the King, but in this case…' Sarah left off her sentence to concentrate on placing a collection of Mathilda's father's ceramic beakers onto a tray, ready for Adam to take out to Eustace's men.

'Handing him over to Ingram would be the right thing to do. After all, not only are we all better off without Richard, if King Edward has one of the Folville family in his grasp, he may be more inclined to give up pressing for the capture of the rest.'

Sarah lifted her shrewd gaze away from her work and levelled it at Adam. 'I can hear the 'but' on the tip of your tongue.'

'But I don't want to risk your safety, or risk losing the rector to the woods, by letting him out of that room any sooner than we have to. Better we send Eustace's men with word to the Folville brothers to tell them of his capture.' As Adam spoke, a flicker of unease showed briefly in his eyes, giving him away.

'The Folvilles? Do you mean Lord John or Lord Eustace?'

'I mean both.' Adam raised a calming palm before Sarah exploded into rage. 'I don't know where they are, but I have a vague idea that Eustace's men will.'

'Of course.' Sarah took hold of herself, 'of course they'd know how to find their master. I'm so foolish…'

'You are far from foolish.' Adam picked up the tray to take outside. 'I wanted to tell you I suspected they'd know, but if I'd told you while Mathilda was here, you might have told her, and believe me, that would have led to trouble.'

'That, I can't deny.' Sarah gave a wry grin as she pictured Mathilda creeping out of Rockingham Castle under the dead of night and sweet-talking Borin into spilling his secret. 'Talk to the men. Lord Eustace may have left instructions concerning what to do should Richard be captured.'

As he reached the door, Adam called over his shoulder, 'I wonder what has happened to my Lord Laurence? Did none of the family have an idea where he was?'

The hope Sarah had felt quickly dimmed. 'I don't think so.'

Robert reined his horse to a standstill and listened.

He couldn't see anyone on the narrow track which led to the side entrance of Sempringham Priory. Nor could he hear any movement, human or animal.

The bell for Prime had finished echoing across the countryside as Robert pressed his horse forward, hoping his kin were already safely gathered there. He had no doubt that Sheriff Ingram would guess he and his brothers would come to Sempringham. Whether he would do anything about that suspicion was another matter.

Keeping a sharp watch as he moved forward, Robert chanted into the rising morning mists,

'Maistar,' than sayde Lytil Johnn,
'And we our borde shal sprede,
Tell vs wheder that we shal go,
And what life that we shall lede.

'Where we shall take, where we shall leue,
Where we shall abide behynde;
Where we shall robbe, where we shal reue,
Where we shal bete and bynde.'

'Therof no force,' than sayde Robyn;
'We shall do well inowe;
But loke ye do no husbonde harme,
That tilleth with his ploughe.

'No more ye shall no gode yeman
That walketh by gren-wode shawe;
Ne no knyght ne no squyer
That wol be a gode felawe.

'These bisshoppes and these archebishoppes,
Ye shall them bete and bynde;

The hy sherif of Notyingham,
Hym holde ye in your mynde...'

~ *Chapter Twelve* ~

Roger Wennesley swung his feet up onto the oak table before him. 'You seem preoccupied, Sproxton.'

'I came to your aid before I had the chance to rearrange things at home. I did not know I'd be gone for more than a night. I was supposed to be elsewhere and -'

Wennesley cut in with a sharp bark of amusement. 'Let me guess: at this precise moment you are either in the wrong place to pay off a debt to someone it's suicidal to owe money to, or you've sweet-talked a gullible female into joining you for a series of amusements.'

'Neither!' Thomas Sproxton lowered his six-foot frame into a chair and grabbed a goblet of wine. 'You speak as if jealous of the fact that I've never had a problem acquiring female company.'

Ingram's voice arrived into the inn's back room before him. 'I don't think any of us would deny your unique touch with Leicestershire's women.'

Sproxton's eyes narrowed as he faced the sheriff. The infernal man had sniped around the subject of their mutual dislike ever since Roger had announced he'd be helping to round up the Folville and Coterel brothers.

'Why don't you just spit it out, my Lord? Then I can deny it all over again and we can get on with the task the

King has laid upon Wennesley. Not on you, not on me, but on Wennesley.'

Ingram remained unmoved by the argumentative tone in Sproxton's voice. 'The fact remains, Sproxton, that you are only here because you owe Wennesley a debt. A big debt. He got you free from a charge of rape, did he not? No trifling matter.'

'A false charge made by a woman out of her wits.'

'How convenient.'

'Convenient or not, Lady Helena de Vere is a harpy.'

Wennesley watched the two men verbally spar for a while, before banging his goblet down on the tale with a hefty crash. 'Enough! We have work to do. I've been charged with tracking men who won't walk easily into captivity. What did, or did not, happen between Sproxton and Lady Helena is irrelevant. Robert de Vere courts disaster and risks his offspring's virtue every day with the felons he invites into the King's castle.'

Sproxton opened his mouth to protest that he'd never raped anyone in his life, but Wennesley raised a hand. 'My friend, I know you did not do what you are accused of, but de Vere has powerful friends. His daughter's word counts for something; even accusing you falsely means something; mostly that you've annoyed the kin of the constable of a royal castle. Time will disperse the cloud that hangs over you, just as it will blow away the cloud that Laurence Coterel's death casts over us.'

Ingram banged his goblet down with even more ire than Wennesley had done. 'Which brings us back to the point. We have sent patrols out to seek our quarry, but we have no way of knowing if we have sent them in the right direction. The men we hunt are experienced, clever and ruthless. They are also likely to be feeling wronged.'

'Wronged?' Sproxton rolled his eyes. 'Laurence Coterel was killed because he tried to murder Roger. We have had the stigma of his death hanging over us ever since. There isn't an innocent man among them.'

The sheriff rolled his eyes. 'If you listened, you would have heard me say that they would have considered themselves wronged. I did not say this was my opinion. However, in the eyes of the people of Ashby Folville and Bakewell, these men, although feared, are respected.'

Wennesley picked up the message the King had sent him. He waved the sheet of parchment out in front of him in frustration. 'It's time to stop pretending, Ingram; we know you're in the Folvilles' pocket.' He rounded on his friend before he could sneer, 'And Thomas, everyone in this room knows that although the rape charge made against you was false, you have light fingers, an eye for the ladies, and gambling debts that money alone is never going to pay off.'

'And you, Wennesley?' Ingram's eyes betrayed nothing of his thoughts as he watched the man's impassioned face, his eyes catching something on the waved parchment that made him frown as he asked. 'What do the three of us all know of you?'

'That I killed a Coterel brother. It was in self-defence, but I still ended his life.'

Silence coated the room. No one bothered denying anything.

A knock at the door broke the spell as one of Ingram's men-at-arms came into the inn's smoke-filled back room. 'No sign of our quarry on the roads to Lincoln, Newark, or Northampton, my Lord.'

'Any word from the posse who headed towards Derbyshire?'

'Not yet, my Lord.'

'Very well. Allow the men to rest. I will issue new orders soon.'

As the guard left, Wennesley focused his attention on the dancing orange flames, 'I wouldn't waste time sending soldiers to Derbyshire.'

'Really? Why, may I ask?'

'Because the Coterel brothers will head to Lichfield. At least, they have the last twice they've got themselves in too deep.'

'And you know this how?'

'Common gossip.'

'And you didn't say so before because you wanted to give the Coterels a head start to get away?' Ingram sounded resigned rather than angry.

'No, Lord Sheriff. While I have no doubt that you gave the Folvilles plenty of warning and time to flee, I did no such thing for the Coterels. After all, I am *not* in their pay.' Wennesley held the sheriff's stare as he spoke. 'I did, however, think we should allow them to get closer to us before pursuing them.'

'A tactic I can't argue with.' Ingram lowered his voice, 'I need to know all you can tell me about the circumstances of these arrest warrants. The *true* circumstances. May I see the document?'

'What I know and what I suspect are different.' Keeping hold of the document Garrick had given him, Wennesley stretched legs out beneath the table. 'While the three of us are alone I see no harm in stating my theory that, although we have no choice but to follow King Edward's orders, it isn't in any of our interests to see the Folvilles or Coterels arrested.'

Thomas's eyes narrowed as he looked from Roger to Robert and back. Eventually the sheriff spoke.

'Under the reign of King Edward's father things were, I think we could agree to say, uneasy. With the usurping of power by Queen Isabella and her lover Mortimer, the situation disintegrated further. Families like the Folvilles and Coterels made the most of the situation. As did de Vere. They used the lack of governance and the corruption of officials to their advantage. I would be foolish to deny that I employed a blind eye when I believed it in the county's interests; but it was only when I thought it was to the benefit of our people. You can think what you like, but when you have a master that is more corrupt than the criminals you're left with the choice of your conscience alone.'

Wennesley smirked. 'A pretty speech; and one I can't argue with. Although we should not overlook how much money our quarry have made from their corruption.'

'Not as much as the Crown has made from its corruption.'

'True.' Wennesley stared at the rolled-up parchment. It was becoming worn from being held so tightly in his hands. 'Yet that choice has been taken from us now. A royal command should be ignored at our peril. What say you, Thomas?'

Sproxton spoke thoughtfully, 'I have not been in anyone's pay, but I owe de Vere for shelter while I was dealing with another affair.'

'What affair?' Ingram levelled his gaze on the younger man.

'I stayed at Rockingham to avoid a gambling debt.'

The sound of the Terce bell from Leicester Abbey broke out. Its solemn peal acted like an alarm call to all three men.

Wennesley leant forward. 'Time passes and we have agreed nothing more than the sending out of our patrols. We might not want to catch these men, but we have no choice.

What happens after they are apprehended is, luckily, not our decision. They will probably buy their freedom. Let's take comfort from that.'

Ingram acknowledged the truth of what his companion was saying, 'This could just be a money-raising exercise for the King's coffers.' He got to his feet. 'Let's discuss our plan of campaign as we ride.'

'To Lichfield?' Wennesley knocked back his remaining ale.

'To Rockingham Castle.' Ingram held his companions' eyes, daring him to argue.

Sproxton was struggling to keep up, his feet itching to be anywhere but in the smoky room with the other men. 'Why Rockingham?'

Awoken by the ache of her cold limbs, Mathilda was surprised to find she'd slept. Without waiting to come around properly, she clasped her blanket around her and headed to the door. Her relief when the lock opened took some of the tension from her shoulders.

She peered down the corridor. There was no one around. Tiptoeing to the Fire Room, she wasn't surprised to find that the door had been locked; presumably by someone who believed that they'd been imprisoning her inside. What did surprise her was that the key remained in the door.

Rotating it as quietly as she could, Mathilda extracted the key and hid it beneath her cloak. Then, taking a step into the room, with the intension of changing into warmer clothing and retrieving her travelling boots so she could take a walk around the grounds, she froze.

A woman lay upon the floor. She was curled up as if asleep, her knees tucked beneath her chin.

A short dagger protruded from between her shoulder

blades.

Nausea swam up Mathilda's throat as she stared, her eyes wide with shock. Despite the lack of apron and linen coif, there was no mistaking the red-haired body of Agnes, servant to Isabella de Vere.

Mathilda's fingers rose to her own hair. Red with wavy curls which often made it appear unruly… just like Agnes's.

Running from the room, Mathilda was halfway along the corridor when she turned back and locked the door again. Keeping the key, her heart thudding in her chest, she forced herself to stop and think. Where was she running to?

To de Vere? Would he be abed, in his working quarters, or in the Great Hall? He'd already told her she had emptied the house of visiting felons; but had he? Clearly one remained.

Wiping her palms on her gown to take off the perspiration that coated them, Mathilda was only sure of one thing as she headed to the hall.

Agnes wasn't supposed to be dead. *She* was.

~ *Chapter Thirteen* ~

'The man on the gate is called Borin. He is clearly the one Lord Eustace left in charge.'

As Adam came into the kitchen, Sarah busied herself unfolding a sheet from a massive pile of dirty linen. 'Was Borin left instructions should the rector be captured?'

Following Sarah's gaze to the fireplace and back again, the steward heaved a pail of hot water from the grate and poured it into a half-barrel Sarah had placed nearby. 'He did. Borin didn't say much. We are to keep the cleric under lock and key until Lord John decides what to do with him.'

Sarah plunged her hands into the steaming water with the sheet and scrubbed it vigorously. 'I'm glad Lord John is the one making the decision about his reverend brother's future. As much as I hate Richard, I would not wish to be the one who sent him to the gallows.'

Adam observed Sarah as she worked. 'Even after all he has done to you and all the trouble he has caused, you would not send him directly to the law?'

'There is less chance of him taking himself out of trouble with his eldest brother. With the Crown he could Bible-talk or bribe his way back into favour.'

'And there I was thinking you'd gone soft.'

Sarah gave him a half-smile. 'No chance.'

'Suppose we should feed him.' Adam spoke begrudgingly. 'Do you have any stale bread?'

'With Eustace's men gobbling every loaf I bake at top speed? Hardly.'

'That's your own fault for making such excellent food, my girl.'

'An odd compliment, but I'll take it anyway,' Sarah winked. 'If you take some bread and water to the rector, you can take something a little more substantial for his guard.'

Robert de Vere's reaction when he saw Mathilda walking towards him from the steps at the corner of the hall was one of blatant surprise. Whether it was shock at her being alive or because once again she'd managed to avoid the constraints of a locked door, she couldn't tell.

There were two other people sat at the oak table nearest the fireplace with the constable. A young woman, who Mathilda assumed was his daughter Lady Helena, and the steward. As she approached them a kitchen maid darted out of the corridor that led to the kitchen, a heavy tray of food and drink balanced in her hands.

Remembering what her husband had told her about acting as if she was the lady of the manor, Mathilda spoke with a confidence designed to be heard by every person in the room. 'My Lord de Vere, perhaps you would care to explain the locked nature of my bedroom door? And further, the point of locking me in, but leaving the key in the door?'

'I... what?'

'You suggested to me yesterday that keeping me confined to the comfort of the Fire Room would be for my own safety. To keep any of the many undesirables who pass through the inner bailey away from me. This loses something of its believability when you leave the means of entry for those felons in plain view.' Mathilda dangled the key she'd taken from the door in front of de Vere's eyes.

A movement at the table caught her gaze. It landed upon the blonde girl of sixteen years. Her gown was immaculate and her hair neat and demurely hidden beneath cream linen.

'You speak boldly for someone the gossips decry as a criminal's wife,' said Lady Helena de Vere.

Two high points of colour rose on Mathilda's cheeks, giving away how much less confident she was inside compared to how she sounded. Nonetheless, she didn't rise to the girl's bait. 'No, I speak boldly as someone who has just found a dead girl on her bedroom floor.'

'Isabella?'

As de Vere whispered the name of his daughter his whole demeanour changed from one of defiance to one of fear.

'No, my Lord. Her maid, Agnes. You should come with me.'

The constable was already moving towards Mathilda when he stopped and swivelled on the balls of his feet to face his daughter, the servant, and the steward. 'Merrick, Bettrys, you will remain here by the fire until I return. You will not pass on anything of what you've heard to a single other human being.' Seeing Bettrys' distraught and anxious face, he added, 'I will explain your absence from duty to Cook.'

As an afterthought, De Vere addressed his daughter directly, 'Helena, you will also stay where you are. Eat your breakfast. Say nothing of this to anyone.'

The girl's eyes narrowed, 'But, Father, how do you even know that this woman speaks the truth? This outlaw's wife could be luring you to your death. It could be your murder that happens here. Agnes might not have been stabbed at all - she could be anywhere.'

'Helena!' De Vere shouted, but Mathilda, used to dealing with men who spoke before they engaged their brains, held up a hand to stem the flow of unhelpful anger.

'I am not in the habit of claiming young women have been killed for the sheer fun of it. I would also be very interested to know how you knew she had been stabbed, my Lady.'

Lady Helena tilted her chin high. 'I was merely assuming. How can you even begin to think -'

'Shut up, Helena!' De Vere was grave as he asked, 'Agnes was stabbed?'

'In the back, my Lord.'

Helena was not content at being made to sit still like the servants. 'Father, I will come with you, I -'

De Vere was obviously used to being the subject of his daughter's disapproval. 'You will do as I ask. For once in your life act as demurely as you pretend to be!'

Mathilda tried not to appear pleased as de Vere admonished his daughter. She knew trouble when she saw it, and Helena oozed conceit and a propensity for manipulation. Mathilda found herself wondering if there was any situation Helena wouldn't be able to twist to her advantage if she saw fit. The fact she hid it behind great beauty was going to be the downfall of many men.

Helena hadn't finished. 'Why does *she* get to go with you, Father?'

'Because Lady Mathilda found the body.'

'A *body* that has a name,' Mathilda snapped. 'You make it sound as though Agnes has deliberately inconvenienced you.'

It wasn't until they were alone, walking up the narrow stone stairwell towards the Fire Room, that Mathilda spoke to the troubled constable. 'I presume that it was my body you expected to find this morning. May I ask how much you were paid to carry out my murder, and who wishes me dead that much?'

'Expected?' De Vere ran a hand through his short hair in agitation. 'What are you talking about?'

Speaking calmly, Mathilda expanded her point. 'A young woman of about my height and build, with similar hair, has suffered a violent death in the room allocated to me. A room in which I was intended to be trapped under lock and key – with the key left in the door so anyone had easy access to my sleeping form.'

As the implication of what his guest was saying sank in, de Vere started to climb the steep stone steps two at a time, almost running towards the room.

Keeping pace by holding up her skirts, Mathilda spoke sympathetically as they reached the Fire Room. 'You were genuinely fearful for your daughter?'

The constable put his hand on the door handle. 'I am sorry Agnes is dead; but if it had been my Bella…'

Mathilda produced the key from beneath her cloak. 'I understand. I wish I didn't, but I do.'

Agnes lay as she'd been left. Curled, face down; red hair splayed outwards in an echo of the phoenix flames on the tapestries surrounding her. 'No one has been here since I found her.' Mathilda surveyed the scene, 'Or if they have, they have neither touched nor moved anything.'

De Vere placed a hand on the lintel as he stared at the slain maid. 'Agnes was a good girl.'

Heartened by the constable's caring tone, Mathilda asked, 'Had she worked here long?'

'Not compared to the others.' He crouched to Agnes's side. 'She came to us from the south, but I never knew her origins. Her master was a felon of the very worst kind.

There was no honour to him. He killed because he liked to kill and stole because he could.'

An image of Rowan Leigh, a similar sort of man who'd done his best to murder her, chilled Mathilda as she observed the fallen girl. 'I know of that type. What became of Agnes's old master that meant she remained here?'

De Vere regarded Mathilda carefully before he spoke. 'I tell you this in confidence, Lady Folville.'

'Understood.'

He didn't take his eyes from the fallen maid. 'I know my reputation; I know how I am viewed. The constable of a royal castle who lets felony pay its way. Well, there is some truth in that.'

'But?'

'But the kings of England, for all their faults, are not stupid men. Nor are their wives.'

'Queen Isabella? Our king's mother?'

'Yes. While she ruled in her son's stead, she sent an envoy here with the conditions of my continued existence clearly stated upon them. I was permitted to remain constable, and to allow felons safe passage and shelter in exchange for funds, on the understanding that those who were not stealing to survive, to help others, or to escape a greater evil, were discreetly delivered into the hands of either the law or the King's military recruiters once their period of safe keeping was over.'

Mathilda thought quickly. What the constable was saying ran in line with the Folvilles' own policy on justice. 'I owe you an apology. I assumed the worst of you. I should have known my husband would not have brought me here if he didn't trust you. I assume you sent Agnes's former keeper to the sheriff?'

'Worse. I sent him to the Scottish wars. With any luck

he'll have been hacked to death. He was vile to Agnes. She is...was...as loyal a girl and as hard a worker as anyone could wish for. Bella will be devastated when…'

As De Vere's sentence trailed off, Mathilda asked, 'Will you let me help find Lady Isabella? If that knife was meant for me, I would like to find out why. As well as why Agnes was in this room in the first place.'

De Vere knelt, stroking the fallen girl's hair. 'Normally I'd sort this out myself with the local bailiff, but as it has happened within my castle I will have to call the sheriff.'

Mathilda felt the hairs on the back of her neck stand up. 'Sheriff Ingram?'

'Of course. I assumed Isabella was sulking somewhere, but now her maid is dead and she is missing…'

'What made you think Isabella was sulking?'

'She doesn't wish to marry Lord William Trussell. He is a good match; better than I'd hoped for considering my position. His parents only need a little more persuasion and the betrothal can be made official.' He shook his head,. 'But now…'

'They needed persuading over the match?'

'They have heard rumours about what happens here. I intended for them to visit to see that nothing was untoward.'

'When are they coming?'

'This week. Or at least, they were. With all this going on, I…'

'Hence the usual visitors being conspicuous by their absence. It wasn't my arrival that frightened them; you've sent them off to avoid an encounter with the Trussells. Your heart must have sunk when you saw me arrive.'

'I confess it was not timely, but you are discreet at least.' The constable raked a hand through his hair. 'I suppose I had better get word to the sheriff.'

Mathilda agreed. 'Lord Ingram needs to know, but I fear he may not be so easy to find.'

Her companion looked blank.

'He is out hunting my husband, my Lord.'

~ *Chapter Fourteen* ~

'Brother, I am heartily relieved to see you,' Robert de Folville greeted Laurence as he strode into the priory's warming house. 'When did you get word to come here?'

'Just past Prime.' Laurence gave the almoner a curt grunt of thanks as he was passed a cup of broth. 'John had no sooner been alerted to my arrival at our Huntingdon home than I was turned on my heels and sent here.'

'Any word as to the reason for the hunt against us?'

'I saw no one to ask.' Laurence de Folville gave a lazy grin. 'I suspect Ingram has been slow in rousing the hounds.'

His younger brother agreed. 'I wish we knew what crime we were accused of.'

'As opposed to all of them, you mean,' said Laurence as Eustace burst into the small room and grabbed a seat by the fire.

'This is no laughing matter, Laurence.'

'I was not laughing.'

'Where have you been, anyway?'

'A merchant in Oakham was not paying his debts. The local bailiff asked me to encourage him to settle his score.'

Eustace grunted. 'Well, now you are finally here, we have a job to do.'

'A job?' Laurence spoke through a mouthful of bread,

spraying crumbs carelessly across the stone floor.

'Of course. We have to pay for our keep here.' Laurence and Robert swapped a knowing glance as Eustace added, 'It's no wonder that our reverend brother is so evil. He grew up in a place like this.'

Eustace gave the almoner a glare which told him clearly that what was being discussed in his warming room was not to be passed on. 'A sad truth, but often truth nonetheless: a priory is the least likely place you'll find charity.' He pointed towards the door. 'Come, brothers, we have an appointment with the cellarer.'

Mathilda had placed a sheet from the bed over Agnes's fallen body before they left the Fire Room, locking the door behind them. Moments later, sat in de Vere's private quarters, she scanned a pile of parchments on the stable as the steward, Merrick, listened to his master's instructions.

'Ingram may not be in Leicester. However, I wish his deputy to give you his promise that this crime will be set before the sheriff as soon as possible.'

An ashen-faced Merrick left the room without a word.

Mathilda closed her eyes. She saw a vision of Agnes's body imprinted on the inside of her eyelids. 'The girl was stabbed with some force judging by how far the knife had been pushed into her. But only once, suggesting it was a deed that someone decided was needed in advance, rather than a sudden attack of passion or desperation.'

The constable raised his eyebrows, but said nothing as Mathilda continued. 'You said Agnes was a good servant. Can you think of anyone who would have confided in her?'

'You think Isabella told Agnes something that it was too dangerous for her to know?'

Mathilda stared into the flames. 'I don't know what I

think yet. If Agnes was the target for the murder, then how did the assailant know to find her in my room? It's possible she was not the intended victim. The killer could come back should they realise they've destroyed the wrong woman.'

'Unless they don't find out.'

'Meaning?'

'That you stay hidden away. Let it be known that the killer got his mark.'

Mathilda frowned. 'You wish me to go under lock and key after all?'

'If it keeps you alive, then yes!'

The passion with which de Vere spoke made Mathilda lean towards him. 'I can keep to the shadows if it makes you feel better, but I can't find out what is going on from behind a locked door.'

De Vere lingered his gaze on the table before him. 'How did you get out of a locked room? I can only assume you were never in there when the key was turned.'

'I wasn't.' Mathilda sighed. 'When did you last see Agnes? Was she in her outdoor clothes?

'Just before midday. She had her maid's apron on.' De Vere, his voice leaden, said again, 'You weren't in your room?'

'No. I have had enough of being held hostage to last me the rest of my life. As soon as I'd understood your intension to keep me under lock and key, I sought alternative accommodation.'

De Vere held his guest's gaze. 'I can see why Folville married you.'

'Thank you.' Mathilda wasn't in the mood for flattery, if that was what it was. 'If I was the target then there is some sense in keeping the identity of the dead woman secret, but I want to know what Agnes was worried about. I offered her help yesterday. The girl seemed troubled. Perhaps she came back to confide in me. Maybe if I'd been there she'd still be alive.'

'Or maybe I'd be mourning two dead women this morning.'

'Cook said she hadn't seen Agnes since she came for my breakfast yesterday. I wonder where she was in between?'

The constable shook his head.

'With Lady Isabella, perhaps?' Mathilda tried to concentrate, but her mind conjured the image of Robert being told he was a widower after less than a week of marriage. Pushing her fears away as best she could, she said, 'My Lord, I wish you to tell me everything from the beginning. Only then can I help you.'

A knock at the door sounded before de Vere had the chance to reply. Bettrys had arrived with a large jug of wine and some goblets. 'I'm sorry I moved, my Lord, but Cook thought refreshment would be welcome.'

'Thank you.' De Vere looked at the young woman sternly, 'Does Cook know what has happened?'

'Not from my lips, my Lord.'

'I didn't suggest you had spoken out of turn, Bettrys. I wondered if she knew anyway.'

Bobbing a curtsey, Bettrys didn't meet her master's eye. 'I didn't ask her.'

'You may go.' De Vere waited until the maid had shut the heavy oak door behind her, 'Damnation. If Cook knows then all know.'

'You believe Bettrys said nothing?'

'The girl has always been a shy one.' De Vere passed Mathilda a goblet. 'I have my suspicions as to who whispered in Cook's ear. My younger child can intimidate anyone if the mood takes her.'

As she was sure she harboured the same suspicions about Lady Helena being the gossip, Mathilda said nothing on the subject. 'You mentioned you assumed Lady Isabella had been sulking. Are you sure you don't know when she went missing?'

De Vere shrugged. 'I didn't notice until after your arrival. Bella is a headstrong girl, she takes after her mother. She doesn't get on with Helena.'

'That must be difficult for you, my Lord.'

'That it is.' De Vere drank deeply from his cup, 'Before we lost Juliana, Helena was quiet and well-behaved. She did her embroidery, learnt enough to be a good wife and daughter, but now…'

'Helena dislikes Isabella?'

'Helena thinks that she should be treated as the eldest child. There is a jealousy there that I have never comprehended and can't cure.'

'Do you think Helena has had something to do with Isabella's disappearance?'

'No!' The denial came out as a yell, which de Vere immediately regretted. 'Forgive me, my Lady. I am worried. I did not mean to shout.'

'You are worried that Helena knows something of this death. I see it in your eyes.'

'Relations between myself and my daughters have not been easy for some time, but recently they have become impossible.' De Vere got up and went to the table which served as his desk. It was heaped with manuscripts, which he leafed through impatiently. Finally, he found the document he was searching for. 'Do you have letters, my Lady?'

'Some.' She took the proffered parchment from de Vere's fingers. 'What is this?'

'An acquittal notice for Thomas Sproxton. Do you know

the name?'

'I have never had the pleasure.' Mathilda scanned the flowery script with speed. 'He was acquitted of rape...'she paused as she read on, 'against...ah. Lady Helena. Did he do it, my Lord?'

'Sproxton has a nose for trouble and he's a gambler, but a rapist... I did believe it at first, but now I'm not so sure.'

'I imagine you threatened him to stay away?'

'Of course.'

'Why was Sproxton here in the first place? I assume he was a paying guest.'

'Hiding from a gambling debt, or rather from the man he owed; I don't know who that was. I find it best to keep questions of that nature to a minimum. While he was here he got talking to my daughters. He and Isabella appeared to get on well enough, but I'm not sure about Helena. When I was around he kept to the cot he'd rented on the side of the hall for a few nights, then he moved on.'

'And the charge of rape?'

'The evening after he'd left Helena rushed into the hall, her face streaked with tears, her clothes grubby and in disarray, with claims of rape against Sproxton. I sent Merrick to have Ingram summoned. When he arrived he arrested Sproxton; who protested his innocence most strongly. A day later Roger Wennesley spoke on his behalf, saying Sproxton had been with him in Melton at the time of the alleged attack.'

'When was all this?'

'The last day of November.'

'Just over a month ago.' Mathilda's brow furrowed. 'How did Helena react to the news of the acquittal?'

'She was furious.'

'Furious, but not distressed? Did she appear afraid that

her attacker was free, or upset that her charge was not believed?'

De Vere's expression clouded further. 'No.'

'Was it about this time that Isabella began to sulk?'

'Yes.' The constable looked surprised. 'How did you know?'

'I didn't. Would you say Isabella and this Sproxton got on, but he didn't take to Helena?'

'He and Isabella spoke often, but he shied from Helena.' De Vere closed his eyes briefly, before opening them again. 'You are suggesting that Helena claimed rape to gain attention? To show Isabella that this man desired her so much he was prepared to go to any lengths to have her?'

'It is a big assumption without proof, but nonetheless that's the scenario I'm imagining.' Mathilda held her palms towards the fire. 'You say it was Wennesley who exonerated Sproxton of Helena's charge? The same man the King has entrusted to hunt down my husband?'

'Yes.'

De Vere was about to expand, when the door flew open.

Daniel, his face flushed, announced, 'My Lord, my Lady, forgive the rude intrusion. The sheriff and two other men approach!'

~ *Chapter Fifteen* ~

Mathilda jumped to her feet. 'They've come here?'

'The groom will be receiving their horses any minute, my Lady. I must go before my absence is noted.'

Daniel was about to flee back to the stables when de Vere called him back. 'Wait. Does Ingram know your face, lad?'

'Yes, my Lord.'

'Then head to the kitchens instead. Tell Cook I've sent you as an extra pair of hands; she will ask no questions. I think it is best your presence here is left un-noted for the time being. I will sort things with my groom.'

'My Lord.' Daniel flicked his gaze to his mistress, who gave an almost imperceptible approving tilt of her head. He disappeared down the corridor.

De Vere was on his feet. He could hear the recognisable tread of Merrick's footsteps approaching. He muttered, 'Does Ingram know where your husband has hidden you?'

'I think so.'

'Then we can safely assume that, if he knows you're sheltered here, he will not have told his colleagues; otherwise he would have steered them away from my door.'

Mathilda shivered despite the proximity of the fire. 'You think they are here hunting for Robert and his brothers?'

'This is an obvious place to start. Rockingham has a reputation for a reason.'

'Too obvious, surely?' Mathilda rubbed her hands over her arms.

'Not if Ingram is playing for time. He will know where the Folvilles are, of that I have no doubt at all.'

'You think so?' A flicker of hope rose in Mathilda's chest, but that hope was not reflected in her companion's expression. 'What is it?'

'I have just issued instructions for the sheriff to be summoned here and here he is. This is all rather too convenient.'

Mathilda walked to the slim window behind de Vere's cluttered desk. The view showed her the front of the castle, beyond the outer gateway. Anyone approaching the castle from the north, west or east on horseback could easily be seen, but anyone approaching from the south on foot, who was careful to keep as tightly to the outer moat as possible, would go unnoticed from this vantage point. 'I can't see anyone.'

'If they have reached the view of the stable lad, then they're already within.' De Vere knocked some documents together against his table, 'I assume one of the men is Wennesley. I wonder who the other one is?'

Merrick's arrival answered de Vere's question. 'Thomas Sproxton is here, my Lord. Shall I remove him before Lady Helena notices and takes fright?'

Mathilda swung her attention from the steward to the constable. 'Sproxton? The man who appears in that acquittal notice?' She pointed to the table of documents. 'This can't be a co-incidence?'

'It could be... Wennesley and Sproxton are known associates.'

'The man who cleared Sproxton of rape is a friend of his?' Mathilda's nose scrunched, up as if she'd smelt something unpleasant.

'I'm not sure "friend" is a word anyone would utter in connection with Roger Wennesley.' De Vere diverted his attention to the waiting steward, 'There's no need for the family to know that we have visitors, Merrick. Please escort Sheriff Ingram and his companions directly here.'

'My Lord.' Merrick bowed and left.

Once his steward had gone, de Vere whirled round to face Mathilda, 'You must go. Head to wherever you hid last night. They must not see you. If Ingram hasn't mentioned you're here, then he'll have a reason for keeping that information to himself. If he speaks openly of your presence, I will own to having seen you.'

'If that happens will you send Daniel to fetch me? There are questions that require answers. I would learn a lot more from talking to these men in person.'

'Such as?'

'Such as, does Thomas Sproxton know of your daughter's disappearance? She may have spoken to him of her plans if they got on well.'

De Vere was stunned. 'You mean to ask after my child and not of your own fate?'

'I don't know why my husband is threatened with arrest and yes, I'd like to know if a specific crime has been laid at his door or if this is a general campaign by the Crown. But whether I know or not isn't going to change the situation. Isabella's future, however, may be something I can do something about.'

Gripping her skirts, ready to stride back to the safety of her night-time hideout, Mathilda added, 'If you can find out everything you can about the pursuit of the Folvilles and Coterels, then I promise I'll find Isabella.'

The constable shook his head. 'You can't promise that.'

'I just did. But to be successful I require more knowledge. Get every pinch of information you can from them about their business, and when you show them Agnes's body, mark every observation. Listen to every word.'

De Vere couldn't help but laugh. 'Anything else, mistress bailiff?'

Mathilda smiled. 'Good luck, my Lord.'

'Where will I find you when they're gone? Which room did you hide in?'

'One that I intend to keep secret.'

De Vere had only just removed Mathilda's cup from the table when Merrick reappeared.

'My Lord Ingram, Roger Wennesley, and Thomas Sproxton.'

'Thank you, Merrick.' De Vere gestured for the three men to come in. 'This is an opportune visit. Not more than a few minutes ago, I instructed my steward to send a man to Leicester to seek you out, Sheriff.'

Ingram's chin tilted up a fraction as he gave the constable a shrewd stare. 'Did you indeed?'

'I would not have said so otherwise.' De Vere pointed towards the fire, 'Please be seated, gentlemen.' So far, the constable had avoided looking at his other two guests and planned to continue ignoring them for as long as possible.

The sheriff, well aware of the situation between Sproxton and de Vere, stoically wiped away the frosty atmosphere with the usual steepling of his slim hands, his fingers habitually winding themselves together as he spoke. 'We have come to search your castle. You will have no objection, I trust?'

'May I ask who, or what, you are searching for?'

'You may ask.' Ingram continued to tiptoe around the

reason for his visit. 'You mentioned that you were going to send a messenger to me. Why would that be? Or are you simply stating an intention that you never had in case we discover something inconvenient while we are here?'

Used to having suspicion cast on him, de Vere didn't even blink. 'I have stated what my intention was, whether you believe me or not, my Lord, is up to you. In the meantime, I have a murdered girl upstairs. An innocent who's been a good servant to this house. Is this of interest, or is the death of a maid beneath you?'

Moving quickly, Mathilda's flat boots took her though the stone corridors, the overlapping dark shadows at the back of the hall and up the stairs towards the Fire Room, without attracting any attention to herself.

Her hand was on the key at her belt before she'd even reached the door. Slotting the key into the lock, with a glance over her shoulder, Mathilda entered the Fire Room to take another look at Agnes's stricken form before the sheriff and his companions arrived.

'I'm so sorry, Agnes.' Mathilda knelt next to the girl. Her pallor had become waxen and her hands icy. The combination of the stone floor and walls, and the fact the fire was nothing more than a glow of embers, had hastened the chill of the corpse. A pool of blood had gathered in the small of her back; it was still and thick. The knife had only gone in once and been left there. Once had been enough.

'Was this meant for me or you?' Mathilda examined the dagger. The tiny amount of blade she could see was tarnished; the rest was buried in Agnes's flesh. Mathilda focused on the knife's plain bone handle. 'A common design, but not a domestic tool. Maybe it's from a workshop? Not a soldier's weapon,' Mathilda mused as she tried to make out if there was anything she could tell about Agnes' attacker from the weapon.

'The blade must have been thrust hard and the lack of struggle means it happened fast. They probably didn't even wait for the girl to turn, so...' Mathilda dropped her voice to a whisper, 'so it could have been meant for me.'

Trying to remain dispassionate, she lay on the ground next to Agnes. Making sure she didn't touch the girl, she stretched out until she judged her feet were level with the maid's. 'Yes, about my height.' Getting up again, she moved to the door and listened. Mathilda didn't know how long she'd have until the constable would bring his party to view the body.

The angle of the knife intrigued her. It wasn't tilted much. In fact, it had gone in almost straight. As if the perpetrator was the same height as the victim, rather than someone taller angling down or someone shorter aiming upwards.

Aware that time was fading, Mathilda gave the room a final survey, reassuring herself that nothing had been disturbed since she was last there. Then, slipping out of the Fire Room, she left the door unlocked and slipped into the empty chamber next door.

~ *Chapter Sixteen* ~

Lady Isabella couldn't remember ever having been so frightened before. She'd been afraid, yes, but nothing like this.

Since the two men and a woman had gone by on horseback early the previous day, she'd neither seen nor heard anyone move through the forest.

Her belly gave an impatient growl, reminding her that she'd eaten the last of the bread over twelve hours ago. The water had run out as well. There was only so much longer she could stay here - but where should she go? If she went home, they'd laugh at her. If they'd even noticed she'd been missing.

Isabella sank further down on her makeshift bed. Helena would have no doubt enjoyed her absence. She wiped the tears of self-pity and betrayal from her cheeks. That was Helena, and she didn't want to think about her father. He didn't notice anyone unless they had a bag full of gold marks in their hands.

As her insides contracted with hunger, Isabella swung her feet off the edge of the cot and forced herself to sit up straight. 'I have two choices. I go back to the castle and act as though I have been there the whole time, or I head to Leicester Abbey and ask for food and shelter until I have a clear idea of where to go and what to do next.'

Even as she spoke the words into the gloom of the run-down hut she strained her ears, hoping for the sound of approaching footsteps. Her love would surely come. He'd merely been delayed. There were so many reasons that could have held him up. He hadn't forgotten about her. He had not changed his mind. He'd sworn that he'd come. He'd sworn it...

Isabella got to her feet. Blowing out the candle, she kept hold of the blanket that protected her from the worst of the creeping fingers of winter which invaded the huts walls.

'I am the eldest daughter of an important man. If anyone questions my absence then I will tell them I wanted some solitude for a while. After all...' Isabella studied the confined space that had been her home for almost two days, 'that is precisely what I've had.'

She pushed open the door, braced herself against the sharp January breeze, and ran towards the castle.

The coming of the New Year was supposed to have been the beginning of a fresh start for her. A life somewhere else with a man she loved. Pushing that notion to the back of her mind, Isabella peered neither left nor right as she ran through the thick woodland towards her home. The idea of lurking cutthroats sped her feet as she ran for the castle's rarely used side entrance.

Despite the thickness of the stone wall that divided her from the Fire Room, Mathilda barely dared breathe as she heard the heavy tread of four sets of booted feet pass the door she'd left ajar. She knew the chance of hearing anything was slim, but she listened anyway.

Resisting the urge to put her eye to the crack in the door, knowing she'd be spotted if she did, Mathilda waited behind the door, so that if any of the men did stick a head into the room she'd be out of sight.

To her relief, the fact that four of them were all trying to stand in the Fire Room at once meant they had to leave the door open. With Agnes' body upon the floor, there wasn't room for them all inside. Although Mathilda was unable to hear precisely what was said, the serious tone to the conversation was unmistakable.

She closed her eyes as she waited, picturing the fallen girl. *Who in this household is the right height and strength to have thrust that dagger home in one go?*

Twisting her body awkwardly to press her ear against the tiny crack afforded by the door's hinges, Mathilda edged forward and listened.

'I should call the bailiff,' Sheriff Ingram spoke as though his duty inconvenienced him, 'but at this time he is engaged on an errand for me. It could be some days before he got here. This young woman does not deserve to be left here until then.'

'You will deal with her case yourself, my Lord?' De Vere tried not to sound hopeful as he added, 'Normally I would take care of it myself with the local bailiff, but as this occurred in my home...'

'I understand. It would be improper for you to act in this case. I will take it in hand.' Ingram exchanged a fleeting look with his comrades. 'As we explained in your study, Wennesley and I are detailed to pursue some felons known to be operating in this area. The fact a murder has occurred just as we start such a pursuit may not be a coincidence.'

Mathilda clamped a hand to her mouth. They weren't going to lodge this at her family's door, were they? Ingram knew the brothers were miles away. He must know... surely he...

Mathilda froze. Of course Ingram knew where her family was. He knew she was here as well. How convenient would it be for him to pin this murder on her? What better way, as Robert had pointed out before they'd parted, for them to capture the whole Folville family than to take her to Nottingham charged with a crime she had not committed? The brothers would try to rescue her and then the trap against them would spring. No wonder Ingram didn't want to alert the bailiff.

'Just one wound.' Wennesley stared at the weapon. 'A forester's knife by the look of it.'

Sproxton nodded. 'The sort they use for stripping bark. A sharp tip for burrowing into wood and two smooth sharp edges for peeling back the bark. A simple but lethal tool.'

'Clearly.' Ingram paused before saying, 'De Vere, can your steward be trusted to keep his mouth shut when required?'

'He works for me, my Lord.'

'Point taken. Let's lift the girl onto the bed. Then call your steward. I want this room secured until I have time to examine the scene at length. Douse the fire completely. If the body remains cold, her condition will not deteriorate too fast. I wouldn't wish to deny her dignity in burial.'

On a gesture from the sheriff, Wennesley bent to the girl. 'Do you wish me to remove the dagger?'

'If you would. And then roll her over. I would like to see her face.'

The sound of the dagger being tugged out of its secure home made each man, hardened as they were to the reality of death, swallow down a retch.

When the deed was done, Ingram peered at the wound. 'Yes. One strike, and little fuss or mess was made. The girl would not have known what hit her. Roll her over. Gently now.'

Wennesley and Sproxton lifted the maid onto the bed. The girl's expression was caught in a moment of shock and anguish. Her eyes were wide open, her mouth slack.

'Who is she?' The sheriff wiped a wave of red hair from the girl's forehead.

'Agnes. My eldest daughter's maid.'

'Is this your daughter's room? Forgive me; this seems more like a guest room than a place of permanent residence.'

'You are correct, my Lord. Agnes was preparing it for a guest. At least, that was what she was about to do the last time I saw her.'

'Which was when?'

'Yesterday, around midday, after she delivered some food to my work room.'

'And the guest?'

Sproxton broke across the sheriff's enquiry. 'Your eldest daughter is Lady Isabella, is it not?'

De Vere's complexion darkened. 'You know damn well it is. Do not seek to humour me with the pretence that you are not familiar with my household, Sproxton.'

'I meant no offence. I was speaking for the benefit of my colleagues who may not know your family structure. Where is Isabella, my Lord?'

'In her rooms, I imagine.' De Vere hoped his eyes wouldn't give away his concern for his daughter and the lack of information he had of her current whereabouts.

'Has she been informed of her maid's death?' Ingram took the knife from Wennesley's hands.

'No. I thought it best to speak to you first, Sheriff.'

'Good.' Ingram looked satisfied, but far from pleased. 'Let us go and speak with her. She may have sent the girl here for a reason we don't yet know of. It is best we inform

Lady Isabella before she begins to think her servant neglectful.'

Mathilda heard the door to the Fire Room close as the sheriff repeated, 'Who was the guest Agnes was making the room up for?'

Unable to catch the constable's reply, Mathilda waited until they were out of sight before edging down the corridor after them. Pausing at the bottom of the stairs, making sure there was no sign of the official party of men, she slipped into the kitchen.

Daniel stood mercifully near the kitchen's entrance, stacking a huge pile of logs ready to add to the open fire that heated a number of vast iron cooking pots.

Keeping to the shadows, praying the busy industry of the servants as they dashed around would work to her advantage, Mathilda crept up to her friend.

Hoping she wouldn't make him jump, she whispered under the roar of the flames, 'Daniel, I need you to ride to Huntingdon. I have an urgent message for Lord John.'

~ *Chapter Seventeen* ~

Mathilda watched from behind one of the giant pillars which helped support the castle's vast roof. The men, led by de Vere, had been talking by the Great Hall's fire, but now they aimed for the staircase on the opposite side of the room.

Assuming it led to the family quarters, Mathilda weighed up the wisdom of following them. If she did, she'd learn more about what was going on, but if they saw her after she'd promised de Vere she would stay out of the way, then his trust would be lost before it was established.

Mathilda debated which way to go. She wanted to think. To do that she needed to be active. Deciding against returning to her hiding place, she picked up her skirts and walked back into the kitchen, but this time with every intention of being seen.

'Forgive my second intrusion into your beehive, Cook.'

A bark of laughter shot from the bounteous woman's lips as she diced a cabbage; the movement of the knife was so fast it made Mathilda's vision blur. 'How may I help you, my Lady?'

'It is more how can I help you. My lad, Daniel, was entrusted to you not much more than an hour since, but now circumstances have sent him on a fresh errand. I've come to offer my services in his place.'

The cook appeared perplexed. 'My Lady, you are generous indeed, but I can't ask you to do what I had lined up for Daniel. Agnes can do it when she gets back.'

Hoping she didn't show any reaction to Cook's oblivious words, Mathilda asked, 'What task was he destined for?'

'Scrubbing the skillets.'

Mathilda couldn't help but laugh at Cook's triumphant expression as she declared one of the messiest jobs in her quarter. 'You think I lack the strength to scrub and clean them?'

'These skillets are old, they do not clean easily.'

'That sounds like a challenge.' Mathilda rolled up each sleeve, enjoying the older woman's look of surprise as she realised her visitor wasn't joking. 'Do you have an apron I may borrow? I did not bring my household attire with me.'

'But, my Lady, it was but a jest. Daniel would have been sent to clean and scrub, but you can't possibly... His Lordship would never permit it.'

Holding up a hand, Mathilda took a step closer to the cook. 'You would be doing me a favour; and your master too. I am the wife to a Folville and two women have gone missing since my arrival. The sheriff is here and he is asking questions. I wish to be out of the way and I need to think. Something is happening in this castle, and it isn't good.'

Cook's eyes narrowed but, although her many chins wobbled, she appeared neither shocked nor disturbed. 'Go on.'

'Gossip will have revealed my reputation for finding things out, and that Lady Isabella has gone astray. As thanks to my Lord de Vere for housing me while my family is in peril, I would like to find his daughter.'

'And help Agnes? You said before that you were worried

for her.'

'To the best of my ability.' Mathilda found she meant it. Agnes had been given an unfortunate lot in life, and the least she could do was to honour the poor girl's memory. 'Now, I do my best thinking when I'm busy. If you have cooking pots to clean, I will clean them.'

Laying the knife next to her chopping board, Cook held out a large red-skinned hand. 'I will show you.'

Ignoring the inquisitive eyes of the household staff, Mathilda noted the general layout of the kitchen, hoping her comments about the delicious aroma rising from the hog being rotated on a spit over the fire, the neat bustle of her staff, and the impressive set of double sinks that were built into the inside of the inner bailey's curtain wall, would make her appear more nosy guest than troublemaker.

As they moved Cook pointed out the highlights of her domain with pride. 'The buttery is through that door. If you walk through it you'll reach the bottlery, where the family's favourite wines and ales are stored.'

An intoxicating hit of spice met Mathilda's nose as they moved away from the intense heat and aromas of the roasting fire towards the storerooms. 'You are equipped well enough to befit a royal visit.'

'We are always ready in case royalty should visit. It would be an honour indeed to cook for such a woman. Word has it that she is a kind and gentle creature. With child as well. The latest messenger from London spoke of plans to have Philippa officially crowned as Queen in March.'

Mathilda, who had little knowledge of the goings-on in London, let alone in royal circles, was intrigued. 'It is good to know a gentle woman steers our King.' She was about to add, *instead of his ruthless mother*, but she stopped her tongue, unsure of who could be listening.

Cook said nothing, but she clearly understood what Mathilda hadn't said. 'A good woman with realistic expectations would be a pleasant change for England.'

As they reached the final section of the kitchen the light dimmed. The pleasant scent of spices, mead, ale, and cooking pork was replaced with sickly sweet sweat, burnt metal, scrubbing soap and all the other aromas of hard work.

'This is where the cooking pots, cauldrons, spits, and skillets are scrubbed down.'

Mathilda goggled at the mound of cookware awaiting the attention of a strong arm and a metal brush. The sheer number and size of the waiting vessels took her breath away. 'Again, I am reminded that this is a castle and not a small manor house.'

Cook's now familiar bark of laughter echoed around the confined space as she picked up a hefty log and threw it onto the blaze in the corner of the room as if it were a twig. A vat of water was being heated over its flames. 'I will not think less of you if you change your mind about your noble gesture.'

Privately wondering what she'd talked herself into, but remembering Sarah's companionable approach to scrubbing cookware, Mathilda spoke stoutly. 'I promised. I admit however that I did not expect to be in here alone.'

'Agnes would be here of a morning after she'd seen to her mistress, but...'

'But she isn't here.' Mathilda put her hands on her hips. 'So I shall get on. If you could loan me that apron, I would be more than grateful.'

Isabella wasn't sure if she'd said too much.

She was sure that it didn't matter. Not anymore.

Agnes was gone, and Thomas had stared through her as

if she was nothing but a whore he'd once known.

Huddled upon the edge of her bed, Isabella struggled to stop the shake in her shoulders. She didn't know if it was a leftover from her time in the freezing hut or reaction to the loss of her friend. There was no doubt that the ache assailing her body was attributable to both those things as well as the realisation that the risks she'd taken for Thomas Sproxton had been worthless.

Worse than worthless. For they had cost Agnes her life.

Lowering her head into her hands, Isabella struggled to think straight. Thomas had known Agnes was aware of their plans to run away together. Therefore, if he had changed his mind...

But if Thomas really had been called away on the King's business as her father had claimed, he couldn't have met her in the hut as they'd planned. Maybe her lover was merely a victim of circumstance, and they'd still flee together.

No. If Thomas had intended to be with her he'd have spoken up. He'd have comforted her when the news of her maid's murder was announced. Sheriff Ingram had spoken of Agnes as though she was nothing more than a deer shot by a poacher.

The only glimmer of light Isabella could take from the last half an hour of her life was the split second of relief that shot across her father's face when he saw his daughter open her chamber door. It hadn't lasted long enough for the others to notice, but she had seen it and took some comfort from the fact her absence had been noted. Perhaps her father had even worried about her.

Isabella's stomach growled once more, but she couldn't face a trip to the kitchen; and she had no maid to send. If her father had noted she'd been missing, then maybe her sister had. The last thing Isabella wanted was a dose of Helena's gloating face as she revelled in the excitement of a murder in the castle.

Mathilda swilled her right hand in some clean water, watching as the blood from her middle finger made patterns across the surface of the liquid.

Hoping she wasn't about to develop another scar, having only just recovered from those bestowed upon her by Rowan Leigh, she glared at the offending weapon.

The spike of the roasting spit mocked her. A tiny lump of her flesh was speared on its tip. Mathilda had a childish impulse to stick her tongue out at it as she pulled her finger from the water and wrapped it in the only section of her apron that remained clean.

Squeezing the wound in its makeshift bandage, she studied her charcoal-stained body. The apron was blotched black, her unwashed hand was smeared grey and, from the tightness of her face, Mathilda suspected she was streaked in old fat, charcoal and grime.

'There's nothing like being a lady of the manor.' An urge to giggle, brought on by fatigue and worry, came upon her as she examined the two skillets she'd scrubbed and polished to perfection before unwisely tackling the vengeful spit. Lifting her skirts, Mathilda tore a strip of fabric from her chemise and wrapped it around her wounded digit.

'The fire in the Fire Room was already lit when I arrived - but no one knew I was coming.' The realisation came from nowhere as Mathilda cradled her damaged hand. 'They were expecting a guest. The room was ready, but not for me. Then who?'

Trying not to let her imagination run ahead of her, the throb of Mathilda's finger informed her she wouldn't be able to carry on cleaning, despite her determination to not let Cook down.

'If someone else had been expected to stay in the Fire Room, who were they, and were they the intended victim rather than me or Agnes?'

Movement behind her made Mathilda spin round.

A maid bobbed an awkward curtsy, her eyes wide as she took in the state of the Lady Folville.

'I've been sent to tell you that my Lord de Vere wishes to speak to you, my Lady.'

'Thank you, Bettrys. It is Bettrys, isn't it?'

'Yes, my Lady.' The girl sounded worried.

'Fear not, I don't know your name because of some misdemeanour. I heard my Lord de Vere address you over breakfast. Are you Lady Helena's maid?'

'No, my Lady.' Bettrys mumbled, her eyes cast low. 'I was, but...' The girl's eyes fell upon Mathilda's makeshift bandage. 'You are hurt?'

'The spit fought back.' Mathilda pointed to the offending article. 'I failed to treat it with the respect it deserves.'

'Forgive me, my Lady, but perhaps I could help you clean up before you go to His Lordship.'

'That would be most welcome.'

Passing Bettrys the apron, she smiled as the girl immediately used it as a rag, dipping it into the water and presenting it to Mathilda. 'If you wipe the worst off your face, then it won't look too bad as we walk through the castle.'

Making sure her smutted face was as clean as possible, with a nod to Cook Mathilda followed Bettrys from the kitchen. 'This isn't the way to the constable's office. Where are we going?'

'There is warm water and a fire in Lady Isabella's quarters. She'd not begrudge you the use before I change the pail and clean the grate.'

Bettrys spoke timidly, but with a guarded edge. Mathilda was sure the girl wished to ask about Agnes, but did not dare.

Waiting until there was no one about, Mathilda said. 'I can tell you kept your word to my Lord de Vere. You have not uttered word of Agnes' fate to anyone?'

A sob leaked from between the girl's lips. 'No, my Lady.'

'I'm sorry. Was she a friend of yours?'

'Agnes kept herself to herself, but she was kind and worked hard. I'd have liked her to be a friend.'

Crossing the hall and heading up the same staircase she'd seen the sheriff and his companions take, Mathilda kept her eyes and ears open. 'Is this the way to the family's chambers?'

'Yes, my Lady.' Bettrys was walking fast. 'This way.'

As they entered a compact square room housing a huge wooden bath barrel, a bucket of lukewarm water and a chair, Bettrys sat Mathilda down and attended to her wounded hand before undoing her dirty hair linen. 'I can wash this if you have another, my Lady.'

'I do, but it is not in a place I can go just now. Perhaps if you could tidy and re-braid my hair, then I'll be presentable enough for the time being.'

Bettrys busied herself without comment.

After a while Mathilda said, 'Was Lady Helena mean to you?'

'I… I would never say such a thing, my Lady.'

'Of course you wouldn't. You didn't, I asked and you wisely did not answer. Your non-answer is sufficient. Thank you. Was she unpleasant to Agnes?'

Bettrys blanched. 'My Lady, you can't think that Lady Helena would kill anyone, I mean…'

'I think nothing of the sort. I'm trying to help Agnes, but

I have no knowledge of the people who live here. I have to start somewhere.'

Bettrys said nothing else until she'd finished tidying Mathilda's hair. 'There you go. Beautiful, my Lady.'

'Thank you. And now I must go quickly to my Lord de Vere, before I annoy him with my tardiness.'

'And I must find some food for Lady Isabella. She must be starving.'

Mathilda spun around on the balls of her feet. 'Lady Isabella has been found? Whole and unharmed?'

'Found, my Lady? She hasn't been anywhere, has she?'

~ *Chapter Eighteen* ~

It was with a lightened heart that Daniel swung his mount into the tree-lined track that led from the village to Ashby Folville manor house.

He could see Eustace's man, Borin, on the gate. He didn't need to wonder if the big man had seen him. Daniel knew that even if he'd been creeping through the trees on tiptoe, Borin would have detected him.

Raising a hand in welcome, just in case, Daniel slowed his horse to a walk as he approached the courtyard. Borin was already striding forward, his hand outstretched to catch the bridle.

'Daniel. Good. Adam in kitchen.'

'Is all well, Borin?' Daniel gave the man a wary smile.

'In kitchen.'

Having been warned Borin had few words and even fewer facial expressions, Daniel left the leather-skinned man, who was already back on the alert for other, less welcome visitors.

'Daniel!' Sarah wrapped the boy in her arms, surprising him with her enthusiastic welcome. Although she was always friendly and kind, Daniel couldn't think of a time when Sarah had touched him before.

'Greetings, Sarah.' He'd only been gone a short time, but the familiar atmosphere of the kitchen was like a welcome blanket. It was another world to the impersonal castle and cold stables. 'Is Adam here? I have news.'

'He's with Lord Thomas, discussing our prisoner.'

'Prisoner?' Daniel's mouth opened to ask who it was and if Lord Thomas was staying at the manor, but Sarah beat him to it with a question of her own.

'Mathilda is well?'

Remembering what Lord Robert did when he had important news, but was unsure if he should be sharing the whole of it, Daniel said, 'She is fit and healthy. I have news, as you clearly have too. Perhaps, if you don't think my Lord Thomas would mind, I should tell my tale to all?'

Sarah smiled. 'You are wise. Owen would've been proud of you.'

Daniel blushed. 'I hope so. I miss him.'

'As do we all.' Sarah, privately cursing mentioning their recently fallen steward, picked up a jug of ale. 'Come, Daniel, bring that tray of beakers, and we'll disturb the menfolk.'

'Are you sure they won't be angry?'

'We are equipped with ale and news. They will not be angry.'

The Canon of Sempringham rocked back in his chair. His great weight tipped him so far that Robert wondered if the cleric would topple, knocking his wits from him as his skull hit the stone floor. He hoped it would, for he did not like what they were being asked to do.

The darkening of Eustace's countenance betrayed his own disapproval. Robert wondered if the canon knew how close he was to being on the savage end of his brother's fist.

Next to the canon, behind a slim oak desk covered in pieces of parchment, ink wells and quills, sat the cellarer of nearby Haverholm Abbey. His apple face glowed in the reflection of the candlelit room. It was this man that Eustace, Robert, Walter, and Laurence watched while they listened to the canon. He was clearly out of his depth. Only desperation had bought him there. The cellarer's chest rose and fell so fast that he puffed with every breath. Robert considered the possibility of the churchman expiring from fear alone before their meeting was at a close.

As Sempringham's chief canon finished laying out his plan, Eustace picked a candlestick off the table and twirled it in his hands. 'My brothers and I gave up our weapons on entry here; a mark of respect to the holiness of your order. I am wondering if that respect was entirely due.'

The cellarer said nothing, but his frightened eyes watched the flame of the candle dance in the air as Eustace played it between his fingers.

'You wish for my family to sabotage a watermill that has been taking trade from Haverholm Abbey. In return you will continue to let us stay here; protecting us from the authorities should Sheriff Ingram and his associates call?'

Neither churchman spoke. There was no need.

Robert leant forward. 'You claim that our presence here will cost the priory in the region of £20. The removal of this watermill will cancel that debt?'

This time the canon responded, 'Correct. The mill in question is causing a dent in the church's profits. Profits we need in case of emergency.'

Walter sneered. 'And what emergencies could the church have?'

'How about the occasional need to harbour wanted men?' The canon's piggy eyes squinted so they were hardly there at all.

'Would you like me to cause a real emergency?' Eustace was on his feet, waving the candle over the table. All it would take to cause an inferno of paper was a tiny tilt of the candlestick.

The cellarer shrieked and pulled back, but the canon remained lounged in his chair. 'Threats, Lord Folville? When you need my help? How foolish.'

Robert put his hand out to stop Eustace from throwing the candle at the desk anyway. 'We are not in the habit of condemning men to die without good reason, Canon.'

'I did not ask for anyone to be killed. Just... their way of life curtailed.'

'You think there's a difference?' Robert heard Mathilda's voice at the back of his mind. He knew precisely what she'd say if she learnt that he was contemplating depriving someone of their livelihood in return for the Folvilles' safety. She'd be quoting Robyn Hode at the churchman with more gusto than he'd ever have attacked his scripture.

The canon leant his bulky frame across the table towards Eustace. Ignoring the candle flame only inches from his face, he said, 'The terms of your continued safety within these walls, and payment for all your previous visits, have been stated. You will deal with the watermill that threatens the income of our sister house, Haverholm Abbey. If you do not, a messenger will be sent to Ingram and Wennesley within the hour.'

Ignoring the threat, Robert asked, 'What do you know of Wennesley's involvement, Canon?'

'Does your enquiry confirm your acceptance of the deal I am offering your family in payment for safety within these walls?'

Eustace answered before Robert could. 'It does. But we

do not like it and we will not forget who asked this of us. Answer my brother's question.'

The cellarer looked as if he might burst into tears as, for the first time since they'd entered his rooms, the canon appeared uncomfortable. 'Roger Wennesley has worked for the Coterel family in the past. I have had dealings with him through them and our colleagues at Lichfield Priory. Not long after we had word from your messenger asking for protection, a messenger came from Lichfield on another matter. He told the porter that the Coterels had moved in for a while.'

Eustace mumbled, 'We predicted as much. Two of them, or are there now three?'

The canon regarded Eustace with care. 'The last I heard, Lord James was still in London. Rumour states he has the favour of the King's wife. Wennesley, I suspect, is King Edward's idea of a joke.'

'His outlaw, even,' Robert laughed, but without humour. 'I wonder, though, do you think...'

As Robert trailed off into thought, Walter picked up his goblet of wine and toasted in his brother's direction, 'Think what?'

'I can't imagine I'm right, but what if it wasn't King Edward's idea to send Wennesley on this mission. What if it was down to James Coterel?'

Eustace banged the candlestick on the edge of the table with such force that a lump of hot wax flew from the candle and hit the unhappy cellarer on the hand, causing him to shrink back further.

Roaring with a strange mix of irritation and amusement, Eustace nodded. 'Robert, if your theory is correct, then this is even more complicated than we imagined. If James Coterel has whispered in enough ears to get his brother's murderer to be the very man tasked with catching his own brothers, or at least to be seen to try to... clever. Very clever.'

Eustace twisted his attention abruptly back to the smug canon. 'The only reason I am not holding you up by the scruff of your neck right now is out of deference to your church. Not out of respect for you, for I have none. Not one drop. Now, tell us exactly what you know about James Coterel's involvement in all this; rumour or otherwise.'

Lord Thomas de Folville had his feet up on the table before the fire in the hall of Ashby Folville. It was unusual for him to be the eldest brother in residence, and despite the circumstances he was savouring the moment.

Adam, his face grave, had explained how Borin and his colleagues had located the Rector of Teigh heading towards the manor's rear entrance.

Thomas was sombre. 'You've acted well, Adam. My brothers will be thankful that Richard is one problem they don't have to deal with.'

'Should we leave him where he is, locked in the storeroom, my Lord?'

'For now; it won't be long before Ingram and his men check the manor. They're bound to make the occasional sweep of the place in case Robert, Walter, Eustace, or Laurence turn up here.'

'Sarah and I weren't sure if we should hand Lord Richard over to the sheriff.'

'In the hope that one Folville would be enough to placate the King?'

Adam sighed, 'I know it's a thin hope my Lord, but...' Adam got no further. Sarah had almost danced into the hall, a pitcher in one hand and a broad beam across her face.

'Forgive the intrusion, Lord Thomas, but I bring welcome news and its messenger.'

'Daniel!' Adam was on his feet as he saw the lad behind Sarah. Taking the tray of beakers from his hands and placing it on the table, he hugged the boy.

Stuttering, unused to being the focus of such attention, Daniel bowed. 'My Lord Thomas.'

'You're a welcome sight, boy. You bring news from Rockingham?'

'I do.'

'Be seated after your ride and speak, Daniel.' Thomas gestured to Sarah and Adam to partake of a drink as they settled to hear what the lad had to say.

'Lady Mathilda is well, but we have a situation at Rockingham we could not have foreseen.'

Sarah stiffened as Thomas asked, 'But Robert's wife is safe?'

'I left the Lady Mathilda safe, but she has stumbled upon a murder. The maid of Lord de Vere's eldest daughter has been killed. It happened a short time after our arrival.'

'Does Lady Mathilda stand accused of this crime?'

'No, my Lord, nothing like that, but the girl that's dead, Agnes, she was found within Lady Mathilda's chamber.'

Sarah jumped to her feet in alarm. Adam put out a hand to her as Thomas said, 'You think Lady Mathilda was the intended target?

'That is our fear, my Lord. Lady Mathilda is investigating, but…'

'But she doesn't know what she is dealing with.' Folville was already striding towards the courtyard, his staff at his heels. He issued instructions at top speed. 'Adam, we need a messenger to go to Huntingdon to tell Lord John of Mathilda's situation.

'Daniel, go and freshen up as fast as you can, then join me for the ride back to Rockingham. I am coming with you.

'Sarah, prepare food for our trip, but first, find Ulric. I need someone to get word to the Coterels. They owe this family a favour or two. Time I called one in.'

The housekeeper's joy at seeing Daniel in one piece and having positive word of Mathilda was in tatters. 'My Lord, you will... I mean...' Sarah faltered. It was not her place to ask anything of her masters.

'I swear upon my life, Sarah, that I will do all I can to care for my sister-in-law.'

'Thank you. I also wonder if you will permit another presumption. We should get word to Mathilda's father. Gossip will soon be rife. Better Bertram of Twyford hears the news of the situation from us rather than others.'

'You are right. Adam, tell Ulric to go to Twyford instead and pass the news to Bertram and his sons.'

Adam was thoughtful. 'My Lord, I wonder; Lady Mathilda's younger brother, Oswin, may be a better choice to take word to Nicholas Coterel as he was in the man's service for a time.'

'So he was, Adam. Oswin then. Now make haste'

~ *Chapter Nineteen* ~

Mathilda was too tired to pace. Thanks to Bettrys, she had a decent amount of bed linen under which to burrow now night had fallen, but she had declined, reluctantly, the offer of a fire in the grate. Having discovered who occupied which rooms and which were vacant or rarely used, Mathilda felt a little safer. She had no intention of staying in any room within the castle for more than one night. And if she could sleep somewhere with no one's knowledge but Bettrys' until she knew more of the facts of Agnes' death, then all the better. The scent of a well-lit fire would draw unwanted attention to her presence.

From Bettrys, Mathilda had learned that Lady Helena had an unhappy knack of destroying any friendship for the taking. Her Ladyship had been, Bettrys had said, sweet to her at first; kind and talkative. They'd shared secrets in the way that maids and mistresses do over the dressing table. Mathilda indulged in the memory of similar happy times she'd shared with Sarah in Ashby Folville, before the recollection was wiped away by what Bettrys had said next.

One day, about six months ago, after Bettrys had been helping Helena into a new dress, prior to a visit from a minor member of the royal household; the maid had spoken to her mistress about how fine the two sisters' gowns were.

Mathilda had bid Bettrys sit down at that point. A shaking had begun in the maid's shoulders and her happy face had crumpled into lines of confused hurt. Bettrys's only crime had been carelessness with words which wouldn't have even been noted by anyone but Helena.

Bettrys had mentioned what a brilliant shade of green Isabella's gown was. Nothing more, nothing less. Lady Helena had flown into a rage. She'd screamed into Bettrys' face, telling her that Isabella was nothing but a troublemaker and that a mere maid had no business saying that anyone, let alone her cursed part-sister, was more beautiful than she was.

The maid had sobbed as she had relayed the incident. The poor lass had no idea what she'd done wrong and in truth, she'd done nothing but hit upon the raw nerve of her mistress's poisonous jealousy. What lay at the root of that feeling, Mathilda wasn't sure, but the fact that Helena couldn't even bear to hear a compliment laid at Isabella's door betrayed a great deal about her.

If Isabella hadn't reappeared, Mathilda knew she'd be considering the possibility of another body being found in the castle, and that the trail from that corpse might have led to Lady Helena de Vere.

Helena, Mathilda mused as she tugged the top layer of her borrowed blankets up over her head to swathe her in darkness as fatigue threatened to overrule her mind, would not like the fact Isabella was back. The unashamed glee on her face over breakfast when Isabella's whereabouts were still unknown was undeniable, as was her dismissal of Agnes' murder. Servants were disposable beings to Helena. Creatures that were there to do what she wanted and say what she desired to hear.

'It's a leap from being a shrew to a killer, though.'

Mathilda closed her eyes and pictured Robert. He'd be safe wherever he was, she was sure of it. She imagined him curled in whatever bed he'd found. 'I will see you soon, Robert. I will.'

Brushing away the prick of tears, Mathilda was glad she had something to occupy her mind, although she wished that something didn't involve Agnes' death.

'Where has Isabella been?' Mathilda muttered into her covers. 'Perhaps she, like me, found a bolthole and never actually left the castle.'

She'd dare not roam forth while she knew the sheriff and his party were in Rockingham. After being found in the kitchen by Bettrys, and taken to de Vere, only to be told that she was to stay hidden for the time being, Mathilda had lost track of whether the men hunting her husband remained within the castle or not. Until she had word from de Vere, she didn't want to risk anyone's safety by trying to find out.

As sleep claimed her, Mathilda's musings morphed into dreams. Her last conscious thought on the first day of the new year was that Lady Helena de Vere and Agnes had been almost exactly the same height.

'You will stay the night, my Lords?'

De Vere made the offer out of politeness, but there was no eagerness to his tone as he addressed the three visitors who remained in his study as the hour crept past midnight.

The question had been levelled at Ingram, but it was Wennesley who answered. 'I think that would be wise, thank you. You have enough rooms ready?'

Ingram laughed, 'The Constable of Rockingham Castle always has a room ready for a guest, isn't that right, de Vere.'

Not rising to the bait, the constable moved to the door

and called Merrick. The steward appeared with his usual magical speed. 'I require space for our guests to spend the night.'

Merrick bowed and left without a word as Wennesley and Sproxton got to their feet.

The constable waved his companions out through the study door. 'I trust you will not find it necessary to search the castle again before you leave, unless you think perhaps that the Folvilles intend to sneak in under the cover of darkness.'

Wennesley, who'd known their trawl around almost every room in the place had been pointless before they'd started, shook his head. 'Your co-operation has been noted, de Vere. We will leave at first light. The Folvilles have clearly gone in another direction.'

The constable's eyes narrowed. 'As you knew they would.'

'As we suspected they might. It made sense to hunt here first though. The King would expect us to, don't you think?'

De Vere inclined his head a fraction, understanding that he was being told the trip here had been purely to give the felons they had been instructed to look for the chance to get a head start.

'I am surprised Lady Mathilda de Folville isn't here.' Ingram held De Vere's gaze with his own. 'If, perhaps, *she* should turn up during the night, it would be most wise of her to talk to me prior to our departure.'

'Have you been told to expect the new Lady Folville, de Vere?' Wennesley added.

'I am rarely told to expect anyone, but should the Lady Mathilda cross my path before breakfast I will ensure she greets you all. Providing she is allowed to keep her freedom, for she is not, if what I have understood from you is correct, included in King Edward's quest against her new family.'

Wennesley, trying to keep a grip on his temper so as not to give away how annoyed he was with the sheriff for continually making it sound as he was in charge of this investigation, added, 'If she is here by the morning, she will be left unharmed and allowed to remain.'

Ingram smiled. 'Lady Mathilda, if her reputation is to be believed, may be of help to us.'

'Help to you?' The constable scoffed, 'You think if she knew where her family was, which I doubt because the Folville brothers do not allow knowledge like that to spread, that Lady Mathilda would tell you?'

'No, I don't. I was in fact, referring to the murdered maid.'

'You think she did it?' De Vere immediately bit his tongue as he realised his suggestion had given away that Mathilda was already there.

Understanding the slip, but not commenting on it, Ingram said, 'No, I think she could deal with the matter for us. Have her, *should* she arrive, at our table in the hall at the hour of Prime.'

Isabella assumed she'd imagined the knock on her chamber door to start with. When it rapped for a third time, with increasingly desperate urgency, she got up slowly, and clasping a blanket around herself and moved to the door. Who could it be? Bettrys would have come straight in.

Agnes?

The brief respite from grief that sleep had provided was washed away in the moment of memory. Her trusted friend was gone. Her only friend.

De Vere was restless. He was also angry.

Wennesley was enjoying himself far too much. He was clearly relishing having the upper hand over the sheriff, who to his credit wasn't rising to the bait.

De Vere didn't like Sproxton being under his roof either. Something else Wennesley must know and be savouring.

Roger Wennesley was a murderer, for goodness' sake. De Vere punched his bedding. He wasn't sure why that worried him. He housed murderers on a regular basis, but this search for the Folville and Coterel families had the feel of a game. It was if Wennesley was aware he had to play, but his idea of the winning mark and the King's winning mark were clearly different. De Vere had an uneasy feeling he could get caught in the middle if he didn't take care.

And now Agnes was dead, and it looked as if the Lady Folville was going to be asked to clear this mess up. He cursed under his breath. If he'd just told them Mathilda was under his roof he could have saved face. Now he was going to have to play games too, pretending she'd fortuitously arrived in the night. There would be polite, false surprise that he had no stomach for.

He was considering giving up on sleep and going to find Lady Mathilda to warn her of what the new day held, when there was a sharp rap at his door and Merrick walked in.

'Forgive the intrusion, my Lord, but we have more visitors.'

De Vere groaned. 'Deal with them as usual, Merrick.'

'In normal circumstances I would, my Lord, but Thomas de Folville is here.'

'What?' De Vere shot out of bed and grabbed his robe. 'Find Lady Mathilda, but have a care. She is not yet supposed to be here yet.'

'I can't just barge into a lady's room, my Lord, but Bettrys knows of our situation.'

'So she does. Get her to find Lady Mathilda and bring her to my study.' He lowered his voice as he followed Merrick through the corridors to the hall. 'Where is Folville now?'

'I bade him wait in the solar. Its cosiness should provide privacy at this time of night.'

'Good. Come on, then. Let's get this charade over with. At least with Thomas newly arrived at the castle we can pretend he escorted the Lady Mathilda here overnight. Perhaps this is a gift from God.'

~ *Chapter Twenty* ~

Bettrys shook Mathilda awake.

'What? I…' Mathilda opened a reluctant eye. She'd been safe in sleep but now a stranger was waking her. For a second she wasn't sure where she was. Comprehension washed over her as the maid's face came into focus. 'Bettrys?'

'I'm sorry to wake you, my Lady, but you must come with me. The constable needs to speak with you.'

Mathilda was on her feet, reaching for her hair linen. 'Help me with this.' The girl looked exhausted. 'Do you know why I'm summoned?'

'No, my Lady. I know we've had more visitors though.'

A childish hope rose in Mathilda's chest. *Robert?* She shrugged it off. He'd hardly come back here openly so soon. *But this isn't openly…*

Saying nothing of her surge of excitement and fear - for if it was Robert then the news would either be very good or very bad - Mathilda thanked Bettrys and bid her go to bed.

Walking fast, grateful for the lit candle Bettrys had thrust towards her, Mathilda realised how lucky she was to have been introduced to the young servant. Not only had Bettrys thanked Mathilda wholeheartedly for thinking of her rest, she had promised to clear up the room too. As soon as the morning tasks were complete, she was going to store away the blankets and remove all traces of Mathilda's presence.

Bettrys had suggested a host of night-time hideouts she was primed to prepare for her and had sworn on the memory of Agnes that she would tell no one but Daniel of Mathilda's future sleeping places, unless a life hung in the balance.

Scrubbing sleep from her eyes as she moved on silent feet through the castle, a list of questions to ask her host formed in Mathilda's mind. The most important was to determine if Lady Isabella was alright, and if she'd even been missing in the first place.

Deciding to keep her suspicions concerning Helena and the death of Agnes to herself, Mathilda reached de Vere's office. The door was open. A familiar voice could be heard from within.

It wasn't Robert. Thomas? Mathilda's heart hit her feet. Had something happened to Robert? Where was Daniel? Sarah? Surely the rector hadn't found her alone and -

Her mind tumbled like acrobats at a fair, with every alarming possibility happening at once. In her haste for answers, Mathilda collided with the steward just inside the doorway. 'I'm so sorry, Merrick.'

'Not at all, my Lady.' The steward gave her a weak grin, stepping out of the way so she could see her brother-in-law. His cloak was on, his face flushed with the excursion of riding hard.

Mathilda gave an automatic curtsey before blustering, 'My husband is well? Daniel, Sarah…'

Thomas's face broke into a soothing smile. 'Worry not, sister. My news is good.'

Sister? No one but her brothers, Oswin and Matthew, had ever called her that. It felt strange but reassuring to hear the affection from a Folville. As Mathilda's pulse eased from a gallop to a trot, she acknowledged her host. 'Forgive me, my Lord, I forgot my manners in my fear for my family.' She dipped her head. 'I thank you for summoning me to meet my brother-in-law.'

Gesturing for his guests to sit, de Vere stretched his weary legs by the fire. 'Dawn threatens to arrive and some sleep would be welcome for us all, I'm sure. We can talk properly in the morning, but there are things it would do us all good to know now.

'First, my Lady Mathilda, you should know that the lad Daniel returned with Lord Thomas, and is safely in his cot in the kitchen. Next, my daughter Isabella is alive and well. She claims to have never been away. I'm doubtful this is the case, but as she is back and unharmed I am inclined to leave well alone.'

Rather than feel reassured by de Vere's decision to leave Isabella unquestioned, Mathilda felt more queries of the girl promptly arrive in her head.

As soon as the constable stopped speaking, Thomas de Folville took over. 'I can tell you that Sarah, Adam, and Ulric are well. They are all the happier now they've seen Daniel and heard you're safe.'

Mathilda's stomach was hit by a wave of nervous tension. 'But I sent Daniel to Huntingdon. Are my friends all there now? Is the manor abandoned?'

Thomas shook his head. 'Have no fear, Mathilda. Daniel rode straight to Ashby rather than Huntingdon. Robert instructed him to do so, should you need to get word to the family. Sarah, Adam, and Ulric send their good wishes, and I have excellent news. Eustace's men have apprehended my reverend brother, Richard. He's locked in the manor's storeroom, with a large mercenary guarding the door.'

Mathilda would have sagged in relief, but the hard,

wooden chair kept her proudly upright. 'You are staying at Ashby for the time being, my Lord?'

Thomas nodded. 'I am, but once Daniel told us of the young maid's death, I knew I had to come here. Not only because I knew you'd investigate, whether you were asked to or not, but because Sarah would have flayed my hide if I didn't come and make sure you weren't lined up to be the next victim.'

Despite her fatigue and concern, Mathilda couldn't help but smile. She could just imagine Sarah giving her firm opinion on the subject. 'I'm glad of your news and I could do with your counsel before you leave again. Is there word on the flight of Robert and his brothers?'

Grave now, Thomas said, 'All I know is that we've had no word from the law, so they have not been captured or arrested.'

'I, however,' de Vere shifted his eyes from where they'd been gazing into the flames of his fire, 'do have some information. I was visited, as you know, Lady Mathilda, by Sheriff Ingram and two of his associates a few hours ago. They were here in an official capacity, searching for Folville and Coterel men with outstanding warrants against them. In fact, although it was sensibly left unspoken, it was clear to me that they were, in fact, here precisely because they knew the brothers were not.'

Thomas raised his eyebrows. 'You mean Ingram was buying time?'

'I suspect so.'

Gratitude for the sheriff ballooned in Mathilda's chest, but it disappeared when de Vere added, 'They are still here. And they have suggested it would be a lucky happenstance if you, Lady Mathilda, would arrive at the castle by breakfast so they can speak to you. Not about your husband, but with a mind to the fallen maid.'

'Agnes?' Mathilda felt wary. 'Do they know I'm here, then?'

'Unofficially, Ingram at least worked it out. Officially you will have arrived overnight. A coincidence of timing, if you like.'

Thomas nodded approvingly, 'A political lie. How fortunate I should have arrived with you, as your overnight escort.'

Mathilda, heartened though she was to have the kindly Thomas with her, was concerned. 'But Lady Helena, as well as Cook and a few others, know I was already here.'

De Vere waved the problem away. 'Merrick has already seen to the removal of your existence from the staff's memories; as to Helena, I will deal with my daughter.'

Isabella lifted her chin and pushed her shoulders back in a fashion she was sure her mother would have adopted were she alive. Her father often said she was like her mother. She was never sure if he was paying her a compliment or criticising her.

Thomas Sproxton loomed in the doorway to her rooms. 'We can't talk here, let me in.'

Isabella copied his tone of hushed urgent whispering, 'I waited and I waited. I was cold, hungry, and frightened. You said you would be there before me, but you weren't and then you didn't come. You didn't even send word with a trusted servant despite what I've sacrificed. And now Agnes…if you'd arrived she'd never have been...'

The words snagged in Isabella's throat. Thomas reached forward to comfort her, but she took a sharp step backwards.

He lowered his head. 'I'm so sorry. I didn't want to let you down, but there are things you should know. Must know, before the morning.'

Shaking, Isabella crossed her arms protectively over her chest. 'Which are?'

'I'm staying in the castle tonight.'

The frown that had been forming cross Isabella's face turned to thunder. 'Staying? What have you done that needs hiding from this time? You promised! You said there would be no more gambling now you had me to help you stop. We were to go away. If you'd turned up we could have been -'

Thomas raised his voice. 'Listen! I have not done anything. I promised to meet you and I wish more than anything that it could have happened. I was prevented by a force that I could not have predicted, nor denied.'

The troubled expression that crossed her erstwhile lover's face soothed Isabella's hurt pride. 'A force?'

'You saw mw with the sheriff and Wennesley earlier. This is all the doing of the King of England.'

Isabella's hand flew to her mouth. 'He comes here?'

'No.'

Isabella gestured to a seat by the fire, inviting Thomas to sit down. 'Then what?'

'King Edward wants the rising criminal tide in this area tamed. It is Wennesley and Ingram who have been chosen to play King Cnut. We are not here because of Agnes's murder. That was but a coincidence.'

Isabella closed her eyes. It was obvious the castle would be a place to start this purge for felons. Fear clutched at her. 'Will my father be arrested?'

Shaking his head fast, he reassured her, 'King Edward has bigger prizes in mind. The Folville and Coterel brothers.'

'Dear God.'

'Quite.' Thomas stared into the fire. Reaching out a tentative hand, he placed it on Isabella's knee; relieved when she neither flinched nor pulled away.

'And your role in this?'

'I am to be their assistant. I was summoned as I was preparing to join you.'

'Why you?'

'I owe Wennesley a favour. Remember?'

Isabella shifted uncomfortably in her chair. 'If Helena sees you she will react badly.'

'Does your half-sister ever react any other way?'

Isabella sighed. 'I have yet to see evidence of that.'

Silence filled the room around them with unspoken questions until Thomas resolutely declared, 'I still want to go away with you. If you will let me.'

Hope swelled inside Isabella. 'You do?'

'Of course.' He clutched her palms, willing her to believe him. 'This situation was not of my making. I will rest easier when it's over.' He tenderly kissed her forehead. 'You will take care while I'm working, won't you.'

The tone of his concern touched and alarmed her. 'Take care?'

'Agnes was murdered. Until we know who is responsible, then everyone under this roof should be wary.'

~ *Chapter Twenty-one* ~

Abandoning her candle and keeping to the shadows, Mathilda headed back to her temporary room. She moved fast, not wanting to be seen by anyone who'd strayed from their chamber.

Just as she reached a buttress which caused a slight curve in the wall just before the family rooms, she heard the shuffle of feet ahead. Freezing to the spot, she glanced behind her. There was no one following her. Taking a step backwards, so she was hidden by the buttress's bulge, Mathilda listened.

She could just see the dark outline of a man, half in and half out of a doorway. He spoke in a low coaxing fashion.

'I promised then and I promise now. I *will* come for you. Until then, we are but people who have met and nothing more. Yes?'

Mathilda couldn't hear the reply, nor did she recognise the man's voice. His manner of speech she *did* recognise. This was someone who had done wrong and was seeking forgiveness. Even with her limited experience, she knew that meant his imploring tones were probably being aimed at a woman.

The sound of approaching footsteps forced Mathilda to press her back flat against the wall. Putting her hand over her mouth to muffle her breathing, which suddenly sounded abnormally loud, she tried to make herself invisible. The man however swept by her insubstantial hiding place. Clearly as much in the wrong place as she was, he peered neither left nor right as he strode towards the hall.

Mathilda stared at the retreating figure. His cropped brown hair was ruffled; making her wonder if a female hand had been holding the back of his head in an embrace. Or maybe he'd been agitated and had torn his hand through his hair in anxiety or exasperation, just as her Robert was prone to do. It was hard to see the man's clothing in the fading gloom of the night corridor, but it was clearly cut of dark cloth. Perhaps this man had a life where remaining unnoticed was essential; like so many men who made short stays in Rockingham Castle.

Telling herself off for seeing secrets where there were probably none to see, Mathilda emerged from the shelter of the buttress and, relieved to see an empty corridor in front of her, ran to her bed. As sleep claimed her, Mathilda continued to mull over who the early morning visitor could be and whom they were visiting. Helena or Isabella? Tomorrow she would discover whose chamber that was.

Roger Wennesley stretched his stiff limbs. He had spent more nights than he could count sleeping on cots that were too short to contain his tall frame, yet he'd never got used to how much his muscles always ached as a result.

Rolling onto his side, he looked across at the snoring figure of Thomas Sproxton. He watched as his friend's chest rose up and down in the grip of his slumber. His boots were on his feet. They hadn't been when they'd gratefully fallen onto the cots hastily provided by Merrick in an alcove off the Great Hall only a few hours ago.

Whatever his associate had got up to do when he should have been resting, Wennesley was sure it wouldn't have been good, and would probably end up costing money Sproxton simply didn't have.

Staring at the ceiling, he tried not to mind that they'd been given such lowly quarters while Ingram had been escorted to a private chamber, no doubt with its own fire and further comforts. King Edward had entrusted this task to *him*. He should be the one receiving the extra touches of courtesy. Swallowing down his resentment, knowing it was pointless, Wennesley listened to the sound of a servant igniting the fire.

The passing of time and rumble of his stomach combined to force him from the crude bedding. Crossing the short two paces to Sproxton's bed, he kicked his colleague's legs. 'Where the hell were you last night?'

Leaping into wakefulness, Thomas's hand grabbed his dagger before consciousness caught up with his brain. 'What? Oh, it's you. Not morning already is it?'

'If you hadn't been up half the night you wouldn't be so tired.'

'What are you talking about? I haven't moved a muscle since we went to bed.'

'Really? You got magic boots then, Sproxton? Ones that get up in the middle of the night and put themselves on your feet unaided?'

Thomas opened his mouth to protest that his feet had got cold and so he'd slipped his boots back on, but something in Wennesley's expression stopped him. Instead, he changed the subject. 'What's today's plan?'

Mathilda could have hugged Bettrys when she arrived holding a hairbrush.

'I thought you might be missing your things, my Lady. If you don't mind me using my own brush, I'll sort your hair out.'

'What a beautiful brush.' Mathilda admired the polished wooden handle that held the bristles.

'Lady Helena gave it to me.' Bettrys began to untangle Mathilda's nest of red hair.

'You're a blessing. I was beginning to feel like a haystack.' Mathilda relaxed into the stroke of the brush, 'It's good to hear Lady Helena has a generous side.'

'She does, but her generosity comes with a price. I was supposed to…' Bettrys abruptly stopped talking. 'Forgive me. I forget my place, my Lady.'

'Not at all. Can you tell me what was expected of you in exchange for such a fine gift?'

'Information. To tell her anything I heard that she'd find of interest.'

'Did you?'

'There was nothing to tell. Lady Helena likes to hear the worst of people; but I don't like to listen.' Bettrys teased out the mess of hair before her.

'Yet she gave you that fine brush. You must have pleased her.'

'I suppose so, but I'm not sure how.' Bettrys blushed as if she'd been caught out. 'Lady Helena wanted me to pay attention to anything that could lead to finding her mother's necklace.'

'It was lost?'

'I don't know. Rumour says it was stolen, but in this castle anyone could have taken it. It went missing the day after Lady Juliana's death.'

'And you were rewarded for news with this brush?'

'I heard someone, a man, speak of a necklace such as

Lady Juliana used to wear, while they were passing through the castle. I told Lady Helena. I wasn't going to, but she was angry with me because I'd spilt some wine upon her gown and…'

'And it does not do to annoy Lady Helena.' Mathilda spoke kindly, 'I understand. I would have done the same in your position. Do you know who the man was?'

'No. Just someone passing through the castle.'

Putting down the brush and applying Mathilda's hair linen, Bettrys changed the subject, 'My Lord de Vere is already abroad. He's in the hall with the sheriff and his associates.'

'My brother-in-law? Is he with them?'

'No, my lady. He bid me fetch you, so you could enter the hall together as if freshly arrived. Lord Thomas is concealed in a room a few doors away.'

'Then I'd best wear my travelling cloak,' Mathilda pointed to the cloak that had been doubling as an extra blanket, 'thank goodness I have it with me.'

Bettrys assisted with the cloak, then regarding Mathilda, the maid said, 'Forgive me, but you do not appear to have just dismounted from a night time ride. Perhaps you should release a little hair from your linen, so it looks as if you've been windblown.'

Mathilda grinned. 'You think around corners. Thank you, Bettrys.'

Easing a stray hair from its bindings in a manner that was usual after a ride, Mathilda followed Bettrys's soft tread, realising that they were heading towards a room not far from where she'd overheard the clandestine conversation a few hours before.

Could it have been her brother-in-law she'd heard talking with an unseen female last night? Mathilda dismissed the idea. She'd have recognised his voice.

Bettrys had no sooner knocked on the door when Thomas, also attired as if he'd just leapt from the saddle, stepped into the corridor and took Mathilda's arm. Wasting no time, he said, 'We left the manor directly after the capture of Richard, agreed?'

Mathilda agreed. 'You are going to tell Ingram one of his quarry is cornered?'

'Can you think of a better way of holding off their march towards Robert's true hiding place?'

'I cannot.' Mathilda's heart beat fast as they headed to the hall, hoping that neither Merrick nor Helena de Vere would give away their subterfuge. 'I will be happier when this party of guests has gone. Although, I suppose, if they stayed to find Agnes's killer then that would be better.'

'Because they'd be occupied here and not my hunting my brothers?'

'No. Because Agnes was a good person and deserves to have her murderer caught.'

Thomas gave his sister-in-law a wink. 'You are a unique woman, my Lady.'

'Is that compliment or a criticism?'

Thomas gave her another friendly wink. 'You chose.'

As the heat of the Great Hall's fire enveloped them, the row of guests seated against one side of the table came into view and the second's levity was lost. Mathilda, wishing they'd had more time to get their story straight, resolved to let Thomas do the talking.

A man had spoken to a woman that night in secret; probably Isabella or Helena. Someone had killed Agnes and someone else was out to blacken Mathilda's name; or kill her. Whether they were one and the same person, Mathilda wasn't sure, but she was confident they'd be in or near the hall this morning.

Her eyes fell on the table. There were two distinct parties arranged along its length, which, Mathilda judged, could easily accommodate twenty people. Two women sat nearest to the fire, while a row of four men, including de Vere, were positioned on the opposite side of the table, too far away to hold a private conversation with the other breakfasters.

The stately figure of Sheriff Ingram sat to the far left of this latter group, his hands steepled and his fingers entwined, in a gesture she recognised as one he adopted when he was thinking. Next to Ingram sat a taller, wiry man. He reminded her of a ferret she'd once seen. Appealing in a lithe muscular way, with an attractive face; yet there was something about him which suggested he would bite the unwary passer-by at any moment. An air of authority surrounded him, but he didn't wear it with any comfort. There was a short scar on his right cheek. *The scar made by Laurence Coterel? Is this the man who killed him? Roger Wennesley; my husband's pursuer?*

As they completed their walk across the flagged stone floor, aware that she and Thomas had been noticed by the gathered guests, Mathilda regarded the final male at the table. He too was of slim build, but perhaps a year or two younger than his companion. They both shared the same short cropped hair, although they didn't have an air of brotherhood about them. This man was a fraction taller, and his hands, as they gripped his beaker of ale, were worn and callused, as if he was more accustomed to manual labour than his companions.

'My Lord Folville, to what do I owe the honour?'

Mathilda had to hand it to de Vere; his act of surprise at their arrival was flawless. But then, she supposed, he'd been running a castle full of felons he had to pretend had never been there, for years. His skills of concealment must be honed to perfection.

As soon as she'd had the thought, Mathilda felt a prickle of apprehension spread across her skin in a bloom of goose-pimples. She had believed everything de Vere had said to her so far - how could she have forgotten that this man survived because of his dependency on skilful subterfuge? *'Trust no one.'*

Dropping Mathilda's arm, Thomas stepped forward. 'Forgive the intrusion.' He dipped his head in deference to Ingram and his companions. 'I see that you may be aware of the reason for our arrival already, Lord de Vere.'

With a glance at the sheriff, who inclined his head to indicate de Vere should continue, the constable said, 'I am forced to conclude that you are here to ask for shelter while the law pursues your brothers.' De Vere turned to Mathilda, 'You are the new Lady Folville?'

'My apologises, my Lord.' Thomas reached out a hand to Mathilda, who stepped forward. 'My brother Robert's, wife. May I present the Lady Mathilda de Folville?'

De Vere bowed. 'Welcome my Lady. Do you require shelter as well?'

'Thank you, my Lord, I do.'

'I however do not,' Thomas interjected. 'I am to return to Ashby Folville to run the manor during this temporary period of disquiet.'

Ingram laughed into his ale. 'Temporary, Lord Thomas?'

'Have you apprehended my kin yet, Sheriff?

'You know we have not.'

'Then the outcome is not certain. So, if I wish to think of this as a temporary inconvenience, then I will.'

Having only seen Ingram in agreement with the Folville brothers before, it was odd for Mathilda to hear the hectoring tones the men adopted. She hoped it was all for show.

De Vere called to Bettrys, who was hovering at a respectable distance behind Mathilda. She moved forward on a signal from her master. 'Bettrys, please see to it that the Lady Folville has suitable quarters for the night. You will attend to our guest during her stay.'

Bobbing a curtsey, Bettrys retreated from the hall, leaving Mathilda wondering if she should risk sleeping in any quarters she was given, or continue to move around, now that her presence within the castle was official.

'Now,' De Vere indicated two chairs opposite the group of seated men, 'your timing is indeed fortuitous. Only last night we were saying how useful your presence would be here, Lady Mathilda.'

'You were, my Lords?'

As Merrick placed extra cups and plates of bread in front of the newcomers, Mathilda felt the eyes of the women at the other end of the table boring into her. Resisting the urge to twist around to see whose glare in particular was scorching her back, Mathilda curtseyed to the Sheriff. 'I trust you are well, my Lord.'

'Thank you, I am.' Ingram gestured to his companions. 'I don't believe you have met my colleagues. Roger Wennesley, Thomas Sproxton, let me introduce you to the unstoppable Lady Mathilda de Folville.'

Tilting her head to one side, Mathilda was glad to see a gleam of mischief in the sheriff's eyes, 'Unstoppable, my Lord?'

'You don't give up until the trap is sprung.' He turned to his comrades, a hint of pride to his voice, 'The capture of more than one felon can be placed at Mathilda's door, gentlemen.'

'And yet she is married to one of the biggest felons of all.' Roger Wennesley's tone was teasing, but there was little fun in his eyes.

'In your opinion,' Thomas de Folville answered the gibe before Mathilda could. 'I think it would be wise to agree to disagree on that mater before we ruin everyone's breakfast.'

'Well said.' De Vere glared at Wennesley. 'The sheriff didn't hope for Lady Mathilda's presence just for you to bait her.'

'I did not.' Ingram spoke gravely, 'I hoped Lady Mathilda's need for a modicum of protection at this difficult time would bring her here so we could seek her assistance in the matter of the maid, Agnes.'

'Agnes?' Hoping she had been successful in her questioning tone, Mathilda asked the sheriff. 'Is there a problem with a maid in the castle?'

De Vere gestured towards the women at the end of the table. 'My daughter Isabella's maid. She was found by Bettrys in the Fire Room, one of the chambers we keep for special guests.'

Marking up another thing she had to thank Bettrys for, Mathilda said, 'This Agnes - she is dead?'

'Stabbed between the shoulder blades.'

'Poor soul.' Mathilda allowed her eyes to fall upon the bent raven head of Isabella, so vivid next to the pale blonde locks of her half-sister. Isabella didn't look up. She mutely played her food around her plate. 'Lady Isabella was close to her maid?'

'She was.'

De Vere said no more and an uneasy peace descended as Mathilda picked up some bread. 'You said you'd hoped for my arrival. May I ask why, my Lords?'

Ingram was about to speak, but Wennesley got in first. 'I have been instructed by King Edward himself to locate and arrest five members of your family and two of the three surviving Coterel brothers - friends of yours I believe. And yet, my assistant here,' Roger gave the sheriff a pointed stare, reminding him of his place in this mission, 'seems to think you would still come to the aid of the law and help find the girl's killer. Why he thinks a woman would be equal to the task, I -'

Thomas de Folville was on his feet, his knife in his hand, the tip aimed in Wennesley's direction. 'You hypocrite! You talk of killers as if you weren't one! And as to the Lady Mathilda's abilities, did you not hear my Lord Sheriff tell you she's already apprehended two such felons?'

Not wanting the meeting to erupt into a fight, Mathilda spoke soothingly, aiming questions at the sheriff. 'You're asking me to do your job for you while you hunt my husband. You wish me to find Agnes's murderer?'

'No, my Lady. We are ordering you to find her killer.' Wennesley seized back the conversation.

'And if I agree, will you explain to me and my Lord Thomas on what charges the King has demanded the arrest of my husband and our family?'

'I don't bargain with the wives of criminals.'

'Oh don't be such a fool, man.' Ingram jumped to his feet. 'I will tell Thomas the details of the indictment. Then if you still wish to know, Lady Folville, you can ask him later. In exchange we require your word that you'll stay here, in safety, to catch Agnes' attacker.'

'I shall need to talk to Bettrys and Lady Isabella to learn all I can about Agnes. I also require the freedom of the castle.' Mathilda looked at her brother-in-law for reassurance. He nodded.

'But as to me staying safe until the killer is caught - only the felon responsible can promise you that.'

~ *Chapter Twenty-two* ~

Having been reassured by Bettrys that Daniel was back in one piece, Mathilda was about to take leave of the young maid when she spotted Merrick heading in her direction.

'Lord Thomas de Folville wishes to address you before his departure, my Lady.'

'Thank you, Merrick.'

Following the steward into the stable courtyard, Mathilda thought fast. There were so many questions to ask, and time was short. Although she most wanted to know what the charges against her husband were, given her task of tracking down a murderer, Mathilda knew she'd be better off enquiring in other areas first.

'Sproxton said nothing while I was at the table. Who is he?'

Folville tested the girth of the saddle, respecting Mathilda's desire for him to get to the point fast. 'Thomas Sproxton is an associate of Roger Wennesley's. He was there when Laurence Coterel died. It appears he's been roped into this round-up of our family. That means he must owe Wennesley a favour. I can't see him doing this out of the goodness of his heart. In fact, from the little I know of the man, I can't see him ever doing anything out of the goodness of his heart.'

'What else do you know of Sproxton?'

'That he is a gambler and possibly a defiler of women - although that could be hearsay.'

Remembering the rape charge that de Vere had detailed, Mathilda asked, 'And the capture of Agnes's killer; am I to be given the freedoms to investigate that I requested?'

'The idea that you could go anywhere in the castle did not sit well with de Vere, but Ingram decreed you should be given full access. The murder is, after all, in his remit.'

'Unlike the hunt for our family. Why Wennesley, do you think? There must be bailiffs who are more suitable for the job?'

Thomas blew out an aggravated sigh. 'I can't be sure, but it is a shrewd move on the King's behalf. He is expendable. If it goes wrong, Edward can simply execute him as a murderer and a failure without losing face, while still being seen to be trying to do something about the crime rate in the midlands of England.'

'Clever.'

'He clearly learnt a lot from his mother.'

Mathilda swallowed before saying, 'Now you have the news Lord John wanted, will you go straight to Huntingdon, or will you visit Ashby Folville first?'

Thomas looked grim 'I shall go via Ashby. Adam and Sarah will be anxious for word of your safety and I'm equally anxious to ensure my reverend brother remains under locked up. One of Eustace's men can take the news to Huntingdon. I will stay at the manor until Richard is collected.'

'What was the sheriff's reaction when he learned Richard was in custody?'

Thomas grunted, 'Hard to tell. Ingram's countenance was as unreadable as ever. Wennesley, on the other hand, looked as if he'd just won a prize pig at the fair.'

'Pleased?'

'Smug.'

'Ah.' Mathilda found she wasn't surprised by this. 'He strikes me as someone who will take credit for the capture although it's not his to take.'

'You have taken the measure of Roger Wennesley.' Thomas opened his saddle-roll and slipped in a hunk of bread he'd taken from the breakfast table. 'The Coterels have worked with him, and I believe Eustace has had some dealing with him in the past. Wennesley is cunning and clever. Treats life as a game.'

Mathilda stroked the horse's mane. 'That's what Robert said; that Roger Wennesley saw things as a game.'

'When he is on your side, I'm sure Wennesley is a staunch ally, but when he's not…'

'And he changes sides all the time?'

'You've got it.' Thomas's eyes clouded. 'You will take care, won't you? I don't like leaving you here with a killer on the loose.'

'I have Daniel and Bettrys is proving very helpful.' Mathilda, wishing she was leaving too, gave him a brave smile. 'Look after my friends for me.'

'I promise.' Thomas leapt into the saddle and circled his horse to face the road.

Placing her hand on the horse's neck, Mathilda finally asked the question she wasn't sure she wanted to know the answer to. 'The charges against Robert: are they real?'

Thomas's response was resigned. 'I fear they are sound. I had hoped the charges were convenient inventions by the King to help his cause, but sadly they are not.'

Mathilda's heart sank. She hadn't realised how much she'd been relying on the warrant being false. 'Tell me.'

'Ask yourself, Mathilda, do you want to know?'

Continuing to stroke the horse, which seemed to appreciate her affection, Mathilda thought. Did she want to know? Whatever it was that her husband had done would have been before they'd met. He had been honest with her from the beginning; never shying from the responsibility of how he and his family choose to live. Folville's Law, as the locals called it, had had positive consequences for the region, but it came with a price. And that price was that they often had to break the law to achieve their version of justice.

'I'd rather hear it from you than Wennesley's gloating lips.'

'They are all indicted, my brothers that is, not the Coterels, on a count of theft. Of stealing chattels worth £200 from the burgess of Leicester.'

Relieved that she hadn't just heard a tale of mass murder, Mathilda asked, 'When did that happen?'

'Last January. All I can tell you for certain is that their hands were forced by events. That theft saved the life of a townsman. As I was not there, I can say no more.'

'That would explain your absence from the warrant.' Mathilda didn't know what else to say. She hated to think of Robert involved in such things. It didn't sit with the man she knew, and yet... 'How did it save a man?'

'Paid his debts and prevented his murder.' Thomas's horse whinnied and tossed its head, as if bored of hanging around. 'I must go. I've messages to deliver.' He regarded his sister-in-law, a worried furrow across his forehead. 'You are sure you'll be alright?'

'I intend to talk to Sheriff Ingram and his associates again before they leave.'

'Why? They can't have had a hand in the maid's death, they weren't here.'

'True. But someone, a man, was roaming the family quarters last night when he shouldn't have been. I know it wasn't de Vere, Merrick or Ingram. And although I know far from every face in Rockingham, I'm sure it wasn't a member of the household staff.'

Thomas paused. 'If you mess with Wennesley or Sproxton now, when Robert is -'

Mathilda held up her hand to stem the warning she didn't need to hear. 'I know. The consequences could be dire for all of us. I will tread with caution.'

'Even if one of them was abroad last night, the chances of it being connected with the maid's death are slim.'

'Slim, but not impossible.' Mathilda shrugged. 'Regrettably there was not time to fill you in on all that happened before our official arrival.'

Thomas inclined his head. 'My brother married well.' With that, he kicked his mount into action. 'Our Lady keep you safe, Mathilda de Folville.'

Mathilda stared at the space where her brother-in-law had been. Envy welled in her chest. He was going home, to where she ought to be. Instead she was destined to stay in this strangely conflicted castle, a place of welcoming unfriendliness, where the emotions and opinions of the inhabitants were split at the seams.

Shaking off her sense of isolation, Mathilda headed to the kitchen. With a courteous nod to Cook, she went to find Daniel. He was finishing off the task she'd started, but more successfully. All his fingers were whole and none of his blood dripped into the washing bucket.

'I am pleased to see you. Thank you for riding to Ashby Folville. My mind is greatly relieved to have word of Adam and Sarah.'

Continuing to work as he spoke, a shy smile curled up the corners of Daniel's mouth. 'You weren't angry that I didn't go to Huntingdon as you requested?'

'You followed orders of which I had no knowledge, why would I be cross? Because you did what my husband asked I have received more information than I otherwise would have done.'

Daniel looked relieved. 'Has Lord Thomas departed?'

'He has.' Mathilda paused. 'Daniel, do you know where my husband is?'

'No, my Lady; on my life.'

'I believe you.' Mathilda squared her shoulders. 'While I'm here, I have been given a task to do.'

'I know, my Lady. To find out why Lord Robert and his brothers have been singled out to be hunted by the Crown.'

'That was correct, but it is no longer the case.'

'My Lady?'

'Lord Thomas used the direct route to discover that information. He simply asked the sheriff, who was happy to share the information. I have a fresh mission, one that ensures I'm kept out of the pursuit of my family.'

'They are blackmailing you into helping them?'

'I suppose they are.' Mathilda sighed. 'I am to find Agnes's killer.'

Daniel's eyebrows met in the middle as he asked, 'Weren't you doing that anyway?'

Mathilda couldn't help but laugh. 'I suppose I was, but now I have to. It feels different now I have no choice.'

Concentrating on a stubborn bit of congealed grease which had been burnt onto the spit, Daniel said, 'Being forced to do something always feels different.'

Mathilda experienced a wave of guilt. She'd volunteered to help in the kitchens. She could have walked away whenever she wanted to - and she had. Daniel had to keep going until Cook said otherwise.

Only a year ago her life hadn't been so different from Daniel's. Running her family's home in Twyford, replacing her deceased mother as the housekeeper, cook, cleaner, washerwoman and account-reckoner for her father's pottery. It was hard, unrelenting work and Mathilda had resented so much of it. Then, like a miracle, it was over. The route to freedom had been unusual, frightening and tough, but she'd made it through and now she was the wife of a nobleman. As Mathilda watched Daniel, she vowed she would never forget what it was like to have so few choices.

'Daniel, I'm sorry you have to do this. Would you like me to help?'

Looking faintly scandalised, the lad smiled. 'Thank you, but it would not be right. Anyway, you have some hard stains to shift - just a different kind.'

With Daniel's words of wisdom ringing in her ears, Mathilda took her leave with a determination to show Wennesley she was more than just someone's wife.

It was time to find out exactly what had been going on here.

~ *Chapter Twenty-three* ~

The Canon of Sempringham Priory leant his vast, habited frame against the pillar nearest the warming house fire. He surveyed the humble but functional room with disdain. He couldn't remember the last time he'd mixed with the lower orders of the house. Typical of the Folville brothers to insist they met in this place rather than within his opulent chambers.

Wanting to get this conversation over with as soon as possible, the canon bent forward and spoke straight into Robert de Folville's face; revealing that the fish he'd eaten the night before had not settled well with him. 'Doesn't your Robyn Hode accept that fees have to be paid for services rendered?'

Drawing back, making no secret of his dislike of the canon's fishy aroma, Robert said, 'I beg your pardon?'

'You baulk at committing this one small service in return for your safety and lodgings under this roof, yet you pretend to follow the word of Robyn Hode.'

'You would do well not to taunt my brother with his devotion to the outlaw tales, Canon,' Eustace growled.

Ignoring the elder Folville, the canon launched into a rhyme he considered his proof,

"And every yere of Robyn Hode,

Twenty merks to thy fee.'
'Put up thy swerde.' Said the cook,
'And felones will we be."

Eustace shot out a hand, and gripped the back of Robert's cloak before he punched the canon into a painfully deep sleep. 'You risk your soul quoting *The Geste* to my brother, Canon. Surely a Bible verse would have been more fitting. But perhaps you don't know any?'

Yanking himself free of Eustace's fist, Robert grabbed the canon by the throat. 'You use the verses to suit your purpose, to convince yourself you're right. But trying to convince me to deprive someone of their livelihood by quoting a verse where Little John and a cook are discussing fair play in the forest, using those very words to excuse your extortion - unwise, Canon. Most unwise.'

As Robert dropped the spluttering cleric, Eustace growled, 'Tell us precisely why the watermill has to burn. Should we agree that it has to be done for the greater good, then it will be done. Otherwise, it will not be done by us.'

His face beetroot at having been humiliated in front of the wisely silent almoner, the canon hissed, 'If you do not do what is requested of you, I will go straight to the king. Surely the "greater good", as you call it, is to protect your new wife.'

The mention of Mathilda and the threatening tone in which it had been spoken was a push too far for Robert. He had re-crossed the room before the canon had got his final word out. Lifting the corpulent figure off the ground and slamming him back against the stone wall, Robert hissed into his ear, 'Man of God? You're a disgrace.'

Letting go of the churchman, Robert watched him slide to the floor before joining his waiting brothers. 'It is no coincidence that Robyn Hode thought so little of the Church, despite his devotion to Our Lady.'

Striding angrily after his kin, Robert felt the palms of his hand tingle in frustration. The canon had them caught and he knew it. However satisfying it had been to frighten him, the cleric knew they would do what he asked because, right now, they couldn't afford not to. They would not forget, though. The Folvilles would never lose sight of what had been asked of them today, and when King Edward tired of playing bailiff, as they all knew he would, they would return to the priory…

Blood hammered in Mathilda's ears. She had tracked down killers in the past, but never by appointment. The first time had been unintentional, a task she'd stumbled upon to save her father's honour and her freedom. The second had come with an even higher price tag. The cost of failure would have been her life.

Now, these previous successes had earned her a third attempt, and Mathilda doubted she was up to the task. In Ashby Folville she had Sarah and Adam to back her up, not to mention Robert and his brothers. Here, she was alone but for Daniel, who'd already had a myriad of household duties heaped upon him.

Would her desire to find justice for Agnes, and her equally strong curiosity to uncover what was going on in the castle, be enough to solve the crime. Or crimes?

Whatever her misgivings, Mathilda's starting point was clear. The sheriff and his associates had not yet left the castle. She wanted to talk to each of them privately. The constable had promised her the freedom of the castle while he'd had little choice but to agree, but would he continue to extend that offer once Wennesley and his comrades had gone to recommence the search for her husband.

Not sure if she was heartened or worried by Sheriff Ingram's claim that she was unstoppable in her pursuit of felons, Mathilda wiped away the perspiration from her palms.

As she walked towards de Vere's rooms, Mathilda forced herself to focus. Even if the arresting party remained with the constable, that didn't mean they would be willing to answer her questions. After all, they hadn't been there when Agnes had died, yet Mathilda couldn't shift the uneasy feeling that it was all connected somehow. She had no logical reason for that suspicion beyond the coincidence of Isabella's abrupt reappearance and the night-time movements of a tall, short-haired man who could have been either of the younger men on the warrant party... or someone else entirely.

Merrick saw Mathilda's approach and announced her arrival to de Vere. The constable was sat next to Wennesley, who was poring over an open document. There was no sign of the sheriff or Sproxton.

Rising to his feet, de Vere displayed no surprise at Mathilda's arrival. His companion remained seated, his eyebrows raised, his expression blatantly curious.

'Forgive my disruption when you have much to occupy you, my Lords.' Mathilda wasn't sure if Wennesley was due the title, but decided politeness was a safe hand to play. 'As you can appreciate, I have many questions to ask to ensure success in apprehending Agnes's attacker.'

Wennesley grunted. 'You intend to apprehend as well as track down this felon?'

'I spoke incorrectly.' Mathilda inclined her head in acknowledgement. 'I will not attempt to apprehend anyone. That would be foolish.'

'At least your arrogance hadn't blinded you to common

sense.'

Not rising the bait, Mathilda spoke to de Vere, 'I believe it prudent to start my enquiry with you, my Lord.'

Wennesley barked with amusement. 'The insolence! You think your host is a killer *and* you are bold enough to ask. Unbelievable!'

'No, I merely thought it polite to check if my host, who has already been kind enough to offer me a room and a maid for my comfort, would object to me speaking to his daughters.'

De Vere was solemn. 'I can see you have to talk to them. I will accompany you.'

Mathilda had foreseen this decision. 'Forgive me, my Lord, but it is possible that, should you be present, I will not hear the entire truth.' Mathilda put up her hand hastily, to stall any objection to the implication of his daughters' honesty being questioned, but there was no need. De Vere had seen the sense in her plan.

'You are right. I recall keeping back more than a little truth whenever I was questioned by my parents.' Smoothing out the document on the table, he added, 'I'd like you to tell me if you learn anything of interest.'

'Certainly, my Lord.' Mathilda curtseyed. 'May I ask a question of you before I proceed? I fear you may find it impertinent.'

'Ask.'

Aware that Wennesley's eyes were fixed upon her as she spoke, Mathilda said, 'Can you think of any reason for Agnes' murder? Is there anyone she has angered, purposely or by mistake? A family member, a servant, a guest?'

'I do not know of such a person.' De Vere kept his eyes on the document as he spoke, making Mathilda sure he was lying. 'Talk to Bettrys. I did not appoint her as your maid by accident. Little goes on in this household without the all-seeing eyes of Merrick, Cook and Bettrys.'

'Why Bettrys? Merrick and Cook I can understand. They have powerful positions with many staff beneath them, but Bettrys is a maidservant.'

'Bettrys is the maidservant who worked most closely with Agnes. She also has the run of the main chambers.'

Mathilda inclined her head in gratitude for this information, adding talking to the steward and Cook in private to her list. 'Then I'll bid you good morning. I will speak to Lady Isabella if she is free. Should I discover anything of consequence you will be informed.'

Before she took her leave, Mathilda turned her attention to Wennesley, while also managing to sneak a glance at the open manuscript on the table. He heart turned over and she struggled to keep her tone calm. 'I trust you slept well last night?'

Wennesley's eyes narrowed. 'I did. Did you?'

'You know I did not. I was travelling.'

'So you were.' Wennesley's mind worked fast. This girl was good. He was sure - or at least strongly suspected - she'd been in the castle all along. She knew someone had been abroad last night, but not who that had been. Cursing Sproxton and his midnight wanderings, he vowed to question his colleague more closely about where he'd been wasting his money this time.

Mathilda regarded her companions with open curiosity. 'Where would I find the sheriff and Master Sproxton this morning? I wish to pay my respects, and plead for a kind hand should you encounter my husband.'

'When will you accept that this is *my* task?' Wennesley shouted. 'Ingram and Sproxton are but helpers in *my* quest.' His palm slammed against the table, unsettling a well of ink, which ran across the document, immediately smearing itself across the top half of the manuscript.

De Vere shot into action to limit the damage and Merrick ran from the door to help clear the mess. Mathilda spoke with a calm she hoped would annoy Wennesley after his pointless and petulant display. 'I will accept it once you have earned some respect. And also,' she lowered her eyes to the parchment that was being flapped dry in front of her, 'when you have decided whose side you are on.'

De Vere scowled at his companion. 'Lady Mathilda can read.'

'But she's just a potter's daughter!' Wennesley spat.

Pulling herself up to her full height in a manner Sarah had taught her, Mathilda focused her green eyes on Wennesley. 'My husband tells me I have never "just" been anything. You would do well to remember that.'

Then, with a satisfying sweep of her skirts, Mathilda strode from the room, her pulse drumming in her ears and her mind full of the name she'd just seen - or thought she'd seen - on the document, and went to find Bettrys.

~ *Chapter Twenty-four* ~

Keen to leave the nasty taste left by Roger Wennesley's words and leering expression behind her, Mathilda couldn't decide if de Vere's assertion that she could read had been made with pride or fear. The document, which had been obscured by Wennesley's childish outburst, had been whisked into de Vere's hands before she could do more than scan a few words.

Mathilda knew she could have misinterpreted the small section she had seen. The handwriting had been thickly inked and written with swirling strokes of the quill. Even if she'd had the paper laid out before her, she doubted she'd have been able to read all of the wording. What she had understood from the larger script at the top of the paper was that it was a legal document, which had been addressed by someone called Master Garrick.

Whoever this Garrick was, he'd been sent out with instructions from the Crown; instructions addressed to Wennesley. Judging that this must have been the document that called for her husband's arrest, Mathilda had felt her heart race as she'd tried to read more, but after that the obscured script had been beyond her reading abilities – except for one name. It had jumped out at her; but she needed to be sure. She had to see the document again, just to be certain.

Wishing Thomas de Folville had stayed at Rockingham, so she could share her sudden fears over the implication of what she'd seen, her fingers caressed the latticework of butterflies carved into her leather belt. Ever since Robert had presented her with it, Mathilda had regarded it a lucky talisman.

Murmuring under her breath, she stole along the length of the empty corridor, the bustle of the kitchen activity becoming louder with each step. 'What would Robyn Hode do?'

If her brother-in-law had been there then, perhaps together, they could have got back into the constable's office to look at the parchment before Wennesley took it with him. Thomas's ability with letters was more accomplished than hers. It was vital the document was checked. Considered guesswork had got her through in the past, but in this instance a guess would be a mistake. Possibly a fatal one.

The growing clatter of sound from the kitchen caused Mathilda to stop dead. She was walking so fast she was getting out of breath in a manner that would not do if she was going to play the entitled lady role Robert had suggested.

It couldn't have been him...could it? A shudder ran unbidden through Mathilda's body as she thought of the name she'd read. If it was him, was it safe for her to know? Did de Vere know she'd seen it before he removed the evidence?

Mathilda swallowed. Robert de Vere had told Wennesley she could read. The more she considered, the more she felt that he'd been passing on this information as a warning rather than as a further claim of her suitability to do a man's job. The only comfort she could find was that at least it hadn't been Richard de Folville's name on the document. The cleric, so often the cause of the family's troubles, was innocent for once, but this man… This name meant trouble.

She was sure of that.

Mathilda rested her back against the stone wall, grateful for its soothing chill. Although sickened by Agnes's death and worried by the knowledge that a killer lurked nearby, only now she had seen something she shouldn't have did she feel afraid.

Tempted to run into the kitchen and ask Daniel to ride after Thomas and request he return to Rockingham at once, Mathilda held fast. If she was wrong, if she'd misinterpreted things, she would look foolish. If she could trust her reading ability it would be different; but she couldn't and it was no good wishing otherwise. She would stick to her plan, find Bettrys and then speak to the Lady Isabella de Vere. After that she'd consider whether to send for help or not.

Wishing she hadn't had to sweep out of de Vere's office in a state of wounded dignity, Mathilda realised she didn't actually know where Bettrys would be working. Unsure in which direction to go, she continued to the Great Hall.

The hall sat like a spider at the centre of the castle web, with staircases and corridors running off it at various haphazard angles. Mathilda saw it would be hard to get to any part of the castle without passing through the hall. Although there were shadows and ill-lit areas in which it wouldn't be difficult to stay undetected for short periods, the fact remained: you had to enter and leave the hall wherever you were going in the castle's inner sanctum.

Lifting her skirts an inch off the floor, Mathilda wondered how easy it would be to enter the castle's heart without being seen. Walking along the corridor, ensuring she made as little noise as possible, she reached the short stairway that ran from the household corridor into the hall and paused.

If anyone glanced in her direction they would see someone, but she wasn't sure if they could see clearly who that someone was. The light in the hall, especially by the fire, was bright and frequently flared as candles guttered, blew out, or were relit. Whenever a lit candle was moved it left a stream of orange light in its wake, which confused and blinded the eyes if you were looking straight at it. *If I was at the main table, could I see anyone standing here? Am I invisible, or simply a silhouette to mark the arrival of a visitor?*

Mathilda's question was partly answered by the arrival of Merrick, who came upon her before she'd noticed, making her jump.

'I'm sorry, my Lady, I didn't mean to startle you. You appear lost. Can I be of assistance?'

Breathing less erratically, Mathilda inclined her head at the steward. 'Forgive me, I was marvelling at how well you do your job. How do you manage to see who awaits your attention here when the shadows must surely play against your vision?' Wondering why instinct was telling her to flatter Merrick but not trust him, she added, 'You must be very skilled at working out who is who from their outline alone.'

Puffed with pride, Merrick bent his erect back a little so he could speak more quietly than usual. 'I confess, my Lady, I do not always know who it is. The family and servants I always recognise, for I see them come and go often enough for their shapes to be familiar. However, unless it is warm enough for a low fire and light enough for no candles to be burning, then often I am only aware I may be needed. I find out who I'm greeting when I reach them.'

'Well, one would never know. You are most skilled at your duties.'

Merrick gave a low bow of acknowledgement. 'Were you looking for someone in particular?'

'I was told Bettrys would be my maidservant whilst I am here, but circumstances saw her sent on an errand before I discovered where she would be at this time of day.'

'And you'd like to be shown your *new* quarters.' Merrick spoke gravely, his lowered tone telling Mathilda that his master had impressed upon him the importance of no one else finding out exactly when she'd arrived. 'At this time of day Bettrys will be attending to the Lady Isabella's bedchamber. Would you like me to take you to find her?'

About to dismiss his offer because she already knew where Isabella slept, then remembering that she wasn't supposed to have that knowledge yet, Mathilda agreed. Taking her chance while she had Merrick's undivided attention, she kept pace with his long stride, glad she was used to walking with Robert. 'I must thank you for helping to conceal my earlier-than-official arrival.'

'You're welcome.'

'I suppose, in a household such as this, as in my own, you become used to following unusual instructions.'

'Indeed.'

'I understand from Lord de Vere that Agnes came to the castle with a less-than-caring master. What was she like? A hard worker?'

Merrick stopped as they reached the foot of the steps that led up from the hall to the family rooms. 'I did not kill the girl.'

Mathilda was surprised and knew her face showed as much. 'I didn't think that you did. In fact, I am sure you did not.'

'You do?' A shadow lifted from Merrick's face.

'Her killer was of a different height to your own.' She regarded the steward more carefully as they began to move again. There was no missing the bloom of red that had crossed his face. Had he cared for the maid more than he was saying?'

Softly, Mathilda enquired, 'You feared I would pick you for the killer?'

'I know the castle better than anyone. I am always there and so rarely noticed.'

She understood what he was saying. 'The familiar is often overlooked. Especially when you are not of noble blood.'

Merrick gave her a piercing stare, but said nothing as they entered the corridor Mathilda had walked only a few hours before. The buttress where she'd hidden in the shadows from the unidentified man lay ahead.

'Did you know Agnes well?'

'Not really.' He sighed. 'She was a shy creature who always assumed others would treat her badly.'

'Agnes had become conditioned to expect ill treatment?'

'Her former master was indeed cruel. He - Reynard, his name was - caused her limp, you know.'

'How?'

'They were acrobats by trade. They'd been practising a trick for their show at the fair. A juggling and tumbling act. Something went wrong and Agnes slipped and broke her leg. Rather than help her, Reynard declared Agnes worthless. He packed his things and left her in the hut in the forest, where they stayed on their visits to Rockingham, without a word to a soul.'

'The swine. It's a miracle Agnes didn't starve to death.'

'She would have if I hadn't found her.'

'You found her? How come you were in the forest?'

'I was bound for Leicester; an errand for His Lordship. I heard sobbing as I passed the hut. The door was wide open. Agnes was frozen to the bone, even though the weather was kind.'

'So you brought her to the castle.'

'It was the right thing to do. I had no idea at the time that Cook would suggest Agnes should stay.' A flush formed across Merrick's cheeks, making Mathilda wonder what had transpired between Agnes and the steward.

'Did you ever have cause to regret her staying here?'

'Never. Agnes was an excellent worker once her leg had healed. He limp never slowed her down. I hoped she was finally beginning to relax and see that perhaps not everyone was out to hurt her, but...'

Merrick's voice trailed off, but whether from thinking better of what he was going to say, or the fact they'd reached their destination, Mathilda wasn't sure.

They had stopped by the doorway to Lady Isabella's chambers. The same doorway where she'd seen the unknown man the night before, and where she'd been cleaned by Bettrys after her wrestle with the skillets.

'Bettrys should be in here.' Merrick went to knock, but before he could, Mathilda gently laid a hand on his.

'What happened to encourage Agnes's belief that all employers, not just Reynard, are cruel?'

'It is not my place to say.'

'Under normal circumstances that would be true, but Agnes is dead. These are not normal circumstances.'

'Felons cross this property on a daily basis, anyone could have...'

Mathilda shook her head. 'Almost immediately on my arrival, every felon in the place fled. That only leaves a few suspects. By telling me who ill-treated Agnes you are helping her. Whoever it was may have killed her, or they may not have. I need to find out.'

Merrick sighed. 'Lady Helena did not treat Agnes with

the respect she deserved.'

Mathilda inclined her head towards the door to indicate that Merrick could knock on it now. 'Thank you. You have confirmed what I suspected.'

The sound of a key in the lock alerted their attention to their door before them. Just before it opened, Merrick whispered, more to the oak-panelled door than to Mathilda, 'I wouldn't have hurt Agnes if my life depended on it.'

~ *Chapter Twenty-five* ~

The chamber door was eased open, but only a crack. Bettrys's face appeared, pushed up against the gap she'd made. Seeing it was Mathilda, she threw the door back. 'Forgive me, my Lady. I was instructed not to let anyone in but you.'

Mathilda stepped into the compact but well-appointed room. 'Lady Isabella does not wish for visitors?'

'Agnes was Her Ladyship's friend as well as her maid. She's taken the news badly.'

'Will she talk to me?'

'I've explained that you are on Agnes's side, my Lady; that you want to find who took her from us.'

'Even if I find that the culprit is someone she would wish to be innocent?'

'Oh, yes. Even then.' The voice that floated through the space from the adjoining room was unquestioningly feminine but lower than Mathilda had expected. It was as if the words had been uttered by someone of mature years and not a nineteen-year-old who was yet to marry or be fully aware of the world beyond the castle. Yet as Mathilda considered the pale, raven-haired girl before her, she realised that the comings and goings within Rockingham had probably provided Isabella with more life lessons than most would ever experience.

Nonetheless, Mathilda felt compelled to underline her point. 'Agnes may have been killed by a friend, or even a member of your family.'

No flicker of disquiet showed on Isabella's face. 'Then they deserve what is coming to them.'

Mathilda sensed the effort the girl was expending on holding herself together as she gestured towards a twin seat by the fire. Folding her hands, Isabella laid them on the pale blue fabric of her gown. Its pastel tone made her skin appear almost pure white against her contrasting midnight hair.

The room descended into silence. Isabella focused on her entwined fingers while Mathilda took advantage of the moment's serenity to examine her surroundings. Split into two distinct sections, Isabella's quarters were entered via the anteroom through which Mathilda had been admitted. It held little more than a table, a place to leave boots and cloaks and a basket of logs ready to add to the fire. This space led on into Isabella's bedchamber by virtue of an open archway. A curtain was pulled back to one side, presumably ready to be drawn across the gap when the worst of the castle's draughts blew and to provide some privacy during the night.

The comfortable short padded seat, on which Mathilda and Isabella sat, was placed near enough to the fire to provide cheer, but not close enough for their gowns to be singed. A large bed was tucked into the chamber's corner and tapestries lined the walls. The hangings did not echo the vibrant colours of the Fire Room, but showed intricate patterns of flowers and leaves which danced together in hues of green and blue. Although the tapestries were undoubtedly works of art, the delicate colours meant they lacked the illusion of comfort and light that such hangings aimed to provide. Only a single woven thread of silver, encircling each flower head, hinted towards illumination.

Bettrys was busy at a table beneath the neat square window opposite the bed. Mathilda could see a hairbrush, pins for Isabella's hair linens, and many other requirements of a lady's wardrobe. A jug and a few cups waited on a circular tray.

Apart from a large chest, which Mathilda assumed held Isabella's gowns, and a smaller wooden box at the foot of the bed which presumably, like her own, held extra blankets, there was nothing. No tapestry stand; nothing to suggest Lady Isabella had any contact with activities - or life - beyond the privacy of her rooms.

Breaking the quiet by passing a cup of warm ale to her mistress and another to Mathilda, Bettrys curtsied, 'My Lady, forgive my asking, but would you like me to stay, or would you prefer me to leave while you speak to Lady Folville?'

Isabella gave Bettrys a smile, and Mathilda was surprised by the change the gesture made to the girl's expression. Her complexion pinked with a glow that Mathilda was convinced would beguile any male she wished it to. 'You are indeed forgiven, Bettrys, for I know you speak out of concern for my welfare. If Lady Mathilda doesn't mind, I will let you get on with your tasks, lest Cook chastise you.'

With a bob of her head, Bettrys backed from the room. Mathilda couldn't decide if the maid was saddened or relieved to be dismissed.

As soon as Bettrys had gone, Isabella, her face eager and imploring, said, 'I had to let her leave. I've already lost one maid due to my selfish ways. If anything happened to Bettrys as well, I'd... I'd never forgive myself.'

Suddenly the young woman's shoulders were shuddering, as if with sobs; yet her eyes remained dry though heavy with sadness.

'You have been away when you should have been here?'

Isabella's frowned, but she did not question how Mathilda knew she had been absent from the castle. 'I have. And a fool I was to go. Such a fool...'

Mathilda considered how to phrase her next question. Deciding there was nothing to gain by side-stepping the issue, she asked, 'Did Agnes know where you were?'

'Yes.' Isabella stared into the flames, before snapping her head around and staring into Mathilda's bright green eyes. 'Agnes was my helper, both my maid and my friend. She was going to join us, but then...'

'Us?'

Isabella's lips tightened. 'As I said, I have been foolish.'

'Will you tell me who he was?'

'Will you tell anyone else?' Her face was beseeching. 'I can bear my own disappointment and even my embarrassment. In truth I am used to it. But there are some in this castle who would take considerable joy in my humiliation. I am not sure I can bear that on top of my grief for Agnes.'

'I give you my word that, providing my silence does not prevent someone getting away with murder, your secret will remain just that. Is that agreeable?'

Isabella nodded emphatically. 'It is.'

Mathilda risked a shy smile. 'You trust I'll keep my word?'

'Bettrys explained your background and why you are here. You have nothing to gain by lying. Perhaps you have as much to lose as I have already lost.'

Unable to argue, Mathilda said, 'You said you're used to disappointment. May I ask why you say that?'

Isabella clenched her hands so tight Mathilda could see the skin whiten to an almost ghostly hue. 'Where to begin?

The loss of my mother, of course... yes, loss... The word sums up my existence.' Pausing, Isabella suddenly shook her head and sat a little straighter. 'Forgive me, I dip into self-pity. A most unattractive quality.'

'You have suffered other losses, beyond those of your mother and Agnes?'

'Three years ago, I was to marry. Giles de Beauchamp, Lord of Alcester. He was a good man. Titled, landed, and I cared for him as much as he cared for me.'

'A rare combination.' Mathilda felt a tightening of gratitude in her chest as she thought how lucky she and Robert had been. 'What occurred, my Lady?''

'My stepmother took against him. She would never say why, but as Giles has royal connections I always suspected she wanted him for Helena. Lady Juliana got what Lady Juliana wanted. Always.'

Thinking of what she'd seen of Lady Helena so far, Mathilda had no difficulty in believing that of her mother. 'Your father didn't stand firm?'

'He did not. Lord Giles married another. Happily, I hope.'

Mathilda allowed Isabella a few moments to gather her thoughts before she brought her back to the present with a jolt. 'Perhaps you would tell me if the man who visited this chamber in the early hours of this morning is the same man you intended to leave Rockingham with?'

Such colour that there had been in Isabella's cheeks drained from her face. Mathilda thought the girl might faint, but she was evidently made of sterner stuff. Mathilda found herself thinking that Lady Helena would have swooned anyway, purely for dramatic effect and the attention it would bring.

'How did you know?'

Not wanting to get Bettrys into trouble, Mathilda waved the issue away. 'Circumstances brought me to this corridor last night. My arrival was timely. I saw the outline of a man. I did not know it was you he was speaking to, I heard no words, but I did recognise his tone.'

'His tone?'

'The nature of his entreaty was of a manner only employed between lovers. From his pleading lilt, I assume he wronged you and was begging forgiveness; and perhaps for a chance to prove himself genuine.'

'Yes.' Isabella's surprised eyes were keen and searching. 'I was to wait for him away from here. He was supposed to meet me. Agnes knew. She was to join us with a few of my belongings.'

'Where were you bound?'

'London. He has family there who would take us in. I would have to work in the household, but better that than waste away as a wallflower; only to be admired when those Father deems suitable view the gardens.'

Impressed by Isabella's willingness to embrace hard work and affection instead of continuing to endure an unhappy life despite being served on hand and foot, Mathilda said, 'The hour and place of your meeting was to be?'

'An old forester's hut in the woods, not half a mile from here. It is rarely used. He was to get there first, by midnight on the night of the thirtieth day of December. I was to follow and join him by the last ring of the church's midday bell. In fact, I arrived early; I was too anxious to sleep. Then, after Agnes's morning duties were complete, she was to head to tidy my chamber as she always did. Instead of cleaning my linen however, she was to gather my clothes and, around mid-afternoon, bring them to the hut.'

'Carrying your pack disguised as laundry, perhaps?'

'Yes.' Isabella was quiet. 'I have since discovered from Bettrys that my father believed me missing for longer than I was. What does that tell you, my Lady?'

'That fathers are not always the men we wish them to be.'

Isabella's eyebrows rose. 'You speak of your own father?'

Knowing that a confidence was better traded in return for another, Mathilda said, 'You will know I am the daughter of a potter. Rumour will not have allowed you to miss that fact. My father is a good man, but when it comes to running the business he is not the wisest. When my mother died he became lost, the debts grew...'

'And so you met the Folvilles. I have heard the story.'

'I imagine you have.' Mathilda shook her head. 'The land is in turmoil and yet people gossip about my marriage. You would think they had better things to do.'

Isabella laughed, it was a light, unexpected sound and, like her smile earlier, it took Mathilda by surprise. Whoever the mystery suitor was, or had been, she could see why Isabella's exotic appearance had attracted him. 'People gossip to take their minds off the mess and muddle that surround us. You are a story now, like the Robyn Hode tales your Lord Robert enjoys so much.'

'He would approve of your analogy.' Mathilda mirrored Isabella's grin before risking destroying it. 'So, you went to the hut as planned? You were not late?'

'Nor was I early. I slipped out through the back of the guardhouse and saw no one from the moment I left the castle until I saw three people on horseback a few hours later as I hid in the hut.'

Mathilda felt a flash of hope. 'Do you know who they were?'

'I do. It was you, my Lady, with your husband and your escort.'

Deflated, Mathilda said, 'You saw no one else as you left. Could anyone have seen you? There must have been guards on duty.'

'There aren't as many guards as you'd normally find at a castle and I know their routine. They are, as you may imagine for such a refuge as my father provides, lacklustre men. I was not aware of any of them having seen me. I frequently move around the castle as if I were invisible.'

Wondering which rooms had windows overlooking the back of the castle, Mathilda said, 'You ran to await your lover, ready to escape the life you have here.'

A lump formed in Isabella's throat. 'I do love my father, but my half-sister is... well... I am better away from Helena and the castle. She will make a better heir for my father. And what's more, she wants the role as a constable's wife.'

'And you do not?'

'To be the wife of whoever my father and the Crown agree should come next? A choice that will never be mine? No, I do not!'

Remembering what de Vere had told her of his hopes of a marriage match for Isabella, but deciding not to reveal what she knew, Mathilda felt a prickle of apprehension as she said, 'Your father already has a man in mind for you? Someone who he considers a good match and a possible future constable of the castle?'

'William Trussell.'

'The Trussells of Hothrope manor in Leicestershire?'

'You know the family?'

'Just the name.' Mathilda spoke gently, 'William, does he know of your intention to leave the castle with your lover?

'Former lover, perhaps. I am unsure of our situation.'

Hearing the slight crack in Isabella's voice, Mathilda gave her a second to compose herself before repeating, 'Did William know of your plans to flee?'

'No.'

'You are sure?'

'Positive.'

Mathilda paused before saying, 'And the man you had decided to flee Rockingham with. Can you tell me: was it Roger Wennesley or Thomas Sproxton?'

~ *Chapter Twenty-six* ~

Once she'd got over the shock of Mathilda mentioning her lover by name, Isabella's story came out through tumbling lips.

She had met Sproxton in the castle some time ago. He'd been lying low, avoiding a man to whom he owed a gambling debt. Unlike the other men who formed the continuous flow of dubious visitors, he hadn't leered at de Vere's daughters, nor had he responded to the demure glances that Helena generally gave any man of a certain age whom she thought should be lavishing her with attention.

'I am surprised Lady Helena would set her sights on someone of lower status than herself.' Mathilda sipped at her wine.

Isabella scoffed, gripping her goblet tighter. 'It is not the men my dear sister is after; not unless they are entitled. It is the compliments. She needs them like the rest of us need water.'

'And Thomas had been unusual in not rising to Helena's flirting?'

'You have seen my sister. She is very beautiful. The men like her appearance, her status, and her habit of looking as if she is inviting them in, even if, should they approach her, she would yell to the heavens themselves.'

Thinking about the claim of rape Helena had lain at Sproxton's door, Mathilda waited for Lady Isabella to continue.

'There were three other men visiting that particular day. Thomas kept himself to himself and sat a little apart from the others, which unfortunately for him located him closest to Helena. He was therefore the target for her coquettish behaviour. In all honesty, she became embarrassing in her ardency.'

'Do you think Lady Helena would have been jealous if she discovered your attachment to a man she'd flirted with to no avail?'

'Helena is jealous of anyone who favours any female over her, and -' Isabella broke off sharply, as she realised what she was implying. 'You think my sister did this to Agnes? Because the girl favoured my company over hers?'

Mathilda spoke gently. 'Could that be possible?'

'Surely not!' Isabella shook her head, but her expression told Mathilda that the possibility, now it had been mooted, would be hard to shift. 'Helena is not pleasant, I grant you, but a killer? Do you truly think so?'

'It's unlikely,' Mathilda owned, 'the concept of your sister getting her hands dirty is not one I can imagine.'

'But she could have.'

'Just as anyone in the castle could have.'

'I didn't.'

'You were not here,' Mathilda saw a new rush of misery flush Isabella's face, 'and if you had been, you could not have prevented what happened.'

'You can't know that.'

'True. But then neither can you know the opposite.' Mathilda gave her companion a stout smile, 'Perhaps we could go back to the first time you saw Master Sproxton.

You said he was ignoring Lady Helena. Was he ignoring everyone? He must have noticed you, surely.'

Isabella ran a hand through her black locks and Mathilda saw it would be impossible to fail to notice de Vere's eldest child amongst so many fair-haired folk. 'He did, but his gaze didn't linger on anyone in particular as far as I recall. He looked and then looked away. I felt it, that look, when it reached me. Do you know what I mean, or do I sound foolish?'

A memory of her first few encounters with Robert ran through Mathilda's mind. 'I know the look of which you speak. But Sproxton neither spoke to you nor sought you out?'

'No. He said and did nothing. Helena began to ask him questions about his life, as well as asking if he liked her gown, her hair, and so on.'

'Does your father not remonstrate with Lady Helena for being so forward with male guests?'

'He used to. He soon realised that chastisement only made her worse.'

Mathilda placed her empty goblet on the floor next to her feet. 'When did Thomas approach you?'

'Two days later, the day before he was due to leave. I was walking in the grounds between the castle and the forest.'

'Where was he going?'

'I don't know if he was going anywhere. He said he'd seen me alone and wanted to make sure I was escorted safely back to the castle. He seemed genuinely concerned that I should be out alone.'

'It is unusual.'

'Not here.' Isabella shrugged. 'My father has long since stopped attending to my presence. I am inconvenient to him. An heir who is not only an unmarried female, but was spawned by a wife thrust upon him; one he never loved and who, to compound to her crimes, died before she could produce a boy for him to cosset.'

Noting that Isabella spoke with honesty and not self-pity, Mathilda said, 'So the fact that you were not noticed missing; and that your father believed you gone longer than you had been, is not so strange.'

'Exactly.' Isabella tucked a stray hair behind her ear. 'Thomas was the perfect gentleman that first time. He walked me back to the castle, asking polite and proper questions, but it was clear we were kindred spirits. Both in places we did not want to be, both seeing a future laid out before us that neither of us wanted.'

'You have told me of your life, but what of his?'

'Thomas knows his weakness for gambling. He wanted to leave that life behind him, to escape those he owed money to and could never repay. We both wished for a new life in a new place, where we could start afresh.'

'In London?'

'He has an uncle there who was prepared to give him a position in his silk importing business. An ideal post for someone good with numbers.'

'Did you not fear Thomas would give in to the temptation of gambling in London? There must be more opportunities for such risky sport there.'

'Perhaps, but he was so earnest. And afraid. Like so many before him, Thomas has been drawn into crime to pay his debts. He didn't want to finish his life at the end of a rope.'

Wondering if Isabella knew of Sproxton's presence at Laurence Coterel's death, Mathilda said, 'You began to swap confidences.'

'Yes. Soon he asked me if I'd like to go with him to London, just as a companion at first. I said yes without having to think. A way out of here was all I wanted.'

'But that changed.'

'Thomas sought me out. Troubling to visit the castle when he had no need to be here. In truth, I sought his eye too. We met quietly in the gardens or the edge of the forest, away from prying eyes. We developed a liking and a week ago Thomas asked me to become his wife once we reached London.'

Tears pooled at the corner of Isabella's eyes, but they remained unshed. 'I agreed, providing Agnes could accompany us as my chaperone and friend.'

'Thomas agreed to that?' Mathilda began to wonder if perhaps he hadn't been eager for anyone to come between himself and Isabella. Had he managed to get into the castle before his comrades and dispose of the maid?

'Readily. He said another pair of hands to do the work was appealing.'

'Did he ever meet Agnes?'

'Not privately, but I pointed her out as she moved around the castle.'

Mathilda frowned. 'When did you and Thomas work out precisely how and when to flee?'

'Two days before you came to the castle.'

'And had Thomas paid his debts here before he left?'

Isabella sighed. 'All but one that he said could never be repaid. I don't know what that meant.'

'You didn't ask?'

'His tone suggested I would be better off not knowing.'

'And Agnes was keen to leave?'

'Oh, yes, she was not happy here either.'

'Why?'

'She would not say, but I think she may have confided in

me once we'd left here.'

Mathilda stared into the fire as questions tumbled around her mind. Did Agnes have knowledge she shouldn't have? Had she already been in fear of her life and Isabella's offer of a way out of Rockingham been heaven sent? Or was Agnes in Thomas' way? Could he have paid someone else to do the deed while he was away? But, then again, Sproxton has no money; at least, that's what he'd claimed. That left Lady Helena.

'Can you tell me what Lady Helena did when Thomas rebuffed her?'

Isabella spoke into the crackle of the flames. 'At first, nothing, but I could feel my sister seething into her dinner as she pushed it around her plate.

'It was a day after he'd left the castle when she made her move. Helena had seen us, Thomas and me, coming in from the woods together. There was no impropriety, but we were smiling. Only a fool would have failed to notice how relaxed we were in each other's company and Helena is no fool. Yet she did nothing until Thomas had gone again -'

Mathilda interrupted, 'The person he owed money to was gone?'

'Apparently he'd given up on getting anything from Thomas.' Isabella shifted uncomfortably as she said, 'In a single moment, the atmosphere in the castle switched from the daily routine to chaos. People were shouting and running to and fro. Maids were attending to a distraught Helena. Father was roaring with anger, yelling for the guards.'

'Which maids?'

'Bettrys and Agnes.'

'I see.' Mathilda nodded. 'Please, go on.'

'Helena was crying rape against Thomas. A crime he could not have committed because he was with me. And she knew it. She knew I would have to tell Father I'd been with Thomas if I was to clear his name. She also knew I would not be able to do that.'

'Your father would have been angry with you?'

'Furious. He would have been fearful that the Trussell family would call off our lucrative union.' Bitterness rang clear in Isabella's voice. 'With her accusation, Helena everything achieved she loved, in an instant: attention and sympathy, my misery, and someone paying the price for not dancing to her tune.'

'Did Agnes say anything? She must have known Helena was lying.'

Isabella clutched Mathilda's arm. 'My God, you really do think… Helena lives in a world of envy and spite, yes, - but murder?'

'As yet, I do not know.'

A hush filled the chamber as each woman became lost in thought. Eventually, Mathilda spoke. 'Your father did not believe the rape charge, did you know that?'

'No.' Isabella glanced up. 'He told you that himself?'

'He did. He also told me that Wennesley, the man who is in pursuit of my husband, is the one who gave Thomas Sproxton an alibi. Saying he was with him… but he wasn't, was he? He was with you.'

'Why would this Wennesley give Thomas an alibi?'

'I can only assume it was to ensure his help in the future, so he could call in a favour when it was needed, as it is now. Sproxton is assisting in the attempt to arrest the Folville and Coterel brothers.'

Isabella drew in a sharp breath. 'So, Thomas told me the truth?'

'I'm sorry?'

'Last night, he came to ask forgiveness for not coming to

the hut. He said he'd been thrust into an errand from which he could not escape. I did not believe him.'

'We have common ground, Lady Isabella.' She fought down the urge to quote a Robyn Hode ballad at her new friend. 'You have reason to doubt the man in whom you trusted and I have every reason to doubt the man he is working for.'

'You are afraid for your husband?' Isabella appeared shocked and it occurred to Mathilda that no one she'd encountered outside of Ashby Folville manor seemed to be taking the Folvilles' enforced migration seriously. Not even Wennesley.

'Lady Mathilda?' Isabella patted her companion's arm gently. 'You have gone pale, are you alright?'

'Forgive me, yes; yes of course... I was just thinking...' Mathilda felt a sudden thrill, but she wasn't sure if it was hope or fear. 'Please, call me Mathilda when we not in public company.'

'Thank you. I'd like that,' the Lady de Vere beamed, 'and you must call me Isabella. We are so close in age; it would be good to have a friend.'

'It would.' Mathilda realised she meant it, but was again surprised. Was she losing her skills at working things out, at making connections? She hadn't even registered that Isabella was only a few years her junior. *But then I don't suppose anyone has ever kidnapped her, tried to kill her, or tried to frame her for murder...*

'What happens next?' Isabella's face had become grave in an instant, 'Do you think Thomas killed Agnes and then ran from here, only to be caught up in the King's business?'

'At first, that's what I assumed; but no, it couldn't have been Thomas.'

Isabella sagged with relief. 'I'd always have blamed myself if he had hurt Agnes. Is that selfish of me? Helena is always telling me I'm selfish.'

Liking Lady Helena less by the minute, and hoping that fact wouldn't cloud her judgement when it came time to talk to her, Mathilda said, 'I can understand why you'd feel like that, but if Sproxton had lashed out at your maid, it would have been for reasons of his own. His doing; not yours.'

Isabella let out a ragged breath. 'Thank you.'

'You've had a shock, I will leave you to rest, but first, I need the answer to a question you may not want me to ask.'

'Ask me anyway.'

'If Sproxton was to return to you now, would you take him back and run away with him?'

Isabella bowed her head and stared at the floor. 'I truly don't know.'

'An honest answer, thank you.' Mathilda, satisfied to hear the only answer she considered could have been truthful in the circumstances, rose to her feet and added, 'If, at any time, you feel in danger while Agnes's killer is being sought, please tell me.'

'But what about you? You will be in danger as soon as word spreads that you're in Rockingham Castle enquiring into a death.'

'I know.' Mathilda was glad of the practise she'd had at appearing to be unafraid even when terrified. 'I am a Folville, remember. Anyone who managed to shorten my life wouldn't live long themselves to relish their victory.'

Isabella rose to fetch her cloak from its hook. It was only then Mathilda realised that she and Isabella were almost the same height.

~ *Chapter Twenty-seven* ~

Leaving his horse with Ulric, Thomas went to find Sarah and Adam. His grim expression lit into a knowing smile as he walked into the kitchen at what proved to be an inopportune moment.

Adam noticed the arrival of Lord Thomas de Folville before Sarah did; pulling away from their embrace with a deluge of apologies.

Sarah, beetroot in the face and for once with no words to sally forth, brushed down her apron and attempted to hide her embarrassment at being caught mid-affection. 'You... you must be thirsty, my Lord. Do you need food?'

Respecting the loyal housekeeper's unspoken plea for no comment to be made about the manner in which they'd been found, Thomas accepted the drink, declined food, and waved away Adam's apology. 'I bring news from Rockingham. Do you have further information to share with me here?'

'No, my Lord. All is as you left it. The rector of Teigh remains captive in the storeroom. Eustace's man appears content to wait at the door until Hell freezes, so we feel safe enough for now.'

Sitting at the kitchen table, Thomas gestured for his companions to join him. 'I am now privy to the nature of the charges against my kin, but I remain curious as to why Lord John and I have been excluded from the hunt. Also, Ingram and Roger Wennesley, the man King Edward has entrusted with the arrests, now know of my Lord Richard's capture.'

'Are they sending men for his transfer to Nottingham?' The prospect of the sheriff entering the manor, when none of the Folvilles were in residence, made Adam feel the weight of responsibility.

'They will in time, but I'm not sure Ingram was that interested. Wennesley looked delighted, though probably because part of his job has been done for him rather than at the actual arrest.'

'May I ask the charges, my Lord?' Adam, still unused to the equal status servants were so often given in the Folville household after years of working for the kind, but far stricter, John de Markham, fiddled with the dagger at his belt.

'The charges refer to a crime committed before your time with us, Adam. An event that I'd forgotten about since it was so minor in comparison to those we *could* have been accused of. I am unsure why, after all this time, the King has decided to deem this particular felony worthy of pursuing.'

As Thomas had not stated what the crime in question was, Adam didn't push his luck by asking again. He was relieved when Sarah changed the direction of the conversation.

'Can we expect the sheriff to come here, my Lord?' Thinking to the necessary household preparations, she added, 'If he comes, he may wish to stay the night if he's on a circuit of the county hunting your brothers.'

'As yet I am unsure, but you would do well to be prepared. I'm sorry I cannot be more definite.'

'I appreciate that you have provided at least some warning, my Lord.' Sarah got to her feet and began to busy herself cutting vegetables. 'Is the Lady Mathilda safe, my Lord?'

'She sends her regards to you both and to Ulric. Daniel is faring well too. They are keeping an eye out for each other, as you would imagine.'

Sensing the air of hesitation that suggested Lord Thomas would have liked to add a 'but' to the end of his sentence, Sarah said, 'And she is keeping out of trouble?'

Thomas barked with humour, 'Can you see the Lady Mathilda staying out of trouble?'

The housekeeper's eyes betrayed her concern. 'She has become engaged in detection?'

'An arrangement has been struck.'

'An arrangement?' Adam pulled a face, 'An odd choice of words.'

'I would call it a deal, but that would have implications which I am unsure apply here.' Thomas drained the remainder of his ale and placed the ceramic vessel back on the oak table with thoughtful precision. 'Mathilda has been asked by the sheriff himself to investigate the death of a servant girl. A maid called Agnes has been killed at the castle.'

'But surely the bailiff -' Adam began.

Thomas shook his head as he cut in. 'The situation suits Mathilda. She was to be confined to her room for her own safety, but she chafed at the bit and eluded Rockingham's best locks. Now, in return for freedom of the castle and being told what the charges against the Folvilles are, she is to solve the riddle of Agnes's murder.'

Sarah sighed. 'She's only been gone a moment and already... The girl attracts trouble like a fly finds honey.'

Adam exchanged a look with Sarah. 'My Lord Thomas, perhaps I too should go to Rockingham. If the Lady Mathilda is to walk around a murderer's lair...'

Folville's hand was already up. 'I am ahead of you there,

Adam. My intention had been to go on to Huntingdon, speak to Lord John, and then run this manor until Robert can come back. However, I think I would be better served at Rockingham with Mathilda.'

Sarah let out a breath she hadn't realised she'd been holding in. 'Thank you, my Lord.'

Adam smiled with relief. 'Would you like a messenger to be sent to Huntingdon, my Lord?'

'It is done. Borin and I sorted that out on my arrival just now.' Thomas laid his dagger upon the table. 'Now, what I'd like more than anything is some of your delicious bread, Sarah. And a cup of your wonderful stew.'

Robert de Folville threw his cloak to the floor. It stank of smoke and sweat. Taking the mutely offered ale from the ever-taciturn almoner, Robert drew a chair to the fire and inhaled the cleaner aroma of the burning logs.

He hated what they had just done. Even more, he hated that they'd been put in a position where they'd had no choice but to do it. Eustace, always the one who advanced unafraid into the jaws of hell, had understood his three brothers' disquiet and taken the matter into his own large, battle-scarred hands.

He'd instructed Laurence and Walter to make sure Quarrington watermill was deserted, while Robert gathered up anything that he considered valuable to those who worked there. Heaping the tools, aprons, ledgers and three pairs of stout working boots under the cover of a clump of trees a safe distance away, he then gestured to Eustace to set the blaze.

The fire, laid so that it would disable rather than destroy the mill, providing the locals were fleet enough of foot to stop the flames, began quietly. The brothers had reached the safety of the forest before the flames took hold; the night time winds showered them in flecks of charcoal and blows of soot.

Now, as Eustace stamped into the warming room he thumped down next to Robert. 'Word has been bought to the priory. The building was all but gutted, but the millwheel is salvageable. The warning has been issued without lives being completely destroyed.'

'It will still be hard for them.'

'If we hadn't done as bid, life would have been even harder for us. And certainly briefer.'

Robert said nothing as he stared into his ale. Walter and Laurence arrived, their own clothing carrying the acrid stench of fire on the wind. The newly arrived brothers took the drinks offered and sank down as Eustace broke the brooding atmosphere.

'The mill owner will find an anonymous donation sent to them with enough funds to rebuild in three days' time. Agreed?'

A smile spread across Robert's face. 'You never cease to amaze me, Eustace.'

'Do not think I grow weak, brother. I simply hate that canon getting what he wants.' He finished his drink and rose to his feet. 'I'm going to get some sleep. Now our debt is paid we need to consider how to turn our king's conquest of corruption to our advantage.'

Walter gave a grimace. 'Impossible, surely?'

'I think not.' Eustace took a handful of bread chunks from a pile on the table, 'I think it's time we met with Nicholas Coterel, don't you, brothers?'

After an uncomfortable meal in the hall, during which she had felt that every single eye in the place was on her, Mathilda went to find Daniel. The idea that the answer to what lay behind her husband's arrest was on the document she'd seen in de Vere's office wouldn't let go of her mind. Until her curiosity was quenched, Mathilda knew she would not be able to settle to the mystery she was supposed to be solving.

There was no point in attempting to see the document alone. Her limited reading made that enterprise pointless. Mathilda didn't want to ask for help, for if she did uncover who had killed Agnes with a man's help, Wennesley would assume he'd done the work, not her - but pride aside, she knew it was the safest way forward.

Reasoning that perhaps playing down her skills in a place like this might make her own position less dangerous and could be a blessing in disguise, Mathilda went to find Daniel.

It was time to send her friend with another message for Thomas de Folville.

~ *Chapter Twenty-eight* ~

At first light the following day, having made sure that Daniel's pony was missing and that he'd already slipped out of the castle towards Ashby Folville, Mathilda made her way to a solitary corner table in the hall away from the family. She could feel Merrick's eyes on her as she moved.

The steward, tall and erect, held his broad shoulders back as though he was bracing himself for action on the battlefield. He watched the family finishing their morning repast, also overseeing the staff and keeping an eye on the fire. Mathilda had taken him for a man of at least four and thirty years, but now she sat and observed him observing her and everything else, she realised she'd made an incorrect assumption based on his serious gait.

Merrick's hair showed no signs of grey, his flesh was unlined, and although he wore the mantle of responsibility with pride, he was not aged by it. *Four years and twenty, maybe - not unlike Robert, though Robert looks young for his age... perhaps Merrick's liking for Agnes was not as unlikely as I first assumed.*

Swallowing a pang of loneliness, refusing to give into the sensation of loss she felt every time Robert's face came into her mind, Mathilda squeezed her fingertips into her palms and forced herself to concentrate. There couldn't be much that Merrick didn't see within Rockingham. Anything he might have missed, Mathilda was certain Cook would know.

While she'd never be able to make a friend of Cook as she had Sarah, Mathilda hoped she had at least gained the woman's respect. Something about that highest-ranking woman on the household staff suggested that she would stalwartly protect 'her' family, just as Mathilda would. Any information Cook gave would be subtly suggested rather than stated outright.

'May I get you anything, my Lady?'

Merrick had crossed the floor on silent feet before Mathilda had registered he was coming. Seizing her chance, she asked, 'I have a question about Agnes if you have time.'

'I have until I'm called away.'

'You cared for her?' Mathilda asked the question at barely more than a whisper, hoping that Merrick wouldn't flee or be enraged by the question.

'I did.' The response was solemn. Sorrow flitted through the steward's eyes.

'Forgive this impertinent question, but were you courting Agnes?'

Merrick's head dipped, but Mathilda had the impression he continued to watch the hall as a whole in case he was summoned, ready to appear magically at his master or mistresses' side.

'I was not.'

'You had hopes, though?'

'Agnes was a lost soul. Her life had left her unable to trust. I tried to change that. I wanted her to trust me, but it was not to be.'

Mathilda hesitated, not sure how to phrase her next question. 'Did you approach Agnes and tell her your hopes?'

'I tried.'

'And?'

'She laughed.'

A frisson of unease shot through Mathilda, 'Laughed as if embarrassed, or…'

'Mocking. It was a scoff.' Merrick's cheeks developed a crimson hue. 'We didn't speak again.'

'I'm sorry.'

'As am I.'

'When was this?'

'Some weeks ago.' Merrick's sad eyes searched Mathilda's face. 'I didn't hurt her.'

'Can you think who'd be happier without her here?'

'If her old master were here, he'd be top of my list, but without Reynard… no. I can think of no one who'd gain pleasure from her death.'

Aware that the steward could be called away at any time, Mathilda quickly asked, 'Agnes was found in the Fire Room. Why would she have been there at that time?'

'To prepare the fire and turn down your bed, my Lady.'

Mathilda nodded. 'The Fire Room is very fine. It was ready on my arrival, but no one knew I was coming. I didn't even know myself until I left Ashby Folville. Is that room always kept ready in case of guests?'

'It is. The Fire Room is kept for the Queen of England.'

'The Queen!' Mathilda gulped. 'You gave me a room kept just in case there should be a royal visit?'

'You are a Folville. My Lord de Vere knows which guests to treat well.'

Abruptly Merrick moved away. Lady Helena was glaring at him, clearly ready to give him the sharp end of her tongue for his less than instant response to whatever it was she wanted.

Mathilda's head whirled. A room for a queen and it had been given to her. No one had been expected; it was always ready in case. As they knew that the Queen was in London, the room had been used for her and now Agnes was dead. Agnes, red-haired like Mathilda, who was not wearing her servant's clothes when she died and who was the same height as the new guest…

Not wanting to dwell on the possibility that she may indeed have been the target - not until she'd exhausted the idea that Agnes was the intended victim - Mathilda reflected on what Merrick had told her. He'd been far more revealing in his responses than she'd expected, but had he been honest? Had Merrick really only told Agnes of his affection a few weeks ago, or had he hounded her for attention for months?

She could imagine Merrick taking his time thinking about how to approach Agnes. He would have planned and hoped and dreamt, watching her as she escaped the clutches of her former master and became part of the Rockingham household. As his liking for the girl grew, when he finally got up the nerve to approach her she had laughed at him. A proud man, Merrick must have felt the humiliation keenly, but enough to murder? Or see her murdered?

Embarrassment and being scorned were not unusual motives for murder, but Mathilda couldn't imagine Merrick risking his position in the household. He was respected there. De Vere valued and trusted him. Not many stewards were that lucky.

Rubbing sleep from her eyes after another restless night in an unheated chamber, Mathilda's thoughts roamed as saw Lady Isabella rise from the table. With a perfunctory curtsey to her father, the lady of the house approached Mathilda.

Thomas de Folville was loading one of Sarah's fresh loaves into his pack when Borin stomped into the courtyard.

'Daniel approaches.'

Adam, overhearing, ran to the gate. 'Why would the lad be back already?'

'I did not like leaving Mathilda in Rockingham with no escort.' Thomas felt his pulse quicken. 'If anything has happened to her Robert will skin me alive.'

'He wouldn't get the chance. Sarah would have killed you stone dead already.'

Thomas's eyebrows rose at the bold statement, but he couldn't deny the truth of Adam's warning.

Guessing that the two men waiting in the gateway would be assuming the worst, Daniel raised a hand in a reassuring salute. As his mount trotted closer, he called out the words they needed to hear. 'Lady Mathilda is well. I come with a request for Lord Thomas to accompany me back to Rockingham.'

'A request from de Vere?'

'From Lady Mathilda. She has stumbled upon a document that needs reading. I was asked to impress upon you the importance of the words being deciphered.'

'I was returning to Rockingham anyway.' Thomas pointed to his prepared mount. 'The idea of leaving Mathilda there without a male escort gnaws at me.'

'My Lady is investigating the crime as she promised, but the document she has seen alludes to something else. I know no more than that, my Lord.'

Immediately despatching a second of Eustace's messengers towards where he knew his kin to be in hiding, to keep them informed, Thomas climbed into his horse's saddle. 'I will leave at once. Daniel, please rest. Go and enjoy some of

Sarah's cooking.' The Folville rubbed at his stomach. 'It is as well I am leaving, for too much of our housekeeper's fare would make me too heavy for my poor horse.'

Daniel dipped his head in reverence, 'You are kind, my Lord, but I am expected back before nightfall.'

'In that case, go and reassure Sarah of your wellbeing. Collect some food to refill your belly and we'll leave together.'

As soon as Daniel had disappeared into the kitchen, Adam took his chance. 'My Lord Thomas, I wish to apologise for the scene you witnessed earlier. Sarah and I -'

Thomas stopped the steward. 'Adam, Sarah is a fine woman who has long been missing a companion in life. All that love is wasted on the likes of me and my brothers. Hold her and never let her go.'

Adam bowed. 'Thank you, my Lord.'

'But, Adam,' Thomas's voice lowered so it was barely audible, 'if you hurt her, there won't be a place far enough away for you to run to.'

'I don't doubt that, my Lord.'

Thomas's expression became serious. 'I suspect you will have a visit from the sheriff and his associates soon. They will be duty bound to make sure my brothers have not doubled back and taken refuge in the manor.'

'We assumed as much. And if they want to take Lord Richard?'

'They know of his capture. There is no need for deceit. If they ask for him, hand him over.'

'Do you think we should have asked for an escort?' Despite having already walked a circuit of the castle grounds and being half a mile into the forest, Lady Isabella was creeping along as if expecting to see peril lurking behind every trunk.

'You had no escort when you went to meet Sproxton.' Mathilda walked on, noting the same row of trees and narrow track that she had ridden with Robert and Daniel when they first arrived at Rockingham. 'If you keep going, this opens out on to a rough road that leads to Leicester.'

'That's right.' Isabella kept surveying the area as she moved, 'I think it's one of the reasons so many felons find the castle useful. You can approach it, almost up to the door, by weaving through the trees. If you avoid coming on horseback, you could be upon the rear entrance of the bailey unnoticed.'

Mathilda suddenly understood Isabella's vigilance. 'How often do men come to the castle for shelter?'

'Daily - until you arrived.'

Keeping to herself the knowledge that de Vere wasn't allowing anyone into the castle in case Isabella's future in-laws should appear, Mathilda said, 'I can't decide if the dearth of felons is an insult, a compliment, or merely a coincidence.' She grimaced. 'The road is narrowing and the trees are becoming thicker, so I'd judge your forester's hut can't be too far from here.'

Isabella's eyebrows rose. 'How did you know?'

'I have ridden through here before, remember?'

'Of course.' Isabella raised a hand and pointed ahead. 'Around this bend, set back a fraction from the road.'

Letting Isabella take the lead, Mathilda took note of every tree, each clump of foliage where it would be possible for an adult to hide, each overhanging branch that could provide shade in the summer and shelter from the worst of the winter.

When they cornered the bend, Mathilda came to a halt. 'Three trees obscure the hut from the road.'

'People only seem to notice it if they are looking for it.'

Isabella said, gesturing ahead, 'If you are coming from the opposite direction, it is completely sheltered from the road, although anyone in the hut can see those who approach on horseback. I'm not sure if they would see someone on foot who was keen not to be spotted.'

Mathilda started to walk again. Twigs, made fragile by days and nights of frost, cracked under her booted feet. 'Is this the way you approached the hut?'

'Yes.' Isabella followed Mathilda along an overgrown path. It led to a rundown building which was more like a tiny cottage than a hut. Although in dire need of repair, it wasn't the insubstantial shack Mathilda had been expecting. 'When was the last time a forester lived here?'

'I don't know. Years, maybe. It is musty and cold inside.'

The one and only door to the dwelling was of oak, solid and hinged with big iron fastenings which had rusted to flecked amber. Although the door was chipped and worn, it fitted the doorframe well. Mathilda didn't think it would let any more draught into the dwelling than a castle door would. 'Are you ready to go in?'

Isabella wrapped her cloak tighter around her body as she readied herself to enter the place she still associated with disappointment and betrayal.

Standing together inside the doorway, the women hovered side by side, one hardly seeing, one examining the scene with intense curiosity.

'The cot has been piled with blankets, were they there when you arrived?'

'Yes. I took it that Thomas had left them for us.'

'But you aren't sure.'

'No.'

'Could it have been Agnes?'

Isabella sounded surprised. 'Well, I suppose it might

have been. I didn't ask her to, but if she was thinking ahead... She knew of the hut as she lived here with her old master for a time.'

'This is the hut where she and Reynard stayed when the fair was in Rockingham?' Mathilda's forehead furrowed. 'Were there candles here, the means to make a light, and any edible food?'

'Yes, not much, but I found some bread and a flask of drink under the blankets. There was a candle, but it could have been there for months. It was very dusty.'

'The bread was fresh?'

'Almost. I assumed that was from Thomas too.'

'Did you expect to stay here long, then?'

'No, just until Agnes came.'

'So, there wasn't any need for the food in Thomas's mind.'

'Possibly not.' Isabella's eyes searched the room. It had felt so exciting, so full of possibilities when she'd arrived here last time. Then the slow dissolving of hope and certainty had hit her, until she'd given in and returned to the castle, her pride dented and her heart sore.

'If Agnes suspected she'd be delayed for a reason she couldn't disclose, would it have been in her nature to provide you with food and drink to sustain you and Sproxton?'

'Very much so.' Isabella sat on the edge of the bed. 'She was kindness itself once you got to know her. We shared so much. Things no maid and mistress should discuss. I don't know what I'll do without her.'

As tears welled up in Isabella's eyes, Mathilda lit the remains of the candle stub and went to the window. 'You're right; you can see anyone approaching from the roadway, but not from between the trees beyond. If someone was watching the hut while you were inside, then you'd never have been aware of it.'

'What? You think I was being watched the whole time?'

'I don't know.' Mathilda sat with Isabella on the bed. 'I doubt you're the only person who knows of this bolthole. How many felons, I wonder, stay here rather than go on to the castle.'

Isabella was horror-struck, 'I never thought…'

'I want you to stay here. I'm going to look outside.'

Walking around the hut, taking her time, studying the ground in a way she'd seen Eustace and his men do when they were tracking others; Mathilda searched for broken twigs, squashed foliage and anything out of place, but to her relief saw nothing amiss.

Rejoining her companion, Mathilda asked, 'You said you and Agnes discussed things no maid and mistress should share. Can you tell me what those things were please?'

Isabella hung her head. 'I don't see how it would help.'

'Nor I, but we need to start somewhere.' Mathilda placed a reassuring hand on her companion's knee. 'For a start, did you share with Agnes your views about your half-sister, your sadness at losing out on Lord Alcester and your possible future husband William Trussell?'

~ *Chapter Twenty-nine* ~

As Eustace's groom, John Pykehose, stepped into his master's temporary quarters, he was greeted with no words. Instead he received a hearty embrace, a beaker of strong ale, and a seat by the fire.

Looking on from the table they were clustered around on the opposite side of the room, Robert, Walter, and Laurence waited for the man to speak.

'Lord Thomas has returned to Rockingham, where it has been discovered that the charges are written thus: that Eustace, Walter, Laurence, Robert, and Richard de Folville are to be arrested on the charge of theft after stealing chattels worth £200 from the burgess of Leicester in January of last year.'

The brothers' expressions darkened as Pykehose's husky growl named them responsible for such a crime. Only when he'd stopped talking did Robert's head snap up. 'Thomas is back at the castle. Why? Is Mathilda in trouble?'

Eustace's tut rang around the room. 'If that wife of yours has fallen into hot water again due to her meddling -'

'Meddling! You encouraged her. You said -'

'Stop!' Walter slammed a hand on the table, aware that if his brothers' bickering wasn't nipped in the bud, it would escalate until it was out of control. 'Let the fellow speak.'

Robert scowled at Eustace, but held his tongue as Pykehose, untouched by the interruption, carried on speaking as if he'd learned the message by heart.

'The boy Daniel came to the manor to ask Lord Thomas to accompany him back to Rockingham. Lady Mathilda has caught glimpse of a document which has caused her to think that something is irregular about your arrest. She is also pursuing the murderer of a maid at Rockingham with Sheriff Ingram's blessing.'

Robert let out a low breath as pride engulfed him. 'She managed it.'

'Managed what, brother?' Eustace snapped.

'I asked Mathilda to keep her ears open. Something about this situation hasn't sat right with me from the start. Now I know the charges levied against us I'm even more suspicious. A theft a year ago. Why that? There are so many other more serious matters that King Edward could have honed in upon.' Robert levelled his eyes on Eustace's, remembering murders in the early parts of the previous year that could have sent them all to hang. 'If Mathilda has discovered something, then we need to know about it.'

Walter raised his ale in Robert's direction. 'That's why you sent her to Rockingham?'

'I sent her there because she's safer there than anywhere else, but yes, Mathilda has skills and de Vere has the King's ear in this region. He harbours, with royal acceptance, felons of varying degrees. I knew Ingram would take Wennesley there in the course of his pursuit of us. I hoped Mathilda would learn much on our behalf.'

'How did you know that Ingram would go there?' Laurence took his nose out of his ale for long enough to prove he'd been listening.

'I asked him to.'

Eustace's face broke into a broad grin. 'Very good, brother. And so Mathilda proves her worth once more. Perhaps we should teach her to read more letters. I assume that is why Thomas is going to Rockingham, to read this document for her.'

'It would make sense.' Robert acknowledged the point, choosing to ignore how changeable his brother could be on the subject of Mathilda's inclusion in their lives. 'My wife would not be able to read a document in detail. She would only recognise a few words. And names, of course.'

'Names.' Eustace scratched his chin. Stubble itched at his fingers, reminding him it was time to shave should he wish to keep his clean-cut, French-style appearance. 'She may have seen a name that alerted her attention, yours perhaps, Robert?'

'It could be any of us. All of us, even; but I'm not sure that would be enough for her to ask Thomas for help. The hunt for us is widely known, so if she saw our names Mathilda would probably assume it was just a repeat of the warrant details. '

'Or perhaps,' Eustace's fingers went to where his dagger should have been, so he could play it between his fingers as was his habit, and immediately cursed the prior for bidding all weapons to be removed on entry to holy ground, 'perhaps your wife saw another name... that of our accuser, for instance.'

Robert was on his feet. 'I must go to Rockingham. If Mathilda stumbles upon -'

'No, brother.' Eustace stepped forward to stop Robert bolting for the door. 'Thomas has gone to her. If you go, then there will be no choice but for de Vere to summon the law despite his personal wishes to the contrary. Sending Ingram and Wennesley there was a sensible move. It bought us time by proving that we are not there and by showing Wennesley that, if you have stowed your wife safely, you are many miles away. He'll have learnt that any pursuit of us will neither be fast nor fruitful.' Eustace paused, his thick fingers fiddling with his belt buckle. 'If you go to Mathilda, the constable cannot deny the fact of your having been there if anyone saw you.'

'Damn!' Robert wished Eustace wasn't right. 'At least Thomas will have the sense to keep her from harm.'

'Robert,' Laurence snorted into his cup, 'from what I know of that wife of yours, it will be her keeping our brother from mischief, not the other way around.'

Eustace rolled his eyes and turned to his groom. 'Are you listening, Pykehose?'

'Always, my Lord.'

'Return to Ashby Folville. Tell Borin to increase his vigilance over the manor. Report to Adam that we are safe and plan to stay where we are until prudence decrees otherwise. Do you have that?'

The man bowed low and repeated the words back to Eustace without error.

'Good.' Eustace clapped Pykehose on the back. 'Now you have completed your mission, is there anything else happening in the world we've missed while tucked away under the arm of hypocritical angels?'

The groom smiled. 'Sarah, Adam, and Ulric are well. They're guarding Lord Richard until Lord John gives orders as to what to do with him.'

Robert's beaker hit the side of the table and shattered into pieces. The noise of the ceramic explosion was lost however, for Eustace and Laurence had let out roars of disbelief and Walter had slammed a palm on the table.

'Our reverend brother is at the manor? Why did you not

say so at once?'

Pykehose frowned. 'Forgive me my Lord. It was not in the message so I assumed you knew. Perhaps Lord Thomas wanted to spare you worry.'

Robert itched to leave again, but this time for Ashby Folville. 'Sarah must be going out of her mind.'

'Perhaps not.' Laurence rubbed his chin. 'She knows where our clerical kin is. Surely that must be better than waiting for him to creep up on her in the dead of night.'

Eustace sat opposite Pykehose. 'Where has Adam got Richard held?'

'Locked in the storeroom, my Lord. My comrades are taking it in turns to guard over his locked door.'

Robert's sigh of relief was even louder this time. 'So Richard doesn't have the run of the manor. Thank goodness.'

'You imagined him taking over the household?' Laurence said.

'I imagined him murdering Sarah in her bed.'

Eustace took no notice of his brothers as he asked his man, 'Did Wennesley capture the reverend himself?'

'No, my Lord, Borin found him lurking near the manor.'

'Did he now? That man is beyond price. And the Lord John knows of Richard's capture?'

'Lord Thomas sent word to Huntingdon at the same time as I was sent here.'

'Does anyone else know?'

'Ingram and his man. They have not been to the manor yet though.'

Robert gave a humourless laugh. 'Wennesley must be delighted that one of his quarry is being held by our own household - less work for him, someone else paying to feed the prisoner, and added humiliation for us.'

'And Wennesley can tell King Edward that he has one felon behind lock and key already.' Eustace shook his head. 'I dislike the idea of a Folville being imprisoned reaching the local gossips, even if it is one who deserves such treatment.'

The brothers were quiet as Pykehose lumbered to his feet. 'I must go, my Lords.'

'Yes.' Eustace gave him a stout clap upon the back. 'You recall my message?'

'Word for word.'

'Then travel safely. If there is news about the Lady Mathilda, Lords Thomas or Richard, or anything concerning our pursuit, I wish to hear about it.'

'My Lord.' The man bowed and went to leave.

Robert stood up, as something that had been nagging at the back of his head, suddenly leapt to the fore. 'Hold on. Did you say Mathilda was tracking a murderer?'

'Indeed, my Lord. A maid at the castle is dead. I know nothing more.'

'Our Lady, protect her!' Robert shook his head, but said nothing. There was nothing to say and nothing he could do to help his wife.

Eustace filled the silence that was left behind as Pykehose left. 'A good man, that; excellent at his job.'

'It was unusual seeing you act kindly, Eustace.' Walter taunted, 'that's twice in one day. Are the holy brothers getting to your soul?'

'Shut up, Walter.' Eustace landed on a chair with a heavy thud. 'Richard is caught. So why aren't we?'

Robert scowled. 'What do you mean?'

'Ingram knows we come here when life pushes us into retreat. Yet no soldiers have sniffed around the priory.'

'The sheriff said he wouldn't pursue us.' Walter frowned.

'He said he wouldn't pursue us *until* his association with Roger Wennesley had officially started. A task that a royal hand pushed him into. The delay provided by a trip to Rockingham has already come and gone   so where are they?'

~ *Chapter Thirty* ~

As night fell, tucked into the cot Bettrys had made up for her, Mathilda thought over all she had learned. She wished she could talk to Robert.

Closing her eyes, Mathilda pictured her husband on the night she'd last seen him. Lying on his back next to her, Robert's arm had been around her, her red curls draping his naked shoulder.

Tell me about your findings, Mathilda. What did you discover today?

Smiling at the image she'd conjured, Mathilda spoke to Robert within the privacy of her room.

'I'm sure Isabella's intended marriage is important. I'm not sure why, though.'

Go on.

'The proposed match between Isabella and William Trussell of Hothorpe manor is not one Robert de Vere wants to jeopardise. Not only would it ally his family name with a respectable lineage, it would bring William to the castle, a man De Vere considers capable of being an excellent constable. A man who, Isabella suspects, her father hopes could clean up the castle and end the supporting of felons. When I asked Isabella why her father didn't simply stop extending a welcome hand to such people, she laughed, saying 'I am not sure your new kin would embrace such a suggestion.'

The girl has a point. What do you know of this William Trussell?

'He is nineteen years of age; Isabella says he is well enough looking and, although not conventionally handsome, is keen to dress the part of an up and coming lord of the manor. As the heir to Hothorpe, whoever William married could expect a life of comfort. When I asked Isabella if, should the king agree to William becoming the next constable of Rockingham Castle, she'd continue to live here or move to Hothorpe, she declared it made no difference. Isabella would still be somewhere she didn't want to be, with someone she cared little for.

'The young couple have only met twice, but apparently William has made it clear he is taken with Isabella.'

Did you ask if Trussell could have got word of Isabella's intension to elope with Sproxton?

'Isabella roundly denied the idea, saying no one but Sproxton and Agnes knew of their plans. But I'm not so sure. Isabella has been let down with a promised marriage before, if her heart is truly engaged with Sproxton's then I'd be surprised if she hasn't sought counsel somewhere.'

Mathilda sighed. The room was warm and comfortable. Bettrys had gone to some pains to make the chamber at the end of the family corridor as pleasant as possible. Now she was officially in residence, Mathilda felt she couldn't continue with her plan to move room each night, so Bettrys had procured an extra key to the door. Mathilda intended to keep it by her side at all times in case someone tried to secure her within. She had enough to think about without worrying about being locked in against her will.

However she played with the facts she'd gleaned so far, Mathilda couldn't see how Isabella could be so sure that no one else had known of her plans. Anyone looking out of a window across the back of the castle could have seen Thomas and Isabella engaged in conversation. If they'd also seen Isabella talking to Agnes...

What if Agnes was forced to tell someone what Isabella was planning?

Robert's voice echoed in her mind and Mathilda's eyes flicked back open. 'Someone prying into Isabella's life might have put pressure on Agnes, forcing her to tell them everything she knew; revealing news that could have enflamed, angered, or even pleased the listener.'

You suspect Lady Helena?

'All I've learned about Helena has convinced me I'm unlikely to ever admire the girl. I can imagine how pleased she'd be if Isabella left the castle. Especially if she did so under a cloud of suspicion or disgrace which prevented her return. That would leave the way clear for Helena to be the eldest daughter by proxy.'

First thing in the morning you should talk to Helena. But take care, wife. Murderess or not, she is clearly a poisonous piece.

'Don't worry, I will.' Turning over again, Mathilda could almost feel Robert's breath on her shoulder.

When was Agnes killed?

'I found her in the early morning, two days ago.'

'On the first day of the New Year?'

'Yes, but she'd been noted as missing before then. She could have been killed any time between mid-afternoon on the last day of December and just before I found her.'

Watching the glow of the fire in the grate opposite her bed, her thoughts drifted to the castle's steward.

'Merrick's a proud man, with a confessed liking for Agnes.'

Was that liking known, or simply suspected by the other staff? Had the family noticed?

'Isabella didn't mention Merrick in connection with Agnes. I'm sure she would have done if there was a liking there; even an unwanted one.'

Unless Agnes said nothing. The girl could have been ashamed of such an association.

'Agnes's short life had been full of incident and hard work. Coming to Rockingham with a master she was afraid of, Agnes had kept herself to herself, rarely daring to speak at first. Then, after Reynard deserted, leaving her alone with a broken leg which set badly and left her with a limp, Agnes had been lost and without employment or hope of a future beyond begging on the streets of Leicester.'

Who found Agnes? If she'd had a broken leg, she could not have come to the castle for help.

'Merrick, but it was Cook who suggested Agnes join the staff. The kitchens are busy and a willing pair of hands is always welcome. For a while Agnes was put to work in the scullery, but her quiet nature, her pleasing looks, and her limp, which troubled her in the kitchen's humid atmosphere, made it clear that she'd be more helpful as a chambermaid.'

Did she work with Isabella?

'Not at first. Helena's maid had walked out of the castle after her mistress had abused her authority once too often, so a replacement was needed. Isabella told me Cook believed Agnes, being used to the sharp end of her old master's tongue, was unlikely to be so affected by Helena's shortcomings as others, so the girl was promoted.'

For a servant to walk out of employment towards poverty, with no guaranteed roof over her head... this Helena must be a harridan indeed.

'Bettrys told me that Agnes was immune to Helena's

complaints at first. If her new mistress claimed her hair linen was too tight, Agnes would loosen it, too loose and she'd tighten it, the wrong colour, she'd change it. If a gown needed mending, Agnes mended it. I'm told Agnes rarely spoke. Apparently, all had been manageable between maid and mistress until the Helena demanded Agnes talk to her.

'Until that point the young maid had gone about her days in comfortable peace. Her survival strategy had been to work and keep her opinions to herself. Apparently, Reynard had encouraged her silence, preferring to enforce his opinion above all others. Helena however tired of Agnes's taciturn ways. The way Bettrys tells it, one day, after a successful dress fitting when Agnes had not responded to Helena's enquiry as to how well her new gown suited her; she demanded the maid use the voice God had given her. Agnes obeyed, of course, but Bettrys said her reply was neither enthusiastic enough nor fast enough for Helena's liking. She accused Agnes of implying she was ugly and did not suit her new outfit. As a result, the first time Agnes had spoken in public in weeks led to someone screaming and shouting at her. Bettrys told me that Agnes wept silent tears and then disappeared for twenty-four hours.

'When I asked where Agnes had been found, Isabella didn't know, but it didn't take long before we wondered if the maid had bolted to the hut we visited earlier today. Maybe that was why Isabella found some food in the hut, maybe Agnes was in the habit of storing supplies there in case she needed to flee? Agnes had served her former master in that very dwelling; there wouldn't be many other boltholes she'd know in the area.'

If Merrick found Agnes that first time, when her leg was broken, could he have gone hunting for her there after Helena upset her? Perhaps he went there for her without telling anyone. Could that have been when his affection for the girl started? Or perhaps he pressed that affection upon her.

'Possibly; and if she rejected him a second time…' Mathilda banged her fist against the side of the cot, 'Oh Robert, it's so complicated! I wish you were here with me.'

"I will be justice this day, doms to deme,
God spede me this day, at my new work!"

Sleep began to claim Mathilda as she imagined Robert reciting lines from the *Tale of Gamelyn* to her.

'Keep safe, my Lord. Come back for me soon.'

~ *Chapter Thirty-one* ~

Dismounting outside the castle, Daniel caught hold of Lord Thomas's bridle as well as his own, then led his master into the outer bailey, hoping to give the air of someone who'd been sent to meet a guest, rather than someone who'd been absent without leave for hours. Explaining to the ostler that the Lord Folville's horse would require stabling for a few days, Daniel promised to return to see to the beast as soon as he'd escorted Lord Thomas into the castle.

Thomas was happy to let Daniel lead the way. Night had closed in fast. A dank gloom had covered the land from mid-afternoon, but now the sky was as dark as pitch. There was not a star to be seen.

Many of the castle occupants were abed, but Merrick remained in the Great Hall attending to Lord de Vere, who sat with a selection of papers before the vast fire.

At the sight of the documents heaped before the constable, Thomas felt his palms itch. Was one of those the paper Mathilda was so keen for him to read?

Merrick saw the unexpected arrivals into the hall and bent to whisper something into his master's ear. Striding towards Thomas, he said 'Lord Folville, back so soon? May I offer you a place by the fire?'

With a nod of dismissal to Daniel, Thomas said, 'That

would be welcome, thank you.'

Allowing himself to be escorted to a place opposite the constable, Thomas raised a hand to de Vere. 'Please, stay seated, my friend. I bring no ill news. I need nothing more than a warm after a bone-chilling ride and, if you will permit it, a bed for the night.'

'Willingly, especially as you bring no poor tidings.'

'I'm here with the minor mission of being able to reassure my family of Lady Folville's welfare. I mean no disrespect to your household when I say this. Mathilda has been through much since she met my brother Robert. There is a desire of her friends and family to know she does not stray into trouble. Something she seems drawn to like a moth to a flame.'

De Vere couldn't help but grin. 'She is a bold one. And brave. Lord Robert chose his wife well.'

Thomas sat, positioning himself so he could see as many of the documents upon the table as possible. 'You're not the first to say so, my Lord, nor will you be the last, I'll warrant!'

'I am making sure Mathilda is cared for. Although she, as I am sure you'll have been informed, is conducting enquiries into the maid Agnes's death, she's not been beyond the reach of a member of my staff at any time.'

Thomas wasn't as sure about that as de Vere sounded. He couldn't imagine Mathilda staying within eyeshot of anyone if she'd decided not to be seen. However, if it was true, he wondered if Mathilda knew she was the subject of such intense surveillance. 'You'll have your work cut out keeping my sister-in-law under a watchful eye.'

'Merrick is more than up to the task. I swear my steward can see around corners.'

Thomas nodded as the steward crossed the hall with a

handful of platters. If Merrick was the one keeping watch on Mathilda, then she would have more freedom to explore the castle than de Vere assumed. His sister-in-law could be asleep in her chamber right now, but she could just as easily be breaking into de Vere's study.

'It is kind of you to take Mathilda's welfare so seriously. My brother Robert will show his appreciation when the time comes.'

'Oh, there's no need for anything like that.' De Vere waved his hand as if to dismiss the thought of any sort of gratuity, while at the same time wondering how much he'd be compensated for his trouble.

'Any word from Ingram and Wennesley?'

'Nothing that has come to my ears, my Lord. However, as they have moved away from here towards Leicester, I'm less likely to have wind of rumour than I was.'

'True enough.' Thomas gestured to the manuscripts strewn on the table. 'Your work for King Edward must keep you occupied enough without having to worry about the likes of us.'

'It is unending.' De Vere swept a hand across the pile of papers in frustration. 'Enquiries, indentures, demesne disputes, arrest warrants for those who may have passed through my gates in the hope I know where they are and can pursue them. Then there are copies of instructions from the royal foresters, and other constables and officials who want to make sure I'm doing my job properly.'

'Sounds rather unnecessary.'

'It often is. Yet if I didn't keep up with it all, you can be sure I'd miss the one vital piece of information I do require!'

Thomas laughed, keeping his eyes on the documents, trying to scan as many of them as he could without making it too obvious. 'And what does our good king want from you tonight? Still hell bent on the cleanup of the midland shires?'

'Once he'd set the hounds upon your brothers his ardour cooled. It is his lady who seems more interested in such pursuits.'

'Lady Philippa? The King's wife?'

'Indeed. She has, so I'm told, little time for those who do not bend completely to her husband's will.'

'Is that so?' Thomas pulled a face. 'She cannot know enough about the problem, surely? She is young and newly arrived from Hainault.'

'Rumour says she has befriended a helper in London who has ignited her interest in the matter.'

A memory pushed itself forward from the back of Thomas's mind, but as yet he couldn't get it to form into anything tangible. 'And this friend, do you know who he is?'

'No, my Lord. I do not.'

Roger Wennesley scowled at Thomas Sproxton. The man was worse than useless. Why had he ever decided to bring him? Still, Wennesley conceded as he watched Sproxton sprawled across a chair, drunk from too much ale and not enough sleep, the man's brawn may yet be a blessing.

Glad they were tucked away at the rear of the Leicester inn where Ingram had the run of the back rooms, Wennesley got up from his seat, abandoned the remains of his ale, and prodded his companion.

'Sproxton! What the hell is wrong with you, man? You've been sullen and surly all day and now you loll in your cups as if you were the one being pursued, rather than one of the pursuers.'

Grunting, Sproxton hurled his legs to the floor, and unslouched his wiry frame. 'I'm fine. Just hadn't banked on spending my days in this manner. I had plans.'

'Such as?'

'It is irrelevant. My plans are null.'

Picking up on the resentment in Sproxton's voice, Wennesley's eyes narrowed. 'I asked you before if you were in debt to anyone. Did you tell me the truth?'

'I did.' Throwing his cup at the fire in rage, Sproxton growled in exasperation. 'Why is it everyone I meet expects only untruths to leave my lips? Even you, a friend, mistrust my words.'

'Forgive me.' Wennesley kept his distance as Sproxton got to his feet, swaying as he moved, 'I am merely concerned. You do not seem yourself.'

Sproxton sank back onto the chair he'd so recently vacated. 'You're right. I'm sorry.'

'Just pull yourself together. The sooner we go through with this lunacy, then the sooner we can all go home.'

Something about Roger's tone hit Thomas, even through the haze of alcohol. 'Lunacy?'

'Oh, come on! We could have captured everyone on that list in a day or two if we'd desperately needed to. It would have cost us a few wounds, I have no doubt, but it would all be over. Instead we have been to Rockingham Castle, where there was never any chance of them being, and now we're resting in Leicester.'

'But we don't know where the Folvilles are.'

'We don't, but Ingram does. I'd put money on it.'

'So why don't we go there?'

'Because Ingram is in their pocket. I bet that tomorrow morning our dear sheriff will arrive from his chamber full of guts and bravado and tell us we ought to give the manor at Ashby Folville a once-over.'

'Only a fool would hide in his own home.'

'Exactly. He knows they won't be there.'

Sproxton rubbed his eyes. 'This is all sounding like a bigger waste of time than ever. If it wasn't for this I could be with…' He stopped himself talking, but it was too late.

'Be with who? Thomas?'

'It doesn't matter.'

Wennesley leapt forward and grabbed his associate by the shoulders. 'Tell me.'

'I had an understanding with a young woman. We were going to leave the area together, but I'm here and she feels hard done by. I will never get such a chance again.'

'A woman? Does she know of your past, of the charges that have so recently been laid at your door?'

'She does. I made a clean breast of things. And what for? I have let her down by simply because I was unable to be where I promised, when I promised.'

'Hence your unease.' Roger frowned. 'You should have said.'

'You would not have let me go.'

'On the contrary, my friend. You're here because I saw a chance for us to clear our names once and for all. If you were far from here, the need would not have arisen.'

Sproxton shook his head. 'What's the point?'

'Freedom. That's the point. Not to be at the King's beck and call. Now, sleep. Whatever happens next, we will need our strength.'

Sheriff Ingram sat by the inn fire eating a hearty breakfast. Raising his eyes towards his sleepy companions as they entered the back room, he passed no comment on the hangover Sproxton was clearly suffering.

'I'm glad you're both here. Today I think we should head to Ashby Folville manor. We need to make sure the brothers haven't doubled back there before we venture further afield, to Lincolnshire perhaps.'

~ *Chapter Thirty-two* ~

'Lord Thomas,' Mathilda curtseyed to her brother-in-law, 'what brings you back to Rockingham so soon?'

'You look well, my Lady.' Thomas de Folville dipped his head as Mathilda crossed the Great Hall, a maidservant behind her.

'I'm being treated like a queen.'

Knowing that Mathilda would not have told anyone of her request for his arrival, Thomas said, 'First of all, I promised Robert I would keep an eye upon your welfare. I know he has no need to cluck over you, but you are yet newlywed. As to the second reason: I bring a request from our steward and housekeeper.'

Mathilda's eyes lit up. 'Are you about to say what I hope you're about to say?'

'If you are hoping that I am about to ask, on Adam's behalf, if you will grant them permission to marry, then yes. Under normal circumstances, I would ask Robert first, but…'

Clapping her hands together in delight, Mathilda beamed. 'But of course! I have no doubt Robert will agree.' Her good humour died a fraction. 'I'm only sorry we are not at home for them to ask us together. What a celebration we'd have had.'

'We'll be together again soon. They plan, should you and Robert agree to the union, to marry as soon as you're home.'

'I appreciate having something so pleasant to look forward to.'

A soft footfall announced the arrival of the castle's steward to their side. 'Would you like some refreshment, my Lord, my Lady?'

'Thank you, Merrick.' Mathilda pointed to a table away from the one the family usually used by the fire, 'Perhaps we could sit over there. I'm sure the family won't want to hear us discussing our manor staff when they come down for breakfast.'

'My Lord de Vere is already in his rooms and Lady Helena and Lady Isabella are breakfasting in their chambers. The fireplace would be more comfortable, my Lord, my Lady.'

'If you are sure we will not be in the way, then we'll take the benefit of the warmth. I swear the winter has penetrated the castle walls this morning.'

'There is thick hoarfrost without, my Lady. I do not envy the outdoor staff this day.'

As Merrick headed towards the kitchen, waving for Bettrys to collect food for their guests, Mathilda lowered her voice, wondering if the steward's mention of the outside staff was a dig towards her lad. 'Did Daniel get back to the stable before anyone noticed his absence?'

'I believe so. When I checked on my horse this morning, he waved at me across the yard. I hear he has duties in the kitchen as well.'

'He helped in the scullery for a while.' Mathilda was pleased. 'The wave will be Daniel's way of telling you all's well.'

'Sarah and Adam wanted to tell you their news themselves, but as I needed a way to explain my return to the castle it seemed the ideal excuse.'

'I'm delighted for them. We'll have to rearrange the manor so they can share a bigger chamber. Sarah's room is so small.'

'Adam's is too. I'm sure Robert would agree to one of the guest rooms being adapted for them. It isn't as though we Folvilles are all in residence together very often.'

Mathilda beamed again. 'I'm so glad you told me. Having that to look forward to will make the next few days easier. Do you think this will be over soon?'

'I can't say.' Thomas shrugged. 'Before we talk about the real reason for my return, I should tell you that de Vere informed me that Merrick has been instructed to watch over you. If you feel he is always nearby, that's because he is.'

'No wonder he is so often in earshot - although I suspect he would be anyway. He is an excellent steward, which means, in a place as big as this, paying very close attention to everyone and everything.'

Thomas peered over his shoulder to make sure they were not overheard. 'This document you saw; what can you tell me?'

'I saw a name - or I think I did. However, I don't know the full nature of the document, beyond it detailing the arrest against our family; I recognised your brothers' names. There was much more listed upon it which I could not read.'

'How come you saw it at all?'

'It was on the table in de Vere's rooms. Wennesley knocked ink over it and de Vere panicked at the thought of it being damaged. The paper was flapped around to dry it and it happened to be facing towards me at the time.'

'And the additional name you think you saw?'

'James Coterel.'

Thomas let out a slow hiss of breath. 'I knew it!'

'You did?' Mathilda sighed. 'Why do none of you Folvilles ever think to tell me the whole of a story before throwing me into these situations? If I'd known this was all about the elder Coterel brother, then I wouldn't have had to risk Daniel's position by sending him for you again and...'

'You misunderstand.' Thomas gave a rueful sigh, unable to argue with the way his family treated Mathilda all too often. 'I had no idea James was involved, although I ought to have guessed. Something doesn't ring true here.'

'What do you mean?'

Thomas was prevented from answering by the arrival of Merrick and a maid carrying food and drink. Changing the subject, he said, 'You must be Bettrys, Lady Mathilda has spoken highly of you.'

Two points of colour pinked Bettrys' cheeks as she bobbed a half-curtsey, 'Thank you, my Lord, my Lady.'

Merrick looked angry. 'Get back to Cook, Bettrys. There may be jobs she needs you to do before you set to cleaning the chambers.'

With a mumbled, 'Yes, Merrick,' Bettrys almost ran back to the kitchen.

Thomas picked up a chunk of bread. 'I did not mean to cause the girl trouble.'

'Not at all, my Lord. It is just that, without Agnes, we are shorthanded. Bettrys can't afford to get ideas above her station.'

Mathilda played her beaker between her palms. 'I believed Bettrys to be a chambermaid, not a kitchen hand.'

'Bettrys does what Cook and I decide she will do.' Merrick's face was an expressionless blank. 'If you will excuse me.'

Waiting until the steward had disappeared into the kitchen, Thomas whispered, 'What was that about?'

'I don't know. I hope Bettrys is alright. She has been a Godsend since I arrived. I will enquire of her later. Now to James Coterel: why do I know so little of him? Until a few days ago I hadn't realised there had once been four Coterel brothers rather than two.'

'After the death of Laurence Coterel, at the hands of Wennesley and in the presence of Sproxton, the other Coterels took the decision to play their brother's death down. They saw it as Laurence's failure rather than Wennesley's success. It was a brawl that got out of hand and Nicholas and John have no time for such things. Laurence was a liability.'

'Like your brother Richard, perhaps?'

'Without the pleasure in cruelty; but the situations are not unalike.'

'And James?' Mathilda chewed thoughtfully, 'He does not live at the manor in Bakewell?'

'He is the eldest and so, like our own Lord John, has more responsibilities to the household name. James Coterel is also a master of manipulation and a devil in disguise. I've met him but once. I will not forget the experience.'

Mathilda felt her insides chill to match the temperature of the room and automatically tugged her cloak closer around her shoulders. 'What happened?'

'James had been cheated by a silk merchant visiting Leicester for the market. The merchant was new to the area, passing through on his way to Nottingham's Goose Fair.'

'Did the merchant ever reach Nottingham?'

'I do not know for certain. We never heard tell of him again.'

'Perhaps he simply never came this way again.'

'Or perhaps James sent his men to make sure he never

went anywhere again.'

Mathilda considered this for a moment. 'Are you saying James does not embrace the idea that lessons must be taught, but fairly?'

'James Coterel is out for James Coterel and no one else. He plays his own game; but his family name means a lot to him. More even than ours means to us, perhaps.'

'And yet he is not known to me. I find that strange. Even before my life spun on its hinges and I was thrust into your lives, I knew of Nicholas and John Coterel. I heard their names whispered in awe and fear - but nothing of James.'

'You are young, and female. Any word of Lord Coterel would've been spoken with caution behind hands over ale, only between men brave enough to admit of his existence.'

'I see.' Mathilda felt her throat go dry. 'How is he involved in what is happening now? Do you think the document I saw also contained a warrant for his arrest?'

'I doubt it. I will have to see that parchment for myself.'

'I have an idea about how to get you into de Vere's study, but whether the document remains within, I don't know. Wennesley could have taken it with him.' Mathilda bent her head over her plate as she said, 'Where is James Coterel now?'

'He went to London some time ago. He has a position in the Royal Court.'

The crash of smashing pottery echoed through the hall as the cup in Mathilda's hands slipped through her fingers and bounced against the edge of the oak table, before shattering on the stone floor.

'Oh my, I'm so sorry!'

Footsteps ran in their direction as Bettrys and Merrick came to make sure they were alright.

'Forgive me, my hand slipped. Clumsy of me. Tell Cook

I will ask my father to replace the vessel. He is an accomplished potter.'

'Thank you, my Lady.' Merrick bowed as Bettrys scrabbled on her knees, picking up the shards of ceramic, 'but that won't be necessary. Accidents happen.'

Only once they'd gone did Mathilda hiss, 'James Coterel works for the King?'

'Worse. The King's wife, Philippa of Hainault.'

Mathilda gasped, and found her hands were shaking as Thomas went on.

'I learned from de Vere last night that it is Philippa whose hand is steering this ship. When he told me that, something began to nag at my brain. Now I know what it was.'

'Tell me.'

'James Coterel became part of Court, as I said. De Vere told me that Philippa has a new favourite influencing her choices. It has to be Coterel!'

'Surely not?'

'He's a charismatic man. Handsome and capable. I have no doubt he has made himself indispensable.'

'But if that is the case, wouldn't he have prevented her pursuit of his own family, if not ours?'

'Or he could have encouraged it. Even arranged the whole thing.'

'But why?'

Thomas leaned nearer to his sister-in-law and lowered his voice. 'Lord John and I were excluded from the arrest warrant. I couldn't understand why, but if James is behind it then that makes sense. John and I have helped him in the past and so it seems we have been spared. My other brothers however have not always seen eye to eye with him.'

'But why pick on his family?'

Thomas took a draught of ale, 'I can only imagine that

it's a blind to something bigger.'

'Like what?'

'If James Coterel is involved it will be one of three things. Revenge, money, or a way to increase his status.'

Mathilda picked at her bread gloomily. 'Or all three.'

~ *Chapter Thirty-three* ~

Oswin of Twyford had not hesitated once Ulric had explained the enormity of what the Folville household was asking of him.

His sister was in need of his help and so he would give it. The danger involved was flapped aside with one of his giant land-working hands. With hasty explanations to his older brother Matthew and his father Bertred, Oswin packed some provisions. Then, taking the family's only horse, a grim determination set across his innocent features, he left the safety of the pottery in Twyford.

It had only been a few weeks since he'd been released from service within the household of Nicolas and John Coterel in far-off Bakewell. Now Oswin counted on their memory of how well he'd served them to secure their help. Although he couldn't see how the Coterels could assist with a situation they were as embroiled in as the Folvilles were.

Ulric had told him to head, not to the Coterels' home in Bakewell, but to the abbey of Lichfield. His message memorised, Oswin's smile widened as the sense of adventure, one he'd developed since his sister had first met the Folvilles, stirred in his placid soul.

The bed, which Sheriff Ingram had used many times over

the years, was crisply laundered and a fire flickered enticingly in the hearth. Sarah scrutinised the chamber with a sense of satisfaction. Since Thomas had gone to Rockingham to help Mathilda she'd felt a weight slide from her shoulders, and there was a comfort in carrying out such familiar tasks, especially as lately her life felt as if it had been repeatedly tilted off its axis.

An image of Adam conjured itself in her mind; Sarah was unable to stop the beam that accompanied it. Never had she envisaged a happiness of this sort for herself, but now here she was contemplating her wedding day. It would be a small affair with, hopefully, the newest Lord and Lady de Folville in attendance.

Returning to the kitchen to prepare the stew pot for use, Sarah glanced up as Adam came in, rubbing his hands together against the frosty morning. A sense of urgency radiated from his rugged frame.

'They approach?'

'They do.' Adam surveyed the spotless kitchen approvingly. 'Borin has sent word. Three men, one of whom is Sheriff Ingram.'

'Then Lord Thomas's prediction was correct.' Sarah straightened her head linen. 'It's a good job we are ready for them.'

'Lord Eustace's men have made themselves scarce, but I am assured they are not far away and have eyes upon the manor.'

Sarah did not need to ask why they'd gone. Eustace had long ago accepted that criminals proved much better guards than honest men.

'Adam. Sarah. I trust you are well, despite the blatant lack of guards protecting the manor?'

Sheriff Ingram leapt from his horse as if he was a man twenty years his junior, handing the bridle to Adam with a knowing look.

'We are, Lord Sheriff.' Adam bowed his head as he took the bridle of the man riding behind Ingram. By contrast, this man's countenance was not welcoming. He looked irritated and tired. 'May I take your horse, my Lord?'

'Naturally.' Roger Wennesley dismounted and pushed his mount towards Adam. 'Hurry up and get off that nag, Sproxton. The sooner we get this waste of time over with the better.'

Biting his lips, familiar with this sort of master, Adam took Sproxton's reins before addressing the sheriff. 'Sarah has prepared food and rooms for you should they be required. The hall fire is lit for your comfort. Permit me to show you in.'

'You are kind, but we are not able to relax in our duties just yet. You will have guessed that we need to search the premises.'

'I can assure you that their Lordships, Eustace, Robert, Walter, and Laurence are not here. Nor do we know where they reside.'

Wennesley snorted. 'Already he lies. We know that the reverend is here.'

'Forgive my companion, Adam.' Ingram laid a reassuring hand on the steward's shoulder. 'If you had listened, Roger, you will not have heard Adam claim otherwise. He did not mention the Reverend Folville at all.'

Wennesley snorted. 'Where is the tainted cleric, steward?'

'In a locked storeroom. Not far from the kitchen.'

'Not the dungeon?'

'He *is* one of my masters, my Lord.'

Sproxton rolled his eyes. 'Is there any point in searching the stables and manor rooms, or will that do no more than exercise our limbs?'

'No one is here but me, Sarah, and the Lord Richard de Folville.' As Adam repeated himself, he tried not to let his dislike of their latest visitors show on his face.

Ingram laughed. 'Sproxton, search each room, the stables and the food store. Then come and join Wennesley and myself in the hall. We will partake of some of Sarah's excellent fare.'

Richard, Rector of Teigh, sat up abruptly. It felt an age since he'd heard voices other than Sarah and Adam's, apart from the occasional grunt from whichever of Eustace's guards was stationed outside his door.

Straining to hear, Richard's heart sank as he recognised the unmistakable sound of the sheriff's voice. He'd begun to dare hope that he would be left there in custody until Robert came home. He was more than content to sit out his temporary confinement at the manor while his brothers untangled the knot they'd got themselves into, rather than facing the wrath of the King's justice.

The arrival of the sheriff and whoever he was speaking to was not good news. Richard had no wish to reside in Nottingham Castle's gaol, and the prospect of being sent back to France was enough to chill him to the bone.

The voices faded before he could make out more than Ingram's distinctive tone. Richard groaned in the darkness as he experienced a most uncharacteristic urge to pray.

Sproxton sank into a chair and grabbed a beaker of ale. 'That was a waste of our time.'

'No, it was a necessary task.' Ingram stared at the younger man. 'Can you imagine what King Edward would have said if we hadn't checked this house, only to discover that Eustace, Robert, and their kin had been here the whole time?'

'It *was* a waste of time, but I suppose it was required,' Wennesley growled, 'I suggest we waste no more time however.' He checked to ensure they weren't in earshot of the family servants. 'You know full well where the Folvilles are, Ingram. Why do you pretend otherwise?'

Ingram steepled his hands together and levelled his stern gaze on Wennesley. 'And no doubt you know where the Coterels are. Tell me this, Roger; do you really want to catch them? Derbyshire with no Coterels. Leicestershire without the Folvilles. Can't you see the consequences if our mission succeeds?'

Watching his companions closely, Sproxton's eyes narrowed. 'What about the consequences if we don't?'

Wennesley's face betrayed nothing as he bypassed Ingram's questions. 'I think we should leave the rector here for the time being.'

Ingram concurred. 'He is secure and the Crown is without the expense of keeping him. A bonus that obnoxious clerk, Garrick, will appreciate, I have no doubt. That man would add four and five together to make twenty if he thought it would earn him credit with the King.'

'Secure?' Sproxton was incredulous. 'Have you seen a single guard in this place? How do we know Folville is even in the storeroom?'

'I told you to look in every room,' Ingram snapped in exasperation. 'I was foolish enough to believe you would do exactly that. Do you need one of us there to hold your hand?'

Wennesley got to his feet. 'For Heaven's sake, Sproxton.

Pull yourself together! If the woman loves you she'll wait, if not, then she isn't worth the fret, is she!'

Ingram's head tilted to one side. 'Woman? Speak now, Thomas. What woman?'

Giving Wennesley a glare which would have culled a lesser man, Sproxton said. 'It is unimportant and not related to our mission.'

Ingram wasn't put off so easily. 'Her *name*, Sproxton?'

'I don't see why I should tell -'

'And I don't see why I should take your word that you didn't defile the de Vere girl. Your reputation with women wasn't good before that. And now -'

'I did nothing to that jealous harpy! Roger himself stood witness.' Thomas swung around in appeal to his friend.

Wennesley dipped his head, 'I did. Was I wise to do so?'

'What?' Sproxton spluttered, a cloud crossing his features. 'Of course you were, I never -'

Slamming his hand onto the table, the sheriff got to his feet, leaning close to Sproxton. 'Tell me.'

'Isabella de Vere,' Sproxton spat.

'The sister of your accuser!' Ingram turned and railed angrily at Wennesley, 'You gave him a false alibi.' It was a statement, not a question. 'Why?'

The sheriff's tone had dropped to a cool calm which was more worrying than hearing the man shout.

'I had good reason.'

'I would like to hear that reason. Now.'

Sproxton raised his voice, 'This has nothing to do with our current mission. The de Veres have not got the Folvilles or Coterels staying with them. You know where our quarry resides. Let's get on with this!'

Hissing between gritted teeth, Wennesley grabbed his comrade by the collar of his cloak and pulled him close.

'Will you keep your voice down! This remains the house of the Folvilles, even when they aren't here. They choose their servants well. You would be wise to remember that.'

Relieved to see no sign of the steward or housekeeper, Sproxton whispered. 'What is it you two aren't telling me?'

The sheriff studied Wennesley for a minute, before he sank into his chair. 'Well, you keep reminding us that King Edward entrusted the mission to you. So, you can decide how the situation is played from now on.'

'Oh, how very convenient for you!'

'Isn't it.'

Wennesley gripped the side of the table and silently counted to ten before exclaiming, 'We will check on the rector. All three of us, together. Then we will eat. After that we will make a plan. A proper one, that doesn't involve chasing spectres which aren't there.'

Ingram nodded. 'And you will also tell me about the reason behind the false alibi you gave Sproxton. In detail.'

~ *Chapter Thirty-four* ~

'Let him in, Brother Simon.'

Oswin turned the brim of his battered hat between anxious fingers, his head dipped in reverence to the surroundings he found himself in.

Nicholas Coterel was not someone he would have associated with holy ground. To see his former employer on his knees before the altar of Lichfield Cathedral felt like an intrusion. Oswin took a few reverential steps backwards as he watched the big black-haired man mutter words to a deity the potter's son was astounded to find a Coterel believed in.

Eventually, Nicholas rose from the stone floor. He gestured to the altar with a flick of his wrist. 'A prayer before bed, just in case there is someone listening.'

Blasphemous though it was, Oswin felt reassured. This was more like the master he had worked for in the past.

'It is good to see you, Oswin. You have a message for me.'

Following Nicholas as he paced down the aisle, Oswin said, 'How did you know, my Lord?'

'Why else would you be here at this time?' As they exited into the January air, Nicholas took a generous lungful. 'That's better. I can't be doing with too much of that dusty atmosphere. So, Master Oswin: your family, are they well?'

'My Lord, thank you; my father and brother Matthew do well enough.'

'Ah… you do not mention your sister. So, what scrape has the fair Mathilda got herself into this time?'

Oswin blushed. 'Forgive me, my Lord. You'll think me presumptive of your help. In truth however, it is not that I come for this time; although Mathilda is again investigating a murder.'

'Is she now? Where may I ask?' Nicholas's shrewd eyes narrowed.

'Rockingham Castle, my Lord.'

'De Vere's place.' Coterel adjusted his cloak. 'I admire your sister's courage. Robert de Folville does not know how lucky he is. If Mathilda ever notices that, I'll be the first in the queue to snatch her away from him.'

Oswin was shocked. 'But, my Lord, I…'

Nicholas laughed heartily and slapped Oswin across his broad back. 'Fear not. I'd never steal another man's wife.'

'I never thought -'

'Your business, Oswin; it is, I presume, connected with my presence here, rather than in Bakewell?'

'It is.'

'And the Folvilles? They reside in their usual bolthole?'

'I do not know, but they are not in Ashby Folville.'

'And Mathilda is in Rockingham. Robert stowed her in safety before the family moved. Good.'

'I am assured she is safe, but the murder…'

Reaching the opposite side of the cloister, Nicholas swung back a heavily panelled door. 'Come inside, Oswin. My brother is within. You should deliver your message to us both.'

Leaving the sharp winter on the other side of the door, Nicholas directed Oswin towards the fire. Already there, booted feet upon the table, his back slouched against a wooden chair, was John Coterel.

'Oswin! To what do we owe the pleasure?'

'My Lord John.' Oswin bowed. 'I bring a message from Thomas de Folville concerning the current situation.'

John's feet were on the floor and his back straight in seconds. 'Then speak it.'

Oswin's cheeks reddened as he found himself the subject of the noble felon's scrutiny. 'My masters know on what charges you are sought. Lord Thomas was unsure whether you were aware of them and bid me come and tell you. He has a mind for the two families to work together to relieve this situation.'

Nicholas and John traded a brief look, the meaning of which Oswin failed to interpret. 'Do the Folvilles know why they too are hunted?'

'They do, my Lord. They didn't until recently. The truth was uncovered at Rockingham.'

This seemed to please Nicholas, who barked with laughter as he lounged next to the fireplace. John pointed to a seat opposite him. 'Please, Oswin, sit down and tell us what is laid against us.'

Doing as he was told, hoping they would not blame him for the ill news he had to impart, Oswin swallowed. 'My Lords, you are charged with the murders of John Matynson and Sir William Knyveton at Bradley in Derbyshire.'

The resulting quiet that filled the room pressed in on Oswin as he waited for the brothers' reaction to the news.

Nicholas was the first to break the silence. When he did, it wasn't with the explosion of anger Oswin had been expecting, but open curiosity. 'Is that so? And tell us the charges against our comrades in Leicestershire.'

'The theft of two hundred pounds' worth of goods from

the burgess of Leicester. My Lords, there is more to Lord Thomas's message.'

'Then speak it.' Nicholas opened his palms in invitation.

'These are the exact words of my Lord Thomas after he explained the aforementioned charges to me.'

'Understood. Begin.'

'Greetings from the Folville manor. We are under the eye of London. The situation needs resolution before mutual future plans can be met.'

Rather than protest his confusion, Nicholas burst into a fresh peal of laughter. 'I don't know whether to be proud or wring his neck. What say you, John?'

'I say we would do well to tread carefully.' Despite the warning in his words, John's rigid features held a reluctant smile.

Oswin looked from one former master to the other and back again. They were making no sense. 'You wish to wring Lord Thomas's neck?'

'No, lad, not him. Thomas is an honest criminal.' Getting up from his chair, John waved an arm towards Oswin. 'Come, old friend; let us badger these canons into finding you some food, ale, and a cot for the night. There is much to consider. Will you carry letters for us until this matter is closed?'

'Willingly, my Lords.'

Nicholas grinned at Oswin's confused face. 'I would also like to hear what Mathilda is doing with her time at Rockingham. You said there has been a murder. I assume she is trying to bring a touch of justice to the situation.'

Oswin didn't know what to say, so he merely mumbled, 'You have the measure of my sister, my Lord.'

Thomas de Folville stared at the outside of the tumbledown

hut for a moment.

'Let's go inside.'

Once again, the dwelling's damp air assaulted Mathilda's nostrils as she sat on the old cot. Thomas stayed by the door and surveyed the meagre space. 'A summary of events seems a good place to start.'

Mathilda, grateful to be able to order her ideas, began to think aloud. 'The steward, Merrick, told me that Agnes was sent to the Fire Room to make up my bed around noon on the day she died. Lady Isabella said she was here at that time; already wondering why neither her maid nor her lover had arrived to travel to London as planned.'

Thomas folded his arms. 'At what time was Isabella expecting her maid?'

'After Agnes had finished cleaning her chamber; so sometime after noon.'

'Did she have Lady Isabella's things with her when she was found?'

'No. She had changed out of her working clothes, though.'

'Did Merrick know why Agnes had changed?'

'No. He also said he was unaware that she was planning to leave.'

'But if he did know?'

'Merrick knows of this dwelling. He found Agnes here with a broken leg prior to her joining the household. He had feelings for the girl and very little love for her old master, Reynard.'

'This Reynard; I assume he's long gone?'

'I haven't encountered him and no one has claimed they've seen him. I'd have thought that if he'd been sighted, he'd have been the first person to have suspicion cast upon him.'

'Merrick is your suspect, then? He's the one who sent Agnes to the Fire Room in the first place.'

Mathilda tucked her hands into her cloak for warmth. 'It has to be considered, although I don't like to think it of him. Merrick held affection for the girl that was not returned. If he felt humiliated and found out she was leaving, then perhaps he struck out. But, then again, if Agnes was leaving what was the point? With her gone, he'd be free of reminders of her refusal.'

'Which leaves Lady Helena.'

'Bettrys tells of a frustrated woman who is obsessed with her appearance and what others think of her. Helena's accusation of Sproxton for a rape he could not possibly have committed is proof that she has no scruples when her will is denied.'

'And she did not like Agnes?'

'Agnes failed to tell her that she suited a gown. For that, Lady Helena dismissed the maid from her personal service.'

Thomas's eyebrows rose. 'I will never understand women.'

'Nor I, when it comes to a woman like that.' Mathilda got up and paced the small space. 'If Lady Helena did kill Agnes, which again I cannot picture because it would involve both effort and mess, then I'm more inclined to think it was jealousy caused by the friendship Agnes and Isabella had. Helena cannot abide anyone favoured above her.'

'And if Isabella was to run away with Sproxton, the very man who had spurned Helena...'

Mathilda nodded. 'Agnes could have been killed to hurt Isabella. It would be easier to kill the maid than Sproxton.'

Thomas began to search the hut more thoroughly. 'Do you think it possible that Agnes was with child?'

Surprised by the question, Mathilda said, 'If she was,

then the child had only recently quickened. There was no sign of impending motherhood, no swelling around her belly. It would have been hard to spot in her aprons, though when she died she wore travelling garb. No one has mentioned her displaying any sickness. Why do you ask?'

'What if Merrick, or someone else, had a desire for Agnes that they could not control and took her forcibly?'

'But if it wasn't Merrick, that would mean Lord de Vere.'

'Or any of the other felons that pass through these doors. The men who stay here are not men of virtue.'

Mathilda shuddered. 'If Agnes had suffered that sort of unwanted attention it would explain why she was so willing to run from the first security she'd ever had. It was a risk travelling into the unknown with Isabella and Sproxton.'

'If she was with child, do you think she'd have told Isabella?' Thomas stared through the dirty shutters into the trees.

'I don't know. In time she'd have had no choice.'

'By then she'd have fled onwards, taking her chances where she could.'

'But why?' Mathilda tried to order her thoughts around this new idea. 'Rockingham Castle takes in all sorts. A bastard child can't be so unusual. Would they throw out a good pair of working hands so easily? In other places, possibly - but here, after they'd already spent time nursing Agnes back to health after she'd been abandoned?'

'Depends who the father was, and if Agnes could be relied upon to keep her mouth shut.'

'Or we could be chasing butterflies.' Mathilda stroked her belt lovingly. 'Agnes showed no sign of approaching motherhood.'

'It can't be discounted as a possibility.' Thomas sat next to his sister-in-law. 'You can't discount de Vere as a suspect either. He is by necessity a devious man and an accomplished liar. If he wasn't, he'd have been killed years ago.'

'True. Nor can we discount Sproxton. By all accounts he is a gambler and womaniser.' Mathilda paused. 'I had ruled him out, but after his late-night tryst at Lady Isabella's chamber door, we know he's capable of getting around the castle unnoticed. Although, that could be said of anyone. I have walked around Rockingham and seen not a soul. '

Thomas lifted the mattress right off the cot as he asked, 'Do you think Lady Isabella would take Sproxton back?'

'The girl wavers. Her heart is not broken, but it is bruised.'

Mathilda came to Thomas's side as he tilted the mattress to one side. A metallic clatter sounded as something slipped from its cover.

Two knives lay on the floor, both similar in size and design to the one Mathilda had last seen in Agnes' back. 'Sewn into the mattress?'

'Part of a set by the look of it.' Thomas weighed them in his hands, 'But were they hidden for emergencies, or because they were precious to an owner who couldn't afford to replace them if they went missing.'

'You think Sproxton dispatched Agnes with a sister knife to these, to keep the journey between Isabella and him a lone venture?'

'I don't know.'

Mathilda rubbed her hands over her arms. 'Let's walk back. I grow cold. Take the knives. I don't like the idea of leaving them here.'

Thomas slid them carefully into his belt. 'I'll hide them in my quarters. I don't think it would be wise to share that we have these until we need to.'

As they wandered through the forest's late morning

light, Mathilda spoke in whispers for fear of being overheard. 'Isabella insists Sproxton was glad of an extra pair of hands to do the manual work in his uncle's workshop. Agnes would have been a blessing to them. I can't imagine him killing her.'

'Makes sense. Sproxton always was a lazy devil.'

Mathilda sighed. 'Perhaps I can't do this. Before, when I sorted out the trouble with Lord Richard and then Rowan Leigh, it was because I had to. My life was in peril. But this suspicion of people I like... I'm not sure I'm made for it.'

Politely holding Mathilda's elbow as they approached the castle, Thomas gave her a grave smile. 'Never forget, you do this to please the sheriff so he is kinder to Robert. It is for all of us. It is for your husband's life, perhaps.'

'I do not forget.' Mathilda was about to suggest they head to the study in the hope of distracting de Vere enough to survey his documents, when she stopped walking. Six people were dismounting from horses in the courtyard. Three men-at-arms, a well-dressed older couple, clearly man and wife, and a younger man of about nineteen.

'Now this *is* interesting.' Thomas gestured ahead. 'I spy William Trussell. What if he has got wind of Isabella's dissatisfaction with their proposed marriage match?'

'So that's Trussell.' Mathilda regarded him with interest. 'I knew they were coming, but assumed in the circumstances that the meeting to discuss the suitability of a union between the families would be postponed.'

'Then you misunderstand what's at stake here.' Thomas spoke kindly, 'It occurs to me that there is another question we haven't asked ourselves. Why did Isabella and Sproxton choose that moment to flee?'

Mathilda gripped Thomas's arm tighter. 'Of course! Because Trussell and his parents were due to visit. She wanted to be gone before then, but what if someone had got to hear about Isabella's intentions?'

'They might have told Trussell or any member of his family or household. Perhaps Agnes was not the target, perhaps it was Lady Isabella?'

'But she had even less reason to be in my room. Thomas, what if…?'

'If you were the target?' He was solemn as they watched the activity in the courtyard ahead. 'It had occurred to me. But your murder here, at this time, would cause more problems that it would solve. This time, sister, I don't think you were the intended mark.'

Mathilda let out a ragged breath. 'It is a relief to hear you say that. I -'

Thomas abruptly tugged Mathilda into the shadows provided by the castle walls. 'You should go and greet them. De Vere will be there any second, if he isn't already. He will entertain them publically before they speak in private.'

'You're going to break into his office to read the document while I'm with them?'

'Just keep Merrick busy.'

With no idea how that was to be achieved, Mathilda strode towards the gathering, hoping her demeanour portrayed a confidence she didn't feel.

~ *Chapter Thirty-five* ~

Lady Trussell's pride radiated across the courtyard. One glance was enough to know that this was a woman who intended to be seen to be going places. Even before she'd heard the woman speak, Mathilda found herself thinking that Lady Helena would make her a far more suitable daughter-in-law.

Holding out a gloved hand for someone to take, Lady Trussell dismounted from her pure white palfrey as if she was the Queen of England herself.

Pushing her shoulder's back as she walked forward, Mathilda searched for Lady Isabella. She wasn't there. Nor was Merrick. Perspiration prickled her palms. Merrick was always there.

Lord de Vere, his face set into a rather unnaturally welcoming beam, waited next to Lady Helena. Demure and radiating obedience and humility, she glowed in a gown of cornflower blue which complimented her yellow hair to perfection.

Mathilda realised she wasn't the only one who thought Lady Helena a better match for the young stag who loitered next to his parents. Helena did too - but whether because she wanted the match, or because she simply didn't want Isabella to have it, only time would tell.

As Lord Trussell helped his wife to the ground Mathilda swallowed a giggle. Her Ladyship was at least four inches taller than her husband and he was doing all he could to diminish the fact. His back and neck were so upright that every one of his muscles must have been taut to the point of pain.

De Vere spotted Mathilda before she had finished her assessment of the scene ahead. 'Ah, my Lords and Lady Trussell, may I introduce our guest, Lady Mathilda.'

Noting the omission of her surname, and knowing it to be deliberate, Mathilda curtseyed to Lady Trussell. 'I'm honoured.'

Talking down her crooked nose, Lady Trussell said, 'You're not one of the resident criminals, I hope?'

Taken aback by the woman's rudeness, Mathilda found herself wishing Eustace was there. He'd enjoy sparing with this woman. 'I can assure you I'm not, my Lady.'

'Out walking alone? Hardly ladylike.'

'I knew the castle was busy preparing for important guests. I did not wish to inconvenience anyone and so took some air.'

De Vere, appreciating Mathilda's diplomacy, interceded, 'For which we are most grateful. Come, let us go within.'

As the party passed through the wide stone corridors, Mathilda watched Lady Trussell. The gleam in her eyes was unmistakeable. A castle was no less than her son deserved. There were no male heirs here. It was ripe for the taking. There was only one problem. Just as the thought hit her, Lady Trussell voiced the words running through Mathilda's head.

'We expected the Lady Isabella would greet us on our arrival.'

De Vere was ready for the sharp enquiry. 'My eldest

daughter wanted to greet you at her best, so I bid her wait indoors for us. She will be by the fire.'

For the first time, William himself spoke. 'The vision of Lady Isabella is always worth waiting for.'

The temperature at Mathilda's side, where Lady Helena walked, dropped violently. Could she be capable of murder after all? Seeing her now, she was certainly capable of planning one.

Shaking her head, Mathilda scanned the hall ahead as they reached the staircase. There was still no sign of Merrick.

Lord William stayed by his mother's side, guiding her elbow as they descended the stairs into the Great Hall. His eyes however were not on his parent. They had found the person he wanted to see; once he'd seen her, his gaze was not to be deviated.

Isabella stood by the fireplace. Her hair was hidden behind white linen, which accentuated her dark complexion perfectly. Her maroon gown swept the floor, its contours matching her body, while her modesty was protected by the cloak at her shoulders.

Mathilda felt Helena's bristling annoyance in the face of her half-sister's beauty.

De Vere moved forward, 'May I introduce my daughter, the Lady Isabella.'

Isabella, who Mathilda had half expected to have run away to avoid this meeting, curtsied reverentially. 'My Lords, my Lady. I'm delighted to make your acquaintance.'

As polite but wary greetings were made, the family gathered around the table. Mathilda sat at the far end, her pulse beating fast. Relief filled her as Merrick and Bettrys appeared. The maid looked flustered and unhappy, while Merrick wore an ever dourer expression.

At least if Merrick was here then Thomas would have no one interrupting his quest to search the office, Mathilda thought, providing he could get through the locked door.

Bettrys avoided eye contact as she poured wine and busied herself with the serving of some of Cook's finest sweetmeats. Every instinct told Mathilda something was wrong, but until this charade was over, there was no way she could enquire about what that something was. Asking a maid of her welfare in front of Lady Trussell would be a black mark in the de Vere family's favour. While Isabella may have welcomed additional reasons to halt the forthcoming union, Lord de Vere was Mathilda's host and she couldn't afford to be thrown out of the castle before her investigation work was complete.

William sat next to Isabella. He said little, but his eyes returned to his intended more often than was seemly. Lady Helena, sat on Isabella's far side, was conversely suffering from a lack of attention from everyone except Lady Trussell, whose expression changed from approval when she looked at Helena to disapproval when she glanced at Isabella and back again at regular intervals.

Wondering if Isabella had made her peace with the fact she'd have to marry the man next to her, Mathilda watched and listened with interest.

'De Vere,' Lord Trussell leant forward so that Merrick could refill his goblet, 'you are certain the King would be favourable to William taking over your role on his marriage to your daughter.'

'If,' added Lady Trussell, 'we agree to the union.'

'Indeed, my Lady.' De Vere gave her a low bow. 'Your caution does you justice.'

'The reputation of this castle concerns me. Although my son informs me he is enamoured with Lady Isabella, I... we have reservations concerning her suitability and that of her station.'

Isabella drew back as if stung while Helena lent forward, her smile more dazzling than ever. Mathilda found herself thinking of a cuckoo throwing another bird's eggs out of the nest.

'I assure you, my Lady, the stigma you refer to is mere hearsay.' De Vere spoke smoothly. 'Shortly, I will ask Merrick to fetch some papers from my office. They prove that the King himself is more than happy with a change of constable and regime here at Rockingham.'

Mathilda tensed, drinking her own wine fast so she had an excuse to call Merrick for more so she could delay his visit to the office at least a fraction.

'One of the benefits of Lord William taking control of the castle,' De Vere went on, 'is that he'd have your family's good name behind him. What better way to curb any lingering fingers of doubt?'

It was a good speech. Lady Trussell sat smugly, pleased at the complement paid to her kin's virtue.

Lord Trussell, who seemed happy to let his wife steer his family ship, lifted his goblet to Merrick. 'Another, please.'

Wondering if only excessive alcohol kept him from strangling his wife, Mathilda was glad of his Lordship's thirst, for it kept Merrick in the room.

As Bettrys served more delicious morsels from Cook's skilled hands, Lady Helena unexpectedly addressed the table. 'Lady Trussell, if you will excuse my boldness, you seem reluctant to let your most worthy son marry into this household. May I ask: is it the role of constable that dissuades you, or the Lady de Vere who has been chosen for this union?'

The second of shock that followed was broken by Bettrys's sharp intake of breath and the clatter of a clumsily placed knife as Merrick leant forward to collect up an empty platter.

Mathilda realised that her mouth had also opened in surprise at Lady Helena's audacity. No one moved.

Lady Trussell however beamed. 'You are perceptive as well as beautiful, my child.'

Isabella's expression appealed to her father who, instead of defending her honour, simply looked down at his plate.

Seconds later, there was a scrape of a chair moving backwards as Lady Isabella rose to her feet. With a bow to her father, she focused on William alone. 'I regret I must leave you, my Lord. I am recently bereaved and am in no mood to be the subject of your mother's slights. Slights based on no knowledge of me whatsoever. I am frank and unladylike, because it appears she respects such unseemly outspokenness. Please excuse me.'

Lady Isabella swept from the table with more regal majesty than Helena could ever aspire to. Just as she reached the entrance to the staircase which took her to her chamber, she called over her shoulder, 'Lady Mathilda, I wonder if you would do me the courtesy of keeping me company?'

With little choice but to comply, Mathilda followed, her mind full of the disaster that could be about to unfold in the hall.

Yet that wasn't what worried her most. If she wasn't there to call Merrick back to the table to request extra food or drink, who would ensure he kept away from his master's office?

Had Thomas completed his mission yet?

~ *Chapter Thirty-six* ~

Lady Isabella ripped the linen from her head. Black hair tumbled around her shoulders like an inky waterfall.

'That spiteful harpy.' Tears streamed down Isabella's face as she sat, knees tucked under her chin, her gown trapped under her booted feet. 'I had just managed to convince myself that life with William Trussell wouldn't be so bad. That maybe we could learn to like and respect each other even if there was no love. And then *she* has to interfere.' Isabella levelled an impassioned face to Mathilda, 'She *must* have killed Agnes. It had to have been her. There is nothing I have that Helena will not try to destroy.'

Anxious to know how Thomas was faring, Mathilda smoothed the knots from Isabella's hair with delicate fingers. 'Lady Trussell was as much to blame. Her eyes were on your sister as soon as she entered the courtyard.'

Isabella sniffed. 'It was Helena's idea that I wait by the fire. She persuaded Father it was better for me to be first seen warm rather than shaking with cold. I actually believed she was thinking kindly for once, but all she wanted was to make a favourable impression herself.'

Mathilda couldn't argue. 'William didn't look at Helena though, did he? He had eyes for you alone.'

Isabella gave her new friend a weak smile. 'You are kind

to say so, but what does that matter now? Lady Trussell rules that family. She will get her way, moulding her weak husband to her will.'

Asking a question which wasn't tactful in the circumstances, but that needed addressing, Mathilda said, 'Do I take it from your distress that you would now rather be with Trussell than Sproxton?'

The eyes with which Isabella regarded Mathilda were wells of sorrow. 'I've lost my friend. I've lost my man. At least if I married William I would be safe from my sister's spite.'

'Sproxton is not lost. He is delayed by a task beyond his control. You haven't answered my question.'

'I know,' Isabella moaned, 'You tell me that Thomas is on the King's business as he claimed. Yet I know full well from my life here that business concerning the English Crown is never over. He is chasing felons - I mean no offence to your husband, but how do I know Thomas will be alive tomorrow? I can't face another loss. The thought alone…'

Wanting to protest that Robert de Folville would never take a life he didn't need to take, Mathilda's tongue stumbled as an image of Eustace's solid frame came to mind. Could she be so sure of all her brothers-in-law? 'I am truly sorry.'

'There is no blame to you here. Now,' Isabella scrubbed her eyes with her sleeve, not caring that she might damage the delicate material, 'enough of this self-pity. How do you progress with the hunt for Agnes's killer? I must be useful or I shall go insane. Can I help?'

'You could assist me in clearing my mind. I can feel the answers prickling at my palms, but something eludes me.' Mathilda got up and went to the chamber's window. Built more for the circulation of air during the summer months than light, it issued a shrill draught as she stared into the fading evening. The woodland, which she knew stretched out behind the castle, was barely visible through the gathering mist, yet the forester's hut could only be half a mile away.

'I've just realised what has puzzled me the most about Agnes's death.'

'What's that?' Isabella joined Mathilda at the window.

'So far I've assumed that the murder was connected to the fact that the killer found out Agnes was due to leave the castle for ever, or that they knew she was due to join you at the hut before your own flight.'

'I don't see how. I told no one.'

'But did she, or Master Sproxton?'

'They swore not.'

Not mentioning that murderers lied by necessity, Mathilda said, 'If the killer did know about your imminent departure, then why kill Agnes in the Fire Room? Why not dispatch her in the forest? The body could have been disposed of in a manner that would certainly delay, if not prevent, it being found.'

Lady Isabella frowned. 'I agree, that makes no sense. Perhaps the person who killed Agnes had no idea of my plans and all this is coincidence?'

'Or they knew, but it was important to them that Agnes should be dead before leaving the castle.'

'Why?'

'I wish I knew. Merrick told me Agnes was in the Fire Room so she could prepare the room for me. Yet what if she was there for another purpose?'

'That room is hardly ever used; what possible reason could Agnes have for going there beyond lighting the fire?

And why would Merrick lie?'

'He had a fondness for her, so it's possible he lied to protect her.'

Isabella appeared surprised. 'Merrick had a liking for Agnes?'

'So he led me to believe.'

'I had no idea, I…'

'Perhaps Merrick knows of a reason for Agnes going to the Fire Room that he hasn't thought fit to disclose.' Mathilda suddenly stood up straight, 'I wonder…'

'What? What do you wonder?'

'I'm sorry, Isabella, but I feel it would be safest that you didn't know of my suspicion at this moment. If you'll excuse me,' Mathilda headed to the door, 'please, draw the bolt behind me.'

Leaving Isabella's stricken face behind, with the sound of the bolt being driven home echoing in her ears, Mathilda tucked her skirts up and ran along the corridor. *Why is this place always so quiet? It's huge and yet there are hardly any servants in the house, while the kitchen and stables are at full capacity - why?*

She stopped dead. *Are there so few guards and staff because it is vital that hardly anyone knows anything here? Did Agnes find something out? Does Bettrys know? I'm sure Merrick would if something big was going on...* A light sweat coated Mathilda's skin as she pressed her back against the stone wall.

Why hadn't she seen it before? A whole staff laboured behind the scenes, but just three - now two - staff served in the body of the castle.

Swallowing, Mathilda resumed her journey. Her brother-in-law must be away from the study by now. Ironically, the knowledge that she was unlikely to be spotted because hardly anyone walked the corridors made her feel less safe. What place could be more perfect for lurking in the shadows, and being up to no good, than a castle where no one patrolled to keep the residents safe from harm?

Thankful that Thomas had been given a room at the far end of the same corridor, Mathilda knocked on his door, uttering up a silent prayer to Our Lady for him to be inside.

Her brother-in-law had pulled her through the door and closed it again before she'd finished feeling relieved he was there. He looked harassed.

'What's happened? Did you see it?'

'I saw it.'

Picking up on his concern, Mathilda's forehead creased into a tight furrow. 'What is it?'

'You were right. The name was James Coterel. The document stated that he is the man who issued the arrest warrant on behalf of the Crown.'

'But, surely the King must know of James' own crimes.'

'Of course he does. James will have claimed that this denouncement of us and his own brothers is his way of making amends.'

'And the King would believe him?'

'James is very charming. It may be enough for the King that the new Queen believes him.'

Mathilda sat down. 'Do you think the warrant has anything to do with what is happening here, in the castle?'

'I didn't until I read more of the document.' Thomas ran an agitated hand through his hair. 'The arrest warrant wasn't news and there was no reason for de Vere to worry about you seeing it on the document. There had to be another reason to hide it if they feared you could read.'

Starting to feel impatient, Mathilda said, 'And the reason? Did you find it?'

'James Coterel has used Rockingham Castle's facilities, just as we and his brothers have in the past.'

Mathilda wasn't surprised. 'It is very easy to move around without anyone knowing you were ever here. It struck me as I was on my way to your room that only Merrick and Bettrys move around inside the castle. It is a big space; surely they alone can't run the whole castle beyond the kitchens? I can't think why I didn't notice before.'

Thomas nodded. 'The perfect place for a criminal to lie low with few people to ask unwanted questions.'

'And the document stated that James Coterel wants to stop that?'

'The document didn't mention that at all. And I suspect that, on the contrary, Coterel wants that state of affairs to continue.'

'But you said...? Isn't James trying to clear the criminals from the area to gain favour with the Crown?'

'On the surface, yes, but after the indictments levelled, the document goes on to say that should the apprehension of felons fail, James Coterel would take over the role of constable himself.'

Mathilda clapped her hand to her mouth. 'He knows it'll fail! He's counting on it.'

'Exactly. Then he can sweep in and take over. This is already a haven for felons passing through the county to evade justice. If James Coterel got hold of it...'

Mathilda suddenly recognised why de Vere was so keen to marry Isabella into the Trussell household. 'But the King said William Trussell may have the constableship if he marries Isabella.'

'And someone is trying hard to stop that happening, aren't they. Agnes is dead. What better than a suspicious death in a nest of felons to put off a marriage union with a well-to-do family?'

Mathilda concurred. 'De Vere has seen the document. He must have worked this out and knows that William wouldn't be constable if it came to light.'

'Unless the mission is successful. Which I presume is what de Vere wants.'

'But Coterel can't have known that Agnes was going to be murdered… unless someone in the castle is feeding him information. Or unless she was killed simply because James was determined for his warrant to fail as much as de Vere wants it to succeed, and ordered a death to ensure that happened.'

Thomas grimaced. 'I think you're right. Someone here has been very talkative. But whether they wanted to be, or whether someone made them talk, we can't know. Agnes may simply have got in the middle of all this by accident. Who is more disposable than a maid with a limp who was conveniently in a place that made her easy to be rid of? That would make some sort of sense, if it wasn't for the thefts.'

'Thefts?'

'After the indictments, the document details the rising number of thefts in the Rockingham area over the past three years.'

'No one has mentioned any thefts.' Mathilda headed to the fireplace, 'Apart from the hairbrush Lady Helena gave Bettrys and the jewels that had been Helena's mother's. But that's two items over a long period of time.'

'Two items that we know of. James Coterel obviously suspects there have been others.'

'Or he could have heard about the two thefts and insinuated or invented others to further his ambitions.'

'It's possible. But this place would be perfect for a thief

to lie low between committing their crime and selling on the stolen items.'

'You think *Agnes* was the thief?' Mathilda found she didn't like the idea - but how well had she known the girl?

'If she wasn't, she may have stumbled across someone living here who was.'

'Or found stolen goods.' Mathilda leapt to her feet again. 'The Fire Room!'

'What?'

'Agnes died in the Fire Room. Merrick said she was sent there to attend to the fire, but thinking about it, the fire was almost out when we got there. I thought she'd been killed before she began her task, but what if she never intended to tend the fire? She was already in her leaving clothes. Maybe Agnes had gone there to collect something?'

'Something that could have paid her way in London?'

'Come on.' Mathilda pulled the key for the Fire Room from her belt. 'Who else would have a key to that room, do you think?'

Thomas put out a hand to restrain Mathilda as she ran to the door. 'De Vere, Merrick, Bettrys, and possibly others. Is the Fire Room unguarded?'

'Bettrys said it was.'

'And what if Bettrys is involved? What will you do then?'

~ *Chapter Thirty-seven* ~

The wait until nightfall had taken for ever. Now, unhooking the Fire Room key from her belt, Mathilda squeezed it in her palm like a talisman. She didn't want to believe that Bettrys was involved, but common sense told her the maid had to know something. Even if it was knowledge she didn't want to have, or didn't realise she possessed.

Thomas had a theory which Mathilda feared was correct. Local thieves, rather than risking their freedom by selling stolen chattels close to home, delivered them to someone within these walls and were either paid for them, or were promised a portion of the money realised after their sale in far-flung parts of England. The castle was the perfect venue for such an enterprise. Felons came to Rockingham from all over Europe, not just from the local hundreds. Not only that, but there were markets and fairs and

Fairs.

Mathilda sucked in a sharp breath, making Thomas tap her sharply on the shoulder to remain quiet as they walked towards their goal. Swallowing her desire to tell him that Agnes had come to the castle after years of working the fairs of England, Mathilda kept moving.

Reynard would've been the perfect man to collect and carry stolen goods. He visited Rockingham at least twice a year for the fair. He could bring not just his tumbling skills, but any profit he'd made from objects sold on. But who would he be giving that money to? A scheme like this would need someone at its heart. A spider at the heart of the web to direct the flies.

The walls echoed with the emptiness of the dead of night, and Mathilda took each step as if she was about to be attacked. As they reached the sweep of the staircase to take them down to the Great Hall, Mathilda whispered, 'It must be almost midnight.'

'And our reason for being out of bed and together at this hour?' Thomas regarded his sister-in-law with an expression of amused affection. 'You do not care what people will think if they glimpse you sneaking around with me so soon after your marriage?'

Mathilda spun around on the balls on her feet, crimson with indignation. 'If they have such empty lives that they wish to think such a thing, then they are welcome to their idle speculation. I have a murder to solve!'

Thomas was solemn. 'But you see, Mathilda, people in a place like this often do have empty lives. The peasants work hard in the fields, their days and nights filled with so much toil they won't ever understand the notion of spare time. For tradesmen it's more or less the same, but those born to money and power... Take war away from the men and thrust sewing into the hands of intelligent women and you get boredom. Boredom leads to thinking. Thinking leads to trouble.'

Mathilda tilted her head to one side, unable to prevent a smile from crossing her face. 'Do you speak for us both in that proclamation?'

'I believe I do. Now,' Thomas took her elbow, 'we should move. I don't think these corridors are always as free from life as they appear to be. Let's move before our luck runs out.'

'If we keep to the walls we can cross the hall and reach the staircase that leads to the Fire Room without being seen. She pointed forward as they hurtled down the steps. 'But we either have to pass the entrance to the kitchen corridor or the main fireplace.'

Coming to halt at the foot of the stairs, Thomas sidled forward a few paces, his back flat to the stonework. 'The kitchen will be busy. Whatever the time of night, there is always the chance that someone will emerge. No one is currently by the fire, but many of the servants that serve in the kitchen will be in their cots behind the screens at the far end of the hall. Even though they must be well used to unknown souls wandering about the castle, I do not think it would be wise to disturb them.'

'But if we cross in front of the fire, our shadows will be sent streaking across the room.'

'Then we must move fast and take care in case any of the servants are paid to watch.'

Mathilda agreed. 'I'll go first.'

Glad that the light of the fire meant no candles had been lit on that side of the hall, so they'd remain mostly in the dark grey shadows that moulded around them as if they were part of the stone itself, Mathilda focused on nothing but reaching the opposite staircase. Quietening her breathing, she trotted forward on tiptoes.

With each step Mathilda became aware of sounds she hadn't registered before. The cracking of heated logs, the murmur of muted voices from the kitchen, the rush of the wind coming down the vast chimney. She could hear Cook, who Mathilda was beginning to think never slept at all, shouting at someone, and the scrape of metal on wood.

Snuffles from a few lucky servants lost in sleep wafted across the chilly air of the otherwise abandoned hall. The atmosphere felt eerie. As Mathilda reminded herself that she didn't believe in ghosts, the memory that both of Lord de Vere's wives had died in this place arrived in her head and refused to budge.

She couldn't hear Thomas, but Mathilda knew he was there because she could feel his breath on the back of her neck.

The fire was only two steps away. This close the heat, despite it being damped down for the night, remained fierce. It seemed so much bigger than it had before. In her imagination, Mathilda had crossed the area of hot projected light in three strides, but in reality it would take double that before she reached the shadows on the far side.

Staring into the gloom, Mathilda paused for a second, before lifting her skirts and running, with Thomas close behind her. The lick of the flames was intense, urging them to go even faster. Seconds later they were at the bottom of the staircase, the momentum they'd gained propelling them past the danger of being burned and discovered within the orange glare.

Not pausing to appreciate the staircase's stone-cold embrace, Mathilda raced up the twist of the stairs, her left shoulder so close to the wall that the material of her cloak rubbed against the limestone.

The key, which she'd been gripping so hard it had formed a pattern in the skin of her right hand, was in the lock of the door and had opened it before either of them dared take a proper breath.

'Lock it again.' Thomas waved a hand to the door as it closed behind them. 'Just in case.'

Mathilda did so, before pointing to the floor. 'There,

that's where I found Agnes. She was lying on her front, a dagger squarely between her shoulder blades. Her hair was loose around her shoulders. She wore her own clothes, presumably from her time with Reynard; not the apron and household tunic she wore around the castle.'

'The weapon matched the knives we saw in the foresters' hut?'

'Yes, and it was in deep.'

'One blow, you think?'

'There was very little blood, so yes. And it was neat and centred. I'm sure the killer must have been skilled with weapons and of a similar height to Agnes.'

'Or they bent down and just got lucky.'

'I suppose so. I've just been thinking the killer had to be like Agnes in stature.'

'And you may be right, but if they are skilled in the business of death they'd have known where best to strike for maximum effect. Or it may have just been a lucky accident, although I doubt it.'

Feeling as if she was in over her head, Mathilda began to search the room. The bed remained without covers and the fireplace was as she'd last seen it, unkempt, with the embers cold and grey, waiting for a servant to clean them up. But which servant?

'Thomas, you recall I was saying that there are hardly any servants here. The kitchen and stables are well-staffed and there are a handful of guards outside, albeit not as many as one would expect for a castle, but inside I have only seen Bettrys, Merrick, and, before her death, Agnes. Do you not see that as strange?'

Thomas flipped open the lid of a wooden chest, unfolding the blankets he found inside, not sure what it was he was looking for. 'I imagine the arrangement suits de Vere well. The castle is open to felons who come and go with little concern for their safety. He has no wife to appease. Providing his daughters have a maid to care of them and the ever-present Merrick keeps an eye on things, then de Vere can let the more dubious activities here go on with a clear conscience. If there is no one to see what is happening, then no one can speak out against it. And if de Vere doesn't know too much about his visitors, then all the better.'

'I can see the sense in that.' Mathilda peered up the chimney. 'I suppose Bettrys must be attending to Lady Isabella and Lady Helena now Agnes has gone.'

'And you as well.' Thomas frowned. 'That's not an arrangement that would work for long.'

'No.' Mathilda paused, 'I can't see Helena standing for it. Bettrys said she was to be Isabella's maid now Agnes has gone, yet I've seen no replacement maid for Helena.'

'If what you say is true, and Helena has alienated every maid she has had, perhaps none of the girls in the kitchen want that sort of promotion.'

'Would they have a choice?'

'Possibly not.' Thomas kept up the hunt for something that could prove or disprove his theory. 'Tell me more about this Reynard. What is the full nature of his connection with Agnes?'

'He was, or possibly still is if he survived fighting in Scotland, a tumbler who toured the fairs.' Mathilda reflected. 'I used to go to all the local fairs with my mother, but I don't recall seeing Agnes. Perhaps I was too young to remember. Anyway, he is, I'm told, the cruellest of men.'

'Aren't we all?'

Mathilda shook her head. 'I can't imagine you breaking a woman's leg and then leaving her alone in agony in that forester's hut we saw, unable to move, so that she'd starve to death.'

'He sounds delightful.'

'The breaking of her leg may have been an accident as they practised, but he still left her there. Bettrys and Merrick told me he was a harsh master.'

'And you say Reynard and Agnes used the hut in the forest?' Thomas paused and turned to Mathilda, who realised what he was about to say.

'The perfect place to leave stolen goods! Reynard may have started this. The Fire Room has nothing to do with it beyond being where Agnes died.'

Thomas nodded, but went back to searching anyway. 'Two people travelling on a regular circuit. They could have made contacts on the way. Agnes would have had no choice but to agree to do what her master commanded of her. Felons who came to Rockingham for sanctuary would pass close by the hut as they arrived or left convenient, don't you think.'

'So, if there was a ring of thieves, perhaps it stopped when Reynard went away? That would explain why I've heard nothing of any recent thefts and why we found nothing of value beyond the knives in the hut.'

'Or perhaps whoever is helping Reynard, or took over from him, is more careful than he was.'

Mathilda went to the window, staring out towards the woods and the invisible hut beyond. 'Merrick found Agnes. He was fond of the girl and she rejected him.'

'So you said.'

'But what if he wasn't? What if he was in Reynard's pay and only bid Agnes come to the castle to ensure she never spoke of his deeds. It is well known in the castle that Agnes rarely talked.'

'Merrick certainly sees everything that goes on.' Thomas's hand paused on the edge of a tapestry. 'There was something else in the document. Another name. It irks me because it's such a coincidence. I have never believed in coincidences.'

'Connected to Merrick?' Mathilda refolded a blanket which had been laid at the end of the bed waiting for a time when it might be needed.

'No. At least, not obviously.'

'Whose name?'

Thomas didn't reply. He was standing by the wall just to the left of the door, holding back a portion of the phoenix tapestry. 'Mathilda, I think you should see this.'

~ *Chapter Thirty-eight* ~

A rectangular gap in the wall, the size of a square building stone, was hidden behind the tapestry. The space hadn't been chipped out, but was smooth and clean as if it had always been there. It was too shallow to hold a candle or be used as a shelf. The space was completely empty.

'This is where a scaffolding post would have been wedged, to help support the castle walls during construction. Normally they're filled in afterwards.'

'An ideal place to hide things.' Mathilda helped hold back the heavy tapestry. 'If a stone block was pushed into the gap, it'd look innocent enough; just as if some masonry had come lose.'

'And being behind a tapestry means few people would look there anyway.'

Mathilda ran a finger around the inside of the stone hollow. 'Dust, but not stone dust. I don't think anything has been placed in here.'

Thomas examined his surroundings. 'Beside the door would be too obvious to hide something, perhaps.'

'Of course!' Mathilda ran her eyes around the Fire Room. 'There'll be another hollow opposite because the scaffolding beam would have spanned the whole room. I wonder...'

Kneeling upon the bed, Mathilda dragged aside another section of tapestry and was presented with the hollow's partner. 'There was something here, but it's gone. Recently I'd say.' Mathilda examined the line in the dust. Something soft, possibly a bag, had been tugged from the space. Again, she put a finger into the space and examined the specks of grit that stuck to its tip. 'Yes; stone dust.'

Dropping the tapestry, Mathilda excused the unladylike behaviour she was about to display to Thomas, and lay face upon the bed. She fished a hand downwards, between the bed and the wall. Her fingers closed around a piece of stone which she held up in triumph.

Placing it by the hollow, it was clear that, despite a few chips and dents, the block fitted perfectly; yet it wasn't quite big enough to fill the gap; leaving space for something to be hidden.

Returning to the bed, Mathilda fished her arm down the side of the bed again to see if there were other blocks in hiding. Instead, her fingertips met something else. Gingerly trapping it between her fingers, she pulled out an empty knife sheath and passed it to Thomas.

'Cheaply made.' Thomas held up the leather sheath, 'This is the sort of cover you'd expect to see house a forester's knife.' He started to flip aside each tapestry in turn as he said, 'I wonder if the killer threw it under the bed in panic, or if it usually holds a knife which is kept there to help ease the stone blocks in and out. If so, where's that knife now?'

As he spoke, Mathilda searched in and around the bed again. 'Wherever it is, it isn't here.'

Thomas found another hollow; this time with a carefully cut stone block still in place. The fit was so good that if he hadn't been looking for it, he might never have noticed the tiny alteration in the shade of the stone. Taking his dagger from his belt, Thomas eased the stone from its wedged resting place as Mathilda held the heavy tapestry up out of the way.

'Wouldn't a guest have found these irregularities in the walls?'

'Castles are cold even in the height of summer. Why would any guest move the very things that help provide a level of warmth and luxury? Did you move the tapestries when you were in here?'

'No,' Mathilda admitted. 'I just admired their beauty.'

'Precisely. If you weren't curious as to what they concealed, then no one else would be.'

'Are you implying I'm nosy?'

'Yes.'

Mathilda smiled despite herself. However, her grin faded as the block was removed and they found themselves confronted with a leather pouch. It had been pushed to the back of the alcove.

Opening the drawstring bag, Thomas emptied the contents onto the bed. A heavy necklace and a fine, polished looking glass, set in a carved wooden oval block, tumbled out.

'Oh no.' Mathilda picked up the mirror, flipping it over so she could see the carving properly.

'What is it?'

Stroking the fine workmanship that had gone into the wooden casing, Mathilda said, 'I have seen this pattern before. It matches the hairbrush Bettrys used on my hair.'

'She used it openly?'

'Yes.'

'Then it is unlikely she knew its partner was stolen. Too risky. More likely she considered it lost, or never knew the mirror existed in the first place.' Thomas picked up the row of polished stones which made up the necklace. 'This is valuable. Stolen from a lady of some quality I suspect.'

Mathilda's head snapped up from examining the glass. 'A necklace was taken from Lady Juliana before her death; Bettrys told me.'

'It appears our theory was correct. This has all the signs of a ring trading stolen goods.' Thomas shook his head. 'It has to be. Such things aren't so unusual, but I didn't know there was one here until now. Clearly James Coterel did.'

Mathilda blinked, her head was beginning to ache. 'He did?'

'The charges placed against his family are for the murders of two men. Those men were leeches. They ran a violent stolen goods ring in Derbyshire. Nicholas and John Coterel cleaned it up, with James's help. They removed the ringleaders and, I suspect, took over running the thing themselves.'

'But James was the one who set the warrant on his brothers. Are you saying he was involved in the same crime?'

'James kept his hands clean, but he was involved in its planning.'

'And our family?'

'The theft from the Leicester burgess was a retrieval of funds, stolen from a man of the city who had previously extracted that amount of money by more extreme means.'

'Did they give the money back to the people it was stolen from?'

'Don't mix my family up with the ballad heroes, Mathilda. Robert may favour the teachings of Robyn Hode's stories, but he is no hero either.'

'Robyn Hode doesn't give the money back. He just takes it from those who don't deserve it.'

Thomas laughed. 'So he does.'

Mathilda sighed as she looked at the beautiful tapestries

that hid so much wrongdoing. As the phoenix danced before her eyes, she said, 'Perhaps Robyn Hode *should* give the money back.'

'If Robert teaches you more letters you could write new versions of the tales. Extend Master Hode's good deeds one stage further.'

Mathilda shook her head. 'I can't see that making me very popular. Anyway, I'd like my favourite stories left as they are, thank you.'

Thomas grinned. 'I have no doubt Robert would be glad to hear you say so.' He pulled back the tapestry on the wall opposite. Another stone drew attention to itself by jutting out at an odd angle.

'Someone's been here, but was disturbed before they could finish the task.' Thomas set his dagger to work and a few minutes later he held a larger leather bag. This time however it wasn't neatly closed. A length of silver chain trailed from its neck. 'Some of this is worth a lot. At least we know now why Agnes died.'

'You think she spotted the ill-placed stone and curiosity made her pull it out and so she discovered this?' Mathilda picked up a silver bracelet. Its latticework was exquisite. 'Or was Agnes one of the thieves?'

'Part of this or not, I suspect she knew of the hiding place and came here specifically to take something to sell to ease her passage through life once she was away from here.'

'A huge risk.'

'If it had paid off, her life would have been more comfortable than that of a maid to a fallen lady and her gambler paramour.' Thomas waved a hand at the objects. 'We need to re-hide these while we consider what to do.'

Working together, they pushed the items back into the bags and placed the stones under the tapestries just as they'd been before. Mathilda flicked her pigtails from her shoulders as she worked. 'The necklaces; I wonder if one of them is the string Lady Helena wanted to find. It was her mother's.'

'I can't imagine anyone stowing such an item for any length of time. It would be worth too much not to sell on, and known too well here to be shown openly. More likely this is a temporary holding place. Thieves are paid to bring goods here, and then others collect them and sell them on for profit elsewhere. A necklace of quality would be taken somewhere it wouldn't be identified to get a better price. If Lady Juliana's necklace was stolen two years ago, then I doubt this is it.'

Mathilda was thoughtful. 'I'd like Daniel to take a message to Adam. Do you think he could get word onto our family and the Coterels?'

'Easily. Eustace's men are there to act as messengers. Can we get to Daniel's cot without going through the kitchens?'

Mathilda groaned. 'I don't know.' As Thomas dropped the last tapestry back into place, she asked, 'Why didn't the thieves move the stolen goods after Agnes had been killed?'

'Once the authorities had been and gone they probably didn't think it was worth the risk of finding a new hiding place. No one else was likely to go poking around in here. How delicious it must be to live with the knowledge that you are concealing stolen property in a room used by queens.'

An unpleasant suspicion crept over Mathilda. 'Do you think de Vere wanted me to investigate because he knew I'd find out about this, or do you think he's fearful that I would? If he knew about it, of course.'

'An excellent question.' Thomas picked a fleck of dust from the nearest phoenix, 'He gave you the maid Bettrys to attend to your needs, didn't he.'

'Yes. Which is odd. Bettrys is Isabella's maid. Surely if she was to serve two women it would be Isabella and Helena, not Isabella and me.'

'Maybe Lady Helena is being punished by her father for being so unpleasant to her staff.'

'If that's true, then that punishment alone may've been enough to encourage Helena to hurt Isabella by depriving her of a maid through murder. The stolen goods may have nothing to do with Agnes's death after all.'

Thomas shook his head. 'The dislodged stone shows that someone was disturbed in the act of hiding or stealing these goods. It makes sense that Agnes was caught in the act of theft here. The killer then stuffed the goods back quickly, but not carefully, after Agnes was dead.'

Mathilda wasn't so sure. 'The more I consider this puzzle, the more Lady Helena has the motive. Although the means escapes me.'

'Could Helena be behind the thefts? Women are becoming bolder by the day, so I'm told.'

Resisting the urge to stick her tongue out at Thomas, Mathilda said, 'She's too lazy. Although I imagine Helena would enjoy benefitting from such crimes.' Mathilda had her hand on the door to leave the room, when she stopped dead. 'Bettrys said Lady Helena had given her the hairbrush as a gift - a bribe - in return for her passing on useful information. I assumed she was after gossip and any news on her mother's jewels. Anything which could be manipulated by a bored and spiteful woman.'

'But now you aren't so sure.'

'Bettrys said she'd heard a man talking about a necklace, but she didn't know who he was. She told Lady Helena and was rewarded with the hairbrush that matches the looking glass we've just seen - presumably before the glass was stolen.'

'Or after it was stolen, and Lady Helena didn't care to keep something that was no longer part of a set.' Thomas wiped stone dust from the blade of his dagger. 'Do you think Bettrys could have lied about knowing who the man was?'

'If she was frightened she may have.' Mathilda sighed. 'When Robert told me to trust no one, he wasn't jesting, was he.'

~ *Chapter Thirty-nine* ~

'He has gone, my Lord.'

Ingram smiled. 'Thank you, Borin. Did he believe all you told him?'

'Enough not to risk staying.'

The sheriff thanked the mercenary, watching as he slid back into the night-time woodland that backed onto Ashby Folville manor. Only once the trees had swallowed up Eustace's man did he retreat to the comfort of his temporary chamber.

'Now we wait.'

Mathilda rested her back against the wall. She felt tired to the bone.

Beyond the curve of the corridor that divided them from the kitchen, she could hear Cook's husky voice biting off each word she spoke. Whoever was on the receiving end of her tongue was not to be envied. Thomas and Mathilda exchanged glances as they listened.

'What were you thinking? Didn't I tell you to take care? If ever there was a time when a little silence would have seen everything left well alone, this is it!'

The unseen target of Cook's ire sniffed, as if battling the urge to cry.

'Don't you dare weep! What use are tears? If you can't hold your own with your mistresses then you have no business in my kitchen.'

Mathilda was torn between wanting to dash into the kitchen so she could confirm her suspicions as to who Cook's victim was, and holding back in the hope of hearing more.

Thomas whispered, 'You create a distraction, I'll go to Daniel.'

Inclining her head, Mathilda, willing her racing pulse to calm, stepped from the cover of the shadows. Three strides later she saw Bettrys cowering below her superior's towering frame. Face lowered, the maid was wiping a work-worn sleeve across the back of her eyes. In two more steps they'd hear her. Cook might already have been aware of her presence. Mathilda wouldn't have been surprised.

'But, if Lady Helena wants...'

Bettrys's protest was curtailed by Cook's face transforming abruptly into plateau of calm, 'Why, Lady Mathilda, what brings you into my domain at such an ungodly hour?'

'Forgive me, but I have so much on my mind that sleep is evading me.' Mathilda pretended to notice the maid for the first time. 'You start early, Bettrys; or are you merely working late?'

Cook's eyes betrayed a flash of uncertainty. Mathilda knew she was wondering how much had been overheard. 'Lady Mathilda makes a good point. You'll be too tired to be of use to me tomorrow if you don't rest. We can finish our discussion in the morning. Off you go, child.'

As Bettrys dashed towards the hall, and presumably the cot that was waiting for her there, Cook turned to Mathilda. 'Would you like a little warm honeyed ale to ease sleep, my Lady?'

'That would be welcome. Thank you. I'm sorry I interrupted you. It didn't occur to me anyone would be here. I intended to walk through the kitchen to take some air in the courtyard.'

'I hear that air can be very beneficial.' Cook spoke as one who considered daylight a luxury item. 'If you have such a need again, you can get outside by going to the end of the corridor past Lord de Vere's office. It's a quicker route.'

'Why, thank you. Again you are most thoughtful.' Hearing the faint sound of retreating footsteps, Mathilda spoke a little louder in the hope of disguising Thomas's move towards the newly revealed exit. 'Don't you get tired? Working the hours you do must be exhausting.'

'I rarely sleep.' Cook spoke as if resting was for weaker mortals as she busied herself heating a jar of thickly honeyed ale. 'You must have concerns about your Lord Robert. I too would find sleep hard in your position.'

Thinking this was an odd thing for Cook to say, Mathilda agreed. 'I confess I will not settle again until we are a family once more.'

'You think that'll be possible?'

Not caring for the surprise in the question, Mathilda said, 'Of course. Don't you?'

'It is not my place to say, my Lady.'

'Yet you have said. You don't strike me as someone who speaks without reason behind an opinion. Nor can much happen within this castle that eludes your notice.'

'Little passes me by.'

'And you have reason to believe my husband's position is hopeless?' Mathilda's hands started shaking. She thrust them into the folds of her cloak to hide the tremors from Cook's knowing expression.

'I've no time for gossip, my Lady. I may hear things.

That does not mean I believe them.'

'Yet you sound convinced that Lord Robert and I will not be reunited.' Mathilda took hold of the table that divided them. Her head felt unpleasantly light. Until that point she'd stubbornly held onto the thought that they'd sort this out, but now the first firm seeds of doubt had been planted.

Cook pulled a wedge of dough for kneading nearer. 'The maids' gossip, the steward shares confidences, the felons come and go, feeling safe enough within my kitchen to speak more openly than they normally would. Even the King's clerk speaks freely here.'

'The clerk?'

'Garrick. Nasty little man. His Lordship despises him, as do many others. He only lives with all his limbs intact because both the old queen and the new one protect him. He's always barging in with word of their demands and desires, most of which are quite unrealistic.'

The Queen? Not the King? Unease swept through Mathilda. Cook was talking too much. Was she deliberately leaving no space in the conversation to avoid being asked questions? Taking refuge in Robert's advice to act like the lady of the manor, Mathilda spoke more sharply, 'His Lordship would not be pleased to hear you talking in such a way.'

'He would not, but although he keeps me to a strict rule here, Lord de Vere cannot prevent me thinking. Anyway, I know too much about the running of this place for him to risk letting me go.'

Holding in the gasp she felt gather at the back of her throat in the face of such confident audacity, Mathilda took the honeyed drink passed to her. 'You mentioned the gossip of the maids; do you think Agnes found something out that she wasn't supposed to? You said everything happens in this kitchen. If there was something Agnes accidentally overheard, then perhaps you could guess what that was?'

'I don't know what took Agnes to the Fire Room. Enjoy your drink, my Lady. If you'll excuse me, I have things to attend to.' Leaving the dough floured but un-kneaded on the table, the big woman sailed from the kitchen like a ship leaving port.

Mathilda was about to take a sip of the delicious-smelling drink when something stopped her. *What if it's been poisoned?*

Telling herself off for being fanciful, Mathilda couldn't shift the notion that Cook would be perfectly capable of killing Agnes. She was skilled with knives and her arms certainly held enough force behind them to dispatch someone with one blow, especially someone as lithe as Agnes...

She couldn't have done it. If Cook had left the kitchen someone would've noticed.

Bettrys. She had to talk to Bettrys. Deciding to let the girl sleep and find out what she knew in the morning, Mathilda put her untouched drink on the table and went to find Daniel and Thomas.

The second she stepped into the chill night air, a hand wrapped itself around her mouth.

Struggling, a muted Mathilda was dragged into the nearest stable.

There was no one in the hut. Thomas Sproxton had checked. Twice. With a dagger in one hand and a sword in the other. He'd also taken his time to study the immediate area to make sure it wasn't being watched by any enterprising guards or hopeful felons. Finally satisfied that he was alone, Sproxton tethered his horse in the forest a safe distance from the hut.

He was tired of playing to Wennesley's tune and now the sheriff knew he couldn't possibly have raped Helena because he was with Isabella, there was no point in staying to play official games. It was what else the sheriff knew, or may know, that bothered Thomas. Was Ingram fishing, or did he see the whole of it?

Either way, Sproxton was not going to risk hanging round to find out. Thankful that security at Rockingham was lax; hoping that would remain the case within the castle as well as without, he edged his way from the hut towards the castle.

Grateful that the moon had refused to shine, affording the protection of a gloomy sky, Thomas tentatively stepped out of the cover of the trees, and sprinted to one of the castle's secreted back doors. He knew there was a corridor leading from the side of the stable block to inside the inner bailey, so he could weave his way past de Vere's office and on into the Great Hall without being seen. After that he'd have to take his chances. At least he knew where Isabella's chamber was.

Increasing his pace, he reached the heavy oak door to the castle's side entrance. No one was there.

He could do this. He'd find Isabella. Then they'd go away together and never come back.

'Oh, for goodness sake!' Mathilda brushed off her brother-in-law. 'What did you do that for? You scared me half to death.'

'Well, I could hardly call out could I? The groom is patrolling the stables.'

'Daniel?'

'He's with the groom. We can't reach him yet.'

'Then we should go back inside and wait until morning.'

Mathilda froze as they reached the entrance of the loose-box they'd hidden in. A figure was running across the open ground and towards the corridor from which she'd just emerged. She knew him immediately.

'Sproxton!'

Her mind whirled. Was Sproxton here because his mission was over? Was Robert arrested? Was he even alive? Surely she'd have felt something if Robert had been stolen from her. On a subconscious level she'd know, just as she had when her mother slipped away after a lengthy illness. Mathilda had been in the orchard when her mother had left this earth. The world within her young heart had stilled while the external world had carried on, uncaring, oblivious to the pain that had wrought her body in two.

Robert is alive. *He is.*

Torn between following Sproxton to see if he headed to the Fire Room or was running towards Isabella, Mathilda felt the weight of responsibility clamp down on her.

Thomas de Folville had fewer qualms. 'Come on! We need to find out where he's going.'

~ *Chapter Forty* ~

'Is the High Sheriff expecting you?'

Gregory, the landlord of Ingram's favoured inn in Leicester, was not fazed by the commanding appearance of the two men who loomed over his bar. Nor was he perturbed that they'd arrived an hour before dawn. The downside of managing the sheriff's unofficial city residence was that he had to accommodate whomever the sheriff told him to, whenever he was told to. The upside of this arrangement was that the sort of men who came calling on Lord Ingram without an appointment were often big drinkers and hearty eaters, and the sheriff made sure they always paid their way. It helped that Gregory was not a stupid man. For this reason he kept a loaded crossbow under the counter. He placed a large hand on it now as the taller of the two men leant closer.

Nicholas Coterel's face creased into an unfriendly grin and placed a palm on the landlord's arm. 'I wouldn't reach for that crossbow if I were you.'

'I would never be so foolish in the company of a man who can see through a wooden counter, my Lord.'

John snorted. 'Respect and lies in one sentence. Ingram must have given you an inflated impression of your value. You have a name?'

'Gregory, my Lord.' The innkeeper tilted his head in the

direction of the back room. 'The sheriff isn't here. I don't know when he'll be back, but you can wait if you like.'

'Gracious of you.' John stared into the man's steady blue eyes. 'Aren't you going to ask us our names?'

'I was going to ask if you would like some ale.'

'A wise innkeeper, whatever next?' John gave a curtailed roar of laughter, before turning to Nicholas. 'Send Oswin to get word to Ingram. Tell him we'll wait for them here. *All* of them.' Refocusing his attention on Gregory, John Coterel said, 'We'll want beds for the night. Oh, and we aren't here. We are, as far as you're concerned innkeeper, completely invisible.'

'Just as you say, my Lord.'

Unable to sleep, Sarah had risen not long after she'd fallen into bed. The excitement of her forthcoming wedding wasn't enough to chase away the fears she felt for her adopted family.

Taking refuge in the art of baking, the Folvilles' housekeeper already had three steaming platters of fresh bread mixed, kneaded, rested, baked, and laid out on the kitchen table when Sheriff Ingram came into her domain.

'Good morning, my Lord.' Sarah bowed, holding up her floury hands to explain the lack of a proper curtsey. 'May I get you anything?'

'Perhaps some of your delicious bread. It never fails to lighten the day.'

'You are most kind, my Lord. Adam has the hearth giving a good blaze in the hall. If you'd like to go through I'll bring you some food.'

'No need. Your homely kitchen will suit me perfectly.' Ingram sat as Sarah cut a steaming loaf into several generous chunks and passed a piece to her guest. As he took a bite, spraying crust crumbs across the table, the sheriff declared Sarah's baking skills as perfect today as they were the first time he'd visited Ashby Folville several years ago.

Disconcerted, Sarah busied herself by clearing as much flour from the table as she could, while one of the most important men of the shire sat before her, giving her a look that could be interpreted as suggestive.

To Sarah's relief, the awkward moment was broken by the arrival of one of her other guests. Roger Wennesley, his face fresh from a brisk wash, his hair damp, stepped into the kitchen.

'Try some of Sarah's bread, Wennesley. There's none finer.'

For once not arguing with his colleague, Wennesley concurred. 'The Folvilles are fortunate indeed to have a cook such as you.'

Blushing, Sarah asked, 'Should I keep Master Sproxton's bread warm, my Lords?'

A voice from the doorway answered the question for her. 'No need.' Adam was troubled. 'A horse is missing. Master Sproxton has left us.'

Wennesley rounded on Ingram. 'Has he now. To Rockingham, do you think?'

'It would make sense.'

Wennesley frowned further. 'It makes no sense whatsoever. In fact it would be suicidal. Which is why I suspect that's precisely what he's done; Sproxton does not think with his brain.'

'A shame.' The sheriff gave a thin smile, 'Such a lack of self-preservation could have been useful at the final reckoning.'

Sarah and Adam wondered what the sheriff meant by that remark, but Wennesley was still talking.

'I bet he's gone for the girl. Well, I wish him luck. *If* he gets as far as London, he'll need all the luck he can get. They both will.'

Standing silently on the other side of the kitchen table, Adam and Sarah failed to keep the confusion from their faces. Suddenly the already meagre party in pursuit of their masters had been cut by a third. Adam took a chance and spoke what had been on his mind.

'Forgive me, my Lords, but does this mean that the men in pursuit of our employers now number just two? It is almost,' he hesitated, unsure whether to go on, 'as if you have no intension of catching them.'

Ingram stared at Adam shrewdly, but gave no direct reply. 'We will be leaving you today. After some discussion we have decided to leave the reverend here. He is safer with you than he would be if two of us tried to transport him to Nottingham Castle.'

'Yes, my Lord.' Sarah curtseyed simply because she didn't know what else to do.

'We are going to Lincolnshire. Should we be wrong about Sproxton and he returns, please bid him ride to Sempringham Priory.'

Adam nodded. 'I will prepare your horses.'

'Is Ulric not here to do that?' The sheriff levelled his eyes on the steward.

'Ulric has been visiting his family. He should get back soon.'

'Has he now? Well, I hope his trip was successful.' The sheriff held Adam's stare and for the first time the steward wondered if Mathilda's theory that the man could read minds was correct. Did the sheriff know Ulric had no family left to visit?

Sarah, unaware of the unspoken conversation going on

between her intended and the sheriff, waved a loaf in the air. 'I will prepare some food for your journey.'

Wennesley picked up the remaining bread. 'I will take Sproxton's loaf as well. It's far too good to waste.'

Oswin couldn't decide which direction to go in. Did he take the road towards Sempringham, or did he maintain his current direction and go on to the priory via a short detour to Ashby Folville?

His stomach growled, answering the question for him. He could tell Sarah and Adam his news, collect some food for his onward journey, and ride fast towards Lincolnshire without losing more than an hour. After all, what difference could such a short amount of time make?

Thomas de Folville stared at his sister-in-law as if she was mad. 'And what if Sproxton's lurking in the shadows and stabs you? You saw the knife in his hand.'

Mathilda was becoming impatient. 'And you know as well as I do that for every second we stand here arguing, Sproxton gets further away. We have to split up. I will run towards Isabella and you go to the Fire Room. He has to be going to one of those places and he is more likely to use violence away from Isabella than near her!'

Defeated by common sense and frustrated by lack of time, Thomas agreed. 'Before you go; the coincidence…'

'What, now?'

'The other name on the document. It was obscured by the ink.'

'What about it?'

'It was Stafford. Sproxton's real name.'

Mathilda didn't wait to hear more. All thought of staying in the shadows was gone as she ran through the corridor, down the stairs into the hall. Stafford? Why change your name unless you had something to hide?

As she reached the fireplace she remembered that Bettrys would be asleep nearby, or possibly awake behind one of the screens that divided the resting servants from the main hall. Diverting from her course, proceeding on tiptoes so as not to wake anyone unnecessarily, Mathilda peered through gaps in the screens until she found who she was looking for.

An exhausted Bettrys was sitting on the edge of her cot, her eyes red, her shoulders hunched over.

'Bettrys? Can you come with me?'

'Lady Mathilda?' Bettrys's voice shook.

'You haven't done anything wrong, but I do require your help. Lady Isabella needs us.'

At the mention of her mistress's name, the maid was on her feet. It wasn't until they were ascending the stairs to the family chambers that Bettrys asked, 'What's happened?'

'Has Lady Isabella ever spoken to you of a man called Thomas Sproxton?'

'I've not heard that name from her lips.'

Mathilda wasn't sure if Bettrys coloured because of the name or because she was tired and confused, as she asked, 'But you've heard others mention it.'

'Yes, my Lady.' Bettrys looked more frightened by the minute, 'He was accused of hurting Lady Helena, but Lord de Vere claimed it a false accusation. He was very angry with Lady Helena. I haven't heard Lady Isabella speak it of him though. Why do you ask?'

'I'll explain as soon as we've reached Lady Isabella.'

They rounded the curve of the family corridor. There was no one about. Mathilda felt tension seep from her shoulders as they faced the closed and locked oak door. 'Do you have a key, Bettrys?'

'Yes, but shouldn't we knock first?'

'Not this time. I do not want to wake Lady Helena or Lord de Vere.'

'But -'

'Please, Bettrys, trust me. This is for Agnes.'

That was enough for Bettrys. The key was taken from her belt and Isabella's door unlocked in seconds. Once inside the antechamber, Mathilda was relieved to see Isabella's travelling cloak and boots in their usual place.

Bettrys ran ahead to her sleeping mistress. 'Lady Isabella, Lady Isabella!'

De Vere's eldest daughter sat up drowsily. 'What's going on, Bettrys?' She realised that her maid was not alone, 'Mathilda?'

'Forgive the rudeness of our interruption. Thomas Sproxton - has he been here tonight? It's important.'

'Thomas? No, of course not. He's in pursuit of your husband, is he not?'

'He was.' Mathilda shook her head. 'But Master Sproxton is now in the castle. I saw him entering by stealth, but I do not know where he went. If he isn't here, then...' She broke off. 'Bettrys, I'm going now. You are to lock yourself in here with Lady Isabella. Do not think about leaving until I say it's safe to do so, even if that means a long wait. Do you promise?'

Isabella interrupted before Bettrys could reply. 'What do you mean, Thomas is here? You can't think he is a threat to us? To me?'

'Please, Lady Isabella. Trust me.'

'But...'

Bettrys looked from one noblewoman to the other before turning to Mathilda. 'I'll lock us in. But please, my Lady, be careful.'

~ *Chapter Forty-one* ~

Oswin was only a hundred feet away from the main gate when he became aware of another set of hooves coming up behind him.

Not sure whether to expect a friendly face or the sharp end of a sword, Oswin was heartily relieved to see the manor's youngest servant. 'Greetings, Ulric, what news?'

Surprised to see Lady Mathilda's brother again so soon, Ulric said, 'I bring a message from Lord Eustace's man, John Pykehose. Did you find the Lords Coterel?'

'I did.' Oswin's round face broke into a beam, 'We should go within. Sarah has been baking, if that delicious scent on the breeze is anything to go by.'

As their horses' hooves clattered across the courtyard, Adam appeared at the kitchen door. Sheriff Ingram elbowed his way past him.

'Ah, Ulric! Fresh from visiting family, and a well-timed visit from Lady Mathilda's kin.' The sheriff studied Adam's face as he added, 'How fortunate.'

The steward stepped towards the new arrivals. 'Perhaps we should go inside to hear any news they may have overheard on their travels?'

'A sensible and diplomatic suggestion, Master Calvin.' As Ingram waved a regal hand towards the kitchen, Ulric and Oswin tied up their horses and did as they were bidden. Sarah, who'd been in the process of passing Wennesley two pouches of ale, looked around in surprise as the messengers returned together. The sheriff appeared a little too knowing for her liking.

'Wennesley, let me introduce you to another loyal Folville servant, Ulric. And this is Oswin. Not strictly a member of the family. More an in-law. He's Lady Mathilda's brother.'

Ulric grabbed the bread Sarah offered him and addressed the sheriff. 'My Lord, forgive me, but I am charged to impart my information without delay.'

'Then give it, young Ulric.'

Still on his feet, as if poised to run for his horse the moment his message had been imparted, Ulric spoke. 'John Pykehose has sent these exact words direct from Lord Eustace. "Go back to Ashby Folville. Tell Borin to increase his vigilance over the manor. Report to Adam that we are safe and plan to stay here until prudence decrees otherwise."'

Then Oswin cleared his throat, 'I must add my message from Nicholas and John Coterel. It concerns all here, including you, Lord Sheriff.'

'Does it now? Go ahead, Oswin.'

'The Coterels await the sheriff, Wennesley, and his associate, as well as the brothers Folville, in the usual place in Leicester.'

Sarah paled as Wennesley snorted, 'They openly invited their pursuers to their side? What arrogance is this?'

'Arrogance you know well, Wennesley.' Ingram turned to Adam, 'Time to end this charade, then. Get the reverend from the storeroom.'

'But, my Lord…' Sarah sat down as she considered the prospect of Richard de Folville being free.

'He will not hurt you, Sarah, nor will he be staying here. The rector is our bargaining chip in case my assessment of the situation is incorrect.'

'And just what is that assessment, Ingram?' Wennesley growled.

'The same as yours. That when the King of England asked you to embark on this quest he believed it would either succeed, or that you would swing at the gallows for the murder of Laurence Coterel. But it isn't the King who is running this show. It's his queen. She dances to a very different tune, and there is more at stake than your miserable life.' The sheriff swivelled on the soles of his boots to face Ulric, 'Back to the priory with you. Tell the brothers they are to come to Gregory's place. No one will hunt them on the way. I give my word. Go now.'

As Ulric disappeared, his young face a picture of confusion, Oswin said, 'And me, my Lord? Shall I go and tell the Coterels you approach?'

'No, you can help us. Father Richard will require more than two men to transport him to Leicester if we aren't to lose him in the forest.'

Wennesley got up. 'Ingram. We need to talk alone. Now.'

On her way to the Fire Room, Mathilda stopped to bang on Lord de Vere's bedchamber door. Waiting no more than three seconds after hearing no response from within, she ran on.

She was at the door to de Vere's study in less than two minutes. Her fist rose to knock as Merrick swung it open.

'Can I help, my Lady?'

Until then Mathilda hadn't noted the steward's lack of appearance throughout the night. Now she was confronted with him, she saw it as odd. 'I need to speak to His Lordship. It's urgent.'

'It's very early, my Lady.'

'I did not ask for a comment on the time of day. I wish to speak to the constable.' Pushing past the steward, Mathilda found de Vere at his table. He was poring over the document Wennesley had spilt ink on. His eyes were squinting over the smudged section.

'It says Thomas Stafford.'

De Vere's head shot up as he realised he was no longer alone. 'Stafford?'

'The name you are puzzling over. The name Wennesley tried to obscure from view by knocking over the ink.'

Glaring at his steward for letting the girl disturb them, de Vere said, 'And how could you possibly know that?'

Not wanting to reveal that her brother-in-law had been poking around the rooms uninvited, Mathilda shrugged. 'As the sheriff warned you, I can read.'

De Vere held Merrick's clouded gaze as he spoke to Mathilda. 'And you are here at this hour because?'

'Because he is here. In this castle. Now.'

Thomas de Folville wasn't afraid of very much. He'd never have lasted as a Folville if he wasn't brave; so he knew it was no use cursing his stupidity. He'd been sure that Sproxton would be intent on his need to grab the treasure and get out again and so wouldn't be listening for anyone following him. He'd been wrong.

Sproxton had been kneeling on the bed when he'd arrived, the tapestry pushed to the side as he replaced one of the stones Mathilda had examined earlier. One glance at his pockets told Folville that the necklace and a few other trinkets were already stowed about Sproxton's person. Pulling his dagger from his belt, Thomas had taken two silent steps into the Fire Room.

Spinning round on realising he wasn't alone, Sproxton

had knocked Folville's knife flying from his hand. It still lay on the floor, where the amber stone in the handle shone, reflecting the light off the dancing phoenix.

Now, Sproxton's breath was assaulting Folville's nostrils as he slammed the intruder's body against the rooms curved wall.

'The ONLY reason I'm not killing you right now is that my life is complicated enough without having a dead Folville on the end of my knife.' Sproxton stank of sweat and ale as he gripped his captive by the throat. 'Take off your belt and hold out your hands.'

Folville didn't move, but as Sproxton waved the knife closer, he offered up his wrists, which were quickly bound behind his back with his own belt.

Thrusting his prisoner backwards on to the bed, Sproxton snatched Mathilda's key from his fingers and patted his bulging pockets. 'You're wise not to ask questions, Folville.'

'Why would I, when I already know all the answers?'

The door slammed and the key clicked in the lock; leaving a cursing Thomas to be the second unwary Folville brother to be trapped in a stone room in Leicestershire in less than a week.

'Bettrys. I asked you what was going on.'

The maid shook her head harder. Her pale face was blotched with pink and her eyes were heavy with frightened tears as Lady Isabella reached out a hand and bid Bettrys sit next to her.

'Come now, Lady Mathilda wouldn't have woken us in the middle of the night for no reason. This has to be to do with catching Agnes's killer. You want that, don't you?'

'Oh yes, my Lady, but...'

'But what?' Finding it hard to hang onto her temper, Isabella said, 'Bettrys, whatever is going on, I want to help. I can't do that if everyone carries on thinking I'm made of sugar.'

Clearing her throat, Bettrys muttered, 'I want to tell you, but if they find out, then...'

'Then what?'

'They might kill me too!'

'Who, Bettrys? Who might kill you too?'

'Whoever hurt Agnes!' Bettrys swallowed, her eyes brimming with tears. 'How do you know Thomas Sproxton, my Lady?'

De Vere's sword was in his hand in seconds, while Merrick pulled a knife that Mathilda hadn't even noticed he carried.

'Where?' Merrick spoke bluntly, his slate eyes glazed as he regarded the woman standing between him and the door.

Understanding in an instant that he already knew where, Mathilda said, 'The same place you'd go if you were him.'

De Vere's fingers gripped the hilt of his sword tighter and swung it round to point at his steward. 'What does she mean?'

Mathilda, feeling time ebbing away, snapped, 'Why are there hardly any staff inside the castle, my Lord? So few guards?'

'What? You are asking this now, when a wanted man is within my walls?

'Answer quickly.'

Thrown by the question, the constable wavered. 'Because of the nature of the guests. I am empowered - no, I am ordered - to entertain after the decree by the King's mother. We've been through this before.'

'And so you employ no one to patrol the corridors beyond Merrick and a couple of maids in case they put themselves, yourself, and the felon in question in peril. But now one of those maids is dead.'

De Vere opened his mouth to protest her impudence, but no words came out.

Merrick strode from his master. 'We have no time for this. If that man is here, we have to stop him.'

De Vere stepped past Mathilda, and held the tip of his sword to Merrick's throat. 'What do you know of Stafford? I've never mentioned that name to you.'

'I am aware of Garrick's messages, my Lord. He has a loose tongue when he visits the kitchen for provisions before leaving the castle.'

'Funny, that's what Cook said.' Mathilda looked grim. 'And you've made use of that loose tongue, haven't you, Merrick.'

'What are you saying, Lady Folville?' De Vere took another step towards the man he'd trusted most in the world. Until now.

'Merrick knows where Stafford is, don't you?'

'I've never even met the man!'

'Not knowingly, you haven't, and yet you are confident about where he'd head, aren't you?'

Mathilda wasn't sure why she was so convinced she was right, but the pallor of Merrick's face confirmed that she was.

'Well if you won't say, I will.' She swung around to face de Vere. 'What do you know of the name Stafford?

'A name I've heard, but not a man I've met. A brigand from London who passes this way sometimes. I've seen his names on warrants before, but I have never captured him.'

Mathilda felt panic rise in her gut. 'We need to get to the Fire Room before it's too late.'

~ *Chapter Forty-two* ~

Sproxton hesitated on the other side of the locked Fire Room. He had intended to go for Isabella; but if Thomas de Folville knew he was here, others might know too.

Keeping one hand on his dagger and the other over his overfilled right pocket, Sproxton sprinted down the corridor towards the stairs.

The stone of the castle walls seemed to give off a half-light, throwing shadows in conflicting directions as the dawn's winter sunshine tried to compete with the sporadically spaced candles that guttered in the breeze of so many ill-fitting shutters.

Comforted by the fact that none of Folville's brothers could be with him, Sproxton was breathing a little easier by the time he reached the foot of the stairs. Although Borin had told him that Ingram suspected who he was, that wasn't the same as proof. Plus, there had been no time for that suspicion to be passed to de Vere. Wennesley had told him of his quick-thinking accident with the ink well, smearing the name he'd given up using since the previous March. Apart from that once. And that hadn't been his doing.

Peering left along the corridor which led past de Vere's office and on towards the Great Hall, Sproxton saw no one. Heading right, he walked fast, not wanting to risk the echoing footsteps that running would make as the route narrowed towards his exit into the grounds and the safety of the forest.

His confidence grew with each step. In all likelihood Folville was arrogant enough not to have told anyone he was going to the Fire Room, too keen to boast the glory of capture for himself. *Typical Folville.*

There was still no one in sight and although he strained his ears, Sproxton heard nothing more than the distant echo of life beginning its daily round in the hall beyond. Perhaps Isabella would be in there now, having an early breakfast. If he turned round he could fetch her, and... *Too dangerous.* He would escape and then send word to her.

With a final peep over his shoulder, Sproxton opened the door to freedom; dashing into the crisp misty air outside.

A shadow detached itself from the castle wall.

'Good evening, Master Stafford.'

'Lady Folville.' Sproxton careered to a halt. 'So Folville was not acting alone. Well, no matter.'

He swung his arm up, but the dagger he held was halted mid-strike by a firm hand gripping his wrist and a heavy punch landing in the small of his back.

Sproxton dropped to his knees like a wet sack. 'I think you'll find it does matter.' Mathilda turned to de Vere. 'You'll probably find a selection of jewellery in his pocket.' Then she addressed their spluttering prisoner, 'The keys to the Fire Room please.'

'What keys?' Sproxton's question came out as a groan as his attempt to stand up was stopped by the constable's boot and the knife of his steward.

'The key you were given some time ago so you could get in and out of the Fire Room. Plus you'll have the key you took from my brother-in-law. You can give them to me or I can ask Merrick here to take them forcibly if you'd prefer.'

'On my belt.' Sproxton glared in anger at the tight-lipped steward.

'If you wouldn't mind, Merrick.' Mathilda gestured towards the prisoner. 'I don't think it would be seemly for me to rummage beneath a man's cloak.'

'Seemly?' Sproxton scoffed. 'Since when did you ever worry about that? You, who run with outlaws!'

Ignoring the barb, Mathilda took both keys from Merrick's fingers and stepped towards de Vere. 'My Lord, I believe my brother-in-law may be in need of my assistance. After I have checked on his wellbeing, I have some questions to ask your daughter.'

'My daughter? Not this wolf?' De Vere stared after Mathilda as she walked away, his mouth open, as she called back over her shoulder.

'I will talk to him in time. Oh, and I wish to speak with Merrick. About Agnes.'

Staring at the place where Mathilda had been, de Vere suddenly gathered his wits. His expression was a mix of begrudging admiration for the girl and revulsion at Sproxton's sprawled figure.

'Before I address this piece of scum,' de Vere bent down, picked up the protesting Sproxton's head by the hair and slammed it against the hard ground; knocking his senses from his body in one go, 'you, Merrick, can decide if you are going to help me or leave my service. Now. Through those woods, never to come back. I don't know what Lady Mathilda thinks you've done, but I will find out.'

'Yet you would let me leave?'

'You have been loyal to me for many years, so I'm giving you this one and only chance.' The constable levelled his eyes on Merrick. 'Stay to explain yourself and face the consequences, or pass me all the keys at your belt and leave now, without setting foot back in the castle.'

By way of reply, the steward stared at the fallen figure. 'As I told you, I've heard the name Thomas Stafford before. I didn't know that was him, though.'

'Does that mean you're staying?'

'It does, my Lord.'

Leaning down to pull a stand of precious stones from Sproxton's pocket, de Vere stared, caressing the stones in his palm. 'Did you know about this, Merrick?'

'That there were stolen goods in the Fire Room? Yes, my Lord. I have recently come to discover a lot of things I wish I did not know.'

'You didn't tell me.'

'I would not have been able to serve you further if I had.'

'Because?'

'I would be dead, my Lord.'

De Vere's complexion darkened further. 'Like Agnes?'

'I believe so.'

'Help me get this man to the dungeon. Then we'll go to my office to await Lady Mathilda.'

'Thank you, my Lord.'

'Don't thank me.' De Vere placed a booted foot on Sproxton's chest as he grabbed his steward by the throat, 'You will stay right in front of my eyes until I know what the hell has been happening in my castle.'

Mathilda's skirts rustled as she wove her way through the castle. The key was outstretched in her hand before she reached the Fire Room's door. Her heart thudded. The last time she'd arrived at this door alone it was to examine Agnes's body. What would she find this time? Not dwelling on the fact that there was a chance Thomas could be dead, taking comfort in the fact that there had been no sign of blood on Sproxton's dagger, Mathilda threw the door open.

Thomas de Folville sat on the edge of the bed; embarrassed and angry. 'For the love of Our Lady, whatever you do, do not tell my brothers I was overcome by such scum.'

Laughing with a touch of hysteria, bought on by relief that he was alive and unharmed beyond his pride, Mathilda undid Thomas's wrists. 'Just get that belt back on before your breeches fall down.'

'Is he captured?'

'We intercepted Stafford as he left the castle. I take it that's his real name?'

'It is. He had good reason to leave it behind.'

'I assume de Vere and Merrick are escorting him to the dungeon.' Mathilda surveyed the room again, in case it was willing to offer clues she may have missed before. 'I don't think either of them knew he was Stafford, although they'd both heard the name before.'

'Do you trust them to keep him captive, or will they be letting him go as we speak?'

'If I'd left him with Merrick alone, then I couldn't be certain, but De Vere appeared genuinely shaken that Sproxton was Stafford. I'm not sure he knows what Stafford has done here, but when I went to alert him to the situation he was trying to read the writing beneath the ink stain.'

'If I hadn't already suspected what I'd see, then I wouldn't have been able to work it out. Even now, it is events that have convinced me rather than the smudged handwriting.'

'You think Wennesley is involved in this?'

'In the thefts,' Thomas waved a hand around the room, 'I doubt it, although he may know of the ring's existence. No, I suspect his involvement is a pure and simple act of revenge. Retribution for the murder of Laurence Coterel, dished out by the clever and manipulative hand of the man's eldest brother.'

'You think Roger dances to James Coterel's tune.' Mathilda surveyed the room as she spoke. 'I think I'm beginning to see the pattern here.'

'How it all connects to Agnes?'

'Yes; but I don't think James Coterel arranged her death. In fact, it's her murder that has exposed the connection he was trying to keep quiet. One that is vital to the success of his scheme.'

Thomas rubbed at his wrists where the belt had dug into his flesh. 'What do you mean?'

Mathilda, still sure that time was running out, said, 'I will explain soon, but first, what happened to you? Was Sproxton here when you arrived?'

Picking up on her urgency, Thomas pointed to the tapestries. 'He was emptying the hiding places. I don't know how many he'd got to before I interrupted him, but his pockets were full.'

Mathilda lifted each tapestry to see how much had gone as Thomas asked, 'Where is Lady Isabella?'

'Locked in her room with Bettrys.'

'So, Stafford killed Agnes.' Thomas looked satisfied as Mathilda's hunt found an undisturbed hollow.

'I didn't notice this one when we came in earlier. It's almost invisible, but a dagger has been in forced between the stones. Looks like you disturbed Stafford before he'd finished.' She emptied a leather pouch of coins onto the bed. 'There are about twenty marks here.'

'A tidy sum to start a new life in London.'

'Much easier to transport and deal with than goods that would need exchanging. Ummm…' Mathilda examined the space in relation to the floor and the door.

'What is it?' Thomas surveyed the circular space.

'Agnes was lying on the floor facing towards where the money was hidden. I hadn't considered the direction she was facing before. There isn't that much floor space, so it didn't seem relevant, but what if she was after these coins? Presumably she put them there, so she'd have known where to head without having to make a lengthy search of the room.'

'And was interrupted before she got to them?'

'The attacker must have taken her by surprise. The dagger was thrust deep and she would've fallen fast.'

'You said she was found curled on her side?'

'Yes.' Mathilda closed her eyes, picturing Agnes as she'd discovered her.

'If the killer had hung around to check she was dead, you'd probably have found her rolled onto her back with the knife removed. I suspect they didn't bother to make sure they'd finished their work.'

'So they were either sure of themselves or hadn't intended to kill and left in fright after they'd done what they'd done.' Mathilda felt bile rise in her throat as she imagined Agnes in the midst of her death throes.

'Agnes must have decided to help herself to some money before starting a new life. It's a cruel irony that the man she and her mistress were due to leave with was the person who helped put the goods in here. Why did he kill her, though? If she hadn't seen him, she could just have had her wits knocked from her. Sproxton knew she was about to leave the area anyway.'

'It wasn't him.' Mathilda frowned. 'Sproxton couldn't have killed Agnes. It would be wonderfully neat if he had, but he wasn't here. I'm not sure he hid anything in here either. He just knew about it, and probably provided stolen goods to be hidden in the first place.'

Looking unconvinced by Mathilda's theory, Thomas placed the coins back in the bag and slid them into his pocket, then led them from the room. 'I want to talk to Sproxton, or Stafford, or whatever his name is.'

'*We* should. But first I want to talk to the daughters de Vere. Then we need to find out how much Cook knows.' They marched along the corridor with Mathilda playing the keys to the Fire Room through her fingers. 'Can you get word to Daniel? We should let the family know what's happening. I'm glad we couldn't reach him earlier now.'

'If you don't think Stafford put the stuff in the room then I bet he'll know who did. He isn't the sort of man who acts without someone pulling his strings.'

'You have a puppeteer in mind?'

'Stafford is not a wanted man in Leicestershire, but he is in London.'

'So why would he want to take Isabella there?'

'Because someone told him to, maybe.'

Irritated by Thomas's inability to get to the point, Mathilda said, 'And that someone might be?'

'James Coterel, of course.'

~ *Chapter Forty-three* ~

Sheriff Ingram was grateful that Daniel hadn't hung around to be seen by Sarah or Adam. The lad had followed Thomas de Folville's instructions to the letter. Imparting word to Borin, exhausted, he'd ridden straight back towards Rockingham. Seconds after receiving Mathilda's message, the mercenary had delivered word to the sheriff while the household remained busy in the manor and Wennesley had restlessly paced the hall.

Now, sat next to King Edward's chosen man, Ingram found himself tempted to tie Wennesley to a chair. 'For Our Lady's sake, Roger. Will you sit down! They'll be with us as soon as it is safe for them to ride out.'

'I still think we should be in Leicester awaiting them.'

'And we will be. But Ulric has barely had time to arrive in Sempringham, let alone deliver his message and help his masters gather themselves for the return trip. It is far more comfortable to stay here while we wait or do you want to be with the Coterels earlier than you need to?'

Wennesley sank on to a seat. 'I suppose you're right.'

Ingram suddenly got up again. 'Come on. I want to talk to you.'

'You just ordered me to sit down!'

'I wish to speak to you. I imagine you'd rather have this

particular conversation in private.

Walking through the courtyard, Ingram pointed towards the manor's heavy timber gate. 'A walk into the village will help us kill time while we wait.'

'It's freezing!'

'Then walk quickly.' Ingram was tired of his patience being tested.

Roger plunged his hands into his pockets, 'So, what did you want to say that couldn't be spoken about next to a roaring fire?'

'That fire, roaring or otherwise, has attendants who pay close attention to every move made within their walls.'

'They are but -'

'If you are about to dismiss Sarah and Adam Calvin as mere servants, then you are a fool. The Folvilles pick their staff with care.' The sheriff paused, watching Wennesley as he added, 'Just as the Coterels do.'

'Considering the lifestyle adopted by those families, they'd be mad not to be careful.' Roger didn't look at the sheriff, but keep walking the length of the tree-lined track towards Ashby Folville village. 'They probably have men in the trees too.'

Ingram, who knew very well that Borin and his company were indeed secreted between the trunks, waiting for when he and Wennesley left the manor so they could go back inside, said, 'They have learned to be cautious.'

'And you, Sheriff; have you learnt to be cautious?'

'Would I be in power if I wasn't? Would I even be alive? Now, tell me what you know of Thomas Stafford.'

Wennesley stopped moving. 'Ahh, I see. I wondered if you knew.'

'I did not know. Not until this morning.'

'How?'

'A messenger came from Rockingham while you paced so pointlessly.'

'Because of the document you thought Lady Mathilda had seen?'

'The very same.'

Wennesley's hand wrapped itself around the hilt of his sword. 'You approach dangerous ground.'

Ingram's gaze dropped to his colleague's hand. 'For me or for you?'

Wennesley's eye's narrowed, but he said nothing.

'I warned you that Mathilda was a capable woman. Lord Robert took her to Rockingham for two reasons. The first was to keep her away from us, so we couldn't force her to tell us where her husband is. Not that she knows, because Robert loves her too much for that. The second was to see if she could uncover why the family is currently under close scrutiny.'

'Why would Lord Robert expect that information to be at Rockingham?'

'Because the constable often deals with arrest warrants. De Vere is nothing more than a glorified clerk.'

'Still a long shot.'

'Either way, as soon as we went there and you flapped that warrant around in front of de Vere's nose in her presence, she began to think. To Robert, his wife's safety was his priority. But Mathilda has skills - and Robert encourages her to use them.'

Biting back the urge to rise against Ingram's implication that it was his fault Mathilda had seen the document, Wennesley said, 'And then she walked into a murder.'

'And more.'

'More?'

'Sproxton is there. Now.'

Wennesley shook his head at his friend's foolishness. 'So, he did go back to fetch Isabella de Vere. Stupid dolt!'

'A dolt, certainly, but I'm not sure he is the empty-headed gambler it serves him to make us think he is.'

'What do you mean?'

'Sproxton didn't just go for the girl. He went to collect the proceeds from a number of thefts that Lady Mathilda has found stowed in the castle. I imagine he was to take the goods to London with them.'

Wennesley scowled. 'Thefts, not gambling?'

The sheriff studied his colleague intently. 'You claim you did not know of Thomas's thieving?'

'I did not.' Wennesley shook his head. 'Fool! A way of paying his debts I suppose.'

'But you did know his real name is Stafford?'

'Of course I did. I was the one who advised him to change it.'

After Mathilda and Thomas had satisfied themselves that de Vere had their suspect in safe keeping, a yawn of unladylike proportions caught her unawares. Taking her firmly by the elbow, her brother-in-law marched her to the nearest empty chamber.

'Sproxton is safely locked in the dungeon and Merrick has allowed himself to be secured within his quarters.' Thomas pushed the door open for her. 'You will need to have your wits sharp if we are to unravel this knot further. A short sleep during the morning's early hours will make no difference to events now we have the culprit in custody.'

Mathilda hadn't bothered to protest that she still didn't think Sproxton was the culprit and, with only a small stab of guilt that she'd left Isabella and Bettrys for so long, had fallen asleep in the process of lying down. A sleep which was punctuated all too soon by a loud knocking.

Squinting into the sunlight that streamed through the crack in the shutters, Mathilda groaned, for however much rest she'd had, it wasn't enough.

The knocking grew louder as Mathilda scrambled out of bed, still fully dressed from the day before.

'Bettrys?'

As soon as Mathilda saw the maid, she guessed what had happened. 'Has Isabella gone?'

'Oh, my Lady! I only let her out because she begged to see her father. I couldn't refuse. She is the lady of the castle after all, and…'

Mathilda held up her hand. 'How long ago?'

'More than three hours.' Bettrys wrung her palms as she spoke. 'We needed food, so I thought I'd fetch some while she spoke to Lord de Vere and then we'd go back to her chamber together but...'

'So you walked with her?'

'As far as Lord de Vere's study. He thanked me and bid me rest despite it being a time when I should have been about my duties. I didn't intend to sleep, but the hall was so quiet. I didn't hear anyone come for breakfast.'

'No one?'

'It felt eerie. Like the castle was deserted.' Bettrys looked as though she'd aged a decade since Mathilda had last seen her. 'I was going to lay awake until Lady Isabella came back through the hall and join her then. But she didn't come. Then I heard his Lordship crossing the hall on his own, so I got up and went to Lady Isabella's room to check if she wanted some food, but she isn't there. I can't find her!'

'You definitely didn't hear her cross the hall before her father?'

'No, my Lady. I heard no one.' Bettrys stared at her feet as if ashamed, 'but I must have fallen asleep for a while, so…'

'I'm not surprised. I'm sorry I raised you from your rest earlier.'

'Where can she be?' Bettrys cried.

Mathilda tugged her cloak around her shoulders and slipped on her boots as she asked, 'Have you told Lord de Vere his daughter is missing?'

'No. I searched and then came straight here. I daren't tell him; he'll be so angry with me. Lady Isabella isn't in her chamber, the hall, nor anywhere I can think of.'

Foreboding crept over Mathilda like fog. Why had she allowed Thomas to let her sleep rather than check on Isabella? Had Sproxton somehow got out? Had Isabella persuaded her father to let her see his prisoner? Were they already running towards London and even bigger problems than the ones they were trying to leave behind?

As questions tumbled through her head, Mathilda wasn't sure which way to go first. Bettrys was looking at her expectantly, as if she should somehow hold all the answers. It took a hungry growl from her stomach to revert Mathilda to the practicalities of life.

'Go to the kitchen. Ask Cook if Lady Isabella has been there and collect us something to eat while we search the castle.'

Bettrys hesitated, her feet shuffling as if her body was wondering why her brain was stopping her from automatically carrying out the orders she'd been given.

Remembering the conversation she had overheard in the kitchen, Mathilda put a hand on the girl's shoulder. 'You're afraid of Cook?'

'I have displeased her. I didn't mean to, but… she is not

forgiving of mistakes and her mood is worse than ever today.'

'Do you know why?'

'Merrick has been helping His Lordship so she has to do even more than usual.'

Realising that word of the steward's confinement hadn't reached the ears of the staff yet, Mathilda said, 'There is hardly anyone to do anything for and yet Cook keeps working. I wonder…' Mathilda stood up straight. 'I want you to be brave for me, Bettrys. I need you to face her again.'

'But what about Lady Isabella?'

'We will find her. Please, trust me.'

Walking through the empty hall, Mathilda frowned. Bettrys hadn't exaggerated. If the usual hive of activity hadn't echoed out of the kitchen, then she'd have assumed the castle unoccupied.

'Why does Cook keep going when there are so few to provide food for?'

'She can never be sure when we'll have extra mouths to feed.'

'But if an important visitor was due, then wouldn't a messenger be sent first?'

'I suppose so.' Bettrys was more anxious than ever. 'I don't know.'

'When Cook was angry with you before, I suspect it was because you'd accidentally told Lady Helena something she wasn't supposed to know. Something you didn't know was a secret, and when Lady Helena asks you something I imagine it's hard not to answer truthfully.' Mathilda swallowed as she saw Bettrys' worried face, 'You told me that Lady Helena had instructed you to keep alert for word on her mother's missing jewellery. Was it to do with that?'

Bettrys stared in amazement. 'How could you know that?'

'I didn't, I guessed. What did you tell Lady Helena?' Seeing Bettrys so uncertain, Mathilda added, 'It could help Lady Isabella and Agnes.'

Rather than being reassured, the maid stopped moving, her face was a picture of panic. 'You think Lady Isabella's dead. That's why you aren't rushing to find her.'

'No! Not at all. I think I know where Lady Isabella is and that she's safe enough. But please, Bettrys, Cook has seen or heard something helpful to us, I'm sure of it. But she has no reason to trust me.'

'She doesn't trust me at all!'

'But if you went to her and explained your situation. Told her that you'd heard something, but were afraid to say anything for fear of upsetting her again.'

'Tell her what, though? I'm not sure what I did wrong last time?'

'Even better.'

Bettrys's eyelids were puffy and blotched. 'I don't think I understand any of this. You must think me very stupid, my Lady.'

'I think nothing of the sort. I think you're worn out and afraid.'

'Cook will dismiss me if I upset her again. I have nowhere else to go.'

'You can come to Ashby Folville if that happens.' Mathilda had an image of Sarah disapproving, but it was too late; she'd said it and found she meant it. After all, Ashby wasn't the only Folville residence. There was bound to be work for Bettrys somewhere.

'I could?' Bettrys's face lit up, the worries of the last twenty-four hours diminishing in her delight. 'Do you mean it?'

'I do. But, Bettrys, you have to tell me know what it is Cook thinks that you know, plus anything that's been going on here that is more underhand than usual.'

The maid wiped her palms nervously down her apron 'Well, ummm... fewer people have been coming to the castle lately.'

'Lord de Vere said he had discouraged visitors while he waited for the Trussells' visit. Plus, it must be assumed there were less people here because I've arrived. A Folville wife might hear things that could cause trouble later on.'

'The numbers have been dwindling since before you came, although they died off quicker afterwards. No offence.' Bettrys bobbed a quick curtsey to underline that she hadn't meant to speak out of turn.

Mathilda was thoughtful. 'It's as if someone has got a whisper of something and spread the word that this is not the place to be around for a while...'

Bettrys's cheeks went pink. 'You don't think the King's coming, do you, my Lady?'

'I doubt it. Perhaps his queen though. And perhaps her helper...'

An image of Nicholas Coterel's stately face came to Mathilda's mind. Thomas had said that James Coterel was more ruthless and far cleverer than his younger brother, a concept she found rather daunting. If James was behind all this, could Cook know and be preparing for his arrival? Could he have somehow convinced her that Queen Philippa was coming to Rockingham? Maybe that was it. Something as simple as the Fire Room needing to be stripped of its secret stash. If Cook knew about it, perhaps she had sent Agnes to do the job; but someone had interrupted and assumed the maid to be a thief...

Or maybe Cook knew nothing, and Agnes had been the thief after all. Or one of them. She'd had a rough start in life, and her master had been…

'Reynard!'

'I'm sorry, my Lady?' Bettrys's looked surprised. 'Agnes's old master?'

'Yes. I wonder…' Mathilda took hold of Bettrys's hands and squeezed them reassuringly. 'Do you really want to come and work for the Folvilles if Cook speaks against you? They are criminals too, even if their motives are often good.'

'I would. Unless Lady Isabella asks me to stay with her.' Bettrys's eyes dulled a fraction, 'Are you sure she's safe?'

'I'm sure I know where she is and that she's alive. The sooner we find out what Cook knows, or thinks she knows, then the sooner we can go and find your mistress.'

'I'll do it.' Bettrys peered into the shadows that led to the bend in the corridor which would bring them eventually to the kitchen. 'I could ask why I upset her and if she could explain the situation so I can be sure never to do it again. 'Cause I really don't know what I accidentally said or did.'

Mathilda beamed. 'You're a brave girl. Thank you.'

Watching the maid thrust her hands into the pocket of her apron and walk towards the kitchen, Mathilda stayed as close to her as the protection of the corridor would allow. Grateful that the castle's lack of staff meant she was unlikely to be noticed, Mathilda prepared herself to listen.

~ *Chapter Forty-four* ~

The furnace-hot air of the kitchen adhered to her skin like a tight-fitting tunic. Bettrys had always associated Cook's domain with heat, but now the searing temperature reminded her of stories her father had told when she was a child; tales of the Devil himself, boiling up human beings in the caves of Hell.

'Bettrys!' Cook's tone was brittle. 'Where have you been? Neither Lady Helena nor Lady Isabella have breakfasted yet.'

'I'm sorry. My Lord de Vere bid me rest after our broken night.'

'Weak! Such flaws will not see you improve your position here.'

'I'm sorry.'

'Sorry won't mend anything. Get on with your work before Lady Helena comes demanding even more of me.' Cook shook her head, muttering, 'I don't know, ladies of the house coming into my kitchen and issuing orders... Well, don't just stand there with your mouth open! Get on with your work!'

Perspiration dotted Bettrys' forehead. Only the prospect of Lady Mathilda's promise to get her out of the castle kept her from running straight to Lady Helena's breakfast tray.

'Please, Cook, I wondered... ummm, when you were angry with me before, what had I done wrong? I truly don't know. I don't want to make the same mistake again.'

Cook laid down the spoon she'd been rhythmically ploughing through a bowl of flour and butter. Her eyes screwed into tiny dots of suspicion, 'You're pretending ignorance on that matter?'

'Truly, I do not know my error.' Bettrys could feel her shoulders tremble as Cook's bulky frame loamed over her.

'Alright, seeing as you are in the mood for games this morning.' Picking the spoon back up, Cook recommenced the stirring; her palm gripping the utensil as if she could use it as a weapon if called upon. 'Lady Helena came in here. Into my kitchen! Twice now she's visited.'

'It's her family's kitchen.' Seeing this was the wrong thing to say, Bettrys added, 'I didn't invite her to come.'

'But you did, girl.'

'I did?' Bettrys murmured, hoping the tears gathering at the corner of her eyes wouldn't leak out.

Cook crashed the spoon against the side of the wooden bowl with a thud that made Bettrys wince. 'Do you recall what Lady Helena told you when she gave you the hairbrush you flaunt so widely?'

'Hairbrush?'

'Don't waste my time by pretending you don't know what I'm talking about. Your position here is perilous enough.'

Panic gripped Bettrys as words tumbled out of her mouth. 'It was a thank you for agreeing to tell her if I heard anything about her mother's missing jewels. She...Lady Helena, said I wasn't to tell Agnes about the brush, but once she was dead I thought... I'd assumed it was alright to use it. I thought I wasn't supposed to tell Agnes so she wasn't hurt that I got a gift when she didn't.'

'Thought? You didn't think at all. You used the brush in front of the Folville woman!'

'Her things were trapped in the Fire Room with Agnes and...' Bettrys paused before asking, 'How did Lady Helena know I had used her gift to brush Lady Mathilda's hair?'

'The outlaw wife must have told her. Now, enough of this! Get on with your work before you lose your position.'

Mathilda sat by the fire in the Great Hall. As soon as Bettrys finished her duties in Lady Helena's chamber, she intended to find her brother-in-law. Together they'd find Isabella. She was convinced the elder de Vere girl would be in the forester's hut; but whether she was waiting there for someone or simply taking time to think, Mathilda was less certain.

Cook's treatment of Bettrys had made her seethe. Mathilda knew she hadn't said a word about seeing the brush to anyone but Thomas. If Cook knew Bettrys had left the brush for her to borrow, then someone, possibly Lady Helena, must have searched Mathilda's new chamber and seen some of her telltale red hair caught in the bristles.

But why the search? If she'd been in her quarters, had it been the brush Helena was searching for, or was it a coincidental find? Why was it so important that Agnes didn't know that Bettrys had it?

Mathilda felt a rough pattern of events begin to form in her head; but until she had a few more answers, she feared she was being fanciful.

Agnes, rather than being hurt that her friend had received a gift when she hadn't, could have recognised the brush as stolen goods, or at least, as part of a set that was hidden in the Fire Room. Had she spoken about her discovery to the wrong person? Maybe that's why she died.

Whichever way she looked at it, Mathilda couldn't make Agnes completely innocent, however much she wanted to. It was working out what the young maid was guilty of that vexed her. Lady Helena was clearly involved somehow; but again, the why eluded Mathilda as she watched the hearth's flames dance like the phoenixes on the Fire Room's tapestries.

A room fit for a queen… There was no question that the hiding place was perfect. The curve of the room, situated as it was at the very end of the castle's corridor, made the wrap of the thick tapestries more important than ever, as the elements hit the outside of Rockingham's walls. It would be a rare visitor who wasn't delighted with the comfortable feel the chamber gave out as you opened the door. There was no reason to lift the tapestries to examine the stone behind. Only the builders and the maids, tackling the spiders who used the gaps between the hangings and the walls as a haven for their webs, would know of the cubby holes left by the scaffolding.

Mathilda watched as the flames dislodged a log from the top of the blaze, causing sparks to flicker across the grate. The question of Lady Helena's potential involvement perplexed her the most. That de Vere's second daughter had taken a single footstep into the kitchen didn't seem in keeping with the elevated importance she gave herself. To visit Cook alone, twice, seemed out of character. Unless Helena had only gone to the kitchen because she was bored and enjoyed throwing her weight around; which Mathilda conceded might be the case.

Her musings were interrupted by the arrival of Thomas de Folville and Lord de Vere.

'Lady Mathilda.' The constable appeared to have aged decades since she'd arrived at Rockingham. A stab of guilt assailed Mathilda. Wherever she went, trouble followed her. Sarah said it was nothing to do with her, and everything to do with the fact that she'd married into trouble that already existed. Here and now however, with only one Folville present, Mathilda began to wonder if she was cursed to carry ill tidings with her.

Thomas pulled out a chair. 'I recognise that look; you have this problem by the heels?'

'Possibly, but each time I think I see the way, I learn something that counteracts my theory.' Mathilda looked towards the kitchen, 'I'm awaiting Bettrys. We're going to find Lady Isabella.'

'Find her?' De Vere frowned. 'You mean speak to her. She'll be in her chamber at this time of day.' He ran a hand through his hair as he sat down. 'I need to speak to her too. We haven't shared a single word since Lord and Lady Trussell departed.'

Mathilda coughed. 'Forgive my boldness, my Lord, but if we are to cure the disease that currently plagues your castle, I require some answers from you.'

'Ask away, my Lady. If I can answer, I will.'

'First, I should tell you that Lady Isabella is not in her chamber. Bettrys has been searching the castle for her, but to no avail.'

De Vere was on his feet, 'Then we must search further, we must…'

Mathilda raised a hand, 'I am certain I know where she is. Although I can't promise her to be in good spirits, I'm sure she is safe. Please, trust me for while at least. It is vital, before I bring her home, that I learn all I can of Stafford, the man who calls himself Sproxton. I also need to know how the business with the Trussells was concluded.'

Only a firm nod from Thomas lowered the constable

back into his seat. 'Lady Trussell scooped up her family as if they were fledging chicks about to encounter a fox as soon as Isabella left the hall.'

'William had nothing to say on the matter?'

'He gave the impression of having plenty to say on the subject, but said nothing. Lord Trussell meanwhile did what he always does when faced with his wife's resolve. Absolutely nothing.'

Thomas de Folville snorted. 'So the proposed marriage is off.'

De Vere clawed his fingers through his hair. 'Nothing was said, but I would be very surprised if a messenger didn't arrive stating that very fact.'

Mathilda played with her wedding band as she asked, 'Would you consider marrying Helena to Trussell instead? That is clearly what Lady Trussell wanted.'

'And Helena,' De Vere sighed.

'No, not Helena.' Mathilda levelled her eyes on her host, wondering, not for the first time, how well he knew his children.

'But she as much as stated…'

'Lady Helena was, I'm sorry to say, enjoying making her sister's life uncomfortable. If William Trussell, who is clearly enamoured with Isabella, wouldn't be an innocent victim of the union, I'd say call Lady Helena's bluff and announce her betrothal to him instead. I imagine she'd be appalled by the suggestion.'

De Vere opened his mouth to protest, but quickly closed it again. Instead he said, 'You are sure Isabella is safe?'

'For now,' Mathilda mused, 'the fact the union between the Trussells and the de Veres is more than likely off will not be a relief to Lady Trussell alone.'

'I knew Isabella was not keen, but I hoped to secure her

future in the castle and '

Mathilda shook her head. 'You misunderstand me, my Lord. Lady Isabella had resigned herself to the role of Trussell's wife as the lesser of many evils. It was not her I was thinking of as the relieved party.'

'Then who?'

'I repeat my earlier question, my Lord: what do you know of Stafford?'

De Vere glanced at Thomas, who dipped his head in encouragement. 'Answer my sister-in-law, my Lord. It's vital to the future of Rockingham Castle.'

'Until today I knew nothing of him other than he was in the company of Sproxton and Wennesley when Laurence Coterel was killed. Rumour also said he was on the run from his home town after a string of thefts at that time. Now I find he was not present with Sproxton, but that he *is* Sproxton.'

Thomas de Folville clarified, 'Which means Roger Wennesley is also aware of this; the man who hunts our family and who gave Sproxton an alibi for the alleged rape of your daughter.'

This time de Vere was on his feet and striding towards the dungeon, shouting, 'I'll kill him! I will…'

Raising her voice, so that it echoed around the hall, Mathilda shouted, 'Sproxton did not rape Helena.'

Swivelling on the soles of his boots, his hands clenching into fists, his face like thunder, de Vere spat, 'And you are so sure because? You, who grew up a potter's child with no concerns but finding the next meal! What could you possibly know? Wennesley is clearly as big a liar as Sproxton!'

Thomas had bunched a fist ready to punch their host, but Mathilda had been prepared for it and caught his arm by the elbow before it could connect with de Vere's jaw. 'Yes, I am only a potter's daughter. You don't have to listen to me.'

Mathilda sat demurely waiting for de Vere to compose himself. He said nothing, but his countenance spoke volumes about his confused frustration and his fear for his children.

Continuing as if there had been no break in conversation, Mathilda said, 'I am sure, because at the time of Lady Helena's invented complaint, Thomas Sproxton was with your other daughter. Lady Isabella.'

~ *Chapter Forty-five* ~

'What?'

The colour drained from the constable's face.

'Please, my Lord. This isn't going to be easy to hear, but I beg you to listen.' Mathilda didn't give de Vere time to reply as she sped onwards. 'I need to speak to Lady Helena to confirm it, but I am afraid her allegation against Sproxton was not only engineered because she was jealous of the way he admired Isabella, as we believed, but because she was told to be his accuser.'

'Told to? By whom?'

'By Agnes. But she, you must understand was delivering orders from someone else. Who that someone was, I am less clear about.'

'Agnes?' De Vere rubbed his forehead as if willing himself to understand what Mathilda was saying. 'Why would a maid tell Lady Helena to do anything? And more to the point, why did Lady Helena agree? Doing what she's told rarely features within her character.'

'Because whoever it was offered Lady Helena something she wanted. Possibly her mother's jewellery, maybe more... much more, perhaps.'

Thomas's mouth dropped open, 'You don't mean marriage?'

'It is only a theory - but it would appeal to Lady Helena, would it not? A castle, lands, and a title; not to mention an open door into the royal circle.'

Shocked, Thomas whispered, 'Not him, surely? He'll never marry. The queen wouldn't allow it, I'm sure… there are rumours that -'

Mathilda held up a hand. 'There are always rumours, and at this time I suspect I'm adding to them. But it would fit, wouldn't it?'

'It would.' Thomas was grave.

Struggling not to slam his palm against the table in exasperation, de Vere barked, 'My steward is under lock and key and you tell me that Isabella is missing, but that she is safe. Then you say Helena willingly accused an innocent man of rape – but then, that the man she accused isn't so innocent, nor is he called Sproxton, but Stafford. Meanwhile, someone else, presumably in London, is planning to marry Helena to control this castle -'

'Almost, my Lord.' Mathilda's head thudded as she battled a wave of fatigue 'I believe the man in London has hoodwinked Lady Helena into believing he wishes to marry her. He has used her vanity, and the affront she feels at being a second daughter, to his advantage. That's why I'm sure: should you suggest she marry Trussell, Helena will be less than delighted.'

'But who would manipulate Helena like that? And what for? If they wanted the constableship of the castle, they could petition to marry Isabella. The King was already agreeable to that.'

'As I said, I have to talk to Helena to make sure I'm right, but, my Lord, you must know who we suspect to be at the root of this. You too have read the document Wennesley obscured.'

De Vere threw his hands up in the air in exasperation. 'The ink spill was an accident, I saw it happen. And it mattered little because the smothered charge was concerned with another part of England.'

'Yet you were curious, otherwise, you would not have taken the time to work out the wording beneath the rogue ink.' Thomas poured the constable some ale. 'There is no coincidence here. Someone, Garrick I imagine, made sure that the charges against my family and the Coterels appeared alongside the charge against Stafford. Did you not notice that the dates of the crimes are not chronological? You were supposed to make the connection, as, I imagine, was Sheriff Ingram.'

De Vere was resigned. 'And I suspect he did, whereas I... It confirms my thinking that it is time I moved on from this post.'

Mathilda spoke kindly. 'You were trying to arrange your daughter's future. Then suddenly you have orders from the Crown to worry about and a Folville wife arrives on your doorstep.'

'Nonetheless, I should have -'

De Vere stopped talking as Bettrys, accompanied by Daniel, crossed the hall. Mathilda addressed the lad. 'You bring news from home?'

'Ulric and Oswin have been playing their parts as messengers well, my Lord, my Lady. Your suspicions about the Coterel connection have been claimed probable by Lord Nicholas. Lord Robert, Ulric reports, is well.' Daniel gave Mathilda a smile as he went on with his missive. 'The assembled brothers agree that the charges laid against them must have been suggested by the same man and that the choice of Roger Wennesley as the hunter rather than the hunted is the sort of thinking that can only be applauded.'

Mathilda exchanged a solemn nod with her brother-in-law before she asked, 'And, now, Daniel? How did you leave the situation in Ashby Folville?'

'Lords John and Nicholas Coterel await Sheriff Ingram and Wennesley at Gregory's inn. Your husband, my Lady, and your brothers, my Lord, are to join them there. A council of campaign will begin as soon as they are together.'

Mathilda prickled with apprehension. 'Does Wennesley know we've established who Sproxton is?'

'I can't be sure, my lady. The sheriff knows. '

Thomas got to his feet. 'I must ride to Leicester. If the families are meeting it is vital I'm there too.'

'They are taking Richard with them.'

As Daniel delivered this last piece of news, Mathilda joined Thomas in a cry of disbelief. 'They're doing what? They'll lose him on the journey!'

Daniel didn't flinch. 'I knew you'd be less than pleased.'

Mathilda folded her arms across her chest as she regarded the young man who'd been a boy only a short while ago. The recent death of his friend, their steward, Owen, had seen him mature faster than she would have wished for him. 'Forgive us, Daniel; it is not your fault you had to impart worrying news.'

Thomas faced de Vere, 'I charge you to care for my sister-in-law. Listen to what she says concerning Agnes and Stafford. Robert will come for her soon.'

Mathilda felt alarmed. 'Why go to Leicester? What's the point of this meeting?'

Daniel spoke up. 'I was told that if that question was asked by you or Lord Thomas, I was to say that the underlying reason is to safeguard future plans.'

'I see.' Thomas was grave. 'If James Coterel wants constableship of this castle, then we have to stop him.'

'James Coterel! Dear God.' De Vere swore under his breath as Mathilda turned to her brother-in-law.

'What is it I'm missing, Thomas? Why would John and Nicholas want to prevent that? Surely it would increase their family's power?'

'It would. And it would also be the end of any tentative alliance between our families. The Coterels within our county boundaries would mean territory disputes and a local war for maintenance.'

'Lord James must know that.'

'I guarantee he does. Why else do all this?'

Mathilda closed her eyes, struggling to see the logic of what she was being told. 'Why would he want our families at each other's throats?'

'For fun. It would amuse him.'

Her husband's voice echoed at the back of Mathilda's memory. 'Robert told me that Wennesley likes playing games. It sounds as if he and Coterel would get on... Oh. I see, that's why Wennesley was chosen to hunt us.'

Thomas was increasingly troubled. 'Plus, if James gets hold of this castle, the possibilities are endless. He has influence in the Royal Court, an already established organised thieves' ring within these walls at his disposal, and the Folville family upon which to blame everything if his schemes go wrong. James wouldn't even have to give up his courtly life. He could install Wennesley to run Rockingham for him.'

De Vere looked more like a hunted man with every passing second. 'I applied to the King for permission for my daughter to marry a man who would be constable in my place. I sought to secure Isabella's position and to guide the castle away from the use that Queen Isabella had sanctioned for it. I thought King Edward would be pleased. That, in light of his pronouncements of cleaning up England, he'd welcome my suggestion.'

'And I'm sure he did. But King Edward has many advisors, and one of them has his wife's ear. That man, James Coterel, is ambitious and cleverer than any I've ever known.'

Thomas signalled to Daniel. 'Prepare my horse. I ride within the hour.'

As Thomas departed for the stables, Mathilda addressed her host. 'I'll be frank, my Lord, I need assurances that I can trust you. My instincts tell me I can, but I have learnt the hard way to have faith in few people. I ask you plainly: did you know of the use of the Fire Room as a place to hide stolen goods before you heard Merrick speak of it? Did you have even the slightest suspicion?'

'That someone was using the Queen's bedchamber in such a way? No. I swear on the lives of my daughters, that I did not. That crimes occurred here, yes, I did know. That's why I petitioned the King. I've had enough. It is hard enough to do my job without worrying about being implicated in crimes myself.'

'Which is why so few people work within or guard the castle? The fewer people here, the fewer eyes there are to see wrongdoing.'

'Or to get involved in that wrongdoing.'

Mathilda gave him an encouraging nod. 'I think I'm beginning to understand. Your method of ensuring that the felonies committed between those who take shelter here are contained amongst themselves has, in fact, become the opportunity that's opened Rockingham to a wider ring of crime. One that, if I'm right, has been in operation since before Agnes entered your service. When did her former master start lodging in the forester's hut?'

De Vere groaned at the implication of what Mathilda was saying. 'At least four years past.' He poured himself some ale. 'Reynard was a foul human being. Cruel to Agnes. You think he hid those things in my castle?'

'Not personally, but I think he's the hand at the rudder. Or at least he was.'

'But not now?'

'I don't know. No one seems to know what became of him.'

The silent figure of Bettrys, hovering near the entrance to the kitchen corridor, pulled Mathilda back to their more immediate problems. 'My Lord, there is much to do. If my family and the Coterels are joining together, then it is vital we act with haste.'

'You aren't going to wait for their help?'

Mathilda was horrified. 'I think we should endeavour to have as many answers as possible before they arrive. Do you want the castle full of Folvilles and Coterels ready to dispense their version of justice?'

'Dear God!' De Vere blanched.

'Quite. Now, I need to talk to Lady Helena. I would also ask that I can have use of Daniel for the remainder of my stay here. I wish to send him to check on Lady Isabella.'

~ *Chapter Forty-six* ~

Daniel hadn't been sure about taking Bettrys with him. His experience of females comprised entirely of Sarah and Mathilda; both capable women. Excessive displays of emotion were not something he knew how to cope with. However, he'd been impressed with how quickly Bettrys had scrubbed away her tears with the sleeve of her tunic once Mathilda had given her something practical to do.

Although distressed, rather than being of no use to Daniel, Bettrys kept her eyes open for trouble as they approached the tumbledown hut in tacit silence. They tiptoed over the icy ground, not wanting to frighten Lady Isabella if she heard them approach - assuming she was inside as Mathilda suspected.

It was only after examining the immediate area to make sure no one was lurking in the dark between the trees that Daniel allowed Bettrys to knock on the gnarled oak door. The result was an instant flinging open of that door and an expression of both disappointment and relief flashing across the occupant's face.

Lady Isabella, her raven hair lank around her shoulders, her uncloaked body heaving with the effects of cold, fell into Bettrys's arms.

Standing back, keeping to the doorway so he could

watch the trees as well as the activity inside the hovel, Daniel listened as the maid beseeched her mistress to go with them to the castle.

Her Ladyship however stepped further into the hut's shadows. 'I was told he was coming and I was to be here. He's late again. Has something happened to him? Do you think the Folvilles have killed him? Do you, Bettrys?'

Isabella's urgent voice spoke of desperation. Bettrys shot a confused glance at Daniel, who said. 'My Lady, the Folvilles are many miles away. Lord Thomas has left the castle to join his brothers. Only Lady Mathilda de Folville remains in Rockingham.'

'But she could have...'

This time it was Bettrys who answered, her voice unexpectedly sharp for a servant addressing her mistress. 'Lady Mathilda has been nothing but kind. Even now she has Agnes's killer in her sights. We must take you back to the castle. Please, my Lady.'

'But I have to wait here.'

'Wait for who, Lady Isabella?' Daniel peered over his shoulder as if he expected to see someone muscling their way through the woods.

'Thomas, of course.'

Daniel looked at Bettrys as he asked, 'Do you mean Thomas Sproxton, my Lady?'

'I -' Lady Isabella suddenly stood up, her previously hunched shoulders wrenched back, an air of defiance crept into her tone. 'It is none of your business who I'm due to meet, boy, nor where I choose to spend my time.'

Unease crept over Bettrys as she saw the look in her mistress's eyes. 'Please, my Lady, who told you to meet him here?'

The overriding theme of Lady Helena's chamber was opulence. Mathilda had the impression of being in the presence of someone trying to appear to be more than she was. Unlike the soothing pastel hues of Isabella's rooms, Helena had copied the feel of the Fire Room. The birds that danced across her scarlet tapestries however were not phoenixes, but peacocks, strutting and proud. Mathilda wondered how long they'd hung there and if whoever had been commissioned to make them had foreseen the child for the woman she'd become.

Lady Helena sat demurely, but her eyes sparked fire as Mathilda folded her skirts beneath her so she could take the offered seat.

'You wish to question me as if I'm a common felon.' The statement was spoken with a girlish lilt, but nonetheless it was laced with an accusatory tone.

'I wish to ask what you know of the recent criminal activity within the castle and if you know where your sister is.'

'My sister's life has been granted to her on a golden platter. She was born first and so has the right to the better marriage. Her mother was of nobler blood than mine, so she has more inheritance. Father hated her mother, yet he dotes on Isabella.'

Jealousy bubbled from Helena's throat as she went on. 'Every eye falls on her heathen black hair, yet she spurns all suitors. Until she is settled and married, there is no future for me.'

There was truth in that at least. Until eldest daughters were safely dispatched towards a future husband, younger daughters had little chance of being found a partner with a good position in life. 'She would have married Trussell.'

'She would not!' Helena spat the words out like shot from a sling. 'My sister's eyes roamed elsewhere. And she is welcome to him.'

'Welcome to whom, Lady Helena?'

'That is of no concern of yours.'

Mathilda realised Helena was enjoying believing she knew more than she did. 'Lady Trussell would have liked you as her son's wife, I think.'

'She would.' Helena preened her hair. 'She knows how to get the best for her son.'

'So you'll be delighted that your father is considering offering you as Lord William's wife instead'

Helena's expression fixed into a waxy smile. 'You must be mistaken. He would not do that to his precious Isabella.'

'I think you underestimate your father's regard for you, my Lady.' Mathilda watched horror light in Helena's eyes, just as she thought it would, but she had to admire the woman's grip on her composure. 'He paid heed to your words, as well as to Lady Trussell's preference for you as a match for her son.'

Helena folded her palms together as she studied Mathilda with the same begrudging scrutiny she would reserve for a dead rat. 'This is not a matter for outsiders. I must talk to my father.'

'Indeed. It is a family concern. However, I was sure you'd be delighted.'

'My delight, or otherwise, is none of your business.'

'My business is to discover how much everyone in this castle knew of a number of ill deeds. Deeds which led to the murder of the maid, Agnes. I am also charged with the task of asking you, again, if you know the whereabouts of your sister.'

'Isabella. I've never liked her; or her name.'

Surprised by this blatant statement, Mathilda replied, 'She shares her name with a queen.'

'Another woman with ideas above her station.' Lady Helena snorted. 'A wife should support her husband, especially when he is the King of England!'

'That's as may be, but Isabella de Vere, unlike Queen Isabella, was born to her station. She is the eldest child. You can wish all you like, my Lady, but that is never going to change. Unless…'

Mathilda felt an icy fear grasp her. She had considered Helena capable of planning Agnes's death but not getting her own hands dirty; but maybe she didn't plan it. Maybe she planned someone else's. Was Isabella the intended victim? How much simpler Helena's life would be without her sister in it?

'Unless what? Are you alright, Lady Folville, you've gone rather pale.' The enquiry lacked every trace of concern; more, it formed a pattern of words that one is meant to say. Everything about Helena felt as if it had been rehearsed. Mathilda was again reminded of the players at the fair, and therefore Reynard.

'Forgive me, I lack sleep.' Mathilda held her hand up to disguise a yawn which arrived as if on cue. 'I asked if you knew where your sister was.'

'You did. And I did not answer.'

'Will you?'

'I have no idea where she is.'

'You mentioned Isabella had a suitor in mind for herself. Who did you mean?'

'You're the one supposed to be finding out things, so why don't you?' Helena rose and opened the chamber door, dismissing Mathilda without another word.

Mathilda's pulse raced as her thoughts darted in conflicting directions. The situation was becoming ridiculous. She was supposed to be narrowing down suspects. Now it felt like everyone in this cursed castle could have murdered the maid.

She still couldn't imagine Lady Helena having killed Agnes; but what if her new theory was right and Helena had believed Isabella to have been the girl in the Fire Room? Maid and mistress were about the same height after all.

'No,' Mathilda muttered under her breath, 'Agnes's hair was red and uncovered, Isabella's is jet black. There is no way they would be confused... unless Helena had her eyes closed so she didn't see what she was doing - but then, she'd never have made such a good strike with the knife...'

Hoping her theory about Lady Isabella being in the hut had been right and that Daniel and Bettrys would have her safely on the way back to the castle by now, Mathilda hurried towards de Vere's office. It was time to hear what Merrick had to say.

As she passed back through the Great Hall, Mathilda's tired mind flew to Thomas de Folville. If he'd galloped all the way, he'd soon be on the approach to Leicester. Her feet moved faster. She had an uneasy feeling that if she didn't sort this out before the brothers all got together, there'd be further bloodshed.

Bloodshed that would result in an arrest warrant no one could talk their way out of.

~ *Chapter Forty-seven* ~

It gave no one particular pleasure to see the disgraced Rector of Teigh freed from his temporary prison at the manor. Bundled into the inn between Eustace and Walter, Richard de Folville, who was considerably thinner than when many of them had last seen him, was squashed in the midst of a trio of kin, Laurence bringing up the rear with his sword waving around like some sort of demonic tail.

The cleric, for once not verbose in protest of his treatment, allowed himself to be dropped into a chair near the fire, with Walter and Laurence remaining close by.

Robert de Folville, who'd never forgive his holy brother for the harm he'd caused Mathilda, felt a measure of relief that Richard hadn't been foolish enough to make a break for freedom between Ashby and Leicester. That would have presented them with another problem to sort out, and right now he wanted to be at home with his wife by his side.

Whatever Mathilda was doing, he hoped she was working to resolve the riddle she'd been presented with. One glimpse of Eustace and Nicholas told Robert that his wife's calming influence was needed here as much as it was in Rockingham.

The unexpected and hasty arrival of Thomas de Folville as dawn broke, his expression set with the importance of the news he had to share, pricked at Robert's sense of urgency.

He watched as Sheriff Ingram and Roger Wennesley, side by side, ignored each other in favour of speaking to Nicholas and John Coterel. They, in turn, were placed on either side of the law keepers. Robert wondered if this penning in of authority was a deliberate move by the Coterel brothers or just a coincidence that might prove useful. He bit back a grunt of derision. Of course it was deliberate. They were conversing politely, but then wolves were known to smile before they bit through your leg.

Robert could see Ulric and Oswin leaning against the door. Both appeared anxious as they fulfilled the dual duties of barring the back door of the inn to unwelcome interruptions and waiting to deliver messages they'd not yet received. His mind flew to Sarah and Adam back in Ashby Folville. Robert had wanted to see them on the way from Sempringham, but they'd all felt the press of time in Ulric's voice when he'd come to the priory, pleading for their urgent presence in Leicester.

'Let's get this straight.' Robert raised his voice against the hubbub of chat that has risen after Thomas had thrown his slingshot of information across the room. The group quietened on the instant. 'You can confirm that Lord James Coterel, from his position within the Queen's court, was the man who persuaded King Edward that Wennesley would be the perfect man to lead this warrant pursuit?'

Robert pointed to Wennesley, who sat, his expression blank, between Ingram and Nicholas Coterel. 'A warrant concerning the murder of two men whose deaths James personally sanctioned and a theft from the burgess of Leicester. Again, a crime we know the elder Coterel approved of?'

Wennesley opened his mouth, but Nicholas Coterel placed a palm over his neighbour's mouth, so Thomas could answer Robert without interruption.

'Yes, brother.' Unhooking his cloak from his shoulders, keeping one eye on the King's outlaw, Thomas addressed the assembly, 'a curious choice until you realise how disposable Wennesley is. Already known to the law as the killer of Laurence Coterel, if he failed in his mission he could be hanged for that death as a more fitting punishment. If Wennesley succeeded, he could be made use of again and again, until he finally failed came and the death of Laurence could be used as an excuse to get rid of him.'

Wennesley's face reddened as they spoke about him as if he wasn't there, but he wasn't foolish enough to swipe away Nicholas's hand. Not yet.

Ingram confirmed what many of them had thought from the start. 'A felon to flush out other felons. In Wennesley here, King Edward has his own outlaw dancing a familiar tune.'

This time Wennesley's palm slammed the table, drawing all eyes to him and causing Nicholas to end his muffling. 'I am no outlaw! No such status has been pinned on me. No threats have been made concerning my future safety if I do not capture you all!'

Eustace's laugh rumbled across the table. 'Well, here we all are, lad. Captured and ready to be corralled off to Nottingham. What are you waiting for?'

'I...'

'Let me guess.' Eustace's eyes narrowed, 'you never had any intention of catching any of us. You were never meant to. If one or two of this group fell into your net, then it would look good in royal circles, but active pursuit was never the plan.'

Wennesley shook his head ferociously. 'All you've done is describe how Ingram has been behaving; not me. The sheriff was appointed to help in your capture and all he did was delay me every step of the way.'

'Because, I think you'll find,' Robert de Folville interjected, 'our sheriff is not a fool, but he knows a foolish order when it comes his way. Even when it's from a king.'

'And who says this order came from the King?!' Wennesley's words were out before he could stop them. The moment he'd spoken he regretted it, but it was too late. The damage was done.

'Ah.' Ingram nodded at Thomas de Folville. 'So, Mathilda was correct and my own suspicions are confirmed. This was done in the name of the King, but not *by* the King.'

Wennesley tried to stand, but two hands grasped his shoulders, one from each of his neighbours, pinioning him to his seat as Eustace demanded, 'Thomas, what is the situation in Rockingham and what do you know of James Coterel's part in this?'

Wennesley slumped in his chair as Thomas launched into the explanation. 'Lady Folville has, with my assistance, pieced together two motives for Lord James Coterel's actions. Actions that have, whether intentionally or not, caused a death at the castle.'

Nicholas Coterel rose to his feet. Resting his weight on the table, he asked, 'Lady Mathilda is well?'

'She is.'

Robert's eyes flickered to Nicholas. He hadn't enquired about his wife's safety. It galled him that a Coterel had got there first.

'Good.' Nicholas tilted his head to one side. 'Two motives for our brother's actions, you say. Let's hear them.'

Thomas gave a humourless laugh. 'First, it will come as no surprise that Lord James remains ambitious and is, if you'll forgive me, my Lords, a most manipulative man.'

John snorted. 'Forgiven.'

'James has a position in the Royal Court and rumour tells us that he's become a favourite of the King's new wife, Philippa of Hainault. A short time ago, de Vere had a visit from King Edward's most trusted messenger, Garrick. From him, de Vere learnt that Edward is eager to rid the country of the remaining influence of Queen Isabella and her dead lover, Mortimer. The criminals allowed to flourish under their rebellious rule have acquired power and lands in quantities beyond which the Crown is willing to tolerate.'

A ripple of unease trickled around the table. 'I can't see James standing for the King implementing that ruling. He can't deny that we have benefitted from the recent upheavals,' Nicholas said. 'So what exactly are you implying, Folville?'

'I imply nothing. I'm telling you what Mathilda has pieced together. Only time will tell if her puzzling is accurate.'

The thud of a dagger being rammed into the tabletop drew all eyes back to Eustace. 'No one will interrupt again.' Tugging his blade from the oak, he used its point to warn each person in the room in turn to remain quiet. 'Thomas, get on with it!'

Refusing to be forced into tripping over his words by his elder brother, Thomas growled, 'For Our Lady's sake! Trying to explain something to you lot is like trying to extract a bad tooth! James Coterel made sure he was the man entrusted, by the new queen, to save the midlands from landowner felons. Men like us. Mathilda believes he also insisted that Wennesley took charge of the mission. That way he could ensure that the enterprise was unsuccessful. I suspect,' he looked at the sheriff apologetically, 'forgive me, my Lord, that it was James who also insisted Wennesley had your help because he knew it would not be in your interests, or the county's, to have the plan work.'

The sheriff's hands came together in a steeple as he rested his elbows on the table. 'Go on, Thomas.'

'To explain Lord Coterel's motives fully, I must tell you what else has been going on.' Pausing only to gulp down some ale, Thomas explained how Mathilda had found Agnes in the Fire Room. How, at first, it had been suggested that Mathilda was the target - but that it was soon evident that was not the case. Something else was going on in the castle.

'Like what?' Eustace's question was blunt as he continued to play his dagger through his fingers.

'Rockingham Castle is more than just a convenient place for the occasional felon to lie low. It is the centre of a web of deception and theft. A hiding place, not just for criminals, but for the proceeds of their crimes. It's clear that Rockingham has been operating as the hub of a stolen goods trading ring for years. Now someone who wasn't supposed to know about it has found out. That discovery has cost a life.'

'And my wife is there.' Robert was on his feet. 'Ulric, Oswin, with me! We ride to Rockingham. Now.'

'No, brother!' Thomas held up a placating hand. 'Mathilda would have you know more before you ride. There is a connection between these events, between our pursuit and the thefts. A name as important to this scheme as James Coterel.'

'And that name is?'

'Thomas Sproxton.'

'I'm coming to Rockingham with you, Robert.' The sheriff was on his feet as he stabbed a finger at Wennesley. 'Eustace, keep him here. He is not to leave your sight.'

'We should come too.' The elder Folville was far from

pleased at the prospect of being left out of the unfolding drama.

'And how would that appear? A horde of Folvilles and Coterels descending on Rockingham Castle? It would look like war!' Robert shook his head. 'If we are not back by nightfall tomorrow, then come. Ulric will join with us. Oswin will remain in Leicester with you, so we have a messenger apiece if we need one.'

Eustace shook his head. 'We'll ride to Ashby. We're vulnerable here. Ashby Folville will provide us with the back-up of Borin and his men.'

Robert approved. 'Word will be sent to Ashby if there's news to share.'

Thomas's forehead creased into anger as Ingram got to his feet. 'What know you of Sproxton that hastens you to ride with my brother, Sheriff?'

~ *Chapter Forty-eight* ~

Mathilda found the constable of Rockingham Castle sitting in the old guard room next to the dungeon. A solitary soldier sat on a chair next to the dungeon door. She judged the place hadn't had more than a token gesture of protection for years.

Dispensing with courtesy, Mathilda asked, 'Anything from Stafford?'

'Not one word since he was cast inside.' De Vere flapped a hand at the closed door behind him.

Mathilda knew they wouldn't be able to leave their prisoner for long if they wanted him to answer any questions. If the castle dungeon was anything like the cell in the Folville manor house, then the chill of such a place would be enough to rob a man of his wits. 'What news from Merrick?'

'Much; by contrast to that felon in there, he could not speak fast enough. I am left feeling played for a fool.'

'You are no fool, my Lord.' Hoping she wouldn't have to waste too much time massaging de Vere's bruise ego, Mathilda asked, 'What did you learn?'

'Mostly, that my steward is afraid. He refuses to say of whom, but I feel they must be close by.'

'I see.' Staring at her folded fingers, Mathilda said, 'I have been speaking to Lady Helena. She was, as I suspected, less than pleased at the idea of marrying Trussell in her sister's place.'

'She would see it as being second choice. That would not appeal to my daughter.'

'I think it was more that Lady Helena has another husband in mind. One who has, although not in person, promised her his hand.'

'You aren't continuing with that preposterous suggestion?' De Vere was on his feet, shouting out his humiliation. 'No man would dare insult my family by not coming to me on this matter first.'

'One would. Especially a man who has been using your daughter's jealous nature to his advantage.'

'You are convinced of James Coterel?'

Mathilda nodded. 'I will explain why as soon as I am sure of what I speak. But please, I must know what Merrick said.'

De Vere tilted his head to one side. 'You speak as though time is running out.'

'I fear it is.'

'Why? The felon is under lock and key. Isabella, you assure me, is with Bettrys and Daniel, while Merrick is cooling his heels in his room. The capture of your family was never my responsibility, so there is time yet.'

'With respect, my Lord, there is not.' Mathilda surveyed the solitary guard. He'd seen many summers and would be of little use in a melee. 'Stafford is a felon, but he didn't kill Agnes. Which means the murderer remains at large.'

'He must have killed her.' De Vere restlessly paced the room. 'Agnes was in the Fire Room and that was the first place Sproxton, Stafford I should say, went when he snuck into the castle. That's where he captured Lord Folville, and _'

'It wasn't the first place he went.'

'What do you mean?'

'When he went to the Fire Room for his property - at least, what he saw as his property - he'd already been somewhere else first.'

'Where?'

'He went to the kitchen.'

'The kitchen? But…'

Mathilda cut through is sentence, pleading, 'Please, my Lord. What did Merrick tell you?'

The atmosphere in the tavern's back room hung heavy with simmering retribution as the brothers made ready to leave.

Ingram's voice soared above the mutterings. 'You saw, did you not, Lord Thomas, the document Wennesley left in de Vere's room detailing the warrant for your family's arrest?'

'I did. It was normal enough. However, it did contain an entry which was out of date by over a year and which was beyond Rockingham's geographical jurisdiction.' Ingram tapped his fingers against the top of his cup. 'Mistakes happen, but not in this case. Not with the ink and quill in Garrick's hand. The man is a blight, but an efficient blight. He would only have made such a mistake if he was told to.'

Eustace growled, 'You know who forced this error from his hand?'

'I do not, but I suspect it was Lord James Coterel.' Keeping a careful eye on John and Nicholas, Ingram went on. 'If Wennesley had not spilt the ink over the document in his eagerness to conceal what was written, I'm not sure we would have attached any significance to what had been scribed above the order from the King to arrest your families for the combined crimes of murder and theft.'

Robert nodded. 'But because of the spillage, your attention was drawn to the damaged area of the parchment in case anything important had been concealed.'

Thomas de Folville agreed. 'The very act of trying to hide what was written there drew our eyes to it. Mathilda knew it was important, but she lacks all her letters so sent Daniel to fetch me.' Thomas watched every face in the inn as he spoke. 'The document confirmed that the arrest orders had come from James Coterel. The ink smudged order above it, showed nothing at first glance, except for the obscured name of Thomas Stafford. It meant little to both de Vere and me beyond the knowledge that we'd heard the name before. But it meant something to you, didn't it, Wennesley. It was only after you realised the implications of showing the document to others that the ink was spilt.'

Once again, the collective gaze landed upon Edward's appointed arraigner who grunted, 'Makes no difference whether it did or not. I received word from the Crown, I admit via James Coterel, to arrest known criminals. As you have already pointed out, I wasn't in a position to argue.'

'And you were told to include me in your quest.' The sheriff's tone remained calm, but light glinted in his eyes as he peered down his nose at Wennesley. 'But you were not ordered to rope in Sproxton. Not officially. So, did you pick him to assist because you value his help as a friend, or because you were given little choice? The man is a gambler, a petty thief, and, if rumour is to believed, a rapist.'

'That rumour can be discounted. The charge of rape was an invention. The thefts were real enough, though. Small trinkets to pay off old and forgotten gambling debts. But that is of no importance,' Roger waved a hand as if bating away a fly. 'I asked him as a friend. A reluctant friend as it turned out.'

'Reluctant because?'

'Sproxton was planning to leave the area.'

Thomas tapped the table as he replied, 'Running away, to be precise. With Isabella de Vere.'

'He's what?' Robert took a step away from the door and swung to face Wennesley.

Thomas laid a restraining hand on his brother's shoulder. 'He isn't running anywhere now. Sproxton resides in the dungeon of Rockingham Castle. Lady Isabella is missing and, if I may remind you, a maid is dead.'

Ingram's expression darkened, 'I'm glad Sproxton is held. Is he suspected of killing Lady Isabella?'

'Not when I left. I have no word on her situation. She may simply be afraid and in hiding.'

Robert repeated, 'And Mathilda is there…' But no one was listening.

Nicholas growled into Wennesley's face. 'You are known to be the murderer of our brother Laurence. You sit with us, alive, because it suits our purpose that you breathe. It also clearly suits James's plans. But we do not forget that Sproxton was with you when Laurence was felled.'

'In self-defence, my Lords!' The taste of panic hit the back of Roger's throat. 'A fact also well documented.'

'Knowing Laurence's short temper and liking for drink, that's probably true.' John was solemn, 'But such an occurrence would bond you and Sproxton. Taking a life leaves a stain that is hard to be rid of. He had no choice but to comply when you asked for help.'

Roger felt the shadow of the Coterels' combined bulk loom over him and gulped, 'We hoped… I hoped… that if we did the job asked of us, we'd be allowed to put the matter aside. That what happened would be forgotten, if not forgiven.'

'And that's why you asked Sproxton to help you? Because you always knew who your orders truly came from.'

Self-preservation took over from Wennesley's determination to say nothing. 'That, and to keep Sproxton out of trouble. If he's with me he can't be gambling; the source of his trouble.'

Robert threw his travelling cloak over his shoulders. 'Is there more to tell, Thomas? If there is, I think you'll have to tell me on the way. I'm leaving for Rockingham. Now.'

'There is much, but Mathilda can explain all. I will stay and share the story with the rest of our kin and follow later. Go with Ingram. Keep her safe.'

'I'm coming too.' Nicholas Coterel was on his feet. 'Do not think to argue, Folville. If my brother is pulling the strings here, I want to know the whole of this confusion, not just the part of it.'

~ *Chapter Forty-nine* ~

Robert de Folville had reason to be grateful to Nicholas Coterel. The man from Bakewell in had proved himself Mathilda's salvation in the past. Robert just wished he didn't talk about his wife with such gentleness. Nothing about Nicholas Coterel could ever have been described as kind until Mathilda had enchanted him.

Choking down the sharp taste of jealousy, reminding himself that Mathilda had shown Nicholas no sign of any liking beyond respect, Robert kept his mount close to Ingram's. With Ulric trotting behind, Coterel flanked the sheriff's horse on the opposite side. Should an outside observer have seen the party in progress along the Rockingham road, they could have been forgiven for thinking that the sheriff was their prisoner.

'Why do you think Sproxton left before this mission was over?' Robert asked as they followed the curve of the lane. 'He couldn't have known Mathilda had worked out who he was. He must believe Roger had hidden his real name with the ink or surely he'd have attempted to completely destroy the parchment, if he even knew it was on it.'

'Ah.' The sheriff reigned in his mount, slowing the groups pace.

'Ah?' Nicholas rubbed a hand over his beard.

'There have been all too many coincidences in this for my liking.' The sheriff chose his words with care. 'Remember, I was in the room when Wennesley shared the document with de Vere. I had already seen part of it before he spilt the ink. Not enough to understand the implication at the time, though. I had been concentrating on what we were supposed to see - the part proclaiming that James Coterel had, apparently, sold out his family.' Ingram raised a gloved hand. 'And before you growl at me, Nicholas, you know me well enough to believe that, rather than trust what I saw. I wondered what game he was playing. James likes games; as does Wennesley.'

'As does Sproxton…' Nicholas nodded. 'You spoke of coincidences?'

'Two established and locally respected, if feared, families are the target of an arrest warrant which focuses on two seemingly unrelated crimes which occurred some time ago. So, why now? Can it be a coincidence that it happened at the same time the constable of Rockingham petitioned the King to appoint another to his position, someone who can clean up the castle and provide a husband for his eldest daughter? It can't be; otherwise what reason is there for James to weave a plan round Rockingham Castle?'

Robert grimaced. 'James knew that you would be duty bound to look for us in Rockingham, Ingram. Even in London, the castle is known to harbour felons.'

'Even so,' Nicholas continued Robert's train of thought, 'my brother knows the venues in which we shelter in times of trouble. None of our safe houses are near Rockingham.'

'James knew his family was safe. He ensured there was a false trail for the Crown to follow.' The sheriff smiled without humour, 'And the only reason to include the specific crimes mentioned within that document was to make sure someone read them and saw their obscurity as a message. Someone in Rockingham.'

Robert peered into the trees that had started to thicken out at the side of the road. 'The same someone who, presumably, was supposed to see the entry about Stafford.'

'But how would they know that Stafford and Sproxton are one man? Nicholas frowned. 'Thomas is a common first name.'

Ingram kicked his horse so that it kept pace with his companions' taller mounts. 'And there was little enough to read once the ink was spilt.'

'But before it was spilt...' Robert stared along the road ahead, wishing them closer to Rockingham and Mathilda.

'Precisely my point.' Ingram was grave, 'I took a leap when Sproxton was with me in Ashby Folville. I mentioned to Borin that it would be interesting to gauge the reaction of Sproxton if it was suggested the man was not all he seemed. No more or less than that. Borin passed on this whisper. Within the hour Sproxton was gone.'

Without consulting the others, Robert urged his horse into a canter. 'Gone towards Rockingham! Where one maid is dead, Lady Isabella is missing and my wife is on her own apart from Daniel!'

'Stafford is under lock and key!' Ingram yelled after Robert, but his words were lost to the winter frost.

'Merrick told me he knew of the thefts, but it was only after Agnes's death that he discovered where the treasures were hidden.'

De Vere slowed his pace so Mathilda could to talk to him as they made their way to the steward's quarters. 'How did he find out?'

'Apparently rumour has been rife in the kitchen for a

while about Lady Juliana's jewellery being hidden in the castle.'

'I've heard that rumour floating around the castle from time to time, but it had just become one of those whispers without substance. Or so I believed.'

Mathilda pointed in the direction of Cook's domain. 'How often do you go in there?

'I rarely need to.' De Vere looked like a man who'd enjoyed many good dinners. 'Cook is not just an excellent provider, but she manages the castle's domestic affairs with a flair both my wives approved of. I find it best to leave her to her own devices.'

'Indeed.' Mathilda surveyed the hall as they crossed the vast space. 'Did you ask Merrick about Reynard?'

'I did. He clearly hated the man, although they can't have met more than a few times.'

'What did Merrick have to say of Agnes?'

'Little, beyond what I already knew, concerning how badly Reynard treated her.'

'You had no sense that Merrick was in love her.'

'Loved her?' He shook his head and immediately started to move faster, causing Mathilda to have to jog to keep up. 'Dear God, how blind have I been within my own castle?'

'Merrick hid his affection well.' Mathilda puffed as she forced her tired body into a run. 'Agnes knew though; she rebuffed him.'

Suddenly, much to Mathilda's relief, de Vere stopped again. 'You think Merrick killed my maid because she didn't return his affection?'

'It crossed my mind, but there has to be more to it than that.' Mathilda caught her breath. 'Where are his quarters?'

'Over there.' De Vere waved to a door near the far edge of the hall. It was of equal distance from the mouth of the short corridor leading to the kitchen, the door to de Vere's private work room, and the main entrance to the Great Hall.

'No wonder Merrick was always so quick to attend. His room is close to everything. Does he have a window overlooking the back of the castle?' Mathilda asked

'I suppose so. I've never been inside.'

'Never?'

'Until today I've had no reason to.'

Oswin patted the neck of his horse as it galloped down the main road from Leicester towards Ashby Folville. He was aware that the speed of his progress was drawing attention, but that was of little consequence. His only thought was to carry out his instructions to the letter. He was to warn Sarah and Adam that a small squadron of mouths to feed was on its way. Then he was to travel on to his father in Twyford and reassure him that Mathilda was well and as headstrong as ever.

At least, Oswin hoped she was.

Daniel and Bettrys sighed with mutual relief as they draped the tapestry curtain across the archway which divided the inner and outer parts of Lady Isabella's chamber.

It had been slow progress from the hut to the castle. Bettrys had held her mistress on one side, while Daniel had supported her on the other. Only the promise that Mathilda had unearthed Agnes's killer had got Isabella there. Once she was in her room however, lying on her bed, Isabella had fallen into an instant exhausted sleep.

Daniel whispered, 'I should leave. It isn't proper that I'm in here. I should find out if Lady Mathilda really has found Agnes's murderer. If not, we just lied to the lady of the castle.'

'For her own good.'

'Even so.' Daniel surveyed the antechamber. 'I always though rich ladies lived in splendour with more space.'

Bettrys smiled; her round face attractively pink with exertion. 'Space is cold, Master Daniel.'

'Just Daniel.' The lad found himself blushing as he hurried to the door. 'Stay with her. I'll get word of what's happening to you as soon as I can.'

Merrick was perched on the end of his cot. The room was all shadows and gloom; the only light came from the un-shuttered window, which afforded little in the way of comfort. These were the quarters of a man who only expected to be within its confines to answer the requirements of sleep.

The unlocking of his door, and the arrival of Mathilda and Lord de Vere, had disturbed nothing more than a few flecks of dust which stirred in the chilled air. The temperature was hardly above that which Mathilda expected Sproxton to be suffering in the dungeon.

The steward did not look up, but maintained his intimate analysis of a patch of grey stone flooring at the foot of his bed.

'Merrick?' Mathilda spoke gently. 'We need to hear the truth of this.'

The steward's complexion was as lifeless as the floor. Mathilda suspected he'd been crying, although would not have offended his dignity by asking.

'I know you had a liking for Agnes. You told me she did not return it and that you'd felt humiliated. Can you tell me when this was? When did you first tell her of your liking?'

'How can that be important now? She's dead.'

'She is. But nonetheless, I would like to know.'

'I thought I knew her, but now... what am I to think?

That she was a common thief dancing to her old master's tune?'

With a patience she was beginning to lose, Mathilda pressed the steward further. 'Why did you think you knew Agnes if you were not close? Why would you take the trouble to get to know anyone who had rebuked you?'

Merrick said nothing, but resumed his intimate study of the floor.

'Unless Agnes didn't reject you.'

De Vere crossed his arms as he leant against the closed window shutters, observing the silent steward. 'If you want to keep your position here, you must answer Lady Mathilda.'

'Why would you not dismiss me anyway, my Lord?'

'An excellent question. I may yet. But if you do not speak now, honestly, then I will hand you over to the sheriff. After that you'd have to take your own chances.'

Exhaling a gust of air, as if he'd been holding his breath for some time, Merrick grasped his hands, twisting his fingers together. 'The first time I found Agnes in the hut I assumed she was dead. Her breathing was so shallow that I almost didn't approach her; thinking to run back to the castle to summon the bailiff.'

Mathilda fought the temptation to rush him, glad that Merrick was talking at last.

'I was at the hut's door before I heard a cough rattle in her throat. She was so fragile, I thought… I thought I could protect her.' He gasped for air, before adding, 'I'd seen her before. Reynard was a regular at the fair and the servants often stopped to see him and Agnes perform their acrobatics when sent into Rockingham on errands. Sometimes, after Reynard had taken to using the hut while they were in the area, Agnes would come up to the castle and exchange pots or some other chattel for food.'

'Stolen goods?' de Vere interrupted, earning a black look from Mathilda and causing Merrick to pause for so long that she feared he wouldn't start talking again.

Finally the steward continued, 'They might have been stolen. I don't know. People often threw coins to them when they were performing. Sometimes people left bread or ale for them.' He paused, before adding, almost to himself, 'I had no idea Agnes was planning to leave the castle.'

De Vere looked at Mathilda, who shook her head urgently, pleading with her eyes for him to keep quiet until the steward had got to wherever his ramblings were taking him.

'You asked when she humiliated me, my Lady; the answer was more recent than I led you to believe. In truth I humiliated myself and in doing so… If I hadn't, she'd be alive!'

'Can you tell us?' Mathilda coaxed the distraught man.

'After I found Agnes in the hut, I tended her there, with Bettrys' and Cook's help of course. Then, when she was well enough to move, I brought Agnes to the castle. Cook agreed that she wouldn't survive if left where she was. Together, we bound her leg and cared for her. She recovered slowly, saying very little about what had happened. We guessed that Reynard had got her in such a state, with her leg broken and bruises littering her body.'

'Not an accident when practising then?' Mathilda felt sick as she considered all Agnes had endured during her short life.

'The leg might have been. The bruises were commonplace punishments for anything he felt like. Reynard drank when he gambled and drank more when he lost.'

A prickle of suspicion tripped across Mathilda's palms. 'A gambler as well. Did he know Sproxton, do you think?'

'It would not surprise me.'

'And if Reynard knew Sproxton, then Agnes probably knew him too…' Mathilda didn't add that Agnes may have also known his real name. Her mind flew to Lady Isabella, wondering if Daniel and Bettrys had got her home.

Had Agnes agreed to go to London to protect her mistress from a man she knew to be far more than he'd claimed to be? 'When Agnes had regained her strength, Cook was happy for her to stay on the staff here?'

'As I said, it was her idea. There was nowhere else for Agnes to go and we're always in need of new maids.' He turned to the constable, 'Forgive me for saying so, my Lord, but Lady Helena gets through maids quickly.'

Mathilda noted the sad inclination of de Vere's head as she said, 'But you were confident Agnes would cope with Lady Helena, because it was her habit not to speak and to obey without question. Two skills living with Reynard had taught her.'

'Yes. And she did please her new mistress for a while.'

'Until Lady Helena tired of the lack of compliments?'

'So I believe.'

'Merrick, time passes.' Mathilda crouched down before the broken man. 'My family and the Coterel family are, right now, meeting to decide what to do. They know that whatever is happening within the castle is mixed up with the warrants for their arrest. I urge you most strongly to help me uncover the truth of the murder before they arrive in force.'

De Vere urged his steward on. 'We have all suffered bereavement here, Merrick. Please tell Lady Mathilda what you know. Whoever it is you are afraid of, they have bigger worries now than you speaking out.'

~ *Chapter Fifty* ~

Sarah was rushing around so fast that she left a swirl of flour dust in her wake.

Oswin had ridden for Twyford as soon as he'd delivered his message, leaving the Folville's housekeeper and steward to prepare the manor for eight hungry, restless, men.

Disappointed by the meagre amount of information Oswin had shared, but hopeful that the arrival of so many of the family at once signalled the recent troubles was close to an end, Sarah laid jugs of ale upon the hall table while Adam stoked the fire.

'Do you think Lord Thomas will have told his brothers about our desire to wed?'

Adam picked a log from the fire basket and weighed it in his hands. 'I advise you not to use words like desire when we are alone in the house, Sarah.' He winked, turning his intended's cheeks bright red.

'Honestly!'

'Don't blame me! I had no intension of falling in love with anyone.' He balanced the log on the spluttering blaze. 'Of course, I'm not sure if I've fallen for you or your baking.'

Poking Adam's shoulder as he worked, Sarah grinned, 'I could say the same about you. One minute a starving outlaw, the next a hardworking, muscled steward of the manor... no wonder I lost my mind and agreed to marry you.'

Brushing his grubby hands together, Adam grabbed the housekeeper, kissing her firmly on the lips, before tilting her chin upwards so he could see into her eyes. 'How about we don't wait? Assuming Lords John and Robert agree, we could get wed the moment they get home.'

'I'd like that.' Sarah enjoyed a few more seconds' comfort in Adam's embrace, before pulling away. 'They'll be here soon if I know those boys. Once they've decided to do something there is no waiting.'

'You sound worried. Shouldn't we be pleased that things are righting themselves and they can come home?'

'I doubt very much they are righting themselves. More likely that Mathilda is righting them, with help I'm sure. But...'

'But?'

'When they are together, especially when they are in the company of the Coterels, the Folville brothers are liable to act without all the thinking required.'

'You are concerned they'll want to do something foolhardy?'

'Almost as much as they'll want my fresh bread and your ale.'

'Very well.' Merrick sat straighter, stretching his arms out before him. 'I will explain for Agnes's sake. But my Lord, please believe me, I never meant any disloyalty to this family. You must understand that I loved Agnes.'

'And she loved you.'

'She said she did, but...'

Mathilda spoke firmly. 'She did.'

A spark lit the corner of the steward's previously dull

countenance. 'It began when Reynard arrived with Agnes before they started lodging in the hut. I know little of the details of how Reynard's crimes first encroached on the castle, but as there's a relationship between Cook and Reynard I suppose it was inevitable.'

Mathilda encouraged Merrick as he confirmed her suspicions. 'Is Cook his sister perhaps, a cousin, maybe even a lover? Logic suggests a connection strong enough to risk imprisonment for. Something beyond greed alone.'

'I don't know; but they are certainly family.' The steward groaned, 'I had no idea Cook was sending the servants to visit Reynard's tumbling show so they could collect trinkets to be hidden in the castle along with the flour and meats we need. I thought she was rewarding their hard work with permission to linger at the fair. You will admit my Lord, the few servants the castle has work tirelessly?'

'With that, I have no argument.'

'The scheme must have worked, for once Cook obtained permission for Reynard to rent the hut in the forest while he was in the Hundred, the visits to the castle began. That was when I saw Agnes properly for the first time.'

The constable's resigned sigh rebounded around Merrick's gloomy quarters. 'It seemed a good idea to allow them permission to stay there. It earned me a little money. I never even considered… and I'm so used to felons that it has always been safer not to ask questions.'

Acknowledging the truth of what his master said, Merrick continued, 'Agnes came up from the hut, often with a money pouch or a gift of pottery. Only recently did I learn that the bags contained jewellery and the pots held items which could not be secreted so easily, and that they were not payment for supplies, but stolen goods to be squirreled away in secrecy.'

Keen to hurry, Mathilda said, 'So the stolen goods were hidden in the castle after Reynard took to renting the hut. Was it always the Fire Room?'

'I think so.' Ruffling his short hair through his fingers, Merrick reached the window in one stride. He stared out, perhaps thinking of the place beyond the trees where he'd found love.

'When Lady Helena dismissed the maid who tended to her before Agnes, I was told the girl had run away because she was afraid. I assumed it was Lady Helena's spiteful temper that frightened her. But just after Lady Mathilda came, Agnes was particularly troubled.

'She never did tell me what had happened to trigger her suddenly confiding in me, beyond that she couldn't keep the truth from me anymore. Agnes said the maid who fled had stumbled upon a terrible secret and had gone because of it. She told me she knew of it too. That was when she explained that the Fire Room, the room we keep for the Queen of England herself, was being used as a stock-house for stolen goods.

'After that, it all came tumbling out. How servants or passing felons delivered items which she would hide under her apron, and then place in the Fire Room when she tended to its hearth. I heard how Reynard had forced her to do what he ordered with threats of violence and how, after he'd gone, someone else had taken over his business.'

Merrick's head hung as de Vere struggled not to take his steward by the scruff of the neck, to reprimand him for not speaking of this sooner. 'I did not believe her. I told Agnes no one in this castle would stoop so low as to use the Queen's room as a thief's cache. I demanded she prove it.' His voice cracked as he added, 'And that must have been what she meant to do.'

Her voice a whisper, Mathilda asked, 'Agnes was in the Fire Room because she was fetching goods to prove she told you the truth?'

Merrick wiped a sleeve angrily across his eyes. 'Someone must have seen her, and...'

'Or someone overheard your conversation.' Mathilda opened the door to the corridor. It was deserted, but the sound of the kitchen staff clattering through their duties met her ears. 'Were you in here when Agnes confessed to you? Was the door open?'

'I... yes, in here. I don't remember about the door.'

'And this was when?'

'Just after noon on the day Lady Mathilda arrived.'

Mathilda nodded. 'I suspect someone overheard you. I'd put money on it if I was a gambler - someone who did not want Agnes to reveal the hiding place.'

De Vere's eyes narrowed. 'If that's the case, why isn't Merrick dead as well?'

Merrick closed the shutter. 'No point in my death, my Lord. Agnes was dead; another body would have drawn more attention to the event. Although I have been alert to the possibility ever since.' He lifted his cloak to show a dagger in his belt. 'I did wonder if they hoped the blame would be laid at Lady Mathilda's door.'

Mathilda nodded. 'I had the same thought. My arrival was most convenient. With my family background, who better to saddle with the crime?'

'I was threatened anyway, though.'

'Threatened?'

'A knife was left in my room.'

'Do you still have it?' Mathilda asked, 'How did they get in, are you not in the habit of locking your door?'

'I always lock it. No one had broken in.' Merrick pointed to his bed. 'It was lying just there. A forester's knife. Short-bladed, like the one I heard was found... in Agnes.' He shook his head hard. 'It was since taken from my room. I don't know who took it.'

De Vere frowned. 'There is no doubt it was a warning - but why should I believe it even happened when you can't show me the knife?'

Merrick stared his hands. All he muttered was, 'If I had believed her, she'd be alive now.'

'You can't be sure.' Mathilda spoke quietly, her mind making fresh connections. The knife sounded a match for those she and Thomas had found in the hut. 'When exactly did you find it?'

'Less than ten minutes after Agnes's confession.' Merrick closed his eyes as he remembered. 'She left here, I went to the kitchen, but I spilt some wine over my tunic, and so I came back here to change. That's when I found the knife.'

Mathilda nodded, 'Agnes knew too much to be safe. Such an end may have come to her in time anyway. Can you tell me who had keys to this room apart from you, Merrick?'

'Only Agnes; and, of course, Lord de Vere has one to every room in the castle.' Merrick roughly cleared his throat. 'It is not a surprise Agnes was keen to leave Rockingham when she was given the chance. She was so ashamed of what Reynard made her do. If only she'd told me before. It would never have occurred to Agnes that I cared enough to leave my home for her. I should have told her, should have...'

Mathilda looked at de Vere, 'We need to make sure your keys are where they should be, my Lord.' She was on her feet, 'Now.'

'You want to make sure this room key is missing?'

'I want to make sure that no other keys have strayed. I

presume there is a spare one to the dungeon?'

The three of them ran to de Vere's private room. Mathilda let out an audible sigh of relief when they found it securely locked. A moment later the constable rifled through a pile of papers and held up an extensive bunch of keys in triumph.

'Well?' Mathilda watched as each key was checked off on the laden ring.

'It's here.' He sagged onto his seat. 'Sproxton remains caged.'

'Is the spare key to my room there, my Lord?' Merrick brow furrowed.

Checking again, de Vere was soon holding up the associated key. 'It is.'

Mathilda's eyes narrowed. 'So the culprit stole the key to your room, unlocked it to put a knife on the steward's bed and then risked breaking back into this study to return it. Why take such a risk twice?'

Merrick shrugged in confusion, an incomprehension that increased when Mathilda suddenly smiled. 'Unless they didn't.'

'Didn't what?'

'Didn't break in anywhere.' Mathilda's brow furrowed as another part of the mystery slotted neatly into place. 'Agnes had a key to your room, you said. So she could be with you when no one was around?'

Merrick coloured, but agreed.

'She did love you then.'

De Vere hid his keys back beneath the chaos of his paperwork, 'Are you suggesting that Agnes left the dagger in Merrick's bed?'

'It was meant to frighten Merrick enough to keep him away from trouble.' Mathilda studied the muddle of parchments on the desk. 'Agnes was trying to ensure your safety. There was a knife kept in the Fire Room. I found an empty knife pouch, but no weapon. I bet Agnes grabbed it, and brought it here, before going back to get the proof you wanted.'

Mathilda was just about to ask de Vere if she could see the document he'd received from the Crown showing the charges against her husband again, when she heard footsteps running towards them.

'Daniel! Do you have Lady Isabella? Is she safe?'

'Safe, but confused. Bettrys is attending to her.'

'Thank Our Lady,' Mathilda, gave him a grateful nod before facing de Vere. She'd expected him to ask Daniel more about his daughter, but all his attention was on Merrick.

'Just now you said you hadn't known Agnes was planning to leave the castle. Where was she going?'

The steward's eyes lit up in surprise, 'Why, to London, my Lord. With Lady Isabella.'

~ *Chapter Fifty-one* ~

They'd arrived in a muted clatter of snow-deadened hooves. The sky, which had hung heavy with the threat of a blizzard all night, had broken first into a picturesque dusting of snowflakes, but know swirled with a thick fall of white crystals.

Rushing to take their guest's cloaks, Adam greeted the group with a combination of respect and wariness. He wondered why they huddled around one horse in particular, until he saw who sat upon it.

Richard de Folville was being returned to Ashby rather than sent on to Nottingham as he'd assumed. Adam met Lord Eustace's glare, ready to question him, but immediately looked away again. The expression on the senior Folville's face alone was enough to inform him this was not the time to ask questions.

After the rector was bundled into the manor, Adam spotted a figure he hadn't encountered before. It had to be Lord John Coterel.

Ensuring the horses were tethered and under cover, Adam rushed inside to help Sarah care for their visitors.

'Are you alright?' Adam whispered out of the corner of his mouth, as the housekeeper bustled around, placing bread on a series of platters.

'They brought him back.' Sarah's face was pale. Her hands were shaking.

'Where have they put him?'

'Back in the store. Borin guards his door.'

'Good.' Adam wrapped Sarah in his arms.

'Adam! We can't do this now.'

'We can.' He held her tight, feeling her tense frame against his chest. 'He's under guard. That man will never hurt you again. I simply will not allow it.'

Kissing his cheek, Sarah rushed off to the hall with some bread in one hand and a jug of ale in the other. The men were bound to be ready for some food, and anyway, she wanted to find out what was going on.

Thomas de Folville looked out of place sat at the head of the table, adopting the stance of authority that his elder brother, the Lord John, took on his rare visits to the family manor house. Uncharacteristically, not one person commented on this as Thomas beckoned Sarah and Adam to join them. 'As I began to explain in Leicester, Robert de Vere recently petitioned King Edward for permission to pass the constableship of Rockingham Castle to someone who would care for the area and who'd also be a suitable husband for his eldest daughter, Lady Isabella.'

Eustace frowned. 'De Vere is willing to give up the extra income harbouring felons has bought him?'

'If the wealth he used to make is still coming in, there is certainly no sign of it in the castle. Provisions are basic and the number of staff is minimal; although Mathilda believes the latter is because the fewer people there means the fewer to find out things they'd rather not know.' Thomas gave a half-smile at the knowing nods around the table. 'No, de Vere seeks a replacement to clean up the castle in the wake of Queen Isabella's influence, and to be a husband for his eldest daughter.'

'The position is not hereditary; does the King approve of his petition?'

Thomas acknowledged Eustace's point. 'It would seem so. De Vere approached Lord William Trussell on this matter.'

'Trussell of Hothorpe?' Laurence leant forward. 'A good choice. I'm sure he'd be glad to escape from that appalling mother of his.'

'Lady Mathilda would agree with that,' Thomas grinned. 'However, Lady Isabella is less than keen to marry William; although Mathilda believes she was beginning to come around to the idea. An idea which, unknown to her, was being subtly sabotaged by an unexpected source.'

'Stop teasing us with facts; spit it out, man!' Eustace's warning growl hurried Thomas to the point.

'As I said, James Coterel wished to get his hands on the constableship of Rockingham Castle. Once he had that, he could employ someone to run the place for him - someone like Wennesley.'

Every eye swivelled to Roger Wennesley. 'How many times? I have no knowledge of this!' Wennesley tried to rise from his seat, but was once again pinned in place by his neighbours as Thomas went on.

'Whomever James Coterel chose to oversee Rockingham, it would have to be a person who'd continue to run the place as a refuge for felons; but with more finesse than before.'

John Coterel thought before acknowledging the possibility of what he was hearing. 'Surely James would want to run the place himself?'

'And leave his life in London?' Thomas's eyebrows

rose. 'When he is having so much fun controlling people in comfort? I don't think so. And why weaken the control you have in Bakewell and its surrounds by asking you or your brother to move to the castle? No, James needs a puppet in charge. Someone he can to control.'

Unhappy with being referred to in this way, Wennesley protested, 'I am no one's puppet.'

Eustace burst out laughing. 'You preposterous fellow! You've been tied with string since this began. Can't you see you have been used? Finally, a bigger game-player than you has noticed how easy it is to flatter you into dancing their jig.'

Before daggers were drawn and blood spilt across her recently cleaned table, Sarah coughed, 'Please, my Lords, if I may ask a question?'

'What is it, Sarah?' Walter took a piece of bread from the nearest platter.

'What about King Edward?'

'What about him?'

'Does he know that Lord James Coterel has deceived him? Surely the King will notice when no one named on the arrest warrant comes to justice, even if he did leave the details to his wife and her advisor? When His Majesty learns that not a single Folville or Coterel has been delivered to justice, won't he pursue you in another way?'

All eyes fell on the sullen Wennesley. 'Well? What do you think he'll do?'

Wrenching himself free from his neighbour's grip, Wennesley stood up; his words simmered with indignation. 'How do I know? I received my orders and followed them. You don't even know that Lord Coterel is behind this. It is just guesswork!'

His hand dived for his dagger, but it wasn't there. 'What

the...'

Walter held it up; the blade glinted in the firelight. 'I'm rather respected for my sleight of hand. Didn't you know?'

Wennesley glowered as Eustace repeated Sarah's question, 'What do you think the King will do when he realises you've failed to catch even a single prisoner? More to the point, when he learns that failure was deliberate.'

'It was not deliberate! And I have no idea what he'll do.' His eyes flitted to the corridor which led to where the Rector of Teigh was held. 'But whatever it is, I'm sure it would be less explosive for all of us if one of you was in custody. Perhaps one whom not even you, my Lord Eustace, would miss?'

The constable's roar of anger was so loud that Mathilda was reminded of Eustace de Folville in a black mood. 'What do you mean? Agnes was intending to leave Rockingham with my daughter? Why would Isabella wish to leave? And to London? There is nothing for her there. No family and no prospects of a good marriage.'

Merrick looked frightened. 'I don't know, my Lord. I swear I didn't know Agnes was going either. Not until she told me of the Fire Room's secret.'

De Vere swung to Mathilda. 'You aren't surprised. You knew as well. Am I the only one in this cursed place who has been kept in the dark?'

Mathilda moved to the window. Snowflakes danced from the sky, dipping the temperature further as dawn rose. 'I knew, but I wasn't sure who else did. You must understand, my Lord; I have not been sure who to trust. I withheld information only with the express reason of finding Agnes's killer.'

'But you can't suspect me!'

'Why not? With all due respect, you manage a castle notorious for its felonious connections. It wouldn't be difficult for you to commit this crime and pass it off as someone else's.'

'I did no such thing!'

'I know that now, my Lord, but you must see I could not take the chance.' Maintaining her placating manner, Mathilda added, 'Not until I comprehended the entirety of the situation.'

'And now you do?'

'I think so.' Mathilda sighed. 'Which is as well, for I can see my husband, with Lord Nicholas Coterel, the sheriff, and their messenger, approaching the castle.'

Despite the circumstances, Mathilda couldn't prevent her smile as she saw Robert approach. His tall, lean body sat proudly, swathed in travelling clothes. As she watched, he brushed flakes of snow from his cropped hair.

'Daniel, please attend to your master and, with Lord de Vere's permission, bid him and his colleagues greet us in the Great Hall.'

De Vere, his expression locked in confused fury, agreed with a motion of his shoulders.

'My Lord,' Mathilda coaxed, 'we must act. Far better this business is closing as my husband and his companions come inside. No one wants them taking things into their own hands the moment they dismount.'

'You think Lord Robert won't listen to you?'

'Oh my husband will listen, as will Nicholas Coterel and the sheriff; albeit out of politeness, but I can't promise that they'll believe what I say.'

The constable was already at the door when Merrick asked, 'My Lord, do I stay here or do you wish me to assist you?'

'Stay there.'

'He should come.' Mathilda's contradiction sounded blunter than she would have liked, but the press of time weighed on her shoulders. 'And I think Lady Isabella and Lady Helena should join us as well.'

~ *Chapter Fifty-two* ~

Not running straight to her husband took effort. They'd only been apart for days rather than the expected weeks, yet Mathilda had missed Robert with an ache that reached her very bones. An ache she'd been forcing herself to ignore, for fear that missing her husband might become a permanent feature in her life.

'Ulric, it is good to see you. Perhaps you would like to wait by the hall door. There will be messages to carry, I'm sure.' Mathilda turned to Merrick, 'Please ensure Cook is at her station in the kitchen. Do not mention anything about what we've been discussing. It is enough for her to know we have visitors.'

With a muttered prayer to Our Lady, Mathilda picked up her skirts. Running towards the family corridor and Lady Isabella's quarters, she left an increasingly redundant and frustrated Robert de Vere by his fireplace waiting for his latest unwanted guests.

Bettrys broke into a fountain of words the second Mathilda called for the chamber door to be unlocked.

'Oh, my Lady, thank goodness! Lady Isabella, she is not herself. I can't get her to eat or drink. Nor can I warm her. Despite the roaring fire and the extra cloaks I've wrapped around her, her flesh stays like ice.'

Mathilda saw at once why the maid was so concerned. The lady of the house was sunk in misery. 'It's alright. Everyone's safe. It's alright.'

Rising from her seat, Lady Isabella flung aside both Mathilda's reassurances and the cloaks Bettrys had so solicitously placed around her. 'Alright? How is any of this alright? How dare you presume to tell me that?'

Isabella railed wildly. 'I was leaving. I had one chance to escape this place with the man I love. Who, for all his faults, I believed loved me too. And now he's let me down again, humiliating me in the process. Yet, I can't think that...' Her anger collapsed into murmured bewilderment, 'Bettrys said Thomas is held prisoner... Agnes's murder...'

Desperately clutching Mathilda's wrists, she sobbed, 'Please, please... tell me it isn't true. Tell me I didn't cause my friend's demise through my desire to get away and...' her voice dropped to barely above a whisper, 'to be with Thomas. He isn't a good man, but with my help, I thought...'

With a gentle squeeze of Isabella's hands, Mathilda struggled to know what to say. Having married a man with his own convenient interpretation of the law, she found she couldn't preach on the stupidity of falling in love with Sproxton.

'All I can assure you of is that Thomas did not kill Agnes. Of that, I am convinced.'

A hint of colour infused Isabella's blotched cheeks. 'You are?'

'He was too far from the castle at the time.' Watching her companion closely, Mathilda took a deep breath. 'Now, Lady Isabella, I'm going to ask you some questions and then, when you're ready, I need you to join me in the hall with your father and some guests.'

'Guests?'

'The hunt for Agnes's murderer is almost dealt with.' Mathilda glanced at Bettrys, who'd settled herself next to her mistress, 'but I fear that you are going to learn some things you would rather not know. For that, I'm sorry.'

Lady Isabella looked as if she was a lost child afraid to ask for help. 'What things?'

'I will tell you all I can in the hall, but first I have an important question. Who told you that Sproxton was going to meet you in the hut this time? It wasn't him, was it.'

Having been reassured by Daniel and de Vere that his wife would be joining them soon, Robert de Folville waited at the hall's main table with Nicholas Coterel and Sheriff Ingram. There were so many questions in his head that having to wait for Mathilda to deliver a clearer picture of what was going on was making him irritable. Beneath the shadow of what James Coterel had thrown over them, another matter niggled at his brain.

'When this is over,' Robert peered around, making sure no one beyond the immediate company could hear, 'we must act on that other business we have brewing. It has been put off too often.'

Nicholas inclined his head. 'The delays we've endured during the last year, although unavoidable, have been aggravating and costly.'

'Costly in lives as well as time.' Ingram's eyebrows knotted in concentration. 'A merchant was found hanging in Nottingham last week. He died by his own hand after being taken for nearly everything he had, including his reputation.'

Robert shook his head. 'Damn my Holy brother! If Richard hadn't been hell bent on humiliating me and hurting

Mathilda and Sarah, we could have sorted the scourge of the justice system by now.' He clenched his fist at the recollection of the Rector of Teigh's resentment of the Folville womenfolk.

Nicholas growled, 'There is no question, only snuffing out the man will...' He stopped talking, the grimace on his face wiped away by a dazzling smile as he got to his feet, 'Why, my Lady Folville, we did not hear you approach.'

Mathilda, despite her joy at seeing her husband, stared at the huddled men with suspicion. 'Who will have to be snuffed out?'

'Why, Stafford of course.' Hating lying to his wife, but knowing if he spoke of the matter they'd taken pains to hide from Mathilda since the day they'd met, she'd object strongly, Robert kissed his wife's hand. 'I have missed you. Daniel tells me you have this puzzle by the throat.'

'Maybe by the ankle, husband. A few more pieces need to be slotted into place, but hopefully all will soon be clear.' Mathilda gestured to the staircase, where Bettrys had been waiting for her signal.

'My Lords, may I present to you Lady Isabella de Vere.'

Pale and walking with the support of her maid, Lady Isabella bowed her head in recognition of the sheriff and his companions. Her raven hair was neatly stowed beneath fresh linen and her shoulders were stiff with the effort of dignity.

'Isabella!' De Vere's cry echoed through the largely empty hall. 'Where have you been, child? I've been worried sick.' Taking in his daughter's miserable demeanour he softened his tone. 'Have you really been in the foresters' hut?'

'Yes, Father.' Her words were hushed with a mix of shame and pride as silent tears fell from her eyes. Isabella stood upright, forcing her body to accept she was the lady of the household even if her mind rebelled against the fact.

'You were planning to leave? With that... that...man?' De Vere choked on his words and Isabella's expression hardened. Not wanting the gathering to fall into argument before any conclusions had been reached, Mathilda coughed with purpose.

'My Lord de Vere, perhaps, if we could all sit down. I beg you to curb your understandable desire to protest at some of what you will learn. I fear it will not be comfortable listening.'

'This is my castle and the girl is my daughter, I will say what I like, when I like!'

Robert got to his feet. He did not raise his voice, but nonetheless his manner was resolute. 'Lady Mathilda is my wife and you will treat her with respect.' He switched his attention to Ingram, 'Sheriff, as the legal representative here, perhaps we could prevail upon you to keep things on track as Mathilda presents her findings.'

'Certainly.' Ingram, his elbows resting on the vast oak table, his fingers steepled into their habitual pose, lifted his chin so he appeared to be looking at everyone at the same time. 'Lady Folville, are all those who you require to be here, here?'

'Not quite, but they will be joining us,' she checked with the steward, 'Won't they, Merrick?'

'They will, my Lady. I believe Lady Helena - ah,' the steward stopped talking as the woman in question swept into view.

Descending the final few stairs into the hall, Helena marched to the table with an air of impatience. 'Am I to be told why my presence was requested in such an insolent manner?'

'No.' It was the sheriff who responded. 'Sit down, my

Lady. You've already kept us waiting.'

Mathilda had to stop herself from applauding as she watched the belligerent expression on Lady Helen's offended face morph into red-cheeked affront. A childish hope that Agnes could see her former mistress being given a taste of her own bad manners, from wherever the good Lord was keeping her soul, crept into Mathilda's mind as she addressed the table.

'There are three issues here. The death of the maid, Agnes, the unexpected arrest warrant issued against the Coterel and Folville families for almost forgotten crimes, and a matter of theft.'

'Theft? What theft?' Lady Helena's brittle query went unanswered as Mathilda went on.

'These felonies are interlinked, although subtly. They have been woven together into a clever net by someone hoping to benefit from this situation. Let us begin to study this mess of smokescreens by looking at the unlikely appointment of lesser noble and known criminal, Roger Wennesley, as the man trusted to arrest five members of my family and two of the three surviving Coterel brothers.

'That, I suspect, is how the master of this charade first saw a way to obtain his ultimate goal. He required a pawn to help steer him towards his aim. Not to kill Agnes, who I am sure was an unforeseen irritant in all this, but to take control of this castle. But you knew that, didn't you, Lady Helena?'

De Vere made to rise to his feet, but Nicholas laid a hand on his arm to stop him interfering.

Lady Helena twirled a blonde hair from her uncovered head through her fingertips, her eyes widened in fake innocence, 'I have no idea what you are talking about.'

Unable to curb his tongue, de Vere said, 'I hope you are not accusing my daughter of murder, Lady Folville?'

Taking strength from an almost imperceptible nod from her husband, Mathilda continued talking to Helena as if she were the only person present. 'You know who is behind this situation, just as we do my Lady. The fact that eludes me is how. How did you come to accept Lord James Coterel of Bakewell's hand in marriage?'

~ *Chapter Fifty-three* ~

Lady Helena's angular chin tilted upwards in defiance. 'You're not as stupid as your roots suggest you should be, Lady Folville.'

She'd been expecting denial or a show of fake tears; she had not imagined Lady Helena would admit to knowing James Coterel. 'I am many things, my Lady, but have never suffered from stupidity. If you could please answer my question?'

Next to a fuming Robert, Lady Isabella stared at her half-sister as if she was a monster. The scrape of the wooden chair legs against the stone floor as she shuffled to distance her chair from Helena's side, to get closer to Bettrys, sounded uncommonly loud.

Laughing, Helena threw Isabella a contemptuous glare. She spoke through lips alight with bitterness. 'It's alright for you sister, with your claim on everything Father has to offer! Even though he hated your mother and loved mine, I have to make my own way. Why shouldn't I search for someone to look after me?'

Anxiety bubbled in Mathilda's stomach as she stated, 'You did not answer my question.'

'Your question is unimportant.'

'On the contrary,' Ingram, his hands together as if in

prayer, flicked his slate-coloured eyes over Lady Helena, 'it is a question you would do well to answer with some urgency before I invite my colleagues to take a walk around the grounds and leave you to talk to Lord Robert and Lord Nicholas alone.'

Helena snapped her neck around to face her father. 'Are you going to let these people talk to me in this manner?'

'Yes.' De Vere glared at his second child in disbelief. 'Tell us all... tell me, and your sister, why you've sought to bring disgrace upon us all by agreeing to marry a stranger without so much as a word to me?'

'Disgrace? I have done no such thing.' Lady Helena got to her feet, her expression full of contempt. 'As you, Father, have failed to tend my advancement, I have secured myself a future. No more, no less. When such a chance came my way, I took it. That is all.'

De Vere's shout of, 'All?' was eclipsed by a loud bang on the table as Ingram signalled that the conversation should hurry forward.

Choosing her words with care, Mathilda said, 'If you told us how that marriage chance presented itself, perhaps we could believe you.'

Lady Helena's lips thinned into a tight line. Her eyes levelled with Mathilda's, but she said nothing.

Sheriff Ingram sighed, 'My advice would be to answer the question, Lady Helena.'

'And if I chose not to heed that advice?'

'We will have to draw our own conclusions concerning the circumstances of your alliance with Lord Coterel.'

Without flinching, Helena replied. 'Then you must do just that.'

Having checked on his reverend brother, Eustace stomped

into the kitchen, where everyone was huddled around Sarah's table. He smiled. The housekeeper was having trouble hiding her annoyance at her territory being invaded on such a scale.

'You're a marvel, Sarah. There's enough for us all to eat at a moment's notice.' Eustace pointed to the pots of stew, open affection for the woman who'd help raise him showing on his face. 'Does nothing ruffle you?'

'I am used to this family, my Lord.'

Eustace's laugh came out as a bark. 'You are indeed.'

Sarah took her chance. 'Will you all ride to Rockingham, my Lord, or do we await my Lord Robert and Lady Mathilda here?'

'If Ulric does not bring us news by this evening, then we ride.'

Adam, his bulky frame squashed against the side of the wall in an attempt to make himself smaller in the overfilled room, stepped forward. 'Should I prepare the horses, my Lord?'

'Do.' Eustace picked a flagon of ale from the table. 'I grow restless. If there is no word soon, I confess I'm tempted to ride out anyway. Whatever it is that James Coterel has done, I want to know sooner rather than later.'

His eyes met those of John Coterel, who blinked silent agreement. There was a tension in the room that neither of them liked. The success of their family's occasional alliances survived on the fact that they respected each other without liking each other. If that bond of respect was broken, then the complications that would cause… Eustace didn't want to think about the consequences. Instead, he said, 'Lord John, I wonder if you'd accompany me to my chamber. We have other matters to discuss.'

Saying nothing, John stood, carrying his bowl of stew

with him.

Ignoring the inquisitive eyes of his brothers and the housekeeper, Eustace waited until they were within his room before he spoke again. 'We've worked too hard for James to ruin things. Do you agree?'

'I do.' John tilted the fine pottery bowl to his lips and chewed his stew. 'Nicholas and I have made sure that James doesn't know of our mutual plans regarding local justice.'

'Few do, that's the beauty of it.'

John asked, 'Does the new Lady Folville know?'

'She does not.'

'Good. She won't be coloured in her opinion of her new husband and family then.'

Eustace gave a sharp laugh, 'A situation that will not stay the same when she does find out.'

John's eyes betrayed his surprise, 'Lord Robert would allow his wife to know our plans?'

'There speaks a man who has never met Lady Mathilda.'

'I'm looking forward to that day. Nicholas has spoken often of the new Lady Folville's fine qualities.'

Something about the way John spoke made Eustace uneasy. 'Nicholas has seen her at work.'

'And admired her for it.'

Committing the knowing expression on John's face to memory to be dealt with later if necessary, Eustace said, 'We need to decide a plan of action in case things do not go well for us today. Then we'll ride to Rockingham; whether Ulric has returned or not. Agreed?'

It was clear that Lady Helena wasn't going to explain how she became acquainted with the head of the Coterel clan, so, with her back to the fire, Mathilda returned to her explanation.

'It is no secret that Lord James has become a favourite in the royal court, particularly with the King's bride, Philippa of Hainault. Having obtained his position by clever manipulation of various officials by means unknown, Lord James has established himself in London as a man to trust.'

Nicholas Coterel couldn't argue. 'A fair summary. My elder brother is clever and wears a mask of innocence that could fool anyone, be they king or pauper.'

Mathilda grinned. 'I would surmise that Lord James's idea to take control of Rockingham Castle first arrived when he learnt of the queen-in-waiting's determination to help her husband scrub away the legacy left by his mother. As my Lord de Vere will testify, the former Queen Isabella made full use of the Crown's influence to use felony to its advantage and control large portions of England through the corruption and bribery of justices.'

'That woman was a snake.' Lady Helena's outburst jarred the room as she repeated in public what she'd shared with Mathilda in private. 'It must be the name. Anyone called Isabella is flawed.'

Lady Isabella and Bettrys took a sharp intake of breath at the intended slight, as de Vere, his voice husky with the effort of not shouting at his younger child again, snapped, 'How dare you speak of your sister like that? You, who sit there as if you are royalty yourself! A child of mine who, for all I know, has a servant's blood on her hands!'

The accusation echoed around the hall, its intensity distilling into a blunt second of shock which Mathilda dispersed by carrying on as if Helena had never spoken. 'James Coterel, however he managed it, had become someone upon whom the young Queen Philippa relies. This means he has contact with a select group of men upon whom she and King Edward entirely depend. The royal messengers.'

'Garrick!' De Vere spat the name.

'Yes. Master Garrick.'

A slow smile crossed Robert de Folville's features as he radiated pride at his wife's deduction. 'You think James has manufactured this situation by bribing the messengers to add to or alter the documents they carry?'

'It would make sense. Garrick's name tops the document at the heart of this.' Mathilda kept her eyes on Lady Helena as she spoke. Her colour had faded so much that should she be thrown out into the snow, she'd have blended into the landscape. 'Either that, or a clerk working with Garrick was paid to meddle with the wording of the messages before they were given out.'

Ingram acknowledged the sense of what Mathilda said. 'If James Coterel, or even Garrick, told a clerk what to write, they would be unlikely to question it. There is so much paperwork involved in the legal profession these days that we do not always take in the words we are writing.'

'So, James could have told the clerk what to write and then paid Garrick to make sure the corrected documents got to the intended recipients.' Nicholas refilled his beaker of ale as he added, 'And perhaps Garrick or James threw in a few coins here and there if additional, unofficial, messages could be delivered by messengers on otherwise legitimate travels.'

Not noticing Robert's discomfort at the way Nicholas was appraising her, Mathilda gave the Coterel a wider smile. 'A role which would also, I suspect, involve a certain amount of information-gathering - and suitable remuneration.'

Basking in Mathilda's grin, Nicholas knocked back his drink, wiping the resulting foam from his lips. 'The pieces fall into place,'

Every pair of eyes levelled on Lady Helena as Mathilda stated, 'A frequent visitor to Rockingham to bring orders to the constable, Garrick is no fool. He told James Coterel that you were here, Lady Helena, disenchanted, ambitious, ruthless and beautiful. Someone who would appeal to the eldest Lord Coterel. Someone he could use to help secure this castle for himself.'

Helena's blue eyes blazed as Mathilda asked, 'When did Garrick first tell you of Lord James' interest in you as his future wife?'

'He did no such thing. Your imagination, Lady Mathilda, is getting away from you.'

'He tempted you with not just usurping your sister as lady of this castle, but through talk of being the Lady of Bakewell Manor with a place in the Royal Court. How tempting that must have been for you.'

Until now, Merrick had hovered, taciturn, as ever at the end of the table. But now hot fury assailed him. 'It was the accusation of rape that Lady Helena falsely threw against Master Sproxton that has to have been the catalyst.' The steward, his countenance bleak, shot every word straight at Lady Helena. 'Agnes told me all about it before she died.'

'Agnes?' Isabella muttered her maid's name through dry lips. 'What did Agnes know of all this?'

'Too much,' Mathilda said gently, 'and it cost her everything. A happy life with the man she loved, years of existing with the fear of being sent to the gallows, and ultimately, her life. For as well as living an enforced life as a thief, Agnes had no choice but to be Garrick's mouthpiece within the castle. Tasked with carrying orders, disguised as requests, from James Coterel, that were first presented to Cook, who then demanded Agnes delivered them to Lady Helena.

'How grating it must have been to take instructions, even ones you were eager to receive, my Lady, from a mere maid.'

A cloaked peace fell upon the room. All that could be heard was the crackle of the fire in the grate and the background muffle of activity from the kitchen as the assembled group took in what they heard.

Glad that no one had protested against what she claimed, least of all the ashen-faced Lady Helena, Mathilda went on.

'The accusation of rape, however - that was made from jealousy, was it not, Lady Helena? It was not an order from on high. Sproxton appealed to you; why wouldn't he? He is a handsome and charming man. Yet he only had eyes for Lady Isabella. How galling that must have been for you. There you were, privately resolved to finding a husband for yourself rather than waiting for your father to do it for you ,and the first man you aimed for preferred your sister.'

'I did no such thing. I…'

Mathilda interrupted. 'I only knew Agnes briefly, but I saw she was afraid. After some coaxing she spoke to me. Of how you treat your maids here, Lady Helena. Then, from Merrick, I discovered Agnes's predecessor left because she was too afraid to stay. The girl was afraid of you, wasn't she?'

'How dare -'

'You made up the charge, a charge that could see Sproxton hanged if found guilty, to punish him for overlooking you despite your best efforts to attract him, as well as to punish Isabella for being his object of affection. Agnes knew this and told Garrick, who told James Coterel; and what a blessing that was for you! An offer of marriage from the head of a wealthy noble family, with royal connections, no less, was the result! Although it came with the demands

I previously mentioned.'

Lady Helena's defiant stare spoke volumes as de Vere shifted uncomfortably in his chair.

Mathilda felt another knot begin to unravel in her mind, 'It was the fact that Sproxton wasn't with Wennesley when the rape was alleged to have taken place which was of most interest to James Coterel. Especially when he learnt that Wennesley, the acknowledged murderer of his brother, Laurence, had defended Sproxton even though he, thanks to Garrick, knew they were not together at the time. What loyalty and friendship, or debt of honour, might that have revealed to him?'

'How could you know that?' Lady Helena's eyes narrowed as Isabella's sad eyes fell to the limp hands in her lap.

'Because Agnes was afraid of someone. Agnes was very used to being frightened. She knew where Sproxton was during the time of his supposed crime.'

'And she told someone.' The words from Isabella's lips were barely more than a whisper.

'She did.' Mathilda's palm dropped from the table and found Robert's hand. Taking strength from his touch, she went on. 'Someone in the castle knows that, once upon a time, under the forced influence of her master, Reynard, Agnes had been a thief and that, against her will, she continued to handle stolen goods. This knowledge was used to blackmail her into passing information to Garrick who, if my theories are correct, passed it onto Lord Coterel.'

'Someone in the castle?' De Vere spun towards Merrick. 'You, steward?'

'No, my Lord!' Mathilda shook her head. 'Not Merrick.'

She reached a hand out to her husband. 'I wonder if you and Lord Nicholas would be so kind as to ask Cook to join us?'

~ *Chapter Fifty-four* ~

The atmosphere choked the air like weeds on a summer river.

Lady Helena's hands remained on the table before her, but as the two men disappeared into the kitchen she curled them into fists.

Sheriff Ingram tapped an impatient finger on the table. 'I suggest you talk, Lady Helena.'

Her features frozen as if she were a statue, Lady Helena stared, unblinking, at her half-sister, but her lips remained defiantly closed as Robert and Nicholas returned with Cook wedged between them, brushing loose flour from her hands.

Cook's stature equalled the men's and her bulk exceeded it. Her huge round face was set in a stance of outrage. Ignoring the majority of the group, she addressed her master. 'My Lord de Vere, I can see this summons must be urgent, but I have much to do if you expect to dine this evening.'

Having used the pause in conversation to gather his thoughts, de Vere rose from his chair and offered it to their latest companion. 'We are well provisioned. Please be seated, Cook. Lady Mathilda would like everyone of importance in Rockingham present. Naturally, as my loyal cook and housekeeper, that includes you.'

Mathilda struggled not to giggle with anxiety. De Vere's

flattery was a masterstroke. The use of the word 'loyal' alone was enough to see Cook seated without another word. The constable however remained close behind her.

Back at his wife's side, Robert placed a palm on her thigh, giving it a discreet encouraging squeeze as she prepared to explain the theories she had woven together. Mathilda was fervently hoping she'd understood the conundrum she'd been faced with. One wrong conclusion and there was the risk of sending the wrong person to the gallows.

'As I said, James Coterel saw an opportunity to take control of Rockingham. The castle however was not the biggest prize. What he wanted most was control of the ring of thieves that runs, or should I say ran, from here.'

She paused. No one spoke. Isabella and Bettrys clutched each other's hands. De Vere stared at the ground in fixed concentration, while Merrick appeared consumed by shame.

'James Coterel is well known as being a gambler. This is something he has in common with two other men in this case: Thomas Sproxton and Agnes's former master, Reynard.

'Now Reynard, as we've said, forced Agnes to do many things that went against her nature, including stealing. She was slim and agile before her leg was broken. Being an acrobat, she was nimble enough to cram herself into opportune gaps to remove goods from other people's dwellings without being seen.

'Their life on the road, moving from fair to fair between London and Nottingham, was perfect for a pair of thieves. By the time anyone suspected their goods were missing, the culprits would have moved on. This worked well until Reynard announced that the constable of Rockingham Castle had granted them the use of a hut in the forest while they worked in the area. Luxury compared to their usual nightly round of entertaining in barter for supper and lodgings, or the countless nights in stables and on roadsides they'd endured.'

Bettrys sighed, 'That's right, my Lady. Agnes didn't speak much of her life before she came here. I always thought she was too ashamed, but she did speak of nights under the stars. Of being so cold she feared she'd never awake the next day.'

Thanking the maid, Mathilda's mind drifted to the many balladeers she'd heard in the past. Where did they sleep each night after she'd been entertained by their Robyn Hode stories? She privately resolved to mention the matter to Robert later.

'Tired of travelling all year, Reynard and Agnes started to spend the winter months in the hut, often coming up to the castle to entertain and to swap goods for food.'

De Vere nodded solemnly, confirming what Mathilda said.

'It seemed natural for you to earn some rent from the hut, my Lord. But I wonder, was it your suggestion that Reynard stayed there, did he ask you himself, or was that seed planted in your head by another?'

'I...'De Vere's brows drew together. 'I don't recall.'

Mathilda looked to Merrick. 'You know who had that original idea though, don't you?'

The steward's shoulders heaved as he uttered, 'It was Cook's idea.'

Cook's piggy eyes almost disappeared into her face as she scowled. 'What if it was? I offered them a kindness. I know nothing of any thefts.'

'But you do, and you always did. Not just that, but you saw how to expand the tumblers' enterprise and how to profit from it.'

Lady Helena sat bolt upright. 'Are you saying that, after all of the accusations you have hurled, including those so cruelly angled at me, that Cook killed Agnes and is a thief?'

Cook's chins wobbled in outrage. Flour dust rose in the air as she snapped, 'I beg your pardon!'

Ingram clapped his hands and a restrained silence cut across the threatening crescendo of chaos, allowing Mathilda to ask, 'You, Cook, are kin to Reynard, are you not?'

Every eye in the hall swivelled towards the woman who had the power to poison them five times a day if she'd so wished.

'You are also the person who, after Reynard abandoned Agnes in the hut and Merrick carried her here, arranged that she stay in the castle. Even though she was left with a limp, you took Agnes on as a maid because you needed to keep an eye on her. She knew too much and could send you to the gallows anytime she chose - plus, she was a very successful thief. Why would you want to lose such an asset? Especially one you could control in your brother's absence?'

Surrounded and seeing no point in denial, Cook spat, 'Only if she sent herself to hell too. Yes, Reynard was my brother. He could still be; I have no idea if he breathes on this earth. I had no part in any theft, mind you, but I'd be damned if I'd let that useless piece destroy us with what she knew of him.'

'Damned is the word!' Merrick bellowed. 'You knew your brother had battered Agnes half to death. Just one of many crimes he committed against her body over the years. When I found her, she was broken in body and spirit. I thought you in acted in kindness, but you wanted to use Agnes, just like your brother did!'

A thick silence fell and Mathilda was glad of the chance to think. There were so many threads still hanging. She longed for the private counsel of Robert, Sarah and Adam. They always knew what to say and how to tease the answers from her over-tired, muddled mind. She was afraid the responsibility of the investigation was clouding her logic.

The respite was over all too soon as Sheriff Ingram asked, 'How does this connection with Cook link back to Lord Coterel and Lady Helena? We await that explanation, Lady Mathilda.'

Closing her eyes in the hope that it would help her concentration, she said, 'The situation is complex and interwoven. Please, bear with me, we will get there.'

Cook laughed, 'You have all the time in the world, Lady Folville. The snow was growing thick when I was wrenched from my domain. No one is leaving Rockingham for a while.'

Exchanging looks with Mathilda, Robert called Ulric from his position by the door. 'Go to the stables with Daniel. If the weather's safe enough, ride to Ashby Folville together. Bid them that we are well and tell them no one is to come here until the storm passes. If you are unsure of the wisdom of attempting the journey once you've seen the sky, return here.'

As soon as Ulric departed, Mathilda said, 'You asked how all this links up, Sheriff. I will explain, but it is best if we examine one puzzle piece at a time.

'In the absence of Reynard, Cook took over an enterprise she'd been at the heart of for a few years -'

'I -'

Cook's words were cut short by the application of de Vere's hastily drawn dagger to her throat. 'I wouldn't bother with denials. Only speak truth if you are intending to speak at all.'

Mathilda watched the dagger blade sink into the folds of

Cook's palatial neck. She wasn't sure if the skin had been pierced as the woman's flesh fell over the side of the weapon, swallowing it up. The result however was that Cook became as mute as stone.

'Agnes was found in the Fire Room. A room I was lucky enough to sleep in. A place usually reserved for the Queen of England.' Mathilda addressed Merrick, 'I assume it was Cook who told Agnes to prepare the room for me?'

'It was. We suspected it amused her to have the wife of a Folville stay there in the circumstances.'

'We?' Robert frowned.

'Merrick and Agnes had an understanding.' Mathilda gave the steward a sympathetic smile. 'In recent weeks Agnes' conscience had been troubling her. She'd been feeling guilty for lying to Merrick, so she told him everything she knew, and sadly, it cost the maid her life. For that confession was overheard.'

Ingram's forehead furrowed. 'And she confessed to Merrick then, rather than before, because?'

'Because of something Lady Isabella had asked of her.' Casting a glance at Isabella, who was staring in bewilderment at her lap, Mathilda said, 'But I'll come to that later.

'Carrying on from where her brother left off, Cook used the Fire Room as a place in which to hide stolen goods; goods which the ring of thieves organised by Reynard brought to her in the kitchen. These felons came here under the guise of wanting to evade justice, just as criminals have come to Rockingham for years.'

Nichols Coterel raked his hands through his hair before stretching out his arms, 'And my brother James' involvement?'

'Reynard was in debt to Lord James Coterel.'

'Ah.' Nicholas's eyebrows rose, 'A gambler?'

'Reynard was a gambler who travelled the country, including stops in Bakewell, Derby, and London. It is not unreasonable that he and James should meet at the betting table. In turn, let us not forget Thomas Sproxton, one of the other knots in this conundrum. He is also a known gambler and was severely in debt to Reynard.'

Lady Isabella's eyes rose and her body stiffened, but she said nothing as Mathilda kept talking.

'James Coterel, thanks to the aforementioned Garrick, knew that Lady Helena was ambitious and jealous of Sproxton's liking for her sister; and was the sort of woman who took revenge in the face of humiliation. He also knew Sproxton had been present at the murder of his brother, Laurence Coterel. This, combined with the knowledge that the Crown was planning a round-up of local felons, gave Lord James an opportunity too good to miss.'

Robert finished his wife's train of thought. 'And so, when Reynard owed him a substantial gambling debt, he demanded the thieves' operation as payment. Then he saw how he could have the castle as well perhaps?'

'We can't know for sure, but I suspect so. The debt might have been abandoned on Reynard's disappearance, but if Garrick had discovered Cook's connection to him, then James could have resurrected the debt, and demanded she deliver on behalf of her kin.'

Nicholas leant forward. 'Lady Folville, how can you possibly know any of this? Do you have proof?'

'Of much of this, no. I'm merely joining threads. But the substance I know to be true, because Thomas Sproxton has been talkative - like so many men who don't wish to hang.'

Lady Isabella began to sob in distress. Bettrys was on her feet immediately. 'My Lady, please calm yourself.'

Patting Bettrys' shoulder gently, Mathilda went on.

'Sproxton also owed Reynard money. A debt Cook wasn't willing to let go. Being an occasional thief himself, a trait he fell back on when gambling debts were mounting, he knew of the Rockingham thieving ring. When Cook's demands became too high, Thomas thought it would serve her right if she was paid back with her own ill-gotten gains.'

De Vere could remain quiet no linger. He faced his eldest daughter with incredulity. 'Isabella, how could you want to leave your home with a man like that?'

The dry sobs that had begun to punctuate Mathilda's sentences were now producing tears. They gathered in pools at the corner of her eyes, but Isabella refused to let them fall. 'The answer is simple. I love him, Father and Thomas loves me too. And he could get me away from *her*.' Stabbing a finger in the direction of her half-sister, Isabella shook her head. 'I tire of Helena's cruelty to me and the servants. She wears me down with criticism and delights in humiliating me. Look how she displayed her lack of sisterly grace in front of Lady Trussell. Thomas offered me a new home and a place of respectable work with his family in London.'

Nicholas Coterel's eyebrows rose. 'Family in London? I'm sorry, my Lady, but I don't believe Sproxton has anything awaiting him in London apart from debts and trouble. He has no family.'

Bettrys edged closer to her mistress as Isabella's porcelain skin paled further. 'Surely, my Lord Coterel, you are mistaken?'

Mathilda sighed, 'He is not mistaken. By courting you, Lady Isabella, Sproxton was carrying out the instructions of another. However, it may be some small comfort to you to know that when I spoke to Thomas earlier, he admitted a genuine affection for you that he'd never intended to develop.'

'It's all too much to take in,' Lady Isabella murmured into her hands.

Robert lifted Mathilda's palm from his lap and placed it on the table, keeping it in full view of Nicholas as he held it tight. 'Are you saying that James Coterel ordered Sproxton to remove Lady Isabella from the castle, ensuring the way was clear for Lady Helena to be the heir here? A lot of trouble for a female descendent'

'Nonetheless, my Lord, that is what happened.' Mathilda felt a wave of sympathy on seeing the misery on Isabella's face, but held back from comment. There was worse yet for Isabella to learn about the man she loved. 'Coterel relieved Sproxton of his debt from Reynard and the tormenting of Cook. Consequently, Sproxton now lives in James Coterel's pocket.'

Ingram's eyebrows rose. 'And Lady Helena?'

'I overheard Cook shouting at Bettrys. She was complaining of Lady Helena coming into her kitchen and throwing her weight around. I couldn't imagine why she would venture near a domestic setting. It only made sense when I realised she'd been visiting the kitchen because she's got into the habit of sneaking around the rooms of the castle. She has certainly been in my chamber and observed a hairbrush I had been lent   as well as her father's study. On a recent visit she saw the arrest warrant.' Mathilda fixed a stare on Helena, hoping no one could tell she was speaking a hunch with no evidence whatsoever. 'Isn't that right?'

Lady Helena said nothing, but her fingers began to fidget in her lap.

Relieved no one had called her bluff, Mathilda pressed on. 'You have your letters, don't you, my Lady? And you, like so many of us here, have read the ink-stained entry on that parchment. I imagine you were searching your father's room for information to send to James Coterel as proof of your sincerity towards his intentions. Am I right?'

The sheriff focused his gaze on the constable. 'You think Lady Helena told Cook about what she'd read?'

Mathilda nodded as she continued to appraise Lady Helena. 'Well, did you? I assume it was Cook who passed on your messages for James via Garrick?'

The younger Lady de Vere said nothing. But the hatred in her eyes confirmed every word of Mathilda's accusation.

~ *Chapter Fifty-five* ~

'I asked you earlier today, my Lady,' Mathilda switched her attention to Isabella, 'who it was that told you Sproxton would be coming to the forester's hut last night. Could you tell us who that was please?'

Licking her dry lips, Isabella twisted her body around so that she was facing her half-sister. 'Helena. Why I believed her, I do not know.'

'Perhaps because you wanted it to be true.'

De Vere's stomach contracted into a knot as, unbidden, Nicholas Coterel stood behind his youngest child, as if to block her between the chair and the table. 'Is this true, Helena?'

After only a brief pause, Lady Helena said, 'Yes, Father.'

'And you were obeying whose orders?'

As she waited for the answer, Mathilda's throat became dry. If she'd made mistakes in her working together the connecting parts of this case, then the whole thing would collapse and she'd be in trouble. It was difficult not to shout with relief when she heard Helena say, 'It was Cook.'

'Does that mean you knew of the stolen goods hidden in the Fire Room?'

Lady Helena's eyes rolled in contempt for her father. 'I knew no more than you did of Sproxton's criminal connections.'

'That isn't what I asked you. Did you know what was stored in the Fire Room?'

'I did not.'

'Then why did you do what Cook asked?'

'Because I hate my sister. I don't need another reason.'

Ulric and Daniel felt the vibration of pounding hooves through the inch of snow that muffled the twig strewn forest floor. Reining in, they moved their mounts under shelter until they could see who approached. As soon as he glimpsed the lead horseman, Daniel broke cover and lowered his hood, 'My Lord Eustace?'

'Daniel? Ulric?' Dropping his own hood to see the boys clearly, Eustace wiped snowflakes from his chin. 'You have news?'

'Lady Mathilda has everyone gathered in the Great Hall, laying out the answers plain. We've been sent to reassure you that all is in hand in case the snow cut us off. We did not expect to meet you, my Lords.' Daniel nodded in respect as Thomas de Folville, John Coterel, and Roger Wennesley rode up behind Eustace.

'The wait for news was proving tedious.' Lord Eustace spotted Ulric's anxious glance towards the snow-filled sky. 'We should keep going. We are nearer Rockingham than Ashby now.'

A murmur of approval met him from beneath the various cloak hoods as the horses stamped.

'Ulric, Daniel, go on to Ashby and reassure Sarah and Adam. Go with care; the roads beyond the forest are caked in snow, but passable.'

The boys chorused, 'Yes, my Lord,' and raised their hoods.

'I could go back with them, Lord Eustace, if you fear for the boys.' Wennesley circled his horse to face back the way they'd come in the expectation of his offer being accepted.

'No, you may be needed in Rockingham.' Eustace felt a prickling in his palms as he eyed King Edward's appointed man suspiciously. 'The lads know the way. Come, this is not a time for lingering.'

Fresh blankets had been fetched from the nearest chamber and the fire stoked so it blazed high. Moved with solicitous care by Bettrys, Lady Isabella was positioned as close to the source of heat as possible. The shivering cold she suffered however was attacking her from within. Mathilda knew from experience, it was the type of chill that heat alone would not cure.

As soon as everyone was re-seated and Cook's hands had been roped to the back of her chair, Ingram drew the room back to order. 'So, young Agnes was an unwilling thief for Reynard and then continued to work for his sister?'

Merrick confirmed this. 'A fact of which she was desperately ashamed.'

'The girl was afraid for her life?'

'Cook had the power to see my Agnes arrested and sent to the gallows at anytime.' Merrick's eyes clouded with distaste as they fell on the lady he'd worked alongside in ignorant bliss for years. 'She never let Agnes forget that.'

Mathilda felt bile rise in her throat. She couldn't put off what needed saying for much longer. If she didn't declare Agnes's killer soon, she might lose her nerve. Swallowing against her dry mouth, she recomposed her summary.

'In recent weeks the pressure of the lies she held within her had been getting too much for Agnes. Lady Isabella had asked Agnes to accompany her and Sproxton to London to his uncle's home. But Agnes knew there was no uncle. Remember, Lady Isabella didn't know that Agnes and Merrick had formed an alliance which went beyond that of steward and maid. Merrick wanted to marry her, but Agnes refused him, and in the moment of emotion that followed, when she tried to explain why she would never be good enough for him, all her confessions came at once.'

Levelling her gaze on the steward, Mathilda asked, 'That's when Agnes told you about the thieving ring and Sproxton and Cook - soon after my arrival in Rockingham?'

'It was. But I didn't believe her.' Merrick's hands came to his face, 'If only I had! If I hadn't got angry and made her prove her words…'

Speaking gently, Mathilda went on. 'Agnes went from your quarters to the Fire Room. First she retrieved a knife that was kept there, and laid it in your bed, hoping it would frighten you enough to stay out of what of what was happening. Then she headed back to the chamber to retrieve some stolen goods to prove her words to you. But someone had been outside of your room listening to your conversation. They had heard Agnes's confession and decided that she'd never share what she knew.

'I can only imagine how conflicted the killer must have been, and how surprised they were to see Agnes return to Merrick's room so quickly, with a knife. A knife they then stole and took up to the Fire Room as they followed in the maid's wake.' Mathilda sighed. 'If Agnes hadn't tried to protect Merrick by frightening him into silence, she may not have died that day.'

Ingram sat back in his chair and regarded Lady Folville with respect. 'Do you think Agnes intended to return to Merrick from the Fire Room, or did she plan to just take some money and run?'

'I don't think she wanted to leave Merrick, but what else could she do? The Queen's Chamber is peaceful. It was the perfect location in which to stop and think about what she should do. After all, no one else in the house had been instructed to go there but her, and if I arrived she could just make a play of tending the fire.'

'And was it so easy for Agnes's killer to have observed their quarry going back and forth from the steward's room without revealing themselves?'

'All too easy. The castle is not well manned and there are shadows aplenty in which to hide.'

The sheriff was solemn. 'You know who did this evil thing?'

'I do. I wish I did not.'

A log slid from the top of the pile burning in the grate, sending sparks of heat towards Isabella. Her nerves already at breaking point, she shrieked, shying away from the spluttering flames.

The interlude was extended by the unexpected sound of a familiar voice resounding through the corridor near the kitchen. As every man drew his sword, Lady Mathilda felt a frisson of fear trip through her.

'That's Lord Eustace.' Mathilda turned to Robert as he sheathed his sword. 'Weren't they supposed to stay at Ashby?'

'Either there's a problem at home or Eustace became impatient.'

'The latter would make sense.'

Eustace advanced upon them, his voice booming, 'Dear God, it's cold. Make room, I do not travel alone.'

Getting to his feet, Ingram embraced his friend, 'My Lord, it's good to see you, but what brings you here? Did you meet Ulric and Daniel?'

'We did. They were well when we encountered them not more than a mile or so away. I sent them on towards Sarah's clucking wings.'

Robert addressed his elder brother with disbelief. 'You have all come?'

'No, brother, Laurence and Walter are looking after the manor while Richard remains under guard in the storeroom.'

A shuffle of footfalls emerged from the far side of the hall as Thomas de Folville appeared with John Coterel and Roger Wennesley just behind him.

Perspiration coated Mathilda's palms. The audience she'd had hanging on her every word before had been bad enough, but this... She laid a hand on Robert's arm and whispered, 'Can we speak alone?'

Sensing the urgency to his wife's tone, Robert muttered under his breath, 'We can't leave here now, you were about to declare who killed Agnes were you not?'

'I was, but as I keep saying, this is a knot which is so tightly bound that only by telling the whole thing will it begin to make sense.'

'And you're afraid you are wrong?'

'No, my Lord. I was, but having gone this far successfully, I find I am now afraid that I am right.' Glancing over her shoulder, Mathilda whispered, 'Who is the man with Thomas?'

'John Coterel.'

'He is not like his brother.' Mathilda regarded the man who was the polar opposite in looks to the dark and broad-featured Nicholas. Slim and fair, John had a dour expression which Mathilda suspected was permanent.

'He is quieter. Less brash.'

Robert's caustic tone took Mathilda by surprise. 'You have fallen out with Lord Nicholas?'

'I dislike how he leers at you.'

It was all Mathilda could do not to laugh. 'My Lord, we are but a few days wed! We haven't had time to spend a week together, let alone had time for my eye to stray. Which it won't. Not ever.'

'You think me foolish, but I don't wish to lose you. When I think how close I came to Rowan Leigh taking you from me, I...'

She swept a stray hair from his face, 'He didn't take me from you. Nor will anyone else. I need your help. Please, husband, listen...'

Mathilda stayed with Robert, whispering her thoughts as Ingram reassembled the enlarged group, and giving them an account of the story so far. It was interesting to watch the expressions on the different players' faces as he explained how James Coterel had used the fact that Reynard had owed him money, the King's desire to clean up the midland Hundreds, and de Vere's request to stand down from his post, all to his advantage.

As Ingram lapsed into silence, Eustace shot a look of distaste at the bound cook, glared at Lady Helena, and beckoned to Mathilda. 'Clearly we've arrived just as your deliberations were becoming interesting.'

Holding Robert's arm for support, Mathilda decided to remain standing, attempting to digest her nerves at being the centre of attention in such a fashion.

'As we know, the reason I came to Rockingham Castle was because my husband,' Mathilda gave him a loving smile, 'wanted to keep me safe while the majority of the Folville and Coterel families were being pursued by the Crown in the shape of Sheriff Ingram, under the guidance of you, Roger Wennesley, and with the help of Sproxton.

'This was, as I'm sure even you will admit, Master Wennesley, rather unusual. You are known to have murdered Laurence Coterel. Why would King Edward send you, a man he could declare outlaw or arrest at any time, to hunt down these two families?

'I know that my kin and Lord Nicholas Coterel have declared it a clever ruse by the King; to send a felon to catch felons, so that, should you fail, you'd be punished with outlawry or the gallows. And it was clever, very clever.'

Eustace began to clap. 'Clever enough for Lord James Coterel, perhaps, rather than the King?'

'Exactly, my Lord.' Mathilda dipped her head towards both Lords Coterel. 'You've said, Lord Nicholas, that your brother, James, is a master manipulator.'

'He is.'

'A fact which has been confirmed by Sproxton.'

'He's been talkative then?' John Coterel's eyes narrowed as he picked up a beaker of ale. 'Well, he is not stupid. Helping now is the only way to avoid the noose.'

Mathilda glanced at Roger Wennesley's face. Not a flicker of expression could be seen as he stared, unseeing, into the fire while listening to the conversation going on around him.

'So you're saying that our brother organised our arrest as part of a way to show the Crown who really rules the Midlands?' Nicholas Coterel scowled. 'That's ridiculous.'

'I promise you, it isn't, not to James at least.' Mathilda wrapped her cloak tighter around her shoulders. 'He used Queen Philippa's desire, to remove the influence of the King's mother, to his advantage. I imagine he had Garrick to make sure the warrants held indictments for crimes committed a long time ago, so that the families involved would be suspicious enough to want to look into the matter. A ruse that you can't deny has worked well. Then Lord James made sure he could control the person investigating those crimes.'

Every eye landed on Wennesley, who sat ready to defend himself as Mathilda added, 'It wasn't just Sproxton and Reynard, and therefore Cook, who James Coterel had a hold over, was it, Master Wennesley?'

'You are saying that Wennesley was also controlled by Lord James?' Lady Helena's piercing voice shrilled through the hall.

Mathilda tilted her head in acknowledgement. 'Wennesley, do you wish to say anything on the subject?'

'I think you are every bit as able as Sheriff Ingram told me you were, but you have overstretched yourself. I'm following the orders of the King. If he was manipulated into appointing me, I can't help that. That I'm disposable is a fact I can't argue with. But I did not murder your maid, nor have I stolen anything.'

'And I believe you.'

Mathilda's firm statement saw Roger deflate with relief and Sheriff Ingram steeple his fingers as he said, 'How do you know this?'

'Merrick learnt much from Agnes before she died. If she'd been spared, then we'd have known about Lord Coterel's plans much earlier. I'm sure her killer had no knowledge of them.'

'You don't?' de Vere frowned. 'But surely -'

Mathilda waved his words away with a sad rise of her palm. 'I have no doubt that the murderer saw what they did as an act of protection which would preserve the future they'd been promised.

'Perhaps they felt they needed to prove their love; and knowing the nature of the man they were trying to impress better than they knew the man himself, they acted in the most uncharacteristic of ways. If they'd waited and got to know that man, they'd have seen someone too far down the road of damnation to be saved.'

The time had come. Mathilda saw every set of eyes swivel towards the two sisters. No one spoke, but nonetheless she heard them demanding her to name the murderer.

Mathilda signalled to her husband, who moved behind Agnes's killer. 'And that's why you took the knife from Merrick's bed and stabbed your maid, isn't it, my Lady. Because you believed Agnes was going to stop you leaving with Thomas Sproxton.'

~ *Chapter Fifty-six* ~

Bettrys dropped her mistress's hand and moved away from her so fast that you'd think she'd been scolded.

De Vere was on his feet, roaring out his disbelief, his eyes fixed on Lady Isabella, who'd neither moved nor reacted to confirm or deny what Mathilda had said. 'Can you prove any of this, *Lady* Folville, or are you concocting answers out of thin air to suit yourself'

Robert threw a punch at de Vere before Mathilda could stop him. His fist landed squarely on the constable's jaw, knocking his chair backwards, so he splayed across the floor with a sickening crunch. 'Don't talk to my wife like that! It isn't her fault your daughter did this, nor that your other child is basking in her sibling's failing.'

As Lady Helena sat, looking as if the King himself had proposed marriage, Nicholas Coterel tugged the constable back to his feet.

Grateful that de Vere's skull had not smashed like an egg, Mathilda's temper cracked, 'For Our Lady's sake! Why can't you all just sit and listen? Robert, there was no need for that at all.'

Nicholas smirked to hear Mathilda talk to her husband in such a way, a smirk which was wiped off his face fast as the new Lady Folville glared at him.

Flushed with ire, Robert hissed, 'There was every need. He lords over a castle kept empty so the felonies that take place here go unnoticed, bleating about what's been going on under his nose, without a word of thanks for your efforts. I will not,' Robert rounded on de Vere again, 'have you disrespect my wife.'

Knowing this was not the time to tell Robert that, while it was good to have her honour defended, she didn't appreciate having it done in this way; Mathilda passed the shocked constable his drink. 'You asked if I can prove this, my Lord? I think I can. Merrick, Lord Nicholas, will you fetch Sproxton, please?'

Mathilda surveyed the group as they waited. Wennesley had a haunted air about him. She wondered if he was calculating the chances of getting out of the hall alive once this discussion was over.

'My Lord Sheriff, you asked why Agnes confessed to Merrick now. It was because Lady Isabella had asked her to leave, together with herself and Sproxton. I believe Agnes wanted to leave the castle with a clean slate; at least between herself and the man she loved.'

Suddenly, as if waking from a trance, Lady Isabella asked, 'Thomas is here?'

'He is.'

'So he didn't come to the hut this time because he was a prisoner, not because he never intended to come?'

'He didn't know you were there. Your sister lied to you about his intentions.' Mathilda swallowed, Lady Isabella didn't seem to have noticed she'd been denounced for murder. Only a few hours ago she'd felt deeply sorry for Isabella; now, she felt nothing but piteous revulsion. 'Does he know you killed Agnes?'

'Killed Agnes?'

'Please don't insult us by pretending to be unaware of your actions, my Lady.' Mathilda felt heavy with responsibility as she continued, 'Earlier today you pleaded with me; asked me to tell you that you hadn't caused your friend's downfall in your desire to get away with him. I thought you were referring to the act of leaving the castle, but you were being more precise. For that's exactly what you did.

'You did go to the forester's hut the day before my arrival, as you claimed. But Sproxton didn't arrive, and so I believe you came back. It is all too easy to move around here without being seen. Cold and hungry, I suspect you stayed in your room, safe in the knowledge that no one ever visited you there. I imagine you didn't know what to do. Should you wait for Agnes to come and collect your belongings as promised, and explain to her the whole thing was over? Would you then remain in the castle and play the dutiful wife to Lord Trussell, or would you flee and take your chances on the open road, or join a nunnery? Or would you go back to the hut just in case Sproxton turned up late? You chose the latter. You were on your way back to the hut, on the day of my arrival, when you passed Merrick's quarters. You overheard Agnes talking. You heard everything, didn't you; about the thief ring and Sproxton's involvement in it?'

Mathilda paused and looked to the steward. 'Merrick, in her desperation to get you to forgive her, did Agnes claim she'd tell the constable or bailiff about those involved in the lawlessness here? Did she mention Sproxton by name?'

Merrick sighed. 'She did, but I would not have let her go to the law, for she'd have been damning herself.'

'But she said it.'

'She said she'd had enough and wanted them all wiped away, Sproxton and everyone else.'

Mathilda turned to her captivated audience. 'And that

was what sent Lady Isabella, not straight to the hut, but into the shadows to think, before seeing Agnes again, only seconds later, holding a knife. A knife which she then took back up off Merrick's bed and, following her maid to the Fire Room, where she struck her dead. Then, Lady Isabella carried on to the hut as planned, expecting to find Sproxton there, ready to persuade him to leave there and then.

'But he still wasn't there, was he, my Lady? After a while you became desperate and eventually you had no choice but to return once more to the castle. When you heard why Thomas had been held up, not because Agnes had spoken out, but because he was working for the King, I imagine you were out of your wits with regret for what you'd done to Agnes. I imagine you've been regretting it ever since. Or, maybe, you aren't. Maybe you still believe Agnes would have spoken against Thomas eventually; something you could not allow. And after all, you had the perfect alibi. You'd been waiting for your lover in a hut half a mile away.'

Lady Isabella said nothing, but stared vacantly into space.

Shock engulfed the hall as Thomas Sproxton, his hands in irons, was led into the room. His clothes were smeared with grime and his teeth chattered. As he blinked against the fire's orange light, his eyes fell on Wennesley. 'Oh, thank goodness, perhaps you could put an end to this outrage, Roger. We have felons to catch and...' As his eyes swam into focus he saw who the other men assembled were. His words tailed into the thin air.

Mathilda forced herself to stop looking at Lady Isabella, whose eyes had lit up on seeing Thomas. She didn't seem to register his irons.

'And the knife Agnes took to scare Merrick?' Eustace remained focused on Mathilda's denouncement of Isabella,

'The goods in the Fire Room are hidden in the old scaffolding holes. A knife was kept handy beneath the bed to help ease in and out the stone blocks that conceal them.'

Thomas de Folville caught his brother's eye, 'I will show you when this is done, Eustace. It is a neat trick.'

Mathilda wished her hands weren't shaking so much. She was desperate for a drink to relieve her parched throat, but she didn't want to show any weakness before she'd reached the end of her account.

'We come to the final thread of this knot.' She switched her attention to the sheriff. 'The document that contained the Coterels' and Folvilles' arrest was cleverly written. I think we can declare that it was either Garrick or an associate who compiled it under James Coterel's guiding hand.

'When Wennesley read the entry above the relevant arrest warrant concerning Thomas Stafford, he panicked when he realised that you'd have to see it too, Lord de Vere, so he made a play of spilling ink over it.' She turned to Roger, 'I assume that part of the document was not something you were expecting to see?'

'It was not.'

As if oblivious to the growing undertone in the room, Lady Isabella whispered, 'Who is Stafford?'

Mathilda regarded Isabella suspiciously. 'The man you killed for. His real name is Thomas Stafford.'

Sproxton's mouth dropped wide, 'Killed for… Isabella, what have you done? Agnes? Why?'

Isabella opened her lips to protest, but the horrified expression on Sproxton's face stopped the words as her face froze into terrified silence, as if the consequences of her actions were finally sinking in.

Mathilda faced the accused directly. 'Your stepmother interceded to prevent you marrying a match of your liking in Giles de Beauchamp, Lord of Alcester, because she didn't wish to risk you being wed to a male of higher station than her own daughter. The thought of your marriage plans being curtailed again - and this time by a mere maid - must have been insupportable. Isn't that right, Lady Isabella?'

Isabella stared at Mathilda as if she hadn't heard a word. 'My Thomas is Thomas Stafford?'

Mathilda began to speak faster. 'Wennesley and Sproxton are old friends. It was your idea, I believe, Master Roger, that Thomas changed his name from Stafford to Sproxton after he'd helped you kill Laurence Coterel. That death was no accident, as you've continually claimed, but an act of rage at the gambling table.'

Wennesley said nothing, but regarded Sproxton as if he were a fool.

'Please don't deny it. The name was on the document you tried to obscure with ink. And it was written there because James Coterel commanded Garrick for it to be there. Lord de Vere and I have spent some time now puzzling over it, and now we have worked out what it says, I shall read it to you.'

Pulling the parchment from under her seat, where it had been hidden, Mathilda read, "Thomas of Stafford struck Laurence Coterel on the head with his sword. Roger Wennesley then struck Coterel with a knife, in the gut, from which he died".

She paused, watching the thunderous expressions around her. 'James Coterel knows it was Sproxton and you who dealt the fatal blows against his kin together, doesn't he?'

This time Wennesley answered, 'He knows.'

Nicholas and John were on their feet. Mathilda spoke faster still.

'And you have been secretly working for Lord James for

how long now, Master Wennesley?'

'Ever since Laurence died.'

Nicholas Coterel wrenched Roger up by his collar. 'Talk. Now.'

The men all started to ask questions at once, causing Mathilda to have to shout. 'If you could show an ounce of patience, my Lords, all will be made clear!'

Holding his palms out in an appeal for calm, the sheriff spoke sharply. 'Wennesley, why would you take the blame for the death alone? James Coterel has publically maintained it was an accident and never claimed Sproxton was involved beyond being there at the same time.'

Avoiding Sproxton's eyes, Wennesley cleared his throat. 'The Coterels accepted the claim of self-defence based on their knowledge of Laurence's hot temper, but one day, when in his cups at the gambling table, Sproxton spoke too much and that toad Reynard heard. I was summoned to the royal court to see Coterel. Let's just say Lord James made me an offer I couldn't refuse.'

'You've been working for him ever since. A deal which guaranteed your continued ability to breathe and a promise that James wouldn't tell his brothers the truth?' Mathilda stated.

'Yes.'

'But Sproxton is your friend, so you advised the change of name as extra protection in case anyone should ever write of the incident. Which worked until Sproxton came to Rockingham. Agnes recognised him as Stafford from her time watching her former master gambling their earnings away.'

John Coterel cleared his throat. 'But why would James let Stafford get away with murder?'

'He didn't.' Mathilda nodded to the shackled man, 'Lord

Coterel was just waiting for a time when Sproxton might become useful.'

'And that time is now?'

'He was instructed to remove Isabella from the castle so Helena was left as the elder. As a woman she would not inherit, but she was still woman in a strong position who is as ruthless as James Coterel himself; a woman he thought he could control would be a tempting proposition.

'Helena agreed to marry James via Garrick, without ever meeting him.' Mathilda studied Lady Helena's expression, 'although I doubt the marriage would have happened. Lord Coterel was more interested in teaching Sproxton and Wennesley a lesson and increasing his hold on the Hundred by taking over Rockingham; all from the safety of the court. Lady Helena was a convenient weapon in his armoury of persuasion. Nothing more.'

Rising to her feet, her hands on her hips, Lady Helena's eyes glared with fury. 'How dare you? Lord Coterel's word is worth more than that of an outlaw's wife.'

Mathilda gripped her husband's arm against the background sound of numerous daggers being drawn. 'You are entitled to believe that, my Lady. Whether you continue to do so after the sheriff has interviewed you from the less comfortable surrounds of Nottingham Castle remains to be seen.'

Not giving his second child the chance to protest further, de Vere, both hands curled into tight fists, got to his feet. His voice held a level of calm that Mathilda sensed could become a tempest at any moment.

'My Lord Eustace, may I prevail upon you for the use of a messenger that you trust. One who cannot be bribed or threatened into changing the nature of his message by any living man or woman?'

'You may. I will send you such a messenger as soon as I reach Ashby Folville. If you share your reasoning I will not charge you for the loan of my finest man.'

De Vere raised his beaker in agreement, 'King Edward needs to know about this.'

Wennesley's hysterical laughter cut through the hall, 'Are you mad? You think the King would believe you once Lord James had spun his own words about us in His Majesty's ear?'

'About you?' De Vere shook his head. 'I am not such a fool as to interfere in any agreement you have to suffer with James Coterel but Stafford owes him money and a certain Master Garrick requires bringing to heel.'

Robert nodded, relieved to see the Constable of Rockingham acting more like his usual self. 'And with luck, the King will be so diverted by that he will lose interest in us, for now at least.'

Nicholas grunted. 'I'm sure he will. If our brother learns his plan has failed, he'll be keen to remove all traces of his subterfuge. Before you know it, the King will think the whole thing a bad idea from a minor servant. Garrick will become the scapegoat, I've no doubt.'

Mathilda gulped as an image of Garrick meeting with the sharp end of a knife flicked through her mind. 'May I suggest, my Lord de Vere, that you reconsider leaving your post as constable for a year or two? Until this matter has been forgotten.'

De Vere regarded his children and nodded with incomprehension. 'And my daughters? What happens to them? In truth, Helena committed no crime, and Isabella only killed a thief.'

Merrick winced, but held his tongue, as with a curtsey to the men folk, Mathilda held one hand out to Bettrys and the other to Robert. 'That is a matter for you and the sheriff to discuss. I leave Stafford, Wennesley, Cook, and Lady Isabella in your capable hands, my Lords. If you have more questions for me, then you can come to Ashby Folville to have them answered. I'm going home.'

~ *Chapter Fifty-seven* ~

The manor shone. The aroma of fresh stew, bread and heated honey assailed Mathilda's nostrils as she embraced Sarah. Waving away requests for news from Rockingham, she held her friend by the shoulders. 'Marriage to Adam. I could not be more delighted. Congratulations!'

'We have your blessing?' Sarah glowed.

'Always.'

A shuffle of nervous footsteps behind Mathilda altered the housekeeper to the fact her mistress was not alone. A shy but hopeful face was peering around the door from the courtyard to the kitchen.

'Come in, Bettrys.' Mathilda beckoned to the maid. 'Sarah, this is Bettrys. Ill-used by her mistresses, I have invited her here until we can find work for her within one of the family manors. I hope you won't be offended.'

Sarah beamed. 'Offended?' Why, my Lady, I swear you are a mind reader.'

'I am?'

Sarah patted the kitchen bench and bid Bettrys to sit with her as she said, 'I am not as young as I was. I am to be wed and I have no child to teach all I know.'

Exchanging a look of delight with Bettrys, Mathilda said, 'What do you think? Would you like to stay here and become Sarah's helper?'

Robert leant against the bedpost. He was playing Mathilda's butterfly girdle through his hands.

'I missed you.'

'And I you.' She smiled, pulling the sheet up over her naked chest. 'Will you tell me where you've been?'

'No.' He winked. 'Safer I don't. Do you know if Reynard is still alive? All this is his fault to an extent.'

'I have a good mind not to say.'

Robert climbed into the bed next to his wife. 'You will though.'

'De Vere sent him to fight in Scotland.'

'Almost certainly dead then.' He teased a palm along her thigh.

'It's so sad. Sproxton did love Isabella. It may have begun as an order from Lord James, but love isn't that straightforward. It doesn't stick to the rules.'

'We are proof of that.' Robert kissed her nose. 'Do you think Lady Isabella has lost her wits?'

'Perhaps. But it would be easy to underestimate her. She has spent a lifetime in a castle with felons; who knows what tricks she may have picked up from them? I'm just glad she didn't kill Merrick too.'

'You think she'd have murdered him next?'

'Maybe.' Mathilda closed her eyes as Robert's fingers teased out the tangles in her hair. 'Do you think she will hang?'

'No, I think her father will buy her freedom. Sproxton and Cook on the other hand are residing in Nottingham's gaol. I doubt they will come out.'

Mathilda sighed against her husband's exploring touch. 'Will the King stop hunting you?'

'For now. I suspect James Coterel will see to that.'

'Won't he be punished himself?'

Robert laughed. 'What do you think?'

'I think I'd like to forget all about it and plan Sarah and Adam's wedding. What about you?'

'I think a wedding sounds like a perfect distraction, but the chances of recent events being forgotten are slim. In the meantime, I'm sure we can find a way to occupy our minds before the next messenger comes knocking…'

~ *Epilogue* ~

February 1330

'This delay is becoming tedious.' Eustace shook the parchment in his hand towards his gathered brother's faces. 'We need to act!'

Not one of them flinched as they sat around the fire of the inn's back room. Nor did they argue. They knew Eustace was right.

Robert raised a calming hand and gestured for his irate kin to sit down. 'You'll get no argument from us, brother. Our plans, so carefully forged, have been delayed too often. I think we are all agreed however that it would have been foolish to act while we were hunted so fervently by the Crown, and the delays imposed upon us by you, Richard, cannot be overlooked.'

Six sets of accusing eyes landed on the Rector of Teigh who, free from custody on orders from their elder brother Lord John, spat into the fire by way of response. 'Decide who your enemy is here, brother. Me or him?'

Robert's eyes narrowed. 'The excesses of the man in question have to end. The Coterel brothers agree.'

Thomas stared into the flames of the fire as he added, 'Lords La Zouche, and Herdwyck will help.'

Eustace grunted into his ale. 'They said they would. But that was before Robert's marriage. We will have to check their allegiance.'

Robert agreed. 'De Vere will certainly assist us. As will Wennesley. They are bound to us now. It is time. We can delay no longer.'

Walter's gravel voice spoke what his brothers were thinking. 'And what of your wife, Robert? What will you tell the fair Mathilda of our plans to murder the Justice Willoughby?'

Historical Notes and References

The ballads and political songs within this story come from the following sources.

Piers the Plowman, Langland, W., <u>The Vision of Piers the Plowman; A Complete Edition of the B-Text</u> (London, 1987), Passus XIX, line 245.

A Geste of Robyn Hode, Dobson & Taylor, <u>Rymes of Robyn Hood: An Introduction to the English Outlaw</u> (Gloucester, 1989), p.112, stanza 456

A Geste of Robyn Hode, Childs Ballads 117.

***

Roger Belers was murdered in 1326 in the field of Brokesby, Leicestershire. The incident was recorded in the Assize Rolls – *Just1/470*

Laurence Coterel was murdered in March 1330 not March 1329. (I have adjusted history by one year to fit my story for reasons that are genuine but dull! Please find it in your hearts to forgive me). The incident was recorded in the Assize Rolls 166m.21 *"Thomas Ifel of Stafford struck Laurence Coterel on the head with his sword. Roger Wennesley then struck Coterel with a knife, per medium gutteris, from which he died"*

Sir Robert Ingram was sheriff of Nottinghamshire and Derbyshire on four occasions between 1322 and 1334. <u>Lists of Sheriffs for England and Wales from the earliest times to AD 1831 Preserved in the Public Record Office</u> (List and Index Society 9, New York, 1963) p.102

***

If you are interested in learning more about Robin Hood and the historical felons of the English Middle Ages, there are many excellent references available. Here a few of my personal favourites.

Books

Dobson & Taylor, <u>Rymes of Robyn Hood: An Introduction to the English Outlaw</u> (Gloucester, 1989)
Hanawalt, B.A., <u>Crime and Conflict in the English Communities 1330-1348</u> (London, 1979)
Holt, J., <u>Robin Hood</u> (London, 1982)
Keen, M., <u>The Outlaws of Medieval Legend</u> (London, 1987)
Knight, S., <u>Robin Hood: A Complete Study of the English Outlaw</u> (Oxford, 1994)
Leyser, H., <u>Medieval Women: A Social History of Women in England 450-1500</u>, (London 1995)
Nichols, ed., <u>History and Antiquity of Leicester, Vol. 3, Part 1</u>
Pollard, A.J., <u>Imaging Robin Hood</u> (London, 2004)
Prestwich, M., <u>The Three Edwards: War and State in England 1272-1377</u> (London, 1980)

Periodicals

Bellamy, J., *'The Coterel Gang: An Anatomy of a Band of Fourteenth Century Crime'*, English Historical Review Vol. 79, (1964)

Kaeuper, R., *'Law and Order in Fourteenth-Century England: The Evidence of Special Commissions of Oyer and Terminer,'* Speculum, Vol. 54, No. 4, (University of Chicago, 1979)

Scattergood, J., *'The Tale of Gamelyn: The Noble Robber as Provincial Hero,'* ed. C Meale, Readings in Medieval English Romance (Cambridge, 1994)

Lightning Source UK Ltd.
Milton Keynes UK
UKHW040625260519
343327UK00001B/19/P

9 781999 350109